ANNA BELL

once upon a leap year

ONE PLACE. MANY STORIES

HQ
An imprint of HarperCollins*Publishers* Ltd
1 London Bridge Street
London SE1 9GF

www.harpercollins.co.uk

HarperCollins*Publishers*
Macken House, 39/40 Mayor Street Upper,
Dublin 1, D01 C9W8, Ireland

This edition 2024

1
First published in Great Britain by
HQ, an imprint of HarperCollins*Publishers* Ltd 2024

Copyright © Anna Bell 2024

Anna Bell asserts the moral right to be
identified as the author of this work.
A catalogue record for this book is
available from the British Library.

ISBN: PB: 9780008467661

MIX
Paper | Supporting
responsible forestry
FSC™ C007454

This book contains FSC™ certified paper and other controlled
sources to ensure responsible forest management.

For more information visit: www.harpercollins.co.uk/green

This book is set in 10.7/15.5 pt. Sabon by Type-it AS, Norway

Printed and Bound in the UK using 100% Renewable Electricity at
CPI Group (UK) Ltd, Croydon, CR0 4YY

Praise for Anna Bell

'Funny and relatable. I love books that blend poignancy
n'
Sophie ct Year

'I feel like I've been on an emotional roller coaster. What
a thrilling ride this novel was – strap in and enjoy. Hilarious
yet heartfelt, this is romcom writing at its very best!'
Isabelle Broom, author of *The Getaway*

'OMG, I adored this book. It's one of the best
I've read for a while and I literally couldn't put it
down. What a gorgeous, poignant story'
Jules Wake, bestselling author of *The Spark*

'Warm-hearted and hilarious. It will make you giggle
and want to hug the book when you finish it'
Miranda Dickinson, author of *Our Story*

'Anna Bell's best book yet, and – given how much I've
always loved her writing – that's saying a lot. It has all of
Anna's unique trademark wit, warmth and wisdom, while
also being an incredibly compelling and brilliant story'
Lucy Vine, author of *Hot Mess*

'Brilliantly written, funny and tender'
Fabulous

'Heart-warming and hilarious'
Yours

'Funny and touching'
My Weekly

Also by Anna Bell

Anna Bell lives in Northern Ireland with her young family and energetic Labrador. Anna can be found walking by the sea dreaming up plot ideas or in a coffee shop trying not to eat too many cakes.

You can find out more about Anna on her website
www. annabellwrites.com
or follow her on
Instagram @anna_bell_writes

For Lyndsey Shepherd.

PART ONE

2004

Chapter 1

Sunday 29th February 2004

*D*on't forget it's leap day, so, ladies, get those knees limbered up, as today, and today only, is your chance to—

'Ugh,' I muttered, switching off the radio. Seriously, can't people talk about anything else on the twenty-ninth of February? Do radio and TV presenters not know that in the twenty-first century a woman can propose to a man on ANY day of the year?

I, more than most people, get how special it is. After all, it's my birthday, and I only get to celebrate it on the actual day once every four years. But still, I wish they'd think of better things to talk about than outdated traditions. What about seizing the day and making the most of having a whole extra twenty-four hours in the calendar? Which is exactly how I see it.

'I can't believe how early it is,' groaned Caz, appearing from what should have been the lounge if our greedy landlord hadn't made it into an extra bedroom. 'Happy birthday, Luce.'

'You didn't need to get up this early. Plus, I'm pretty sure that you wished me that every time we ordered shots after midnight last night.'

She groaned again, and held on to the back of a chair to

steady herself. 'Is that why my head feels like there's a samba band drumming inside it?'

I laughed. 'Quite possibly.'

Despite the chilliness of the room, she was wearing a skimpy pyjama set with a towelling dressing gown draped over the top. She tied her hair into a messy knot, exposing even more of her midriff.

'You'll get sick, it's freezing in here.'

She rolled her eyes at me, but she tightened up the dressing gown anyway. 'Better?'

I reached over to the clothes horse in the corner and pulled off a pair of my thick slouch socks, which were just about dry, and chucked them at her.

'Thanks, Mum,' she said, catching them.

'The landlord's doing his best to kill us off in the cold; we don't want to give him a helping hand.'

She hopped on one leg putting the socks on, and from the look of delight that spread over her face, I knew that was the last I'd see of them.

'I don't get how you're up and all chipper,' she said, mid-hop into the second sock. 'You're worse than Amy.'

'Should my ears be burning?'

Caught off balance, Caz almost fell over. She hadn't seen Amy glide into the kitchen. Despite having the same – few – hours of sleep as Caz and me, Amy looked bright-eyed and bushy-tailed; all freshly showered and made up. I'd showered but it had done little to wake me up and I'd shoved my wet hair into a towel on top of my head where it was no doubt a matted, frizzy mess now.

'Speak of the devil. Seriously, what's wrong with you? Who

looks that awake or that good on a Sunday morning?' said Caz. She'd initially tried to shake her head in disbelief, but she'd stopped mid-shake and clutched at her temples.

Amy shrugged her shoulders. 'Being a morning person is both a blessing and a curse. But today, it's more blessing as it means I'm up to play Fairy Godmother for Lucy here who doesn't look like she's in a fit state for her big romantic date.'

'It's not a big romantic date. For starters, it's Will,' I said, flicking on the kettle. If I was going to have to deal with Amy being this perky, I needed more caffeine. 'Will, who you're always trying to point out does not have a romantic bone in his body.'

'And you're always trying to convince us that there's more to him.' Caz lowered herself gently to the table with a wince.

It wasn't a state secret that my friends hadn't gelled with my boyfriend. But they didn't see the same Will I did. He wasn't a people person. He didn't ooze charisma or light up any room he walked into. He was the kind of guy that was great when you were on your own with him. He listened, had interesting things to say, but put him in a group situation and he'd find the side of an argument that no one wanted to take, just to provoke debate. A characteristic not on my ideal boyfriend wish list, but it wasn't like I was going to date him for ever. I was a realist when it came to relationships. I was never going to marry a guy I'd met when I was an actual teenager.

When *I was* a teenager. I was now officially in my twenties. I swallowed a lump in my throat; that was going to take some getting used to.

'You know what I mean. It's not like he's going to be whisking me off for a day in Paris or something. We're probably just going to Margate for some fish and chips.'

Caz wrinkled her nose. 'Please don't mention food.'

'Did he not give you any clues? What if it's a super-fancy restaurant?' asked Amy.

'He just said to dress comfortably.'

I dug around in the fridge and passed a can of Coke across the table to Caz. 'Drink this, you'll feel better.'

'Dress comfortably? What does that even mean? Tracksuit bottoms? Jeans? Trainers? Or comfy heels?' Amy was blinking as her brain flicked through the options in her mind.

'He didn't say. If it makes you feel better, I'll text and ask.'

I tapped out a quick message.

Amy was twitching behind me. She was one of life's planners. She would no doubt have interrogated Will when he first mentioned this day trip until she had a full itinerary and a packing list. But I'd been so grateful that Will had even suggested anything, I hadn't wanted to spook him by asking too much.

'I can't believe you're this calm,' said Amy. 'Aren't you even going to do your hair? I can straighten it if you like? Get those back bits flat.'

'Would you?'

'Of course. I told you. I'm Fairy Godmother.'

I unwrapped the towel and my half-dried hair fell about my shoulders.

'Hmm, I'm going to need more than a magic wand for this.' She tugged at my hair.

'Oi, that hurts.'

'Go blow-dry it and I'll warm up my hair straighteners.'

*

6

Amy unpinned another section of my hair, and fed it through her fancy GHDs. My phone beeped and I lurched up to get it, but she pushed me back down in the chair.

'Hold tight, I'm almost done,' she said, a slight hiss escaping as she caught a patch of not quite dry hair.

Caz's head was rested on the table and her eyes kept closing. Every so often she'd jolt as she jumped in her near-sleep.

'But it might be from Will.'

Amy sighed. 'Just this once.'

She leaned behind her and presented me with my phone.

'Is it from him?'

'From my mum.'

Happy 5th Birthday Darling Girl. Hope you have a wonderful time. Wish I was spending the day with you. Kisses xxxxx

I smiled. My mum always counted my leap year birthdays as my proper birthdays. I sent a quick message of thanks.

'I'm surprised she didn't come up today.'

'We're going to Bluewater next weekend.'

Amy was raking her hands through my hair and she stopped abruptly. 'Jealous. I love a big shopping trip.'

'It'll mostly be window shopping.'

Neither of us had the healthiest of bank balances.

'Sometimes those are the best trips, when you're not stressed out looking for something in particular.'

'Absolutely. Give us time to potter round.'

'And have plenty of time to catch up on her dating stories. Has she been speed dating again?'

'No, thank goodness. Ouch.' Amy grazed the side of my head with the hot plate.

'Sorry. And that's a shame for her.'

My mum had recently started to date again, which I fully supported right up until she started oversharing. Since my parents' divorce, the two of us had become more like friends than mother and daughter, which would be fine if not for my mother's emerging sex life. Whilst I was excited that she might find someone that makes her happy, I dreaded the idea of hearing about anything more than a peck on the cheek at the end of the night.

'But not a shame for me. I haven't quite got over her and Mr Carrington.'

Amy snorted then stopped herself.

'It's not funny. It was bad enough that she went on a date with one of my old teachers, let alone . . . ' I shuddered at the thought of what had happened when he'd dropped her home.

I could see Amy in the mirror we'd put on the table to pretend we were in a proper hair salon. She was biting her lip hard, doing a terrible job of trying not to laugh.

I couldn't help but smile too. As much as Mum's dating life made me cringe, I was pleased she was at least getting out there again. When Dad left, the sparkle had left her eyes, and now, four and a half years later, it was only just starting to return.

We'd come a long way in those four and a half years. I thought of my last leap year birthday. I'd planned a sixteenth birthday party at the local hockey club and invited what felt like my entire year. For one night only it was supposed to be all about me. I was going to be the popular one. The one that everyone made a fuss of. Only I spent the entire time trying to keep my parents in separate rooms to stop the bickering. I'd barely acknowledged my guests and I'd definitely not partied on the dancefloor with my friends.

I was about to put my phone back on the table when it beeped in my hand.

'It's Will. What the . . . "Jeans. Trainers. Something warm."' I gasped, before I read out the rest to Amy. '"And forgot to say, you need your passport."'

'Passport,' shrieked Amy so loud that Caz startled and sat bolt upright.

'What's going on?' she rubbed at her eyes and stared between us.

Amy prodded me until I snapped out of my shock.

'My passport,' I said, leaping out of my seat and grabbing Amy by the hands. We danced around in a circle. 'Will told me to bring my passport.'

Amy stopped and I almost crashed into her.

'Oh my god, you're going to Paris.'

'We're not going to Paris.'

'No, she's right. You know you can get the Eurostar from Ashford, don't you?'

'Exactly.' Amy pointed at Caz. 'That's exactly where you're going.'

'Can you really get it from there?' My mind was racing. Surely Will wouldn't actually do something that romantic, would he?

'That's why it's called Ashford International,' said Amy, hands on hips.

'I thought they were just being fancy.'

'This is so exciting,' said Caz. 'You realise you'll need better make-up than that.'

'I haven't got any on.'

'Why not? What time's he coming to get you?'

'I'm meeting him on campus in an hour.'

'An hour?' said Caz in alarm. 'We don't have much time.' She stood up, no longer acknowledging her pain, this mission clearly more important than her hangover. She took in my giant fleece like she hadn't noticed I'd been in it for the past hour that we'd been in the kitchen. 'And that is not what you're wearing.'

'She shouldn't be wearing it any time,' said Amy, pulling a face. 'How many times have we told you to bin that thing?'

'It's so cosy.'

It might be unflattering, and a bit bobbly from the frequent wash and wear, but I swear it had saved me from getting hypothermia living in our freezing house.

'It might be, but it's also ugly. You can't wear that to Paris. Come on, let's sort you out.'

They pulled me up and guided me out towards my wardrobe, leaving the table, and seemingly any form of free will with it.

An hour later, I walked onto campus, tugging at my roll-neck that I was convinced was trying to suffocate me. It was Caz's and a little too small for me.

Amy and Caz had come up with an outfit that they called *Parisian chic*, the roll-neck paired with a corduroy skirt, chunky knit tights, cream-coloured knee-high suede boots with the tiniest hint of a heel, topped off with a knitted flat cap on my head. It might have seemed chic in my bedroom, but standing on campus on a Sunday morning, watching people do the walk of shame, I felt more ridiculous than they looked with the bed hair and last night's clothes.

'Bloody hell, I said jeans and trainers,' said Will, walking up behind me. He leaned over and tapped me on the bum as he gave me a kiss. 'You look good though.'

'Um, thanks.' I took in his jeans and a sweatshirt that – from the ketchup stain on the cuff – looked like he'd been wearing it all week. Still, Paris, I thought to myself. It didn't matter how we were dressed, the fact we were going was the main thing. 'Caz and Amy said I should make an effort, it being my birthday and all.'

He closed his eyes for a second and then flicked them open.

'Right, happy birthday,' he stuttered. 'I . . . um . . . I'm going to get you a present when we're there.'

'Ooh, lovely. Something special to remember the day by.'

Will pulled a face before he shook it off. 'Yeah. Um. So did you have a good night last night?'

'We did. Caz got me up on stage and the DJ made everyone sing "Happy Birthday" to me, the Stevie Wonder version, not the normal one.'

His eyes were glazing over and I could see he didn't really care. He had an aversion to our student union, not understanding what we saw in it. It had been one of the things I'd liked about him at first, as it meant that he didn't want to come with us on nights out. Which, after having a boyfriend in first year who followed me round the club getting in the way, suited me fine.

'It was fun,' I said, trying to supress a giggle at the memory of Caz falling down the steps onto the dancefloor and styling it out with a forward roll. 'How was your Call of Duty tournament?'

'Awesome.'

I nodded, convinced my eyes would equally glaze over if he elaborated. 'Are we going to head down to the train station or . . .'

'Nah, we're getting a bus from behind the student union.'

'A bus?' I didn't know of any bus from here going to Ashford.

'Yep. In fact, we don't want to miss it.'

He shoved his hands in his pockets and motioned with his head for us to get walking.

Campus was quiet, as it always was before midday on a weekend, but it seemed that anyone that was braving the early morning start was heading in that direction.

When we got to the car park, there was a large coach with students milling around it. Someone I recognised as one of the student union officers was by the door, holding a clipboard and discussing something with the driver.

'Here we are,' said Will.

'Here we are where?' I looked at the mostly male students hovering around the coach. Most were dressed in tracksuit bottoms and jeans. Not another carefully selected Parisian chic outfit in sight.

'The bus. For the booze cruise.'

'The booze cruise.' My voice was flat.

'Yeah. Dover to Calais. It was only a pound a ticket, bargain!'

'A pound a ticket.'

I realised I was parroting back to him what he was saying, but I was in shock.

'Did you remember your passport?'

I nodded, now rendered speechless.

'Chug it, chug it,' chanted one of the guys near the front of the queue. His friends joined in clapping and shouting until the boy in the middle of their group downed a tin of beer.

I shuddered. It wasn't even eleven.

'It's going to be awesome,' said Will. 'My housemate went

over a few weeks ago with his parents. Brought back a whole boot of booze. Obviously, we'll only have what we can carry, but I've got my big rucksack.'

He showed it off proudly as he led me to the back of the queue. I didn't resist, still mourning my trip to Paris that never was.

'I thought you'd be more excited. Getting to go to France for your birthday.'

'You're right.' I tried to find some enthusiasm. 'Actual France. How long are we going for?'

'I think we get three hours.'

'Three hours? Is that all?'

From the few French family holidays I'd been on as a child, I knew you could barely eat a meal there in three hours.

'Don't worry' – he squeezed my hand – 'it'll be plenty of time to buy everything. All the big shops are together.'

'We're not going to sightsee?'

Will laughed and then stopped when I didn't join in.

'That's not really what a booze cruise is for. Clue's in the name.'

How was I going to explain this to the girls? They were expecting me to come back with stories from the Eiffel Tower, not hypermarkets in Calais.

'Don't worry, though. There's a shopping centre with clothes shops too.'

'Great,' I said, thinking of my trip I had planned with Mum next week. Any surplus birthday money had already been earmarked for that.

'Happy birthday, babe,' he said, putting his arm around me as the queue started to move. He handed over our £1 tickets and we were on our way.

The coach journey was nothing like the trip I'd envisaged on the Eurostar. I'd pictured the two of us sitting while looking into each other's eyes, setting the tone for our trip to the city of love. Instead, we were crammed next to each other, surrounded by what seemed like the entire men's rugby team. They must have been the only people to bring booze on a booze cruise.

'Passports,' said the student union rep. 'We're almost at Dover and we just need to get them ready for passport control.'

I dug around in my bag and handed mine over.

He took Will's and gave it a quick scan, before doing the same with mine.

'Your birthday's the twenty-ninth of February?' He held the passport closer to his eyes before looking up at me. 'It's your birthday today?'

I nodded. 'This is my birthday treat from my boyfriend.'

He looked at Will and nodded his head. 'Awesome present, dude.'

The two high-fived. Men really were different to women.

'You know, there's a guy near the front whose birthday it is too,' he said, turning to point to a few rows in front of us, but all I saw was a sea of rugby players. Maybe a birthday amongst them explained why they'd been so spirited this morning. 'I don't think I've ever met anyone born on the twenty-ninth before, and there I am meeting two of you in two minutes. Amazing. What are the chances of that?'

He didn't stop to ponder the odds and off he went. I'd never really thought about it, but I'd never met anyone who was an actual birthday twin either. I'd met people who celebrated on the first of March like I usually did, but never one born on the twenty-ninth.

'It's weird, isn't it? Two leaplings,' I said to Will who had rolled up his coat against the window and was nestling his head against it.

'Not really.' He shuffled in his seat, trying to get comfortable. 'This is a cool thing to do for your birthday. I'd expect there to be even more of you.'

Before I could respond, he'd closed his eyes. I looked over the sea of heads, trying to catch a glimpse of my birthday twin, but really it could be anyone. There was a one in fourteen hundred and sixty-one chance of being a leapling, but what were the chances of two of us being here and on this very bus?

Chapter 2

When I'd dressed in my cream boots, I had imagined mooching between bars in the Latin Quarter under blue skies, not dashing across supermarket car parks in between breaks in the rain. It had been teeming it down all day and the suede was getting soggier by the minute.

So far, Will had stocked up on nearly every variety of flavoured vodka and some wine, and I'd stretched to a bottle of Baileys and a slab of Smirnoff ice. We'd stored them in the bus, and were headed over to the mall entrance for some window shopping in the dry, only to find all the boutique shops and anything not hypermarket related were closed.

'Why aren't they open?'

Will scanned the opening hours on the door. 'They're shut on Sundays.'

'All of them?' My voice came out in a squeak. It had been the only thing keeping me going round the hypermarkets, that at least I could stay in the warm and dry and potter round the rest of the shops.

I should have known that they'd be closed. I could remember holidays in France when it seemed like whole villages and towns shuttered up on Sundays, with no signs of life.

'Oh well,' said Will with a shrug. 'Might be a good time to buy some ciggies to sell.'

'Really?'

I don't know what grated on me more: the fact that he used the word ciggies, or that that's what he suggested we do with our new-found free time.

'Might as well make back some of the money for the trip.'

'You mean the two pounds you spent on the tickets?'

'And the lunch.'

'Right.' My birthday lunch: a soggy burger from an unknown chain. 'How long have we got until the bus goes?'

He looked down at his watch. 'About an hour and a half.'

I looked at the waiting taxis all lined up across the road. 'Why don't we head off into town and do a little sightseeing?'

'In Calais?' He wrinkled his nose. 'Babe, I think it's just hypermarkets.'

'It can't be. There must be a real town with at least a little bistro that we could go to.' I tried to put on my most seductive voice, but it was hard in the biting wind and the rain.

'You heard what they said on the bus – if we're not there, they'll go without us.'

'But look, we could get a taxi there and back. There's plenty of them, it's not like we'd get stranded.'

He looked between the line of cars and the big warehouse shop next to him.

'I did promise Gareth I'd bring him some Marlboro Lights.'

I sighed. 'I thought this was my birthday treat.'

Will took a step back and let out a deep breath. 'I bought you a ticket to come abroad. I'm spending the whole day with you. Not to mention I bought you a burger, and that bottle of wine in the last shop.'

'It was buy two get one free.'

'Yeah, but I could have kept the free one.' He folded his arms across his chest.

I looked down at my boots, now a sludgy brown colour, and thought how they, like me, deserved better than this.

'Well, I'm going to go and see the town, even if you're not.'

'Fine,' he said. 'I'm going to shop in here.'

'Fine.' I folded my arms to match his. For a split second neither of us moved, each waiting for the other to cave first. But when it became clear that neither of us was going to back down, Will swore under his breath and went inside the shop.

I cursed loudly, pulling my arms closer into my chest, unsure whether it was for comfort or to warm myself.

The taxis were there with their lights like a beacon, and yet I knew deep down that I was never going to go alone. I wished that I was brave enough to do it. If Caz was here, she'd go on her own. She was fearless.

I fiddled with the four-leaf clover charm on my bracelet, which somewhere along the line had become a talisman for when I needed courage, only it wasn't working its usual magic.

A lone tear rolled down my cheek, followed by another, and another. Before I knew what was happening I was full-on crying. I don't know whether it was that I'd got my hopes up for Paris, or that I'd ruined my favourite boots, or that I was starting to see the side of Will that my friends did. Whatever the reason, my tears were matching the rainfall.

'Hey, are you OK?' I turned to see a guy that I vaguely recognised. He'd been on our bus, but I'd seen him around campus too. He had one of those faces that always seemed to be smiling, only today the smile didn't want to stay on his face. He was doubling over in pain.

'I feel like I should be asking you that,' I said, wiping away my tears.

'I'm not the one crying.'

'And I'm not the one clearly in pain.' I tilted my head in concern. 'What's wrong?'

He bent over again. 'I had some oysters, when we first got off the bus, from the little truck in the car park.' He shook his head; his face was practically green. 'They did not agree with me.'

I pulled a face. Oysters were definitely not on the list of French delicacies that I'd be willing to try.

'Do you need me to get you some help?'

'Nope, I've taken some stuff to try and um—' He paused and I worried he was going to be sick, but instead he let out a deep breath. 'Anyway, tell me why you're crying. It might take my mind off it.'

'Really?'

'Really.' His voice was going a little pitchy as he spoke.

'My boyfriend brought me here on what I thought was going to be a romantic trip, only it was really for him to stock up on booze, and cigarettes that he can sell on.' The guy was not looking good and he was fidgeting, so I sped up in case he needed to make a sharp exit. 'And I started to cry because I wanted to get a taxi to the port, but I'm not brave enough. So instead, I'm probably going to just stand here looking at them for the next hour and a half, burning with bitter resentment and becoming even more like a drowned rat as if I haven't ruined my outfit enough already.'

'Or you could get in the taxi and go.'

'I know it's pathetic, but I'm scared to go alone.'

'It's not pathetic, it's probably pretty sensible.' He looked around and then broke out into a smile. 'You could go with my mate Noah. He'll be up for it. He was just moaning that everything's closed.'

'Oh no. I'm not going to go with some stranger.'

'He's not a stranger. He's Noah.'

I stared at the guy, wondering if he was for real.

'But . . . ' I said, deliberately slowly ' . . . he's a stranger to me.'

'Maybe, but you'll like him. Everyone likes him.'

'Listen, you seem really nice and I'm sure he would be too, but I'm not just going to—'

'Noah, mate,' he interrupted, calling to a man in a blue cap further down the car park, phone to his ear. 'I'm Paul, by the way.' He motioned for his friend to come over.

'Lucy,' I muttered, but I was distracted staring at the man who hung up his phone and jogged across to us.

'Noah, mate, this is Lucy. Lucy, this is Noah. Her boyfriend's a knob and she wants to go into the town,' Paul said, his voice getting quicker and quicker as he explained, a sheen of sweat appearing on his forehead. 'I said you'd go in a taxi with her. Got to run to the toilet again. See you on the bus later.'

Paul had barely finished the sentence before he started to sprint to the supermarket.

'Bloody oysters. Who even eats oysters?' said Noah. 'Let alone ones you get by the side of the road.'

He pulled his cap off his head and stroked his hair down. It was the kind of longish hair that was almost spiky, like boyband members seemed to be fond of. He replaced his cap and looked down at me.

'Right, Louise.'

'Lucy.'

'Right, *Lucy*,' he corrected. 'Sorry, I'm terrible with names. What's this about getting a taxi?'

'Oh, don't worry about it.' I waved a hand to bat the idea away. 'I don't need you to do that. Your friend Paul was just trying to be nice.'

'He does that a lot. He's a nice guy. It's a bit of a liability.'

'Must be an awful characteristic.'

'It is really. He's nice, and polite, *and* he goes out of his way to help strangers.' He pulled a face. 'It's a nightmare.'

'Yes, sounds it, having such a nice friend.'

Noah laughed. 'It is, because he's always roping his mates in to his good deeds.'

'Like escorting strange women to industrial French towns?'

'That's what it is this week, but last week it was walking our elderly neighbour's German Shepherd. You have no idea how big the poos were I had to pick up. Three bags,' he whispered under his breath and it made me giggle.

He smiled at me laughing, then stopped. 'Are you OK?'

I'd forgotten that I was probably a tear-stained mess, and I wiped at the sticky trails on my face.

'I'm fine, really. You can go about your shopping. Honestly. I'm not going to head into town; I might just wander round the shops here. Buy some stinky cheese or something.'

'So that you can find some friends on the bus home? Who doesn't love sitting next to someone with stinky cheese?'

'Exactly,' I said.

'And who knows, it might be better smelling than the rugby team.'

'Or at least mask their smell.'

Noah laughed harder.

'Right, well, I'll let you go on your important cheese-buying adventure. I'm going to continue my search to find Goldschläger.'

'What's that?'

'What do you mean, what's that? Only the best, most prestigious shot-drinking experience you can have.'

'I don't think I've had it.'

'Cinnamon tasting, with real gold in it?' He raised an eyebrow and I narrowed my eyes further.

'You drink real gold?'

'They're only flakes and yes.'

'Fancy.'

'Exactly. I can't usually afford it, but I was hoping it'd be cheaper here.'

There were green flecks in Noah's hazel eyes and they seemed to dance as he spoke animatedly; watching them was almost hypnotic.

'Well, good luck with that.' I bowed my head, like I was a fair maiden sending him off on his quest.

He bowed back. 'And you too, with the cheese. If I don't smell it down the back of the coach, I'll be disappointed.'

I smiled, looking towards the hypermarket, only my heart wasn't really in it.

'Thanks for being nice. It's been such a shitty birthday so far, and you being—'

'Hold up. It's your birthday?'

'Yep.'

'Today?' He narrowed his eyes and looked me up and down.

'All day.'

'Fuck, it's mine too.' His smile was wide now.

'You're *the* leapling?'

'What, like the chosen one?' he said, with a theatrical tone.

'No, you're the leapling the student union guy was talking about.'

'Oh right, yeah, he made a big deal out of it when he saw my passport. Which he should as we're so bloody rare. I mean what's the chance of being a leapling – one in a thousand?'

'One in one thousand four hundred and sixty-one.'

He gave a low whistle.

'Bloody hell. That's specific.'

'I'm good with remembering little details.'

'Uh-huh, right. I've honestly never met anyone with the same birthday as me before.'

'Me neither.'

He looked around the grey car park.

'This feels a bit of a momentous occasion that we need to celebrate.'

I followed his gaze to the chain restaurant where I'd had my infamous soggy burger, and another restaurant that doubled up as a bar that was bulging at the seams with most of the rugby players from our bus.

'What's in the town you're so desperate to get to?'

'Something other than a car park?' I ventured.

He laughed. 'Come on then, let's go.'

'But what about the Goldschläger hunt?'

'I kind of get the impression that's a bit like a needle in

23

a haystack. Plus, we do only get to celebrate this birthday once every four years.'

'That is very true.'

'We might as well do some sightseeing. See what Calais has to offer.'

The taxi ride into town didn't take long, and it turned out there was more to Calais than industrial estates and shopping centres. We walked through impressive public buildings in the centre only to find, like the shopping centres, everything was shut.

'Fuck,' said Noah, as we walked down another street without signs of life. It was like something out of the zombie apocalypse.

'Where's everyone gone?' I cupped my hands, peering into a shop window.

'There's got to be a bar or something open, somewhere.'

The rain had eased off but my boots were well and truly beyond salvage. Water had seeped right into my tights and there was a squelch each time I took a step. I stopped to pull up my soggy tights, wishing I'd put on the jeans Will had suggested.

'That's quite the outfit for a booze cruise,' he said. 'Very chic.'

I snorted with laughter and Noah looked at me, alarmed.

'Sorry, I didn't mean to laugh like that. It's just what my friends were going for when they dressed me – Parisian chic.'

'I'm not sure where to start with that.' He rubbed at his forehead. 'The fact that your friends dressed you or that they named your outfit Parisian chic. Although I guess with the hat . . . ' He pulled a face like he was appraising it.

'The hat that's now doing damage control for the frizz ball underneath.' I tugged at it, but it was soaking just like the rest of me. 'We thought I was going on a daytrip to Paris.'

I looked down the deserted street; it was about as far from the bustling cobbled streets of the Latin Quarter that we could get.

'Oh, Paree,' he said, in a French accent. He wrinkled up his nose. 'I'm getting a sense of why the birthday isn't working out so well.'

'Uh-huh. Great expectations.'

'Yeah,' he said, with a nod. 'It's hard not to with the big birthdays, isn't it? I'm the same. Although this birthday had all the hallmarks of being epic, the plan was to buy booze here to use at our house party tonight. Only Paul ate that oyster.'

I shuddered again. 'Who even eats oysters?'

'I know, right?'

'But a party. That's cool.'

He shrugged. 'Yeah. I just hope Paul's recovered in time. But I guess it's not all bad, this sightseeing is . . . ' He didn't finish as the rain started up again, harder and heavier than before. 'For fuck's sake.'

We ran to the nearest awning for shelter.

'Should we get a taxi back? I think we've seen the best the town can offer us on a Sunday,' I said, shaking my head with disappointment. 'We should have gone on the Goldschläger hunt instead.'

'Hang on.' Noah looked over my shoulder, face lighting up. 'Do my eyes deceive me, or is that place open?'

I snapped my head round and saw what looked to be a shop-front with lights on. At this point it wouldn't have mattered what it was, but the word crêperie written over the door made it heaven sent. A sign from the universe that this might not turn out to be the worst birthday after all.

Chapter 3

The door jangled as we entered. The crêperie was busy, which wasn't surprising with everything else seemingly closed. But there were a few tables free and a waitress directed us over to one.

'Of all the things to be open,' I said, picking up the menu, my eyes lighting up as each line seemed to add something more delicious and naughtier to the crêpes.

'How's your French?' Noah squinted at the menu.

'Good enough to order a pancake. There's ones with Nutella.'

'Even I could translate that one,' he said, with a mock roll of the eyes. 'Ooh, this one's got rum on it, has it? Rum and potatoes?'

'Apples,' I corrected.

'Right, sounds good to me.'

He closed his menu and put it down.

'Just like that?' I peered over my menu at him. 'There's all this choice and you've picked already.'

'What's the point in spending ages looking when I've found something that sounds great?'

I stared at him, my mouth dropping that much more.

'Don't tell me,' he said, folding his arms and resting his elbows on the table. 'You're one of those people. Always looking for something better to come along. Too scared to make a decision in case it's the wrong one.'

I put my menu down.

'I can make a decision.'

'Uh-huh, what are you going to have then?'

I blinked, trying to do a mental coin toss between Nutella and Chantilly cream, and bananas with chocolate. Every time I opened my mouth to speak, I changed my mind.

'Bananas,' I said, eventually. 'See, decisive.'

'Hmm,' he nodded. 'And to drink?'

'Beer?'

'Beer's a solid choice; I'll go for one too.'

We stumbled through ordering in our rusty French and I was pleased when our drinks arrived and they were indeed beer. It gave me a bit of hope that we were going to get the food we thought we'd ordered.

'Cheers, to us.' Noah raised his beer glass. 'To our big birthday. Happy fifth?'

He raised an eyebrow and I nodded back.

'Happy fifth birthday to you too.' I chinked, making strong eye contact with Noah in order not to anger the gods of bad sex.

I sipped my drink, which was the best beer I'd ever tasted.

'So, is your boyfriend on the rugby team?'

'No, why?' I couldn't think of anyone less likely to play such a physical contact sport than Will.

'Because we're on a rugby team booze cruise?'

I blinked, trying to process the information.

'We are?'

'Uh-huh. Didn't you feel like you were on the team bus on the way over?'

'I didn't know.' I closed my eyes in disbelief and sighed. At this point nothing about this trip surprised me. 'So, does that mean you and Paul are on the team?'

'No.' He spluttered a laugh. 'I'm far too uncoordinated for that. Our housemate Bruce is on the team and they had a few spare tickets.'

'Right, I guess Will got us each one of those too.' It was all starting to slot into place. 'Bloody Will.'

'So let's get this straight: you were supposed to be going to Paris and you ended up on a rugby team booze cruise? There's a bit of a difference between the two; how did he mess that up?'

'He didn't exactly mess it up. I mean, he never said Paris. I just kind of assumed . . . '

'You just kind of *assumed*?' His eyebrow was raised and it made me feel even more ridiculous.

'Will was surprising me and he said I needed my passport.'

He narrowed his eyes. 'And you thought that because you needed a passport, you were going to Paris, out of all the possible places you could go.'

He started to laugh and I noticed a little dimple appearing in his left cheek. If he wasn't so infuriating, it would almost be cute.

'It's actually a very logical assumption. Ashford is only a few stops on the train from Canterbury, and the Eurostar stops there on its way to Paris.'

Noah stopped laughing.

'Actually, that is logical.'

'I know,' I said a little too loudly. I attracted glances from the nearby table and I pulled an apologetic face. I leaned in closer and lowered my voice. 'That's what Caz and Amy thought.'

I was getting used to his eyebrow raising now.

'My housemates,' I added. 'They thought I should make an effort, hence the outfit. But we didn't factor in the weather. Do you have any idea how awful wet tights are?'

'I don't.' He shook his head. 'But if it makes you feel any better, my jeans have gone cardboard-like from the rain too.'

I laughed and he smiled back.

'So, what happened to the boyfriend then? Why isn't he sitting here instead?'

'He's buying cigarettes to sell.' I shook my head. 'He wouldn't even come into town to try and make it a little more special.'

'He sounds like a great guy.'

Noah reminded me of Amy and Caz.

'To be fair to him, he never pitched this as a big romantic day out. He just told me he'd booked something for us. It was me and the girls that got carried away with our imagination.'

Noah shrugged his shoulders. 'I don't know, if it was my girlfriend's birthday and she only got to celebrate it once every four years, I'd want to celebrate with her, do something special. I mean, my girlfriend's at uni in Aberystwyth so we couldn't make it work this weekend, but we met up last weekend and celebrated then.'

My body tensed when he mentioned his girlfriend and I couldn't understand why. We were discussing my boyfriend after all.

'What did you do?'

'We spent the weekend at my parents' house in the South Downs. Country walks, romantic meals. Normal couple stuff.'

It bristled when he said normal couple, like me and Will weren't.

Before I could respond, the waitress put our crêpes down in front of us. They looked and smelt amazing.

'*Merci* bucket, I mean, *merci beaucoup*,' said Noah, cringing. The waitress tutted as she walked away. 'We always used to say that when we were younger.'

'Glad you said it after we got the food with the look she just gave you.' I pulled a face.

'I know.' He picked up his cutlery and pointed at mine with his knife. 'Yours looks good.'

'Hmm, yours too.'

I didn't want to admit that his looked and smelt even more amazing than mine. We were both silent for a while whilst we enjoyed our pancakes.

'So how did you end up with a girlfriend in Aberystwyth?' I asked him just as he put another fork full of crêpe into his mouth.

He had to chew as quickly as he could to answer. 'I met her during my gap year.'

'You took a gap year? You're a first year?'

'I did, and I am. You know, I think this is the longest conversation I've had with anyone since coming to uni where we haven't established that in the first sentence.'

'Along with where are you from and what are you studying,' I said, remembering the monotony of fresher's week.

'The typical *Blind Date* questions.'

'Please don't talk about *Blind Date*; I'm still in mourning about Cilla leaving.'

'Yeah, it won't be the same without her.'

'It definitely won't. So where did you go?'

'Where did I go where?'

'On your gap year. Let me guess . . . you did the backpacker trail in Thailand.'

'Actually, I taught primary kids in Ghana.'

'Oh.' I was surprised by his answer. 'That must have been amazing.'

'It was. It made up for the six months before that where I had to work as a temp in a fish finger factory to pay for it.'

There was something about the way he spoke that drew me in. He had such an easy-going manner that it felt like he was spinning a story.

'And before you ask, no, I have no desire to ever eat fish fingers again.' He shuddered. 'But then I went to Ghana, and it blew my mind. I made great friends and the kids were brilliant. They taught me so much.'

He looked a little glassy-eyed as he told me about his year. I asked questions and he took thoughtful pauses to consider them before answering.

'You're making me wish I did a gap year. Beats listening to someone telling me how they bummed around Asia. There are only so many times that I can hear about ping-pong balls and Khaosan Road.'

'Is this a bad time to mention that I did spend three weeks in Thailand at the start of my year? Before the fish finger factory. And I tell you what, I'd go back to Khaosan Road in a heartbeat. I take it you haven't been?'

I shook my head. I hadn't really been very many places.

'You should go, if you get the chance. I want to go back and explore more of Asia. I want to go to Vietnam and Cambodia.'

'Sounds like you've got the bug.'

'Yeah, and luckily so has Hayley.'

'Hayley.' Despite knowing nothing about her, in my head she was some sort of adventurous Lara Croft type. 'She's the one you met in Ghana?'

'Yeah.'

'And you think long distance is going to work?' Now it was my turn to do one of his eyebrow raises.

'Seems to be working so far.'

'Three years is a long time.'

'Oh, I see,' he said, taking a final bite of his crêpe. 'You're a pessimist.'

'I'm a realist.'

He put his knife and fork down and took a sip of his beer.

'So am I. And I met the woman that I can imagine marrying, so why wouldn't we try to make things work?'

'You're going to marry her?'

'Well, not now, obviously. I just mean one day. I feel like I couldn't imagine my life without her. Isn't that what relationships are supposed to be about? I mean, what's the point of being with someone if you don't think you're going to end up with them?'

I thought of Will and my heart sank.

'I just think that we're only twenty – ha, doesn't that sound weird – and twenty is so young and now's the time to be dating unsuitable people.'

'Well, your boyfriend certainly sounds unsuitable.'

'He's not as bad as I made him out to be.' There wasn't a lot of conviction in my voice, but he didn't know Will and perhaps I'd not painted him in the best light. 'But it doesn't matter. I'm sure that I'll date loads of Wills before I settle down. If I settle down.'

I took a last mouthful of crêpe, wondering if the waitress would judge me if I ordered another one.

'At least it's real with him. I know what I'm getting.' I put my cutlery on the plate. 'It's not just fake romance.'

'Fake romance? What does that even mean?'

'It's just . . . all the romcoms that you see, it's all over the top, it's not real. We're all sold this idea of what love should be and how we're all going to live happily ever after, but that doesn't really happen, does it?'

'Doesn't it?'

I thought of my mum who had raised me on a staple of Disney movies, swooning with me every time the prince came along and swept the heroine off her feet, but then Dad had left, and we'd come back down to reality with a bump. Life wasn't a movie.

'My parents have been married twenty-four years,' he continued.

'Lucky for you. My dad left my mum for his secretary.'

'Ouch.' Noah winced, before he started to soften. 'Recently?'

'Four and a bit years ago,' I muttered. 'Not long before the last leap year birthday.'

Noah tilted his head. 'I'm sorry, I didn't mean to sound snarky or anything.'

'You didn't. And I shouldn't have made it seem like your relationship won't last. I'm sure it will. I think it's just . . . watching my mum go through the process.' I thought of the nights we'd curled up on the sofa eating ice cream from the tub, her crying on my shoulder. 'I guess I'm not in any hurry to have my heart broken like that.'

'It was a messy break-up then?'

I nodded. 'My dad didn't go about things the right way.'

'Is there a right way?' He signalled to the waitress for another two beers.

'I'm guessing that if there was, having an affair and then moving straight in with her and her daughter wasn't it.'

'Oh shit.'

The waitress deposited our new beers and took away our plates, and I resisted the urge to order that second crêpe.

'*Café?*'

'Coffee?' I said to Noah and he shook his head.

'*Non, merci.*' He poured the fresh bottle of beer into my empty glass. 'That does sound rough.'

'Yeah, it wasn't the best. He sort of sidestepped from one readymade family to another.'

Noah whistled through his teeth. 'And what about your mum now. Is she OK?'

I thought of how much she'd gone through, and how she always dug deep to overcome the things thrown at her.

'Yeah, she is. She's recently started dating again.'

'Good for her.'

I smiled. 'It is.'

'And your dad?' His face crumbled into an apologetic mode. 'Sorry, I feel like I'm interrogating you.'

'It's OK. Things with my dad are complicated.' I started to peel at the corner of my beer label, but it wasn't budging. 'He wants me to be part of his new family – he's always inviting me over to theirs for dinners and stuff – but it feels disloyal to my mum, you know?' I studied his face but there wasn't a hint of recognition; he didn't know what it was like. He'd said his parents were happily married. 'Anyway, it's complicated. So, do you get on well with your parents?'

34

'I do.' He wrinkled his nose up. 'Sorry.'

'Why are you sorry? That's great. Uncomplicated.'

'Are you OK?'

I could feel my eyes sting as I fought back tears.

'Yes, I'm fine.' I took a deep breath. I wasn't going to cry for a second time.

'OK. It seems to have got very deep, very quickly. Let's change the subject.'

'No complaints from me there,' I said, dabbing under my eyes, relieved that at least so far my waterproof mascara was working.

'So, I think we can pretty much assume that a rugby booze cruise was not how you pictured the big birthday, but what would you pick, if you had the chance?'

'If I had the chance?' I said, relieved to be distracted. 'Hmm . . . '

'And money was no object.'

'New York,' I said, without a skip of heartbeat.

'Wow, that was quick. No deliberation there.'

'Because there's no need. I've always wanted to go. Have you been?'

I could tell his answer from his expression. 'Of course you have. Is there anything in your life I don't need to be jealous of?'

He laughed. 'Plenty, and you'll learn when you get to know me better.'

There was something comforting about the idea that that was a possibility.

'And yes, I went to New York on a school trip,' he said.

'What kind of a school did you go to?'

'Just a bog standard state school, but we had an American exchange.'

'An American exchange? That doesn't sound bog standard at all. I've heard enough.' I raised my hand to get him to stop.

He picked up his beer again, honouring my wishes, but I waved my hand to get him to continue. 'Was New York as amazing as it looks on TV?'

He paused to think.

'Better.'

I knew it. I hadn't met a person yet that had been who hadn't fallen head over heels in love with the city.

'What did you do?'

'We were only there for two days, one night, so it was real whistle-stop stuff. The Statue of Liberty and Ellis Island. Empire State Building.'

'Bloomingdale's?'

He pulled a face. 'Macy's.'

'Good enough. Uh, it just really makes me want to go.' I tried to shake the feeling off. 'I'm totally jealous. So how about you?'

'How about me? Am I jealous of my younger self for the trip? Absolutely .'

I laughed. 'No, I meant where would you spend your dream birthday?'

'I'm not sure . . .' He paused like he was taking the question seriously. 'There are a lot of places I want to go: Australia, New Zealand, Costa Rica, Borneo.'

'Now who's undecisive.'

'The whole world's a big place, it's not like a little menu. But you know, New York wouldn't be a bad place to go back. I barely saw any of it.'

'I want to go ice-skating outside.'

'At the rink in Central Park?'

'Yeah,' I said, nodding. 'That's the one. Now, not that I like many romcoms, there's this one, *Serendipity* . . . '

'John Cusack, yep, seen it.'

'You've seen *Serendipity*?' There weren't many men that I'd met who would so freely admit they'd seen such a cheesy romance, but Noah didn't seem ashamed in the slightest. 'Why am I not surprised you've seen it?'

'What? My sixth-form girlfriend wanted me to take her.'

'Your sixth-form girlfriend?'

'Bethany.'

Of course he'd had a girlfriend in sixth form. I wouldn't be shocked, from the way he talked, if he hadn't spent a day single in his life.

'Right, well, then you know there's that scene where they're at the ice rink at night, and I guess I thought that was cool.'

'Uh-huh. Because that's the main mushy bit?'

'Definitely not.' I didn't want to admit that it was one of the few movies where I actually liked the mushy bit. 'Because it looked amazing with the backdrop of the buildings, all lit up and twinkling, and it's Central Park.'

Noah smiled.

'Central Park is cool.'

'Still jealous.'

The waitress appeared again and asked us in English if we wanted anything else. When we declined she presented us with the bill.

I fumbled in my wallet for the euros I'd hastily exchanged on the ferry.

'I'll get this,' said Noah.

'No, really. I'll get it. Thank you for coming with me.'

The two of us wrestled with the bill until I finally won, placing the notes on the table.

'Thank you, It was a nice birthday treat.'

He slipped on his puffer jacket, drips of rain falling onto the table.

'So what's the plan now?'

Noah pulled back his coat and looked at his watch.

'Shit, it's past three. What time was the bus leaving?'

My blood ran cold.

'How is it so late?' I said, pushing my chair back. 'It leaves at quarter past. What if we miss it?'

'We're not going to miss it,' he said, in far calmer manner than I could muster. He thrust the little silver dish with the money at the waitress. 'No time for change though.'

The waitress finally cracked a smile when she saw the generous tip we'd left.

'Which way's the taxi rank?'

'How am I supposed to know? I've been here as long as you.'

He took a few steps one way then turned and walked the other. The more he scanned the road, the more panic crept over his face and he was no longer the laid-back, well-travelled Noah that had been in the crêperie.

'Fuck,' he muttered, taking his cap off and rubbing his head. 'The bus driver said they wouldn't wait, and I've got the party.'

'And you think I want to be stuck here? Let's try this way.'

We ran up a deserted street in the hope that we'd find a taxi nearer to the main square where it had dropped us off.

'What's the actual time?' I said, trying to keep myself from freaking out. 'Were you talking one minute past three, or ten?'

'It had literally just turned three.'

'OK, OK. We've got time, it was only five minutes by taxi on the way here.'

'True.' Noah nodded his head. 'And it's not like there's going to be traffic with the apocalypse having happened to the town.'

'There is that.'

It was one of those situations where we could either laugh or cry, and thankfully we chose the former.

We got to a main road where a few cars were passing, and we stopped to get our bearings and I bent over a little to catch my breath.

'Look,' I shouted, whacking him on the arm. 'There's a taxi.'

There was a white car with a little green illuminated box on the top heading in our direction.

The two of us stuck our arms out and waved furiously, and we watched in horror as the car sped past us.

'What the—' but as I went to stick my middle finger up at the driver, I saw that he'd stopped further down the road in a layby.

Noah grabbed my hand and he pulled me along to reach it. We climbed in the back and I didn't even wait for the driver to ask where we wanted to go.

'Um, *je voudrais* . . . ' I froze, looking at Noah. 'Um, the grand supermarket.'

'Carrefour,' he said.

'That's it. Carrefour, *très grand*.'

The taxi driver nodded and pulled away from the kerb. The little red clock above his meter said it was five past three, which meant there was still time.

'Blimey, that was close,' said Noah, trying to get his breath back. It made me feel a little better that I wasn't the only one not in peak physical fitness.

'Tell me about it. Imagine if we got stuck here.'

'Don't. My mates would kill me if we didn't make it back with the booze for the party.'

'Wouldn't Paul take it back?'

'That's true. Then actually no one would really care about me, they'd still go ahead with the party.'

I laughed.

'True friends.'

'Absolutely. What about you? What do you have to go back to tonight? You hitting . . . I was going to say the town, but Canterbury's a bit like Calais on a Sunday night.'

'Yeah, that's why we had our big one last night. I think I'll just hang out with Will, if we're speaking again when we get home . . . And if we're not, I think my housemates were going to have a movie night, so I can always crash that.'

'Some great romcom to cheer your heart.'

'Or turn it more to stone.' I sighed.

'You know, you should all come to my party.'

'Oh,' I said, trying to think of a polite way to decline, 'I don't know.'

'What, are you too cool to hang out with a load of first years?'

'Well, you know, you're OK, but the rest of them, they're so much younger.' I was never a big fan of drinking lukewarm wine and making small talk at the best of times, let alone with first years who always seemed so eager.

'That year makes all the difference.' The sarcasm was thick in his voice. 'But if you must know, Paul took a gap year too, Terry's a fourth year, Jan is a Danish exchange student, and Bruce, well, I doubt he'll even make it to the party given how much he was drinking before he boarded the coach.'

I loved his descriptions of his eclectic mix of housemates and part of me did want to go.

'Plus, we probably could do with people to help us drink all the booze we bought before Paul started feeling queasy.'

'Well, when you put it like that.'

I watched out of the window at the passing scenery, goosepimples spreading up my arms because nothing was looking familiar.

'Noah, is it just me . . . ' I started but didn't finish. I was too busy watching in horror as we drove into an industrial estate and up to a gigantic hypermarket that looked incredible, but nothing like the one we'd left.

'Oh shit. It's the wrong one,' said Noah. 'But it looks huge, exactly the type of place that would have Goldschläger.'

'Focus, Noah, focus. Um, *excusez-moi*. Wrong Carrefour,' I said, turning my attention to the driver. '*Il y a beaucoup Carrefour?*'

I tried in my best pidgin French to convey the situation, but I was so worked up it would be hard even if I was explaining in English to an English driver.

'Are there others?' said Noah pointing. 'City Europe.'

The driver made some guttural noise and sped off, the car screeching.

'Do you think it's far?'

'Let's hope not,' said Noah, digging his phone out of his pocket. He started to tap away at the keys and held it up to his ear. 'I'm trying Paul.'

I nodded, knowing my phone wouldn't work as I didn't have roaming.

'No bloody answer.'

'I hope he won't miss it too; he didn't seem well.'

Noah pulled a face. This was becoming more hopeless as the minutes passed by. I went to play with the charm on my bracelet, but my wrist was bare.

I shook out my sleeve, hoping that it had fallen off into my jumper, but there was nothing.

'Shit,' I muttered, looking around my lap in faint hope.

'What's wrong?'

'My bracelet's gone.'

'The four-leaf clover?' he asked.

'You noticed it?'

'In the crêperie. Maybe it came out when you put your coat on. Was it valuable?'

'No, I bought it at a craft market years ago; it's just one of those things I put on when I was doing my GCSE exams and then I've sort of always worn it, for luck.'

'Did you want to go back?'

He was being sincere and part of me wanted to hug him for being so sweet, but I knew we couldn't go back for that.

'Like we've got time? No, it's fine. Honestly.'

I'd grown used to fiddling with it when I was stressed; I'd have to find something else to distract me instead.

Noah's phone rang and I sighed with relief. That must be Paul. He could delay the bus until we get there.

'Hey, you.' There was almost a purr in Noah's voice, giving me the impression that it wasn't Paul. 'Yeah, having a nice time. Listen, I'm just trying to race back to the bus, so now probably isn't the best time . . . uh-huh, ah, yeah . . . in a taxi . . . uh-huh, no with Lucy . . . she's just a mate. One of the guys really . . . yeah, I'm sure you'll meet her when you're next down.' He shut his eyes tight for a moment. 'Yeah, OK, love you too. I'll call when I'm back.'

He hung up the phone.

'One of the boys?' I arched an eyebrow.

'Yeah.' He looked sheepish. 'I've found that's the worst part of long distance, it's easy to imagine things that aren't there. Best make sure she knows straight away there's no need to worry.'

My fragile ego was a little affronted that there was no need to worry, but I understood his logic.

'I guess that makes sense.'

I saw the clock on the dashboard change to quarter past.

'How long do you think they'll wait?' I was going for light and breezy in my tone, but my voice came out pitchy. 'What time is the ferry? Isn't it at four?'

My stomach was churning. Why hadn't I just stayed and gone on a cheese hunt?

'I think it's four,' said Noah, looking out the window at the hotels we were whizzing past. 'Looks like there are plenty of places to stay if we get stuck.'

I stared hard. It would be Sod's law that I'd have to use all my birthday money to stay in one of them overnight.

'Don't look so scared,' said Noah, putting his hand on my arm. 'I'm just teasing – we'd be able to get back on another ferry as foot passengers.'

'Right.' I nodded. I hadn't let myself consider what would happen if we missed it, but it was slowly sinking in that it could be a reality. My breathing was getting shallower and my palms sweatier.

'Lucy, stay with me,' he said, reaching for my hand. 'It's going to be OK.'

He gave me such a sincere smile that it spread calmness all over my body. I looked out the window, still aware we were holding hands, but doing nothing about it.

'Oh my god, there it is, City Europe.' I tapped on the glass to point at the archways coming into view.

'Any sign of the bus?'

I craned my neck, trying to spot it out the window.

'I think this is the wrong car park, wasn't it over the other side of that Tesco's?'

I looked beyond it but the driver had already flicked off his meter.

'I've got this one,' said Noah, handing over the euros. 'It'll be quicker to cut across there.'

We hastily thanked the driver and started to run. My boots were slipping and I couldn't keep up with Noah, so he grabbed my wrist and helped keep me upright.

'I can see it,' he shouted.

The bright-blue bus stood out in the sea of grey. Noah and I waved frantically and the closer we got the more faces I could see gawping out of the windows at us.

'They waited,' he panted. 'Fuck, we actually made it.'

We waited for the electronic door to swish open.

'You two are bloody lucky,' said the Student Union rep before we had a chance to step onboard. 'We were just about to go. This one made us wait.'

He gestured to Paul who was sitting in the front row, resting on the safety rail that ran along in front of it. He did at least try and raise a hand in our direction.

There was a cacophony of cheers from the rugby team, who all looked as worse for wear as Paul, when we climbed the steps up to the seats. The only person not cheering was Will. His face was like thunder as he marched down the aisle towards us.

'Where the hell did you go?' His hands were placed on his hips and it reminded me of the times before Dad left that I'd tried to sneak in after curfew.

'Into town. I didn't mean to cut it so fine. The taxi took us to the wrong supermarket.'

He stared over my shoulder at Noah and then back at me. He tutted loudly and turned and stormed back the way he came.

'I take it that's the boyfriend,' whispered Noah as the coach lurched and we hastily sat down in the seats behind Paul.

'He was just worried.'

'So worried that he was on the coach, ready to go?'

I shook my head. Now wasn't the time.

'I should go and sit with him.' I looked down the back of the coach and I could see the top of Will's head halfway down.

'Sorry, I'll stop, but,' he said, gesturing to Paul, 'you know you're welcome to stay here, seeing as he's replaced me with a bucket.'

Paul gave us a thumbs up without lifting his head.

'Thanks, but I better sort things out with Will.'

Noah smiled. 'Thanks for today's mystery tour.'

'It's me that should be thanking you. Thanks for being that white knight.'

He laughed. 'Anytime. And I meant what I said, about the party tonight.'

I saw the look that Will gave Noah earlier. Going to his party would probably be like pouring fuel onto a fire.

'I'll see.'

'In case you change your mind. I'm at 22 Ellenden Court, over in Parkwood.'

'OK,' I said, getting to my feet only to find myself sitting down again. 'And if I don't make it tonight, it was nice to meet you.'

I stuck my hand out for Noah to shake. It was an oddly formal end to the afternoon, but I somehow didn't know how to say goodbye to him.

Noah smiled and shook my hand, with a firm grip. 'It was nice to meet you too, fellow leapling. Enjoy the rest of our birthday.'

I gave a wave and headed down the coach, gripping the tops of the seats as I went. I got the impression that the driver was trying to get us to the port at breakneck speed to make up for our tardiness, and I almost ended up on the laps of a couple of the rugby players.

I made it to my seat next to Will, and he shuffled across so that I wasn't touching him in the slightest. To make his point even further, he turned so far that he was almost looking at the back of his seat rather than out of the window.

I stared at the back of his head, incredulous. He really wasn't going to attempt to make this better.

'You're the one who wouldn't come with me when I went into town,' I said, almost in a whisper.

'And you're the one who's been ungrateful about this whole trip.'

I gritted my teeth. What was I doing sitting next to Will? Why was I putting up with this?

There was a tiny knot starting to tighten in my stomach as I thought about this afternoon. I wasn't sure if it was Noah's opinion on Will and how he thought he should have treated me, or the way he described his own relationship and how much he believed in it. Or maybe it was that spending the afternoon with a guy who was actually interesting, and funny, and nice, had made me realise that Will wasn't really any of those things, not anymore.

I should have sat next to Noah. I looked at his blue cap, like a beacon at the front of the coach, and I wondered if, when we got back onto British soil, I should text the girls and see if they fancied going to his party.

I leaned back into the seat and closed my eyes, relieved to have made it on to the coach. A small smile crept over my lips as I replayed our frantic taxi ride to get here, the anger starting to ebb away as I imagined the story I'd have to tell the girls when I got home.

Chapter 4

'Why are we going to a first year's party?' Amy folded her arms over her light denim jacket as soon as we got out of the taxi.

'Don't say it like that.' It was the same tone I'd had earlier when Noah had called me out on it. 'They're our age.'

'But they're in *first* year. They haven't had as much life experience as us.'

I could see her breath as she spoke. The chill had really descended and I was sure her jacket was much more suited to a balmy summer evening than a frosty night out in February.

'Noah taught at a school in Ghana, and worked in a factory to pay for it. I'm pretty sure that he got more life experience doing that than we did bar hopping and arriving at lectures still drunk.'

We heard the party before we found it. The thump of the bass and hum of chatter coming from the corner of the cul-de-sac of tiny houses.

'There's the mention again – Noah,' said Caz, putting on a husky voice when she got to his name.

I raised a finger in protest, worried that he'd somehow over-hear. 'You're barking up the wrong tree. He has a girlfriend, a long-term-love-of-his-life-type girlfriend.'

'I notice, Lucy Adams, that you didn't say that you have a boyfriend.' Caz flicked her hair over her shoulder, like she'd won the point.

Whilst Will and I hadn't officially broken up, neither of us had spoken to each other on the trip back on the ferry. It felt very much like we were just waiting for the final nail in the coffin to be tapped in, but neither of us wanted to be the one that hammered it. Instead, I had spent my time with Noah and Paul during the tiny respites of his sickness.

We got to the house and the front door was ajar. Caz pushed it open and squeezed her way past the people in the doorway and into the kitchen. I followed tightly behind her.

It was busy, busier than I'd expected it to be, and the downstairs of the house was full to the brim with students.

'Let's find this free booze,' said Caz.

'Hey, you made it,' cried a voice behind me. I spun round and almost didn't recognise Noah without his cap. He looked even more like a boyband member now with his shaggy but styled longish hair and a button-down shirt hanging over his jeans. He leaned in and gave me a hug like a long-lost friend.

'I take it these are the famous housemates,' he said, as I introduced him to Caz and Amy. 'I'm so glad to meet the outfit pickers. I'm disappointed there's no Parisian chic tonight.'

'We thought we'd tone it down for a house party.'

'Student chic, I like it. Come on, I'll get you drinks and introduce you around.' He motioned with his hand as we tried to make it down the packed kitchen. He was different to this afternoon. It wasn't just that he was doused in Hugo Boss and he'd made an effort with his clothes, he seemed more confident too.

'Here, we bought you this.' I handed the free bottle of wine that I'd got from Will's multibuy offer.

'Thanks, that's really good of you.' He took it and studied the label before nodding his head in approval. Caz poked her tongue out at me. She was one of those teenagers that drank wine with their parents growing up, and she'd taken one look at the bottle and told me it was dessert wine and best given away at any available opportunity. 'Did you want a glass of it now?'

'It's not chilled,' said Caz, quickly.

'Right you are. Not sure there's room in the fridge.' He placed it down on the worktop. 'What else can I get you? I think we've got nearly every flavour of vodka.'

'Any Goldschläger?' I peered along the bottles.

He put his hand over his heart. 'Oh, hit me where it hurts why don't you. How about Aftershock? It's not quite the same, but it'll still give you that cinnamon hit. Shots?'

We all nodded. He found some novelty shot glasses in a cupboard and filled them to the brim.

'To the birthday boy and girl,' said Amy, raising her glass.

'To us.' We all chinked our shots together, but it was Noah's eyes that met mine as we shot the drinks back.

It burned as it hit the back of my throat.

'Bloody hell, that felt stronger than usual,' said Amy. She looked almost as green as Paul was earlier.

'I think I might have been a little over generous with the measures. How about some vodka cocktails instead?'

'Perhaps I might pour them,' I said, reaching for the lemon vodka. 'I want to make it home tonight.'

'Very wise.'

He dug around, trying to find us some glasses and when he

couldn't find any, he handed us some mis-matched mugs. Drinks made, he tried his best to introduce us around the party before he was torn away to greet someone.

It wasn't long before I lost Amy and Caz to the party too. Amy was last spotted talking to one of Noah's housemates, and Caz was deep in conversation with a group of Danish students on their year abroad.

'Hey, Lucy.' I turned to find Paul, holding a beer in one hand, and what looked like a pint of water in the other.

'Wow, you're looking a whole lot better.'

'I don't feel it.' He frowned. 'I feel bloody awful.'

'Well, at least you've got some colour now. And you're drinking again.'

He checked over both of his shoulders before he leaned closer to me.

'Don't tell anyone but I poured it into a glass for someone else to drink, and I filled it with water.'

'You're pretending?'

He startled and looked around. 'Don't say it so loud. The boys . . . Peer pressure. You know what it's like.'

I laughed. I'd never understood why men had to egg each other on when it came to drinking.

'Oh, I met your friend earlier,' he said, brightening up. 'The nurse.'

'The nurse?'

Neither of my friends were nurses; in fact, I wasn't sure that was even an option offered at the university.

'Yes, she said that she'd go home to get her kit to take care of me if I needed.' He scratched his head. 'I think she was a little offended when I said no, but there's nothing she could have done about it, really. And I didn't want her to go to any trouble.'

I went to open my mouth to correct him, but he waved his hand up in the air at someone that had just arrived.

'Sorry, Lucy, I'll be back in a second.'

I found myself alone again and the way that Paul greeted the new arrivals I didn't think he'd remember he was mid-conversation with me. I edged over to the corner of the room, perching on the windowsill, trying to make myself as small as possible. Caz was still deep in conversation, and I saw Amy weaving through the crowd as if she was looking for someone. I held my hand up to wave at her.

'Hey you,' I said, as she got closer.

'Hey. Isn't this a great party?'

I pulled a face in mock surprise. 'What *this* party? This first year party?'

She pursed her lips, not wanting to admit she'd been wrong.

'I've barely met a first year yet,' she said, 'it's such an eclectic mix of people.'

'So eclectic.'

'Where's Caz?'

I pointed to where she was holding court in the centre of the room.

'Look at her, how does she do it?' I watched her bring someone standing on the sidelines into the conversation. She was nodding and tapping people on the arm when they said something funny.

'How does she do what?' asked Amy, her eyes narrowing as she watched her.

'I've never known anyone like her. She can go into any social situation and talk to anyone.'

'It's not like you're a shrinking violet. You're the one that spent this afternoon touring a foreign country with a man you just met.'

'You make it sound like we were driving around the countryside on some epic adventure. We went into a town centre and had a crêpe.'

'Well, I was impressed. I didn't know you had it in you.' Amy swilled her drink round before she finished it off. 'Do you want another one?'

I looked at my second lemon vodka drink; I'd barely started it.

'I'm alright, thanks.'

'I might get another,' she said, peering over to the other end of the kitchen again. She was taking great interest down there and I wonder if she'd found what – or, more accurately, who – she was looking for. 'And I might just go and talk to that guy again.'

I followed the end of her finger that could have been pointing to any number of men. And with Amy it would be hard to tell.

In the year and a half that I'd known her, I'd learned that she didn't have a strict type like I might. She was attracted to what she called a person's energy. Which meant, I'd seen her date short men, tall men, ginger-haired men, curly-haired blond men. The only thing that they had in common is that she didn't go out with them more than once or twice. She didn't see the point in carrying something on if it didn't have the potential to go anywhere.

'Wish me luck.' She adjusted her fringe in the reflection of the window.

'Good luck.'

I watched her strut off and get swept off into the crowd. My fingers automatically reached for my bracelet, the disappointment sinking in when I realised that it was no longer there. I tugged at my sleeves instead, straightening them up, trying to overhear conversations nearby in case there was one I could join, but the nearest group to me were talking about bands that I'd never heard of.

I was trying to pretend that I didn't feel massively self-conscious, but I wasn't good at pretending. I wasn't Caz, or Amy, and I'd used up my daily allocation of bravery talking to Noah in Calais. The back door opened as someone walked in and I saw it as an escape and headed outside.

I made my way past the small group of smokers by the door, and found myself in the communal garden at the back of the houses. It was surrounded by hedges and flower borders, and once inside it was like a secret garden. I spotted a bench and sat down.

'Party getting too much?'

I almost jumped back up in shock, and my hand flew to my chest in reflex.

'You scared the crap out of me,' I said to Noah, who was sitting on the top part of a bench further down, his feet resting on the seat. He climbed down, shoving his illuminated phone in his pocket.

'What are you doing out here?'

'Trying to scare unsuspecting victims.' He put on a villainous laugh that he couldn't really pull off. He stopped abruptly and got up and walked over to my bench. 'I don't get any signal in the house. So, how are you liking the party?'

'It's good,' I said, shuffling along to make room for him.

'So good that you had to escape?'

I smiled weakly. 'It's not that I don't like house parties, it's just sometimes I find them a bit exhausting. Having to talk to people.'

He laughed. 'That's kind of the point of a party.'

'Yeah, I know. I'm just more of a hang out in a pub with friends type of person. I hate it at parties where you're talking to one person one minute and then you have to start afresh with another the next. It's always trying to find that common ground, or feigning interest in something that you know nothing about, and having to be witty—'

'And breathe.'

'Sorry.' I sighed. 'It's just—'

'—parties.'

'Parties,' I agreed.

'Well, I won't speak to you, if you like. Give you some space to sit here and look at the stars, which are looking fabulous by the way.'

I smiled, about to protest that I didn't mind speaking to him, but my mouth dropped open at the sight above me. Where we lived in town, and even on the main campus, there was a lot of light pollution, but over this side there was nothing and the view was incredible.

It was one of those crisp, cold nights that weren't conducive to sitting on a bench without a coat, but it did mean that the sky was dark black and the stars were shining brighter than diamonds.

'I always look for Pisces,' said Noah, scanning the sky. 'But to be honest I never see it.'

I looked for our star sign, even though I knew the chances of seeing it were slim.

'I think I read once that you can only really see it in autumn,' I said.

'I guess that shows you how little I know about astronomy.'

'I don't know anything either, to be honest,' I said, unwrapping the hoodie from round my waist and slipping it over my head.

There was a moment of silence between us. It was the kind of silence that was rare to find when talking to someone new. Neither of us were rushing to fill the void and that was OK.

'You said you were out here for a phone call,' I said, changing the subject.

'Yeah, Hayley usually rings me around this time to say goodnight.'

Part of me wanted to be revolted at the slushy sentiment, but a pang in my chest let me know how I really felt about it. In all honesty, it sounded nice. In those moments late at night, when the house is still and feelings of loneliness descend, it would be quite nice to have someone to remind you that they care about you.

'I know, you think I'm a soppy git.'

'Obviously.'

He smiled.

I wrapped my arms a little tighter around me to shield me from the cold. The hoodie hadn't really done enough now that my body had cooled down from the party.

'Do you want my coat? You must be freezing.'

'I'm OK; it was really hot in that party.'

'I know. It's hot in there on a normal day as we've got no idea how to turn down the thermostat, let alone when we've got half the campus in there.'

'It's nice so many people came out for your birthday.'

'Oh, I'm under no illusion that they came for that. They came for the free booze.'

'I'm sure they didn't.'

He raised an eyebrow. 'They're students, of course they came for the free booze.'

'I didn't.'

He turned to look at me and in that split second it was like all the breath was sucked out of me. I coughed and looked back up at the stars, my cheeks starting to burn with embarrassment. But on the plus side, at least it was warming me up.

'I take it, from the fact you're here tonight, that you didn't work things out with the boyfriend.'

I felt my shoulders tense at the mention of him.

'I figured that it was perhaps best if we had a little space.'

'For good?'

I shrugged. I wasn't sure about that yet.

Noah shook his head.

'What?'

'I don't get why you'd stay with someone who treated you like he did today.'

'Well, I'm sorry, but we can't have all found the love of our lives at twenty, can we?' It came out harsher than I meant it to and I bit my lip. I shouldn't be taking out my frustration on him. 'I'm sorry; I didn't mean it like that.'

I wondered how it was possible that I was jealous of something that I didn't even want.

'No, it's me. I shouldn't have poked my nose in. You're an adult.'

'Doesn't feel like it,' I said, with a smile.

He smiled back. 'Look, I am fully aware that this is none of my business, and I only said it because I think you're a nice person, and you should be dating one of the good guys; there are quite a lot of us out there.'

'Are there? Single ones?'

He winced. 'Yeah, I guess that's the challenging part. But really, don't hang on to a wrong one because you can't find the right one.'

'That sounds like the kind of advice you'd get from a *Just Seventeen* agony aunt.'

He stroked at his chin. 'Agony aunt, or I guess agony uncle; I'd be good at that.'

'How to keep the romance in your relationship.' I put on a faux American accent. 'Step one, have a bedtime phone call.'

'Now you're taking the piss.'

'I'm not, it's sweet.'

'Yeah, yeah. Miss pessimistic thinks it's sweet now?'

'Realist, not pessimist. I don't know, I think I can take or leave a lot of relationship stuff, but that kind of sounded nice, you know, being someone's last thought at night.'

I don't know where it came from but my eyes started to well up.

'Oh, hey, you're not going to cry, are you? I'm sure there are lots of men that think about you in bed.'

I spluttered. I guess that was one way to stop the tears.

'Wait, that's not what I meant.'

'Not quite agony uncle language.'

'I just meant, that from what I've known from meeting you today, you're sweet, and kind, and intelligent and funny – well, sometimes – and I guess you already know you're pretty.'

My cheeks were starting to burn as one after another the compliments rolled off Noah's tongue, and my heart beat faster. I wasn't sure if he was leaning towards me, or if I was leaning in to him, but suddenly our faces were mere inches apart.

'I think any nice guy would be crazy not to want to call you to say goodnight,' he said, in almost a whisper. I could feel his warm breath on me.

Deep down, I knew I couldn't kiss Noah, and I could tell from how he hadn't closed the gap between us that he knew it too. And yet, we stayed in that almost moment for longer than we should have, my heart wishing for something my brain knew I couldn't have.

'I'm sorry,' he said, moving back.

'Yeah.' I turned and looked up at the sky again, letting out a long breath.

I'd been seduced in that moment not by Noah, but by the idea of what a relationship could be; perhaps what it should be. I couldn't stay with Will.

Noah's phone rang.

'It's Hayley,' he said to me unnecessarily; we both knew it would be.

'You should get it. I'm going to go back to the party.'

'Look, it's no longer our birthday.' He pointed at his phone screen. 'And the four-year wait for the next one begins.'

He raised an eyebrow and hit answer. He walked away, phone to his ear and I listened to the sound of his voice getting fainter as I walked out of the hedged garden.

Four years until the next birthday . . . I couldn't help but wonder where I'd be then.

Text message – Noah to Lucy: March 2004

Hey! Thanks for coming to the party. It took me days to recover. Think your nurse friend made quite the impression on Paul. How about we all run into each other at a pub one night so we can get them together!

Text message – Lucy to Noah: March 2004

What happened last night??? Is Amy still at yours???? Still wetting myself that Paul thought she was an actual nurse. Imagine if he'd have taken her up on the offer and she'd trotted back to your party in her naughty nurse costume. LOL. But seriously – Amy and Paul???

Text message – Noah to Lucy: October 2004

Hoping I've timed this right and you've moved in already and don't need any help ;) You and Caz fancy a pint? Amy's just arrived and I don't think her and Paul are looking for a third wheel tonight.

Voicemail – Lucy to Noah: May 2005

NOOOOOOAAAAAHHHHHHH! Where have you been hiding? I am officially done with uni, last exam this morning, so you better get your arse in gear and hang out with us before we leave for ever. Hayley visiting is no excuse – you know we love her more than you. Just kidding, just get your arse out.

Email – Noah to Lucy: September 2005

To Lucy,
Sorry I've been crap at emailing. You'll be glad to know

that I'm working like a dog out here. I might be lapping up the Greek sunshine, but the only sun loungers I get to see are the ones I'm hosing down. The hotel is brutal, although definitely a work-hard play-hard mentality. Hayley, of course, has got some cushy job on the reception desk. Looking forward to going back to uni next month for a rest. Good luck with the grad scheme; I know you'll be great. N x

Text message – Noah to Lucy: March 2006
Are you ever going to come back and visit? What happened to 'we'll be down all the time because London drinks are too pricey'? We've only got a couple of months left before we leave so you better make the most of it.

Text message – Lucy to Noah: December 2006
Is Paul telling the truth? Are you and Hayley really off to Oz? We've only just got used to having you living in London with us. You better not be leaving before our Xmas bash.

Email – Noah to Lucy: January 2007
Hiya,

I'm so sorry we missed you before we left. It went proper mental trying to fit in so many goodbyes. But really a year and a half will fly by and there's always Oz. You can visit. Use some of that holiday that you're so fond of accruing. Pretty sure that place will still be standing if you take a break, you know. Just saying.

Anyway, we've got a few days in Singapore, then we're headed to Sydney on Thursday. And before you ask, yes,

I've packed plenty of mosquito repellent. Plus, Hayley's got a whole medical bag with her too. No need for you to worry.

Catch you soon,

N x

Phone conversation – Noah to Lucy: February 2007

L: (groggy) hello

N: Luuuuuucy!

L: Hello? What time is it? What?

N: Lucy, Lucy, Lucy, Lucy.

L: Oh, god, Noah is that you? Fuck. What time is it? Bloody hell, it's three in the morning. What time is it there and why are you so drunk?

N: I figured that it's kind of our birthday, you know, right now, in the middle of the twenty-eighth and the first for you, so it's our birthday right?

L: I'm pretty sure it's technically the first. (Groans)

N: Then it's your birthday. Let me be the first one to wish you a happy one.

L: Thanks. You know you could have waited until I actually got up.

N: I know, but I don't think I'm going to be up for long. Yesterday's birthday shenanigans were intense. Thanks for the card.

L: You're welcome.

N: And next year we'll celebrate our actual birthday.

L: If you're back.

N: You could always come here.

L: Look, Noah, I'm so pleased you rang, but I've got a presentation tomorrow and—

N: OK, OK. Happy birthday, Luce.

L: Thanks, make sure you drink water before you go to bed.

N: Thanks, Mum.

Lucy's Facebook status: September 2007

Lucy is excited as she just got a new promotion!

Comments

Mags – Huge congratulations, sweetie, but don't get too comfy in your new cubicle, I still won't give up on getting you to come work for me.

Lucy – @Mags Don't you mean with you?

Mags – @Lucy Do I? Joking. Of course, with me.

NOAH – Way 2 go Luce!!!! Hope this means you'll move out of the shoebox into a flat that I can kip on the floor of when I get back.

Lucy – @Noah Ha ha ha. Amy and I have already signed a new lease.

Noah Facebook relationship status: December 2007

Noah Matthews is Single

Email – Lucy to Noah: December 2007

Just saw Facebook. Is it true? Please tell me you were hacked? If not, and it's that brutal – hope you're OK? Skype?

Voicemail – Noah to Lucy: 28th February 2008

I'm just about to start the long, long trip home. I don't even want to think about what time I'll get there, but with changes of flight times and stuff, I think I get into Heathrow at four thirty in the afternoon. So hopefully it'll give me time to have a quick nap before we head out in the evening? I hope that works with you and your plans for your day off? I'm guessing in London you probably couldn't leave the key under a mat for me? But perhaps send me a text and let me know if you'd be in? Laters.

PART TWO

2008

Chapter 5

Thursday 28th February 2008

I hung up my phone and slipped it back in my bag. The sun was matching my mood today and there was less of a chill than there had been this morning. If it wasn't for the buildings plunging me into the shade I'd have no need for my woolly scarf.

It was the tiniest hint that winter was almost over, and between that and Noah's voicemail, it was enough to put a spring in my step.

'Look at you, like the Cheshire cat. Take it easy; smiling gives you wrinkles,' said Mags. She was smoking outside the revolving doors to our office block. She'd managed to find herself a sliver of sun to stand in.

'So will those things.' I pointed to the cigarette.

'Touché. I'm quitting.' She took one last puff before she stubbed it out.

'Uh-huh.'

'I am, honestly. I'm just finishing up my last pack. Don't want any around to be tempted.'

'You could throw them away.'

'At the prices they charge? I'm getting my money's worth.'

She dug out a little metal pill box of mints from her pocket and popped one on her tongue. She held the box open to me.

'I'm good, thanks.'

'So I can see. What's with the big smile?'

'What big smile?' I said, trying to push the corners of my mouth down, but it was no use; they kept springing back up.

'You know what I'm talking about. It's got to be a man. Is it the guy from My Single Friend?'

I shuddered. 'Definitely not. You know he dumped me in the end for his mate that wrote the advert for him?'

'What?'

'Yep, apparently when she wrote his profile to attract other women, she realised what she was missing. It was the last straw when he started dating me.'

'And of course, he just happened to be in love with her?'

'Always had been.'

We flashed our badges at the security guard and headed towards the bank of lifts in the centre of the lobby.

'Tale as old as time. You know, men can never be friends with women. It's a known fact. No one has a platonic male friend.'

'Yes, you can and people do.'

'No, you can't. It's the gospel. And the whole point of *When Harry Met Sally*.'

We squeezed to the back of the lift as other people filed in.

'Which is a good movie. But that's not real life. Besides, I do have a good male friend. And we're just that. *Friends*.'

I hadn't really noticed that I'd never had a male friend before I met Noah. I'd hung around with boys in sixth-form college, and we had a couple in our university group but I wouldn't have called any of them real friends. I wouldn't phone them up for a chat, or turn to them in my moment of need. But the day I met Noah, all that changed. I'm not sure if it was just that we'd had our mini adventure in Calais, or because we were born under the exact same star alignment that cosmically meant we were destined to get on, the truth was he was one of the few people that I felt comfortable around. Comfortable telling him what I thought. Comfortable in silence.

And for the last year and a half he'd gone and messed that all up doing his working holiday visa in Australia.

'I don't believe you. One of you will have fancied the other at some point.'

'Nope,' I said, almost with conviction. There had been a few moments over the years when I'd questioned whether there could be something more, but as quickly as the thought popped into my mind, it popped out again. 'He's like my brother.'

'Your brother?' Her eyebrow arched. 'Let me get this straight, you're telling me you've been friends for how long . . . '

'Four years.'

'You've been friends for four years, and not once have you had a drunken hook-up?'

'Nope,' I said, thinking of that first night and how we almost kissed, too lost in the fantasy of what a relationship could be. 'Not once.'

'No drunken snog?'

'Nope. Just friends. I mean, he's had a girlfriend for pretty much most of it.'

'Ah, that explains it.' The lift doors pinged open and we pushed our way through the others to get out. 'You never got the chance.'

It hadn't even crossed my mind when Noah and Hayley briefly broke up when he was in second year.

'Honestly, it's not like that. Even now that Noah's single I still wouldn't.'

I could tell from the look on her face that she was having none of it, and I rolled my eyes at her, and headed straight for the coffee machine.

'Surely you have at least one platonic male friend,' I said to her. 'Who was the guy that came to your Christmas drinks? Teddy?'

'We slept together that night.'

'You did not?'

She shrugged like it was no big deal.

'We're each other's go-to fuck buddy when we're lonely and single.'

'You were still with Aiden at that point.'

'Huh, OK, we're each other's fuck buddies when we're lonely.'

I squinted at the new coffee machine that was so complicated it felt like you needed a master's degree to work it out. I pressed on what I hoped was a decaf latte.

'Well, OK, *you* might not be able to have platonic male friends, but I can. His name is Noah, and the reason that I was smiling is that he's been living in Australia and he's coming back tomorrow for our birthday.'

'Our birthday?'

'He's a leapling too.'

The coffee machine started to make horrendous noises, a good sign that it was working.

'Right, and that massive smile was just for a friend?' She shook her head. 'And you're both now single? No, I don't buy it for one second.'

'You don't have to buy it,' I said, stepping back from the

billowing steam coming from the milk frothing, 'but that's the reality. Look, we've known each other for years, we've spent countless nights sleeping on each other's sofas and honestly we're just mates. Plus, he's one of those god-awful hopeless romantics and I'm—'

'—a woman with a heart of stone?'

'I was going for realist, but if the shoe fits.'

'Ummhmm.'

'Whatever. You know, he's more your type than mine. Always looked like he'd stumbled out of a boyband. Don't you like them preppy?'

'Oh no, don't let me get involved. I don't want to go through what you just did, I get set up with this great guy only for you to realise you had feelings all along and swoop in.'

'Honestly, never going to happen.'

'Yeah, yeah. Anyway, I'm looking forward to a full report on Monday about your night out and how you guys hooked up.'

The coffee machine finally stopped whirring and I took the cup, warming up my hands.

'Aren't you coming tomorrow? I thought you were swinging by on the way to your dinner?'

'Yeah, I will, if I get a chance, but I hadn't realised that the dinner is in Surbiton. I've got to catch a mainline sodding train.'

'Oh, well, if you can stop by, I'd love to see you. You know I only get these birthdays once every four years.'

I did what I hoped were puppy dog eyes.

'I'm going to make the effort, just to see you and your "friend".' She did air quotes around the word friend.

'I'm leaving now.'

I headed back over to my desk, and, no matter the teasing

from Mags, I couldn't stop smiling. I'd missed Noah. I'd missed that male perspective that's hard to get through a ten-hour time difference when you're only communicating in snippets of messages and emails, sometimes with weeks in between when you forget to reply.

I thought of what he'd missed out on in the last eighteen months. I'm sure if he'd still been living in London, he'd have seen through the bullshit of Barney, a guy I'd dated for a few months, and he certainly would have picked up weeks before I did that I was never going to hear from Michael, my first foray into online dating, when he said he'd ring after he got back from his work trip to Yemen. It took me a hangover and a day binge watching *Friends* to get that reference.

Of course, I reported the Yemen story to Noah, but it wasn't the same seeing the response typed out: ha ha ha. You didn't get the high-pitched squeak that he had when he was laughing from the pit of his belly. Or the little crease on the bridge of his nose, or that dimple on his left cheek that put in rare appearances.

'Ah, Lucy,' said Francis, marching up to my desk and jolting me out of my memories of Noah, 'I wondered if we could have a little word.'

'Absolutely.'

I put my coffee down and braced myself, waiting to hear what it was I'd done wrong this time. Francis and I had started work on the same day, on the same graduate scheme, and yet he'd risen through the ranks at double the speed whilst only doing half the amount of work. He liked to tell us at length that it was nothing to do with the fact that he was on first-name terms with the CEO – the CEO that his dad had shared a house with at Eton once upon a time. Pure coincidence. Just like the coincidence that Mags and I, the only women on the scheme, always worked with the smaller clients.

'I think you should come to my office. Better to have some privacy, don't you think?'

I huffed as I stood back up. There was something about the way I had to follow him ten feet to his office, almost just for him to prove that he had one. Not that there was much to Francis's office. It was cold, dark and dingy. Much like his personality. I'm sure in any other floorplan it would have been a broom cupboard. But to Francis, it was everything, and didn't we have to know about it!

I squeezed into the chair, breathing in as he shut the door.

'Now,' he said, walking sideways to squeeze behind his desk, 'it's come to my attention that you're taking on Mackenzie Field as a client.'

'That's right, I've just sent the prelim contract over to legal to check and—'

'It's just,' he said, not letting me finish, 'that you'll know their parent company is P&R, who, as you're aware, I manage.'

I took a deep breath. 'Yes, I am aware of that. I did look into their company history before I went for the initial meeting. But they're owned as a separate subsidiary so they're fully autonomous and are a separate entity to P&R in daily operations.'

'Well' – he hunched his shoulders and I steeled mine for what was to come – 'you see, that's not how we do things around here, is it? It's a bit like poaching a client.'

'It's not poaching a client; you've still got the big fat fish. I'm just picking up the minnow.'

'The minnow that's already attached by line to the other fish.'

I gritted my teeth. The annual billing for Mackenzie would

be about a twentieth of that of P&R. He didn't need it for his portfolio. He didn't need it for any status. He was just messing with it to let me know that he could.

'I was speaking to Clive on the squash court last night and he agreed that it would look better if I took on both clients. You know, for continuity.'

There it was, Clive, the CEO. The name drop, the flex of the muscles.

'Right, Mr Horner thinks so, of course he does. When you suggested it.'

'I'm merely trying to keep the synergy.'

I nodded and squeezed my lips together so hard that I thought they might burst.

'Synergy.' I looked at the latest bestselling business book on his desk and wondered if that little gem had come from there. Although, there wasn't any bend or crease to the spine and I doubt it had even been opened; perhaps it was for show, like everything else. 'Fine. I'll message the client and let them know that you'll be taking over, and I'll send you over the contract for you to review.'

I could imagine what Mags would say when she heard about this. The same thing she always said, that this was another sign that the two of us should start our own business. We were never going to get anywhere here. No matter how hard we worked, we couldn't escape the fact that we didn't belong to the same club. We were the wrong sex. We'd been to the wrong schools.

'That's great. Thank you, Lucy, for being so understanding. I'm sure that you'll find another client to bring on board. You're so good at finding new business.'

'Hmm,' I said. I wish the same could be said for keeping it;

there often seemed reasons to move them to someone with more capacity or someone with a corner office.

'Anyway, send it across and I'll introduce myself ASAP, let them know that they're being handled by a senior account manager; those kind of titles always impress people. Makes them think that they're getting that extra special treatment, don't you think?'

'I personally think all my clients are happy with me. I haven't had any complaints.'

Francis laughed, and I smirked back. Mags was right, we needed to get out of here.

'I'll go and do that all right now,' I said.

'That's great. And if you want to send over any of the account work you've already done. Brainstormed ideas, initial proposals, that would of course be helpful.'

'I'm sure it would.' I wondered if he wanted blood next.

'Great, thanks, Lucy.'

He turned his attention back to his PC.

I walked back across the office and with each step I took I felt angrier and angrier at the injustice of it all.

I'd been over the moon to get on the graduate scheme at a London marketing firm, which was a stepping stone to an account manager role along with a decent wage, pension and bonuses. But sometimes I wondered if the financial stability was worth all the crap that came with it.

I took the long way back to my desk, so I could sneak over to the sales department where Mags worked.

'What's Fucking Francis done now?'

'How could you tell?'

She patted the top of her desk for me to perch on.

'The flaring nostrils. What is it?'

'Oh, just the usual,' I said with a sigh. 'He took my new client because they're a subsidiary of P&R.'

'That cheeky—' she said, stopping herself short of swearing. 'What's wrong with him? It's not like he earns commission; he doesn't need to scoop them all up.'

'It's all point-scoring, isn't it?'

'You just know he's going to outsource all the work to you.'

'Yep, I do all the work, but this way he gets all the credit.'

Mags took off her glasses and rubbed her eyes.

'You know what we've got to do, don't you?'

I nodded my head.

'One day, Mags, one day.'

She rubbed her glasses clean and slid them back on.

'They're a nice shape; are they new?'

'Hmm,' she said, 'I bought them off the internet.'

'Since when can you buy glasses off the internet?'

'I got them from the States, about half the price that they are in the opticians here.'

'They're nice.'

'Thanks,' she said. 'But stop distracting me.'

'What?'

'Complimenting me on my glasses. I know what you're doing, missy. You want me to stop talking about you know what.'

It was true, it made me nervous when she hinted at leaving the company whilst we were at the office. I got nervous enough when we talked about it outside of work. I might hate working with Francis, but there was something to be said for having a steady job. One that paid well. I was earning enough to start paying back my student loan, unlike a lot of my friends, and

76

I rented a flat in Battersea that was light and bright without a hint of mould. I couldn't see how I could still do that and have seed money to start a company. Let alone coming up with an idea that's good enough to be viable.

'When you come up with the million-pound idea,' I said, with a shrug.

'You'll be the first to know.'

I started to shift uncomfortably in my seat wondering if I'd be brave enough to make the jump with her when the time came. I got the impression that it wouldn't be long before she thought of something, I'd never met anyone quite so determined.

'Just be ready for when I work it all out.'

'Yeah, yeah.'

I headed back towards my desk and what would presumably be a cold coffee by now, because that was just the kind of day I was having.

Chapter 6

Friday 29th February 2008

It had been gone 10 p.m. by the time I got home from work last night. Too late to start faffing around cooking, or even to wait for a takeaway to be delivered. Instead, I'd snacked on some crackers and cheese and drunk a large glass of wine. I'd just about brushed my teeth, done some questionable make-up removal and flopped into bed. The only highlight was deliberately not setting my alarm as I had the day off for my birthday.

It was going to be a full-on day. First there was late lunch with Mum, and then Noah would be arriving, making our night out by the skin of his teeth. Knowing him, he'd be charged up on energy drinks and still manage to stay out later than us.

But the most important thing was that all that fun started from midday, which meant I was going to get a full, uninter-rupted night's sleep. Even Amy was staying over at Paul's, which meant I wouldn't get woken up by the sound of her hairdryer or the clicking of all her make-up boxes as she applied it in the hallway mirror. A lie-in surrounded by peace and quiet was exactly the birthday present I wanted to give myself.

I was in the deepest sleep when the doorbell started to ring.

I sat bolt upright in panic; at first I thought it was the fire alarm, but then the silence of the flat and the darkness from the window made me think that I'd dreamt the whole thing.

I took a couple of deep breaths, trying to calm my pounding heart down, before it buzzed again. It was longer this time and more of a stop/start motion.

'Who the bloody hell is that?' I squinted at the clock on my bedside table. It was 5.36 a.m.

Besides the milkman, I didn't know many other people that got up at such an ungodly hour, and for a minute I just lay in bed. It was bound to be kids or someone that had got the wrong house. Amy and I didn't have anyone dropping by to see us at the best of times, let alone at this time.

The bell rang again, almost like it was punching out morse code with a buzz-pause-buzz pattern and I finally threw back the covers and climbed out of bed. I hunted round for my slippers and dressing gown and stormed off downstairs to give the person a piece of my mind.

'OK, I'm coming,' I shouted to stop the ringing. 'It better be a bloody emergency.'

I didn't care that it could be a serial killer on the other side; at this point I was so mad and the only person in danger of getting murdered was them.

'Who the bloody hell do you think you are ringing the doorbell at this—' I grumbled as I opened the door. The man's face was obscured at first by the darkness and the lamppost behind and I was in full-on rant mode, hands on hips, before I realised that standing in front of me was Noah.

A look of utter relief washed over his face, followed by a large grin.

'Finally,' he said. 'I thought you were going to have me standing here all day.'

Frozen in shock, I wondered if I was still dreaming. I rubbed at my eyes and blinked, but my eyes weren't playing tricks on me.

'Strewth, Sheila, are you going to let me in or what?' he said, with a dodgy Australian accent.

'That hasn't improved since I last saw you,' I said, my brain finally accepting that it was indeed Noah on my doorstep.

'No, it hasn't, and neither has the bloody British weather. It's freezing.'

'Oh yes, of course.' I opened the door wider for him and his backpack to squeeze in. We lived in the upper flat in a two-storey house with a narrow stairwell to get to our flat. I loved that we didn't have any communal space with our neighbours, but it did mean that it was far too narrow and not quite wide enough for him and his backpack.

'Surprise.' He leaned over to give me a hug.

I put my arms around him and I found my whole body squeezing him.

'I might need some air left to breathe.'

I pulled out of the hug. 'Sorry, I'm just so excited. I can't believe you're here. I thought your flight didn't land until four-ish?'

'Yeah, well, I um, got that a bit mixed up. I thought it landed at four-thirty this afternoon and it landed at four-thirty this morning. No queue at passports, unsurprisingly.'

'What a shocker.' He'd only been here less than a minute, and already my cheeks were aching from all the smiling. 'I'm glad you're here. It was worth getting woken up for. Come on up.'

I stood flat against the wall to let him and his giant backpack pass.

I paused ever so slightly to look at myself in the hallway mirror as I went by, instantly wishing I hadn't. I had black bags under my eyes as big as saucers, and tell-tale red wine marks in the creases of my lips. I quickly rubbed them away and retied my hair into a messy bun. I pulled my dressing gown tighter around my mis-matched, misshapen PJs.

What was I doing? This was Noah, a man that had shared a tent with me at V Festival where I hadn't showered for three days, who had held my hair back when I'd vomited after too many gins at our third-year summer ball, and who had held me when I'd cried ugly tears after break-ups.

Instead of focusing on what a state I looked, I should have been concentrating on the fact that he was here. Here in my house. I'd been thinking about seeing him all week, excited about the moment that I got to hang out with him again and now that he'd arrived early, I couldn't believe it. My tired mind was all abuzz and whirring at a zillion miles an hour to process it.

'Blimey, this is nicer than your flat in Shepherd's Bush.' He paused walking into the kitchen and blew a whistle through his teeth.

'I know. No black mould thrown in for free.'

'Or drug-dealing neighbours.'

'Not that I know of,' I said, with a smile. 'But you know, it's always the quiet ones.'

'Always.'

In the light of the kitchen, I could finally take him in. His hair was shorter than I'd ever seen it, not quite buzz-cut short but close, and his skin was much darker. He'd filled out too. Not that he'd put on much weight – he was still skinny like he'd always been – but he was carrying the weight differently now. Almost like he'd grown into his body.

'I tried to call you and warn you that I was coming, but it kept ringing out to answerphone.'

'Yeah, I was knackered last night and put it on silent.'

He pulled a face.

'Sorry to wake you up; I'm guessing you were planning a lie-in?'

I nodded but my nose started to scrunch up. I couldn't even pretend to be mad at him.

'I was, but if ever there was a reason to get up at stupid o'clock in the morning, it would be to see you.'

He leaned against the worktop.

'Steady on, you sound like you missed me when I was away. And I know from the lack of Skype calls that that wasn't the case.'

'Hang on.' I flicked the kettle on; I might be excited to be up and seeing Noah, but it didn't mean that I wasn't in desperate need of a coffee. 'I Skyped you.'

'Once.'

'Once? No, I spoke to you more than that. We called you last year, on your birthday.'

'With Amy and Paul.'

I felt sheepish, wondering if that was true.

'OK, so I was a bit crap with the Skype; I'm blaming you moving somewhere with a ridiculous time difference. But at least I emailed, and I texted occasionally.'

'That's true.' He sat down at the table. 'It's just not the same, is it, when you don't get to see a person? You look different.'

'Ha.' My hand flew up to my messy hair. 'It's called being woken in the middle of the night and not having brushed my hair or put any make-up on.'

He shook his head.

'It's not that. You were blonde when I left, and now look at you.'

A bit of my natural brown hair had fallen out of my bun and I tried to tie it back round.

'I've been dying it for so long that I thought I'd give it a rest for a bit.'

'It suits you,' he said, nodding. 'It brings out your eyes.'

He stared at me for a moment and it caused me to shudder. The kettle came to a noisy boil and I snapped round.

'Coffee?' I offered, desperately needing to change the subject.

'Yes, please.'

'And then I'm guessing you'll want to sleep? We've got a super comfortable sofa bed in the lounge that we've earmarked for you. But if you want a real bed you can use mine. I won't be in it,' I added with a hurry. My cheeks were starting to burn. Since when did my cheeks burn talking to Noah? 'I mean, I'm up now, so I'll probably stay up.'

'As tempting as a bed sounds after travelling for god knows how long, I'm actually quite awake. I slept pretty much the whole way and they served the strongest coffee known to man. Not sure I'll get much sleep before next Tuesday, if I'm honest.'

I went to pass him the cup of coffee and hesitated. 'Are you sure it's a good idea to have another one?'

'More coffee is always the answer, but I tell you what I really want to do.' He took hold of the cup as I held it out to him. His hand brushed against mine and I almost dropped it with the jolt.

83

'And what's that?' I hadn't meant it to come out sultry or flirty, but that's exactly how it sounded.

'I really want a fry-up. Like the greasiest, most artery-clogging fry-up that you could ever imagine. Sausage. Eggs. Bacon. Baked beans. Mushrooms. Tomatoes. Toast. Hash Browns. Black pudding.'

I pulled a face. 'I don't believe people really eat that.'

'Don't knock it until you've tried it. And all washed down with proper builder's tea.'

'Well' – I looked over at my fridge, which might have a soggy mushroom and some wrinkly tomatoes – 'I can run out and grab some. There's a Tesco's not far away that's twenty-four hours.'

He shook his head. 'Not that I don't believe that your cooking skills have drastically changed since I left.'

'Hey,' I said, knowing full well that I had recently used a cookbook to work out how long to boil an egg.

'I'm just kidding, but seriously, we have to go out to eat, it's our birthday.' He screwed up his face. 'It is our birthday, isn't it? I'm so confused what time it is and going forward and back in time.'

'You're right,' I said, stirring a bit of sugar into my coffee. 'It's today. Happy birthday.'

'Happy birthday.' He put his coffee cup down and reached into the small pocket of his backpack. 'I brought you a present.'

He dug around, pulling out what looked like dirty clothes and shoving them further in. How could he ever find anything in there? It would drive me mental. I knew there was a reason I'd never been backpacking. Give me a suitcase with compartments to separate things any day.

After a couple of minutes, he finally found what he was looking for and passed across a small present wrapped up in a brown paper bag.

'Yeah, sorry about the wrapping, I didn't get a chance.'

I turned it over in my hands, unable to guess what was inside. Tugging at the Sellotape, I opened it up. Inside was more tissue paper and buried deep in that was a small silver bracelet. I pulled it up and saw a little charm hanging off it in the shape of a four-leaf clover.

'Oh, Noah.' I looked up at him. 'That's just like the one I had. How did you remember?'

He shrugged his shoulders. 'It's that really cheesy line: I saw it and thought of you.'

I turned the bracelet round in my hands. It was just like the one I'd lost in Calais.

'It's not cheesy, it's really thoughtful. And it makes the present I got you look really crap.'

His face lit up like a little kid. 'You got me a present?'

'Don't get too excited. It was more for later on.'

I opened up a cupboard and reached for a gift bag and handed it across. Noah opened the bag up and pulled out a bottle of Goldschläger. He laughed.

'Figured I could afford to buy some now.'

'Oh god, I don't think I've drunk this since uni. Wow, now I feel like I've made it.'

'Do you think it's actually really gold?'

He turned the bottle round in his hands.

'I think so. I'll have to look it up online, but someone told me that each bottle has about twenty pence' worth.'

'Huh. That much?'

'Fancy a shot? It's five o'clock, right?'

I shuddered and shook my head.

'Pretty sure that refers to the PM.'

'We'll save it until later then. But in the meantime, I'm starving. Let's get some food.'

It was funny catching the Tube into town with Noah, surrounded by a sea of commuters doing their best to ignore each other. We, on the other hand, were perched on one of the padded bumpers, laughing as we reminisced about nights out and Tube rides from before he left. The time that we decided to run up the stairs at Covent Garden trying to beat Paul and Amy in the lift, only to keel over halfway from exhaustion, or the time that Hayley was so hungover that she fell backwards on the Tube and landed on the lap of a very disgruntled man.

I'd suggested staying local, but when Noah heard I was meeting Mum for a late lunch at Claridge's, he suggested we head into central London and play tourist. Apparently he'd missed the city and was craving historic buildings.

After eating the greasiest breakfast in a traditional café just outside of Waterloo, we were well and truly stuffed.

'I can feel my arteries clogging already,' said Noah.

'I can't believe out of everything you could have had for your first meal, that was what you craved.'

'Well, a decent vindaloo and sausage roll were a close second, but I didn't quite fancy either for breakfast.'

I pulled a face.

'Plus, I didn't see you complaining as you ate yours.'

'I admit, it was a nice change from my usual cereal. So, I've got a couple of hours before I meet Mum, what do you fancy doing?'

'I dunno,' he said as we walked under the arches heading towards the South Bank. 'How about we walk to Trafalgar Square, up through Horse Guards, pay my respects to the Queen if she's at home.'

'When you said play tourist . . . '

'Do you know I've never actually done it?'

'Done what?'

'Played tourist in London. I've spent the last eighteen months travelling round all these sights, going to see long overgrown temples, and the place where Captain Cook first landed in Australia, and yet I've never done any of that stuff here. I've never even been to Windsor.'

'What? How did I not know that?'

Noah shrugged. 'It's not the kind of thing that ever really comes up, is it? But when I was in Oz everyone either asked me about places or told me their stories of visiting them. Telling me about the time they went boating on the Serpentine or how they went on the London Eye.'

'Didn't you go when you were younger?'

'I only remember coming up to London on a school trip once to see a show, but we never did any sightseeing.'

'And your parents never brought you? You only lived in Sussex; that's so close.'

'I know. My dad's always had a thing about cities – hates them. He used to come out in hives if he had to go into Brighton.'

Noah's parents still lived in his childhood house, on the edge of a town in the South Downs not too far from Brighton, in a home where the sound of laughter always rattled round the walls.

'Well, it's something then that we can definitely put right

over the next few months. Speaking of your parents, when are you seeing them?'

'Tomorrow. Paul's driving me out and then he's staying for the night.'

I was a little jealous of Paul getting to stay in the Matthews household. I have so many fond memories of our trips there when we were at uni. There'd usually be a whole gang of us, sleeping like sardines on the floor of the lounge. His mum Sandra making us bacon sandwiches in the morning to rid us of the hangovers.

'Then are you coming back up to London? Have you sorted somewhere to live yet?'

'My mate Liam's flatmate is moving out in May, so I'm going to move in there. In Balham.'

'Nice.'

'Yeah. I just need to get a job by then so I can pay the rent.'

'Ah, and how goes the job hunting?'

It was so lovely being able to fire off questions and get immediate responses, after the last year of emails where it felt that every message threw up more unanswered questions.

'Not well, it's been hard to do it from internet cafés. I've applied for a few things, but it'll be easier at my parents'. They've got decent broadband, at least.'

'Are you still looking to work for a charity?'

'I've been applying, but I'm also thinking that I might try something different.'

'Different?'

'I just wondered if it was worth changing before I got too stuck in the charity sector,' he said, as we started to climb the bridge over towards Embankment.

'I thought you liked it. Making a difference and all that.'

'I did, I mean I do. It's not like I hated my job, not like you.'

'I don't hate my job.' I bit my lip. 'I just hate some of my colleagues and some of the working practices.'

He raised an eyebrow.

'I love my clients, and I love what I do day to day.'

'Which you can find at another company.'

'Yeah, but,' I said, knowing he was right, 'I've only been there a couple of years. It would look bad if I left after so little time.'

'By that logic I'm screwed,' he said, with a laugh.

'That's different. You've worked and travelled. I just probably need to get a little more senior before I move.'

'Always playing it safe.'

I bit the inside of my cheek. He was starting to sound like Mags; she was always pushing me to go for bigger things.

'Not safe, I just worry about what comes next. What if I move to another company and it's worse, or I get shitty clients? And I've effectively walked away from a job with a decent salary and good bonuses and benefits, all because I got pissed off with the golden boy in the office. I know you like to live on the edge.'

Noah popped his hand on my arm. 'I was only teasing. There's a lot to be said for earning a decent salary. That's why I'm thinking of changing industries. Following the money.'

'Really? Mr I don't want to be part of the corporate machine is going to go over to the dark side?'

He steeled his jaw.

'I didn't say I was going to the dark side, but maybe I'll look at ethical for-profit companies.'

Noah stopped on the bridge and took hold of the railings, staring over at Somerset House and beyond, towards the City.

Now that he'd got me looking at the London skyline, I couldn't help but spot everything. He was right. There was so much history crammed into every square mile and usually I walked head down, not seeing anything.

'I helped out my boss in Oz with some of the projects he was working on, and I quite liked the project management side of things. So I thought maybe I'd do a qualification.'

'I think you'd be great at that,' I said, nodding.

'We'll see. I think I'm going to have a bit of an uphill struggle trying to find something.'

We started to walk along the bridge again.

'You'll find something. You'll be saving for the next trip in no time.' If there was one thing I'd learned about Noah, there was always another place on his bucket list to tick off.

'I think I've got all that out my system, for now,' he said.

'Really? You're not going to let us get used to having you back and then disappear off again?'

'Never say never,' he said, tucking his hands in his pockets. 'But I think I'm going to be sticking around for a bit. I had a great trip, but I missed here.'

'Like the fry-ups and the buildings?'

'And the people.'

'But you looked like you were having a ball in your photos. All those barbies on the beach.' My Australian accent was no better than Noah's and we both cringed.

'It's easy to make it look like you're having a good time in a photo, and it helps when you've got dazzling blue skies overhead all the time. But I don't think I'll keep in contact with anyone I hung out with over there, other than on Facebook.'

'Really?'

He shook his head. 'It was really hard to make proper friends out there.'

'But Aussies always seem so friendly.'

'They are friendly, but they've also got their friends. Most people tend to stay local to go to uni, so they just continue hanging out with the people they went to school with, and they weren't that interested in making friends with someone who was only going to stick around for a year.'

'I guess I can see that. It's always hard saying goodbye to people. But it only makes it better when you get to say hello again.' I nudged him with my elbow.

'You missed me too?'

'I didn't say I was talking about *you*.'

He laughed.

'But seriously,' he said, turning his head to look at me, 'you know, when you're on the other side of the world, it makes you realise who you really care about and who you really miss.'

My foot slipped on wet leaves near the bottom step and I felt my balance go. Noah grabbed my arm and kept me steadied.

'You OK?' I was holding on to both of his arms and a look of concern crossed his face.

I nodded; I couldn't seem to get any words out. My heart had started to beat fast. I didn't let go of him and he didn't stop looking at me.

'Excuse me, coming through,' said a voice behind us. Noah dropped my arm and I stepped to the side of the railings whilst a man carrying a bike over his shoulder came down.

'Well, um,' I said with a laugh, 'I should be more careful.'

'Good job I was here to catch you.'

'That would have made a memorable birthday.' I took hold

of the railing as I went down the remaining steps. 'Spending the day in A&E after falling down stairs.'

'Could you imagine? It would make getting almost stuck in Calais look uneventful.'

'That day. I've learned my lessons from that one and I'm not setting my expectations too high this time.'

'Why not? I'm pretty sure that last time exceeded all of my wildest expectations.'

I thought back to almost missing the bus and the fraught taxi ride.

'We got to meet each other,' he said.

'Geez, what happened to you in Australia? Or is it the jetlag? You've turned into a right soppy bastard.'

'As I said, I've worked out what it is that I really missed.'

I could feel his eyes burning into me before I turned my head to meet his eyes. What was going on here? Apart from the moment in the garden when we first met, there'd been nothing between us. When Amy and Paul started dating, we saw each other a lot and we'd slipped into a comfortable friendship where Noah was just Noah. Like a big brother.

Only my brain seemed to have forgotten that. And now there was this man before me that had grown up so much in the year and a half, and he seemed even more comfortable in his own skin – something I didn't think possible.

He zipped his coat up right to the top.

'Man, I'd forgotten how cold it could be in February. This is doing nothing.'

'We should get you a scarf.'

'And a hat.'

'And gloves.'

'And maybe a thicker coat.'

'Bloody hell,' he said, muttering through his breath. 'Remind me why I came back to this tiny, freezing island?'

'Because you missed us.' I laughed and slipped my arm through his. 'Come on, let's find somewhere to warm up.'

Chapter 7

After a warming coffee, we headed to Hyde Park. I had the perfect idea of how to play tourist.

'I get the sentiment,' said Noah, staring at our reflection in the water, 'but do you not think we should do this when it's warmer? I'm back for good now; we could do it any time.'

'Come on, you know what life is like. You'll be on the merry-go-round of work and brunches at the weekends, and you'll never do it.'

I looked around the park. It looked majestic today under the bright-blue sky. It was cold and crisp and the grass was almost sparkling with the frost.

Noah breathed out steam. He giggled and did it again.

'I haven't done that in ages,' he said.

'See, you've missed the cold, too.'

He shivered and bounced a little on the spot.

'Maybe I have, but I also missed sitting in pubs by fires and drinking warm beer. We could do that instead?'

'No.' I took hold of his arm and gently pulled him towards the pedal boats on the edge of the lake. The man took our money and showed us on a jetty to our boat.

'I can't believe we're doing this. What if we fall in?'

'Ha, listen to you. Aren't you always telling me to take more risks?' I climbed in the best I could in my heeled boots. The pedalo rocked and I saw that the floor of it had the same icy white sheen as the grass. I was starting to doubt that it was a good idea, but I felt that I'd gone too far to turn back.

Noah took his place next to me.

I popped my foot on the pedal and immediately slipped off. I quickly put it back on, not wanting Noah to spot any weakness.

'I'm not sure you're dressed for this,' he said as I tugged at my wool coat that was in danger of hanging down in the bottom of the boat.

'It'll be fine.' I gritted my teeth, hoping I wasn't going to turn up for afternoon tea a sweaty, bedraggled mess.

'Uh-huh.'

He watched as my heels slipped again, the non-existent grip on the soles doing nothing.

'Sure you don't fancy that pint by a fire?'

'Stick with this, I'm sure we'll get warmer.'

He threw me a look that let me know he wasn't convinced.

'I guess there's that.'

'Do you think we should have at least done any limbering stretches first?' He turned his head to look at me, and the smile was at least returning.

'Probably. We're getting old now; my muscles aren't what they used to be.'

'I know, we're positively ancient. Twenty-four, eh?'

We pedalled gently, and there was something comforting in hearing the boat push through the water. There were only a couple of other boats on the lake, far over the other side.

'Do you know, up until I went to uni I thought I'd be married with kids at twenty four?' I said.

'Really?'

'Uh-huh, it seemed like a really grown-up age.'

An image of me in dungarees with a baby bump and a paint roller popped into my mind. I'd always had this weird fantasy of painting a nursery in a London townhouse. The kind that, now I lived here, I realised I'd never be able to afford, along with the husband that was too perfect to ever exist.

'Yeah, anything over twenty felt ancient. But I guess in our parents' generation that would have been our life. My parents met and got married at twenty-two. I'm already behind schedule on their plan.'

I watched a duck nearby put his head under the water and it made me shiver at the thought of the cold.

'I bet they wouldn't have dreamed that at that age their son would be unemployed and technically homeless,' he said, a hollow laugh escaping.

'I'm sure they'd have been proud of your bravery and all that you'd seen on your travels.'

My legs were starting to burn from the exertion of the pedalling. We'd started to increase the pace and it was highlighting how much I needed to start using my gym membership for something other than their power shower.

'Is that what you think?'

I nodded. 'Yeah, I do. I know loads of people go travelling, but it's one thing to go on a gap year before uni, before you've got anything to lose. You went when you'd finally got on the career ladder.'

'Don't remind me.'

'But look at the work experience you had in Sydney,' I pointed out. 'Sounds like it turned out to be a good move.'

'Yeah, I probably shouldn't have left that too. They offered to sponsor my visa, you know.'

'What? And you didn't take it?' I cringed at the tone I'd used, wishing I had been able to hide my disbelief that he hadn't stayed.

'Things with Hayley at that point weren't great, and I felt that if I got a visa that would probably be me living there indefinitely. My parents would have killed me for starters.' He let out a deep breath. 'Coming back here, though, seems terrifying too. More starting again.'

We'd almost come to a standstill with our pedalling.

'You've done it before; you'll be fine. Plus, we're not that old, I promise. You've barely got any wrinkles.'

'I have.' He stretched the skin by his eyes. 'Look, here.'

'They're laughter lines, and they just mean that you're fun. I reckon I'm going to get scowl lines.' I scrunched my forehead.

Noah chuckled.

'You know, you did that look a lot a couple of times when we were on our jaunt around Calais and at points I wondered if you were going to murder me if you didn't find somewhere open.'

He pursed his lips, trying to stop himself from laughing harder.

'Ha, ha, very funny. I can't help it. If I'm daydreaming I just kind of stare off into space.'

'And look like you're planning someone's demise.'

I pushed him a little and it only made him laugh harder.

'Actually, I think it's kind of cute.'

'Kind of cute?' I tried not to blush at the compliment. 'Me looking like a murderer? Oh, I get it, some kind of sadomaso-chistic fantasy?'

97

'Now you're talking.'

I shook my head. Noah was the only guy that could take me from moaning about getting old to talking about bedroom kinks.

'You're doing it now,' he said.

I sighed loudly and tried to push my face into a more neutral position, but I was having trouble.

'You've opened a Pandora's box in my mind with me now thinking about whips and—'

'Go on.' He turned to look at me.

'Noah Matthews. I think we'd better change the subject.'

'Hmm, yeah maybe.' He started to pedal again, but I moved my feet further back, just taking in the scenery and watching the life in the park. Dog walkers. Tour groups. Runners. There was something for everyone. 'Do you ever think about that day in Calais?'

'What, about how close I came to murdering you?'

'I mean,' he said, raising an eyebrow, 'about how we met. You know, it's our anniversary today.'

'Our anniversary? That makes us sound like an old married couple.'

He shrugged. 'But it's true. We met four years ago today.'

'Does that mean it's our first anniversary? If this is our sixth birthday?'

He paused, as if he was weighing up the answer.

'Quite possibly.'

'It's funny to think that we've known each other four years.'

'It's gone past in the blink of an eye though, hasn't it? I mean, so much has changed since then.'

I thought back to the woman I was at university. So naïve

in so many ways, dreaming big, living small, and I wondered if anything had really changed.

'I guess it has,' I agreed. 'Although I think you've crammed more into yours than mine. I've pretty much just spent the last three years chained to my desk.'

'Well, you know my thoughts on that one.'

I nodded. Do something different. Take a risk.

'I wonder sometimes if I should take a leaf out of your book.'

'Don't tell me you're going to quit and bugger off travelling when I've just got back?'

My heart swelled a little at the genuine look of disappointment on his face.

'No, I mean, maybe I should be a bit braver. Mags, one of my work colleagues wants us to set up our own business.'

'Doing what?'

We were drifting close to a bank and Noah managed to steer us back in the other direction.

'That's the million-dollar question with hopefully a million-dollar answer.' I'd never met anyone like Mags before. She was desperate to be an entrepreneur and I was utterly convinced one day soon she would be. 'It's all pie in the sky at the moment.'

'Could be exciting.'

I smiled. Of course Noah found it exciting. He was one of life's risk takers.

'Could be terrifying.'

'But what have you got to lose?'

'A load of money we don't have,' I said, with a laugh. It sounded ridiculous talking about it out loud. That was sometimes the problem with dreams. They existed in a secret part of your brain and could be cultivated and nurtured, but when exposed to the elements they shrivelled up and died. 'Perhaps I'd be better off just changing jobs.'

'Perhaps,' he said, 'but then you might end up with another Francis.'

My heart sank. 'Fucking Francis.'

I started pedalling again. It was getting cold, and as much as my muscles ached, I wanted to keep warm.

'In answer to your original question, though, I do think about the day we met sometimes. When I need a good laugh. Our faces when the taxi driver pulled up at the wrong supermarket.' I closed my eyes.

'Don't. I'm now that traveller that arrives hours early for flights and ferries in case of taxi problems.' He started a low giggle. 'It's random, when you look back though; we just let Paul talk us into going when we were complete strangers. But it felt like we'd known each other forever.'

'The mark of a true friendship,' I said, tilting my head to the side.

'Hmm.' He kept his head straight and looking forward, over the park.

My phone started to buzz in my bag and I rooted round to find it.

'It's my dad.' I picked it up, miming a sorry to Noah as I said, 'Hello.'

'Hey LuLu, happy birthday.'

I almost dropped the phone in shock.

'You remembered, on my actual birthday?'

'Hey, I send you a card and phone every year.'

'The last one you were a day a late. And you don't send it, Tania does.'

'Oh, the last leap year, yeah, well, maybe it's easier today as it's a work day. I can't get away from the date. And everyone is talking about it on the radio.'

'I know, why do they do it? It's like this day only comes round once every four years or something.'

He laughed down the phone. I could hear the sounds of a busy office and it made me think of work and if I'd done enough for things to run smoothly without me being there.

Noah pulled a face and I realised that he was mirroring my scowl. I tried to relax and tune back into what Dad was saying.

'We should be on our way back from Birmingham in time for lunch, so Tania said she'd book a table for half past one. Not far away from the station, if that's still OK for you to head down?'

'Yeah, I'm still good for that.'

'It'll give you time to get over tonight's hangover. Are you doing anything nice?'

'Just out with friends.'

'Great stuff. Well, looking forward to hearing about it. Just wanted to wish you a happy birthday. Tania and Gilly do too.'

'Thanks, Dad.'

I hung up the phone and stared at it for a moment before I tucked it back in my bag.

'Your dad remembered on the day?'

'I know,' I said. 'Crazy, huh? And there's my mum saying that men don't change.'

Noah patted me on the leg.

'All men, believe it or not, have the capacity to change. Sometimes it just takes us a while to work out what's really important.'

'Good to know.' I wondered if we were still talking about

my dad. His hand lingered on my leg and my eyes fell to it, and he moved it away.

'So,' he said, with a cough. And unzipping his small day pack, he pulled out a camera. 'I've got a couple of pictures left on the film.'

'On the film? Surely you must be the only person alive who hasn't gone digital.'

'You know me, old romantic. I love the element of surprise when you get the photos back.'

He held his hand out to try and take a picture.

'You know, you're probably only going to get our chins?'

'I was hoping for my bald spot, actually.'

'Bald spot? You don't have a bald spot, do you?' I started preening his hair like a monkey.

'Not yet, but I tell you it's thinning.'

'We're getting old.'

'We're getting old,' he agreed, and he stretched his arm out. 'Say leapling.'

I started to laugh as I heard the mechanical click.

'Oh, that'll be attractive,' I said, trying to get the laughter under control. 'I guess we'll see.'

'One more to go.'

'Do you want me to take one of you, immortalise your first London tourist trip?'

'No, no. I've got an idea for this one, just you wait.'

Trafalgar Square was always busy but lunchtime had made it even more so.

'I still don't get it. What do you want me to do?' I asked, scanning the scene in front of me.

'I'll turn my back, you go off and stand somewhere in the crowd, somewhere not too obvious, but somewhere you can see me, or be seen by me, and I'll take your photo. Then when I get the picture back, it's like Where's Wally.'

'And I'm the Wally? Right?'

'Well, yes. But come on, it'll be a laugh. Adds something to getting your holiday photos back, you get to remember the day and have a little fun.'

'Right, OK, and how exactly will I know that you've finished taking the photo?'

He nodded his head. 'OK, fair point. I'll put my hand up and wave and you'll know it's safe to come out.'

'And you'll turn round again.'

He laughed. 'Now who's taking this seriously. Yes, I'll turn around. It shall be a mystery until it comes back from the developer.'

'OK. OK.' Only Noah would suggest this kind of thing. 'Let's do this.'

He turned around and I weaved my way through the crowd, turning my back to check I could still see him and he could see me. I was laughing to myself, a childlike giddiness coming over me.

I found the spot I was going for. At the very base of Nelson's column. I stood by the plinth feeling ridiculous as I put my hand over my chest, mimicking Nelson's pose. A couple sitting eating sandwiches looked up at me and I smiled. Noah always got me to do the most stupid things.

I watched him turn around to scan the crowd and the sight of him took my breath away. It was like I'd seen him for the first time all over again. Butterflies fluttered in my belly. I wanted him to find me, to lock eyes with me, but at the same time I wanted him to look for me in the photo. He put the camera up to his eye and the next moment he waved his hand, like he was waving for his life, and turned round again.

It took me a moment to get my feet to move towards him, because I didn't feel like I was walking to my friend anymore. All those times I'd told people that we'd only ever be platonic, but if someone asked me now, I'm not sure I'd be able to say it with any conviction.

Chapter 8

I'd never been to Claridge's before and it was even more opulent than I imagined. I tugged at the jumper I had on under my coat, hoping that it would be smart enough. I'd paired it with skinny jeans and boots, but looking around the restaurant I felt that a skirt or dress might have been better, or to be dripping in pearls like many of the other diners. I sighed relief on spotting my mum in a lilac blouse. She waved at me and I raised my hand back.

'Can I help you, madam?' asked the maître d' as I approached the seated area.

'I'm meeting my mother. She's just there.'

'Of course,' he said, with a bob of his head. 'Do you need to put a coat in the cloakroom before you take your seat?'

'I don't think so.' My long wool coat right now was the smartest bit about me, and I was reluctant to take it off.

'Very good.'

I felt ridiculous being led across the restaurant floor to my mum but I guess it was that kind of place and I couldn't help but giggle.

'Thank you,' I said as he pulled out my seat for me. I'd barely sat on it when he pushed it in again. I leaned over and gave my mum a hug. 'This is fancy.'

'I know. Trust Marion to get me something like this for Christmas. But knowing her, she probably thought I'd bring her along.'

I almost wish that Mum had taken Aunt Marion with her. Not that I didn't like afternoon tea – who didn't like eating their body weight in tiny sandwiches and cakes? – but I never felt comfortable in places like this. I always worried that everyone would know that I was using the wrong fork or judge me for putting the jam on my scone before the cream, or some other kind of faux pas.

'Now I feel bad; you should have brought her.'

'And hear more about her oriental pond? If I learn any more about it I'll be able to go on a quiz show with it as my specialist subject. No, I'd much rather be here with you.' She leaned across the table. 'So, how does it feel to be twenty-four?'

'Don't remind me. I'm in my mid-twenties.'

I picked up the menu, wanting a distraction, but my mind swam with all the choices of teas.

'What I wouldn't give to be that age again.' Mum sighed. 'You don't know how lucky you are.'

I rolled my eyes.

'Just you wait till you get to my age; I'm going to be fifty-two this year.' She pulled a face then hid it behind a menu. 'Believe me, it's no fun getting old.'

She put the menu back down on the table and I looked up at her face. She didn't look like she was in her early fifties; all I could say was that I hoped that I looked that good in thirty years' time.

'Have you worked out where you're going tonight or is it a kind of see where the night takes you?'

'See where the night takes us with Amy coming? She's planned it all. What bar we're meeting at, guest list tickets for the club.'

'What a useful friend.'

'I know. If it had been left up to me we'd have ended up at the pub down the road.'

The waiter came over to take our tea order, and complimented me on my choice, even though I just pointed to a random one in the middle of the menu.

'And Noah's still on schedule to make it back in time?'

'Actually, he arrived this morning. Woke me about half past five, hence the huge amount of eye make-up I've got on.'

Mum squinted like she was trying to spot it before she registered what I'd said.

'He's back? That's great news. I was worried when you said he had all those connecting flights. Imagine if he'd had to spend his big birthday alone in some airport terminal.'

Mum really did have a knack of worrying about worst-case scenarios.

'Well, luckily he didn't.'

I sat back as the waiter put our teapots in front of us.

'I'll be with you shortly with your sandwiches.'

I turned back to Mum, who was leaning forward with both elbows on the table and her hands under her chin, like she was waiting for something.

'So . . . how was Noah?'

'Oh, you know him. Same as ever.'

I thought of us on the pedalos today and how that wasn't remotely true. I felt a blush creeping over my cheeks.

'He's had some trip, from the sounds of it. Imagine getting

to live in Sydney.' There was a wistful hint to her voice. Mum had gone backpacking around Europe when she was in her late teens and I got the impression that if her life had been different she would have been off to much more far-flung destinations.

'He said he had a great time, but he's been pining for old buildings and history.'

'He has?'

'Yeah,' I said, smiling at the thought of hiding in Trafalgar Square for his Where's Wally photo.

'Imagine that. But still, good on him for going.'

'You know, you and I keep talking about that New York trip; we should stop putting it off.' We've been talking for a few years about going Christmas shopping, and hearing about Noah's travels has made me think we should do more than just talk about it.

'Hmm, yeah.' She sat back, and started to pour her tea.

'We could go this December, get an early booking offer?'

She kept on pouring, and I wondered if she was going to leave herself any room for milk.

'There's no rush, is there?' She finally stopped pouring, and put the teapot down. 'What?'

She looked up and smiled at me and I realised I'd been staring.

'Nothing,' I said, a quick shake of the head. 'Is everything OK, you know, money wise?'

My mum's spoon chinked on the sugar bowl and she put it down, giving me a firm stare.

'You're like a sniffer dog at the airport. Things are fine, thank you. It's just I had a big bill for the boiler again and—'

'Mum, not again. I keep telling you, let me help you get a new boiler; there's only so many times they can fix it.'

'I'm not having you pay for it,' she said, a little loudly until she realised her surroundings. Self-consciously she looked around at the other diners but no one was looking.

'But, Mum' – I leaned forward and lowered my voice – 'I've got the money. It's not like I'm doing anything with my savings; I'm never going to be able to afford to buy a flat.'

'You should be spending it on something exciting for you. Something you want to do.'

'Like going to New York?' I lifted an eyebrow. 'I could buy us the tickets.'

I hoped that a holiday would be less offensive in her eyes than a new boiler.

Mum laughed. 'You are as stubborn as your father. Look, we will go to New York, and I'll pay my own way, OK. But it might not be this year.'

I fixed her with a hard stare, but I knew there was no point arguing.

'You know that there's help if you need it.'

She nodded her head, not saying anything. Mum was determined, after Dad left, that she was going to do everything on her own. I don't think she would have taken the maintenance money from Dad if she didn't have to.

'I know, and I appreciate it. But spend some money, Luce. I know you're saving, but make sure you have fun whilst you're young. Before you know it you'll be pushing mid-fifties.'

'Again, stop thinking you're old. You have a better social life and a better dating one than I do.'

'Oh, please.'

'Speaking of which,' I said, lifting the lid on my teapot and checking the colour of the tea, 'are you still seeing that gardener?'

'Jimmy?' She wrinkled up her nose. 'No, I ended things.'

'Oh no, I thought you liked him!'

'I did.' She picked up her tea and cradled it towards her. 'He had the most amazing hands. You know, proper worker's hands, all callusy and rough.'

Now it was my turn to make a face.

'Sounds lovely.'

'You didn't see that version of *Lady Chatterley's Lover* on the telly; I think you would have been too young. We'll have to watch it. Once you see Sean Bean in that, then you'll get it.'

'So I take it Jimmy wasn't a patch on Sean?'

'He was alright to look at, face as well as the big hands,' she said, with a cackle that made me cringe. 'But it was more that I found myself zoning out when we were talking. We had nothing in common, and then once, when he was kissing me, I found myself planning my shopping list and I figured that something was off.'

'No chemistry.'

She turned her nose up. 'More's the pity. You know, I think, to be honest, I could take or leave all the sexy stuff, but what I really want is the companionship. You know? I miss having that banter and that friendship.' The waiter went past with a tray of cakes and both of us followed with our eyes. 'I want what you have with Noah. What is it you always call him, your agony aunt?'

'Hmm.' I didn't want to tell her about the tiny butterflies that had started to creep into my belly.

'I just want to find that. You know, it all gets so complicated when sex and feelings get involved. I just want a mate. A male one. You don't know how lucky you are.'

Mum's eyes widened like saucers when a three-tiered stand of sandwiches, scones and cakes arrived.

'Do you think they'll let us take a doggy bag home?' she whispered as the waiter left.

'I reckon we could polish it off now.' I couldn't quite believe I could possibly be hungry after the big breakfast I ate.

'I guess you do need to make sure that you eat enough so that you can drink more tonight.'

'And I worked up an appetite this morning. Noah and I went on the pedalos on the Serpentine.'

'In this weather? Are you two mad? That sounds fun.'

I giggled. 'Yeah, it was.'

'See, I need a Noah in my life.'

'Everyone needs a Noah in their life.' There was a pang in my heart as I said it. He was back, and back for good this time and I was going to make the most of it.

Chapter 9

I was buzzing after Claridge's. Mum and I had stopped for a couple of glasses of wine at All Bar One near the station before I saw her off on the train and headed home.

'Friday night, and we're looking pretty cool,' sang Amy. She had a short skirt and top on, with her hair wrapped in a towel turban. 'I can't remember the last time I was this excited for a night out and it's not even my birthday. I wish that Noah would wake up soon; I want to crank up the tunes.'

We were doing our best to get ready without waking Noah who was passed out face down in a star fish pose on the sofa bed in the lounge. I had my dress on, but still needed to do my make-up.

'Should my ears be burning?'

We turned to see Noah walk into the kitchen in a pair of multicoloured trousers and no top. My eyes instinctively headed down his torso, over his pecs and those toned abs and . . . I snapped my head up.

'Hey,' said Amy, flinging her arms open and embracing him in a hug. 'Look at you. Look at that tan. I'm jealous.'

'Not that I'm going to get much of a chance to show it off over here, in this weather.'

'That's true. Oh, it's so nice to have you back,' she said, rustling his hair. 'Paul is over the moon. You know he's left work already? I can never get him to leave work before eight usually, and look: first day you're back he leaves at six. Six!'

'What can I say?' He winked and my legs went weak. I blamed the afternoon wine with Mum.

'Look at us, all hanging out together.' I took hold of the chair back to steady myself, still not believing he was here. 'I can't think when we were all last together.'

'Noah's leaving do, surely,' said Amy.

'I couldn't make it. Maybe that Foo Fighter's concert in Hyde Park?' My mind instantly went to when Noah put me on his shoulders and I'd screamed until I got there and saw everything from above, and then I clung to him for dear life.

'Or was it Hayley's birthday? When we went to see that band in Camden,' said Amy.

'Yeah, that was probably it.' Noah nodded. I had to stop looking at him, my eyes kept wandering from his face. I turned and busied myself in the cupboard, trying to find some glasses. 'Blimey, that was far too long. And weren't you with that guy? What was his name?'

'That guy with the Bart Simpson haircut.'

I knew without looking at them that they'd be pulling faces. He wasn't one of my finest choices of men.

'That's right,' said Noah, I could hear the mirth in his voice. 'What was his name?'

'George?' offered Amy.

'No, not George.' said Noah.

I turned around and put them out of their misery. 'Greg.'

'Greg, that was it,' Noah said pointing to his nose and then at me.

He wasn't one of the best men I'd ever dated. In fact, it had been Noah who had warned me about him. He hadn't thought it was a good sign that Greg ordered for me all the time; he'd thought he was too controlling. And he'd been right. Greg had started to take over more and more of the decisions in our relationship and I'd seen where it was heading.

'Well, I'm glad that the gang will be back together, minus Greg,' said Noah.

I wanted to point out that Hayley would be missing too but I couldn't. Whilst we'd mentioned her in passing this morning, I noticed that he'd never said anything about their break-up. I know from Paul he'd taken it hard. Even though it sounded like it had been a pretty mutual decision, it didn't mean to say it hurt any less after all that time together.

But it wasn't just going to be Noah that missed her. Amy and I had spent a lot of time with her over the years too, and she'd come out with us on multiple girls' nights. That was one of the weirdest things about being an adult. You spent an increasingly large portion of your social life welcoming other people's partners in to be one of your friends, but if they split up you lost them. Now, we were relegated to being Facebook friends. I knew that she'd come back from Australia before Noah, and had settled back in her home town of Newcastle. It was unlikely our paths would cross again, unless Noah and her got back together.

Amy started to pour the vodka into our glasses.

'You want one of these?' She gestured to Noah.

'I'll grab one in a bit; I'm guessing I need to get ready.'

'Unless you're going to go out like that,' said Amy.

He nodded. 'You two are looking good by the way. Nice dresses.'

Amy put her hand on her hip and struck a pose, whereas I tugged at the hem suddenly self-conscious about the amount of leg I was showing.

'We do our best' – Amy was still pouting – 'but you, on the other hand, I think your outfit needs work. Although nice abs. Working out down under, I see.'

'Turns out spending ninety per cent of your free time on a beach is quite the motivator to actually work out. I'm going to head in the shower, if that's OK? Just checking that no one needs it first.'

'It's all yours.' I tried not to stare too much at his bum as he walked back out.

'Oh my god,' whispered Amy to me. 'Noah got hot.'

I shook my head at her. 'He looks like he always did.'

'Oh no.' She shook her head again. 'He looks different and you're not telling me it's just that amazing tan.'

'Everyone looks better with a tan.'

'I don't, out of a bottle or otherwise.' She gave me a knowing look before pulling the cranberry juice out of the fridge and topping up our drinks. 'He's not going to be single for long looking like that.'

She handed me a glass and gave me a pointed look.

'What?' I said.

'What do you mean, what? Come on, you're single, he's single.'

'What are you talking about?' I hoped that my cheeks were less rosy than I thought they were.

'Well, when has that ever happened?' Her eyes were practically dancing.

'There was that time in our third year when he broke up with Hayley.'

'They were always going to get back together then. We all knew that. And he dated that rebound girl.' She took a sip of her drink and shuddered. 'That is an excellent drink.'

'Even if you do say so yourself. But look, it's not like that with me and Noah, it never has been. Us lot have always been a gang hanging out.'

'Yeah, but me and Paul are in the gang and we bump uglies.'

'Bump uglies.' My nose wrinkled. 'But no, we're just mates.'

'Pur-lease, I saw the way that you were drooling at him.'

'Pretty sure that was you.'

She held out the bottle of vodka that had been in the freezer.

'For your cheeks, because they're telling me something your lips aren't.'

I instinctively put my cold drink to my face. 'It's just hot in here.'

'Hmm,' she said. 'You can't blame the downstairs neighbours for all the heat.'

Her eyes were twinkling and she didn't need to spell out what she was thinking. I've known her long enough to know how her brain works. No doubt she's planning us double dates.

I heard my phone ringing from my room and Amy pointed a finger at me. 'Don't think you've been saved by the bell.'

I had a bit more of my drink, and hurried down to my room, but before I could answer it, it rang off. It was Mags. I tried her back and got her answerphone. I took my phone with me back to the kitchen and back to my drink, and I bumped straight into Noah.

He was now wearing even less, with a towel round his waist, and his tanned chest was glistening with water droplets.

'I'm so sorry,' I muttered.

'It's my fault. Forgot to take my clothes in.'

'Right.' The two of us stood in the hallway, neither stepping back or moving. He smelt so good, his shower gel all musky and manly; it was the kind of smell that drew me in closer and closer. I could almost feel the heat radiating off him.

'I . . .' he started but nothing else followed and still we were unmoved.

The key went into the lock of the front door, and it was followed by thundering footsteps up the stairs, causing us to step back. The spell was broken.

'Mate,' screamed Paul at levels that would no doubt have the neighbours banging on the ceiling.

'Hey, buddy.'

Paul and Noah embraced like long-lost brothers.

'You're all wet,' said Paul, pulling out of the hug, but only for a moment. 'I can't believe you made it back for the big birthday bash.'

'Well, I wasn't going to miss it, was I? No matter how hard the bus breakdowns and the airlines tried to make it.'

'And happy birthday to you too.' He spun round, almost as if he'd just clocked that I was here. He leaned over to give me a hug.

It wasn't long before Amy came to see the commotion in the hall.

'So, Noah, that's an improvement on those ghastly trousers from earlier, don't you think?' Amy's eyebrow was raised and her lips pursed as she stared at me. 'Although, I don't think they'll let you in the bar in a towel.'

'Not to mention that it would put the rest of us with beer bellies to shame.' Paul patted him on the back and steered him towards the lounge. He clapped his hands together. I hadn't seen him this excited since England got into the World Cup quarter-finals a couple of years ago. 'Drink?'

'Yes, let's get on it,' said Amy.

It wasn't long before Noah was in the kitchen wearing a long-sleeved shirt and jeans, and we all had drinks in our hands and the music was blaring from Amy's iPod speaker.

There was a knock at the door and I wondered if it was the neighbours complaining about the noise.

I brushed down the sequins across the front of my dress and planted on my best apologetic face as I pulled open the door.

'Hey, sweetie, surprise,' said Caz.

My mouth dropped open. She threw her arms up, bottle of wine in one, bracelets sliding down the other.

'Oh my god, you're here. I thought you were in Brussels.'

'We closed the deal early, so I got a flight to London rather than Manchester. Organised it with Amy at lunchtime.'

'Oh, I'm so glad you're here. I thought April was too long a wait.'

I flung my arms around her and gave her a big hug. The comforting smell of her trademark perfume hit me.

'And how's Nick? I take it he's not coming?'

'No, he's not, but he sends his best.'

I pulled her into the flat and she wheeled in her little cabin case and started to de-layer. Being Caz, she was dressed all in black, but there was a hint of sparkle in the plunging neckline of her top.

'Drink?'

'Always,' she said, handing me the bottle. 'And oh my goodness, happy birthday.'

'Oh, yes, thank you.' I smiled as we climbed the stairs into the kitchen area. Caz and Noah were here – what better present could I have asked for?

She immediately worked her way round hugging everyone. She stopped when she got to Noah, looking him up and down.

'Look at you. So tanned and grown up.'

I noticed her and Amy share a look, which I didn't want any part in. The two of them were just as bad as each other when the three of us got together. Just because they were both dating.

'I don't know about that,' he said. 'Although that journey home aged me.'

'Well, it looks good on you.'

Amy handed her a drink and we automatically split into boy and girl ends of the kitchen.

'I'm so pleased you're here,' I said. 'It's been too long.'

'Uh, why do we always say that, and why do we let it be?' Amy waggled her finger at Caz. 'It's all your fault. If you hadn't buggered off up North, this would have been a weekly occurrence.'

'I could say the same about you guys. You should move up to Manchester; you'd have a flat four times as big plus money in your pockets.'

We'd been having the same conversation for the last three years, ever since Caz broke the news that she wasn't following what seemed like the whole of the third year in their mass migration to London after graduation.

We soon got into the nitty gritty of what we'd all been up to and the minutes ticked by, feeling like seconds, as the five of us caught up and drank.

'Right, weren't we supposed to be leaving at eight?' asked Caz, glancing at her fancy watch.

'That's right,' said Amy. 'I told Helen that we'd be at the bar at quarter past. What time is it now?'

'Ten past.'

'Shit, drink up, people. I need to find my coat.'

'We haven't even done a birthday toast yet.' Paul opened the cupboards and pulled out our mismatched collection of shot glasses; we only had four but he improvised with an egg cup.

'Not only is it Lucy and Noah's actual birthday, which seems like it's been a long time coming, but I also need to acknowledge how pleased we are to have this one back.' He slipped his arms around Noah's shoulders. 'It has not been the same without you.'

Amy hit him in the chest. 'Does this mean that I'm never going to see you now your buddy's back?'

'Afraid so.'

'Thank fuck for that. I might get a social life back,' she teased and Paul winked at her before giving her a quick kiss. The two of them might always be bickering and pretending they didn't really like each other, but it was plain to see how much they were in love.

'To Lucy and Noah, happy birthday,' shouted Amy.

We raised our glasses and threw them back. There were a lot of strained faces and shudders.

'I better go grab my bag.' Amy headed out of the room, Paul following hot on her heels, trying to grab her bum with her slapping his hands away.

'And I want to reapply my lippy.' Caz hurried out.

'You know we haven't toasted to our anniversary,' said Noah, as we found ourselves alone in the kitchen.

I almost laughed until I looked him in the eye and the breath caught in my throat. Where once his face was always smooth and boyish, now it was coated in a thin layer of stubble. It wasn't just the long journey, he did look older.

He was holding my gaze. Something had shifted in me this morning, and I wondered if Noah felt it too?

When he'd said it earlier, it had sounded like it was all about our friendship, but now he was looking at me in a way that made me think there was something more.

'Our anniversary,' I said. The words came out a little squeaky. He'd moved in a little closer. The sound of laughter from Amy's bedroom seemed to fade away and all I could hear was my heart thumping loudly.

I felt drawn to him. Like every time I was in the same room as him now, I was sucked into his orbit. I didn't know whether it had always been like that and I'd resisted because of Hayley or if this was something new.

There's that feeling you get when you spend time with friends and it leaves you all charged with endorphins, but this left me with butterflies. The kind of butterflies you get at the start of a relationship when everything feels exciting and magical and like your life isn't going to be the same again.

His face crinkled and the dimple appeared. I hadn't realised until that moment how much I'd missed those little details of his face. The kind that the grainy skype pictures didn't show.

He was still looking at me and my breath caught in my throat.

'Do you ever wonder what would have happened if I hadn't been with Hayley and you hadn't been with Will when we first met?'

'I . . . ' I didn't know what to say. I thought about it some-times, usually in the moments when I'd been on a date with another man who got his phone out to work out the bill to the exact penny or one who didn't call me after a few dates. In those moments that made me consider every single decision that could have taken me in a different direction. Wasn't that what he was doing? He hadn't been broken up with Hayley for long, and he couldn't be over it already.

But the butterflies. Maybe I wasn't the only one feeling them.

'Sometimes,' I muttered, surprised at my honesty.

I felt that he was taking in every detail of my eye, and yet I didn't look away. I stared harder, searching his for an answer to what I was feeling.

We shouldn't be doing this. We were such good friends and this was only going to end in tears, like most relationships, wasn't it?

'Right, drink up,' said Amy, coming over and pushing the bottom of my glass. She had her coat on and her bag over her shoulder.

I shot Noah a look, but he'd already headed out of the room.

'Did I interrupt something?' Amy's eyebrow was raised in expectation and she looked like an excited puppy dog.

'No, just catching up.'

I smoothed down my sequins and let out a deep breath.

'Hmm, looked like it,' she said. 'Now get that coat on. The sooner we get to the bar, the sooner this party can carry on.'

Chapter 10

We spilled out of the packed bar into the street, and headed towards the club.

To give Amy her dues, she'd done her research and made sure that we didn't have too long a walk between venues. Her military planning wasn't always welcome when it came to our cleaning schedule, but on nights like this it was a godsend.

We stopped outside a bank en route and Amy and I stood with Noah and Paul whilst the others got cash.

'You realise now, Noah, that you're basically never going to be able to leave again,' said Amy. She was swaying, and I got the impression that her looped arm through Paul's was more to hold her up than any kind of romantic declaration. 'This one was an absolute wreck when you left.'

'I wouldn't say a wreck,' Paul protested, but the way that he'd hung off Noah's every word tonight said otherwise.

'Come on, you were practically sobbing.'

'I wouldn't say sobbing.'

'Don't worry,' said Noah, jumping in before the two of them started to bicker about whose recollections of events were true. 'I told Lucy I'm not going anywhere anytime soon.'

'Too broke?'

'That's part of it.' He turned his head to directly look at me.

'Plus, there are things that I want to do. Things I should have done before.'

I shuddered. Amy and Paul's eyes were burning into me.

'So where is this Cheesefest?' asked Noah, and Caz let out a groan.

'I still can't believe you're spending your one-in-four birthday there. When I tell my mates I'm heading to London for the weekend, they're always like, where are you heading to? – Shunt? Or Fabric? – and I have to admit where we're headed.'

She wrinkled her nose up in mock disgust, but no matter how much she pretended to hate it, I know she would have been secretly disappointed if we hadn't ended up there. She loved the place as much as the rest of us, even if it did mean taking a credibility hit.

The first time we'd gone, it had reminded us all of the student union, and there was that nostalgic feeling to the cheesy music and sweaty bodies not taking themselves seriously that we'd all latched on to.

'I can't wait to finally go. Paul's been bigging it up for months,' said Noah.

'It's so your type of place,' said Amy. 'They even have a meat raffle.'

Noah put his hands on his hips. 'Why didn't you say before? What are we waiting for? Lead on.'

He gestured with his hand and we started to walk.

'Just be prepared,' I said, wondering if my attempts to pace myself at the last bar were ill-advised. The club we were heading for was better the more liquid courage you had.

'Oh, I'm prepared for it all.' Noah smiled and I smiled back and we fell into step, a little further back from the others.

'Hmm, I'll remind you of that. Ben and Alex might have had the right idea jumping ship early.'

'Lightweights. I mean, what kind of an excuse is the last Tube anyway. Who doesn't love a night bus adventure?'

I groaned.

'You know, I feel like you've remembered London with rose-tinted glasses. Don't you remember the time that guy threw up all over you, and we had to sit there with you covered in sick for forty minutes.'

He winced; it was the kind of memory you'd want to bury deep. 'Yeah, I'm not sure what was worse about that. The fact I had to sit like that for so long on the bus, or the fact that I took off all my clothes, showered them and didn't shower myself? I stank so bad when I woke up the next morning.'

I couldn't help but laugh; it was so disgusting.

'Or what about the time when we were sat at the top of the bus and that awful guy started hitting on Caz.'

'Oh, I remember that. What was he, some shiny-shoed estate agent?'

'Yeah, that was it.'

'No one does put-down lines like Caz.' I was laughing and it was not helping the fact that I'd needed to wee since stepping out of the last bar. 'We've got to stop, or I'm going to wet myself.'

'OK, no fun.'

'No laughing.'

'Got it, I understand the mission. So what to talk about . . . hmm.' He stroked his chin, looking ridiculous.

'Not helping.'

'What? I was going for my best serious pose. Right, OK,

boring conversation. Remember that time that Paul made us all go to that lecture at Christmas? Now that was boring.'

'Oh, I'd forgotten that. What was that even about?'

'He'd thought they were showing *It's a Wonderful Life*.'

'Yes, that was it, and instead we had to sit through advanced physics.'

'And Paul snored in the middle and the lecturer whacked a ruler on the desk.'

'This is not helping.' I didn't think I was going to make it.

'Look, we're almost there.' Noah pointed at the club entrance like a beacon. I looked up and Amy was already at the VIP line sorting things out; god bless Amy.

I had reached the level of drunk where I had every confidence known to man. I'd become more tactile with everyone and the odd word was slurred.

Cheesefest delivered on so many levels. Noah loved it as much as the rest of us.

Chesney Hawkes' 'The One and Only' came to an end and it was replaced by a Madness song. I stopped dancing, thanks to my irrational hatred of their music, and Noah leaned into me.

'Wanna sit this one out?'

I nodded and we left the others who were dancing round and pulling up their imaginary baggy trousers.

I started to walk and found Noah's hands on my hips as he helped to steer me through the dancefloor that had spilled out from its confines and across most of the open space. I could feel the heat of his touch. My hand came to a rest on top of his like it was the most natural thing in the world.

He steered me past the bar and up the stairs to the seating

area, where we found a table with the kind of PVC seats that I would be in danger of sticking to with my short dress if I hadn't been wearing tights. We sat down next to each other and it might not have been as loud up here, but we still found ourselves leaning in to talk to each other.

'You still hate Madness then?'

'I do. I've tried to like them, but I don't know what it is. Must be all the fun.'

'Must be. You being a big killjoy.'

'The biggest.'

We were both grinning, my heart aching at how much I'd missed this.

A couple walked past us, a tall woman, dragging a shorter man to the corner, where they sat opposite each other at the table, neither looking at the other.

'What do you reckon their story is?' asked Noah, leaning even closer.

'Oh, I don't know. He's in trouble for pinching the bum of some girl that walked past.'

Noah nodded. 'Could be; he looks like he has wandering hands.'

'They're not doing much wandering there. Those body language experts you get in magazines would have a field day. His feet pointing that way, hers the other.'

'Her folded arms.'

'The biting of the lips.'

'Classic argument.' Noah glanced around. 'And what about them? What's going on there?'

I looked to see a woman on all fours on top of the PVC seating, crawling towards a man. The man looked a little startled at first, and then she tilted her head to the side.

'Oh, goodness. Let's see. I reckon he's Bill and she's Mary. They're actually married, but they like to come to clubs and pretend they're complete strangers and then, oh my.'

I held my hand over my eyes to shield the fact that Mary had climbed on Bill's lap and had wasted no time sticking her tongue down his throat.

'I hope you're right with that one,' said Noah, pulling a face. 'And what about us, what do you think someone watching would say is our story?'

I turned towards him, to tell him and he rested his hand on my thigh, just at the line where my dress hit my tights.

Goosebumps shot up my arms and my whole body started to tingle in all the right places. He didn't take his eyes off me as he started to trace shapes just under my hem line. I closed my eyes for a split second and let out a small moan.

I wanted him in the same way that Mary wanted Bill. I wanted to climb on him and to have his hands run all over me. I wanted his hands to stop teasing and go higher. I wanted to trace my fingers over that chest I saw earlier.

'What would they say about us?' he whispered in my ear, his nose nuzzling at my neck as my hand found his waist. I went to say something and I felt his mouth meet mine. It was as if a thousand volts of electricity pulsed through my veins and I knew that anything I had felt today hadn't been imagined. My whole body was aching for him. Aching to be touched. Aching to be kissed.

But not like this. Not here. I didn't want to be Bill and Mary. I didn't want this to be some drunken fumble in a club. That wasn't what I wanted the start of our story to be.

'Noah, we can't.' I gently pushed him back. He'd taken my

breath away, and I cleared my throat to tell him not here, not like this, and how I wanted it to be special.

'Right,' he said, shuffling back, and running his hand through his hair. 'Of course, I'm sorry, I—'

'Noah.' I reached out a hand.

'There you two are,' shouted Amy, flopping down in between us, unaware of what she was interrupting. 'I've been looking for you everywhere. Look who came.'

She held her hands up and I saw Mags standing in front of us.

'Oh my goodness, you made it.' I struggled to get to my feet to give her a hug; my legs were like jelly. 'Wow. You look amazing.' She was wearing tight leather trousers and a tight red top. On anyone else it would look cheap but somehow Mags, with her platinum blonde hair, looked a million dollars.

'I thought I might feel a little overdressed, but it seems anything goes,' she said, as a person in a Crayola crayon outfit walked past.

'It's that kind of place.'

'You look great too.' She stroked the sequins on the long sleeve.

I tugged self-consciously at the hem. I'd tried to go for sexy, but I don't know how sexy constantly pulling down my dress was.

'I feel like I'm two months late for Christmas.'

'No, it's glitzy and glam; it's perfect for your birthday. Happy birthday, by the way.'

'Thanks, although I'm pretty sure it's no longer my birthday.' I turned to look over my shoulder at Noah who was talking to Amy. I tried to throw him an apologetic look, sorry that we'd been interrupted, but he wouldn't meet my eyes.

'So, is this your famous male friend?' She didn't wait for an answer. She turned to him and stuck her hand out. 'Hi, I'm Mags. I work with Lucy.'

'Ah, yeah, I've heard all about you. I'm Noah.'

'Nice to meet you, Noah. I hope you've heard all good things,' she said, raising an eyebrow in my direction. 'And I've heard all about how you're Lucy's platonic male friend.'

He looked between me and her.

'I always say men and women can't be just friends, but Lucy assures me that you guys can.'

He turned back to Mags and nodded, a smile on his face. 'That's us. Just friends.'

I watched the hurt appear in his eyes. I knew I should reach out and touch him; tell him that I had been wrong, that there was more. That I wanted there to be more. But I didn't. I watched that door close for us.

It was like Amy bounding up had jolted me back to reality. Made me see that getting together with Noah wasn't a good idea. Because I loved having him back in my life and I was scared if something went wrong it would fracture our group apart.

'Mags, you need a drink. In fact, we all do. I'll go get us some,' he said. 'Shots?'

'Brilliant idea, but I'm buying. You guys are the birthday boy and girl.'

Noah stood up and I wanted to grab his arm to explain that it wasn't how it sounded, but Amy took hold of me and pulled me down and I watched as they headed to the bar.

'Hey you, you can't leave me as well,' she slurred into my ear. She stroked my face. 'You know how much I love you, have I told you that?'

'You have, Ams. Every time you're drunk. And every morning when I bring you up a cup of tea.'

She smiled and closed her eyes.

'That's why you're the best housemate. Please, never leave me.'

I watched Noah and Mags at the bar; they were talking and I could feel pangs of jealousy thinking of how a few minutes ago those eyes had only me in their sights.

'I think it's you that's going to leave me.' I tried to prop Amy into a more seated position. 'I reckon you'll be moving in with Paul soon.'

'No, I'm not moving in with a boy. They leave the toilet seat up. And they smell. No, let's live together forever. Ooh shots.'

She sat bolt upright and started to clap as Noah put a round in front of us.

'Wait, what are we toasting?' Mags asked.

'To friends,' he said, shooting it back and not waiting for the toast. 'Will you excuse me, I'm going to find Paul.'

'Tell him I'm staying with Lucy forever,' called Amy.

He gave her a thumbs up and went off.

'Oh my god, what are those two people doing?' Mags recoiled.

'That's Mary and Bill. Don't worry, they're married.' Both women looked at me and I wished that Noah was here to share the joke. But he was heading down the stairs, his face unreadable.

I had a sinking feeling in my stomach that I'd ruined whatever moment was between us, but that same sinking feeling told me that maybe it wasn't a bad thing. That maybe I saved the friendship that everyone seemed to be trying to find.

Chapter 11

Saturday 1st March

I woke up with a pounding headache and a throat so dry it was like someone had sucked all the moisture out with a vacuum cleaner. I risked opening my eyes, the light streaming in through the curtains.

I tried to take in the scene of my room and piece together what had happened. I was wearing a vest top and pants, the top back to front. My clothes from last night were trailed along my floor and there was a pint glass on its side on my bedside table.

'Shit,' I muttered, trying to mop up the spillage on the floor with a rogue towel, hoping it wouldn't stain the carpet.

I needed water and headed out to the kitchen. The living-room door was shut; no doubt Noah was still fast asleep. The jetlag had caught up with him and he'd been asleep most of the taxi ride home, and had collapsed as soon as we'd got in.

I downed a glass of water, then another, my head still pounding. And I started to replay the moments of last night. Noah and me laughing, dancing, then I remembered the feeling of his fingers running up my thigh. How close we'd come to kissing.

The front door slammed, and I heard footsteps coming up the stairs.

'Morning,' called Noah, far too chirpily for my liking.

I pulled my dressing gown tighter around me.

'Morning. You're up early.'

'Couldn't sleep.' He took his bag off his back and started to unpack. He had a large bottle of orange juice, what looked like a paper bag of croissants, and a pack of photos.

'Is that your last film?' I said, filling the kettle up.

'Uh-huh, I dropped it in yesterday afternoon, popped in on the off-chance they were ready and they were.'

He started to flick through the pack, smiling at each one. 'Koh Phi Phi.' He held out a photo of the classic Thailand beach shot with long-tailed boat, turquoise waters and golden sands.

'Stunning.'

He flicked through the others and then he stopped. His smile changed, before he handed one to me. 'Here.'

It was the photo Noah had taken in the pedalo. It did have our faces in it, and it wasn't the most flattering of photos, my nose was scrunched up and my eyes were shut, but my smile was wide and I could almost hear the laughter.

'I'm proud of that. Both faces in and everything.'

'No bald spot though.'

'No,' he said, laughing, 'but maybe an extra chin of mine I didn't know I was carrying.' He stroked at his face.

I went to hand it back but he stopped me.

'You keep it, I'll get a copy. Pin it on the fridge or something.' He pointed at our messy fridge that had magnets holding back masses of takeaway menus, letters and photos, and then he went back to the pack in his hands. 'Now I just have to spot you in here.'

I looked over his shoulder, of course spotting myself

immediately, but I could see how it wouldn't be easy for Noah to find me in the sea of faces.

He brought it closer and then he laughed. 'Got you.'

'Already?'

'I'm a seasoned pro.'

I flicked on the kettle, and set about getting the cups. 'I take it you want coffee?'

'I'd kill for one.' He pulled up a chair at the kitchen table, and I got some jam out of the fridge for the croissants. 'It was a good night last night.'

'It was.'

'Quite drunken.'

'Uh-huh.'

'Look, Luce, I'm sorry about, you know, that bit near the end where I got a bit touchy-feely.'

'Oh yeah, I was going to talk to you about that.' My voice was a little shaky, unsure what I was going to say, my mind flip-flopping between my heart and my head. My heart telling me how amazing it would be and my head telling me that if it went wrong I'd lose Noah from my life.

'It shouldn't have happened,' he said, opening out the paper bag. 'I'd had far too much to drink and I think it's new for me being drunk and feeling soppy and not having a girlfriend and—'

My heart burned and my stomach sank.

'I get it. It's fine.' I raised my hand. Not wanting to hear any more. Because that's something I hadn't considered. That this wasn't about us, but him being a bit drunk and single after so long. 'Good job we stopped it.'

The words came out a little bitter, but if I'd been doubting my decision to push him away, I was now glad I had.

I couldn't imagine what it would be like if we hadn't stopped and then had to have this conversation after.

'Good job,' he said. 'Now, do you want one of these croissants?'

'Actually, I'm going to head into the shower.' The kettle came to the boil and chirped, but I couldn't stay to make the coffee. The tears were starting to sting behind my eyes.

'I'll try not to eat them all,' he said, as I hurried to the bathroom.

I flicked on the shower and shut the door, resting against it and letting the tears fall.

An hour later, dressed, hair blow-dried and neatly styled, I had breakfast in the kitchen whilst Noah showered.

'What are you going to do for the next big birthday?' Amy was flicking through Noah's holiday snaps. 'Perhaps we should go here. It looks awesome.'

She flashed a photo of a jungle on the edge of a beach.

'Looks amazing. Might be a bit extravagant for a birthday though.'

'I think we should go somewhere. A city break?' said Paul. 'I'm sure you could put Amy on the case.'

'You certainly can.' She sighed as she took in another beautiful beach. She finished up the pack, not even giving the one of Trafalgar Square a second glance.

'I should probably get my stuff together to go to Noah's parents.' Paul stood up and winced in pain. 'Bloody hell, I think I pulled a muscle in my bum last night.'

'Don't look at me,' said Amy, holding her hands up.

'I think it was when I was on that podium. Your friend Mags is a bad influence.'

He pointed at me and I shrugged back. Seeing him and Mags do *Coyote Ugly*-style dancing to 'Pour Some Sugar on Me' had been one of my highlights of last night.

'What are we all laughing at?' said Noah, towel drying his hair. Luckily he was fully dressed. His hoodie had none of the effect his dripping wet torso had had on me yesterday.

'Paul dancing on that podium with Mags.'

'I didn't know you had it in you, buddy.' Noah patted him on the back, and Paul flinched again.

'I don't think I did; that's why my body's now in shock.'

He hobbled out of the kitchen. Noah put the kettle on and picked up the cup in front of me. 'Coffee?'

'Thanks,' I said, not meeting his eye. I'd given myself a bit of a pep talk in the shower. I knew that this feeling would pass, and in time I'd be pleased that we hadn't jeopardised our friendship, but right now I felt a plethora of emotions: gutted, upset, but mostly foolish.

'Your mate Mags seemed like a lot of fun.'

'She is.'

'She gave me her phone number.' My stomach lurched. 'She said to call her as she might have a friend that could help about a job.'

'Oh, you should do that,' I said, relieved that that's all it was about. 'She's an excellent networker.'

'That sounds like it could be promising.' Amy drained her glass of juice and filled it up with more.

'I'll take any leads at this point.'

The shrill of our doorbell rang out.

I raised an eyebrow at Amy. 'Postman?'

'It's probably my parents.' Noah started towards the door.

'They're coming here?' The kitchen that looked like we'd had a full-on party here the night before. There were discarded glasses everywhere, and it probably stank of booze.

'They've seen worse.' He shook his head and went downstairs to answer the door.

Amy and I shared a split-second look, before we started to work at making the kitchen presentable.

'I thought they weren't coming until later,' she said, flipping open the window as I collected empty beer bottles and put them in a plastic bag.

'I thought the boys were catching the train?'

'I don't think they trusted the boys to actually make it. They thought they'd be too hungover. And between you and me, I don't think his mum could wait any longer to see him.'

We heard Noah's parents' voices carry up the stairs and I hastily started to stack the dishwasher. By the time they made it to the kitchen, it looked semi-presentable.

'Hello, girls.' Sandra, Noah's mum, held her arms wide and gave us both a squeeze. 'Look at you two; so grown up, so grown up.'

She stroked my cheek.

'And look at this place. I can't believe you live here. Look at this natural light. Oh, it's so gorgeous. Such a contrast to those dingy houses you all rented off-campus.'

'Yeah, we've definitely lucked out with this place.'

'It makes me shiver just thinking about how cold those houses were,' said Amy.

Noah walked in, closely followed by his dad.

'Hello, hello.'

'Hello, Mr Matthews.'

'Lucy,' he sighed. 'I thought we'd dropped that. Mr Matthews is my father, and whilst I might have gone grey like him, that's where the similarities end. It's Peter.'

I nodded, smiling at how this was a well-rehearsed script that me and Peter read off each time we saw each other.

'No ring on that finger yet then, Amy?' Sandra grabbed at her ring hand to investigate.

'No, not yet.' She blushed. 'Not sure we're quite there.'

'You know, by your age, we were married with a toddler. I don't know why you all leave it so late these days.'

'So that you've retired by the time we have kids and we get free childcare.'

She giggled and playfully hit Noah on the arm.

'You wouldn't believe with his cheek that I'd miss him.'

She beamed at her son, and he wrapped his arm around her.

'And where is Paul, anyway?'

'He's gone for a shower.'

'Right, so we've got time for a tour of the house?'

I pulled a face. 'I don't think you want to see the rest of the place; Noah slept in the front room.'

She raised a hand.

'Say no more, I used to clean his bedroom.'

'Hey, I'm right here.'

'I know.' She tugged at his cheeks. 'It's so lovely to have you all in the same room. I wish you were all coming back with us.'

'They wouldn't all fit in the car,' said Peter.

'I wasn't suggesting it. But you know that you're always welcome, right? Noah's staying with us indefinitely.'

'Until May, when I move in with Liam.'

'If you get a job by then; if not, you'll be with us.' There was a tiny bit of hope in Sandra's voice that she almost wanted him to not get the job so that he could stay.

'There's the positivity. I'll be fine.'

Paul walked into the room, giving Sandra and Peter big hugs.

'Right, we better get going to beat the traffic.' Peter hadn't stopped checking his watch since he'd arrived.

'What traffic?' said Noah. 'It's Saturday.'

'There's always traffic in London. Plus, kick-off is at two and I don't want to miss it.'

Sandra chuckled. 'And there's the real reason. Take my advice' – she leaned towards me – 'never marry someone obsessed with sports . . . Are you dating anyone, Lucy?'

'Not at the moment.'

She took hold of my hand and gave it a squeeze. 'It'll happen. Lovely girl like you. You'll soon be snapped up.'

I caught Noah's eye and he looked away. Just not by him.

'Right, we better be off,' said Peter. 'Pleasure as always to see you two.'

'Don't be a stranger, girls.' Sandra gave Amy a hug, before turning to me. 'I know Noah would love it if you came to stay whilst he was there.'

'Mum,' he said, almost prising her off me. 'Thanks for having me, Luce.'

Unlike the warm hug that his mum had just given me, he barely gave me a tap on the back. It was the kind of hug you did when you were trying to make as little contact with someone as possible.

'I'll see you out,' said Amy, ushering everyone down the stairs, whilst I stayed in the kitchen.

I glanced at the fridge at the photo we took yesterday. How

much could change in twenty-four hours? Look at us grinning at each other. It's the type of photo that we'd have proudly framed if we'd got together. The type that you'd laugh and say, that was the moment when we knew.

Only we didn't. And now it's just another photo of us as friends.

'Happy birthday, me,' I muttered, not knowing how my proper birthday had started on a such a massive high and finished with me feeling this low.

Text message – Noah to Lucy: April 2008
Hey, I'm back in London tomorrow for an interview – thanks to Mags' friend. I'm meeting her after for a drink to say thanks. Wanna come?

Facebook messenger – Lucy to Noah: June 2008
L: Hiya, long time no see! How's the new job over at the dark side working out? Do you fancy meeting for drinks Saturday night? We can get the gang together.

N: Actually, I've asked Mags out on a date for Saturday.

L: Wow! I'm so happy for you guys :) Wait, did she say yes?

N: Yes, she did. Can't quite believe my luck. And thanks, we'll see what happens.

L: I'm missing out on all the gossip now we work on different floors.

Voicemail – Noah to Lucy: January 2009

Hey Luce, sorry we missed you last night. We'd been planning to make your party, but the drinks at Mags' friend's was more of a sit-down dinner than we'd expected. There were name tags on the table and everything. Fancy. Anyway, I tried to call but all the lines were busy. New Year's, eh? Hope you had a good one. And um, happy new year. Hope this year goes well for you.

Facebook messenger – Gillian to Lucy: February 2009

Hey Lucy!!!! I'm not sure if Dad called you??? Me and my mate Delia wanna go see Katy Perry at KOKO. Can we crash at yours? Do u live nearby???

Email – Mags to Lucy: April 2009

OMG – I've been looking into this online glasses idea in the UK and I think there's something in it. If only so I can stop paying bloody customs fees for mine. But have a look at the links below; think it's worth considering??? And, no, just because you've changed jobs does not mean that I'm going to let you off the hook from joining me. PS Mega proud of you. Fucking Francis is raging! PPS Do you fancy coming out with me and Noah at the weekend?

Text message – Noah to Lucy: October 2009
Noah:

Just heard that Amy's moving out. You OK? You got anyone to move in?

Lucy:

Thanks, I'm super sad, but pleased for her and Paul. I'm sure it'll be like a second home! I'm going to advertise the room. I did think of Mags but she told me that she might be getting a different roommate soon. Happy for you guys .)

Voicemail – Amy to Lucy: March 2010

Holy shit, Paul proposed. I'm ENGAGED! Can you believe it? You're a bridesmaid natch. We've not set a date or got any idea where it's going to be, but all I know is I will look fantastic and you and Caz will be by my side. Call me as soon as you get this, I am literally climbing the walls not sure what to do.

Email – Mags to the Group: July 2010

You guys – I am now officially a CEO – LOVELY LENSES is now online and open for business. Obviously I'm looking at you, Paul, as the lone glasses wearer, but to the rest please share far and wide. And, Lucy – get that resignation letter typed and ready to send. I have a feeling this is only the start :)

Email – Caz to List: Amy's Hens: October 2010

Ladies! The time is approaching to give Amy the send-off she deserves. We thought it only fitting that we'd take her back to Canterbury to all the old haunts where her and Paul met. Expect trips to The Canterbury Tales, pub crawls, Mexican food in the best Mexican restaurant outside of Mexico, and whatever that club in the town with all the floors is called now. Bring lots of booze and your dancing shoes.

Facebook wall posts: February/March 2011

Happy birthday, Mr Matthews! Hope you and Mags have a good time skiing. XX

Happy birthday, LUCY! Have a good one x

Text message – Amy to Lucy: August 2011

Thank you for going above and beyond and being the world's best bridesmaid. Gutted that you didn't catch the bouquet. Not quite sure I see Mags being the marrying type . . .

Also, if you get a chance, chat to Caz before she heads back home to see if she's OK? I think she's having problems with Nick. She kept rambling when she was drunk about a French man called Bert something xx

Voicemail – Noah to Lucy: October 2011

Hey, I am just ringing as a totally impartial person that may have just read the expansion plan that Mags put together for the loan. Tell me you're going to finally jump on board, mainly so that she stops telling me how much she misses you at work? But seriously, it looks solid, and she in no way is making me say this, ouch, no tickling . . . sorry, um, anyway call me, call us. No, apparently call Mags. Laters.

Facebook messenger – Lucy to Noah: December 2011

Hey! Just wanted to see if you and Mags are both free on the 28th? I've managed to pin the newlyweds down and I've invited Graham over too. I know you guys were keen to meet him. I thought if we couldn't all get together before Christmas, this would be the next best thing.

Text – Caz to Lucy: January 2012

Hey, hope you're OK! Just a quickie. Do you think anyone would mind if I brought Bertrand to Dublin? He said he'd fly over from Paris to meet us? Don't know if it made the group too big? Xx

Email – Mags to Lucy: February 2012

Hey, just checking in to see if you've made a decision? Sorry to push, I know it's a big one to weigh up and I know that I'm not offering as much as you're on now, but I promise you this is only the start and it'll grow and you'll be cruising to the office in a Porsche before you know it – or actually probs still the Tube as the parking is shocking around the office, but you know what I mean. Either way, let me know as if you don't want to take it, I'll have to try and find someone else. M xx

PART THREE

2012

Chapter 12

Tuesday 28ᵗʰ February 2012

Amy opened the door, tears streaming from her face.

'Oh, sweetie.' I pulled her into a big hug, banging into her ever-increasing bump.

'I'm sorry to have called. It's just I was on top of everything and then Paul said he had to go into the office and I lost it. He hadn't even packed, and I ran around finding his bits. He was like, I only need three pairs of boxers and a couple of T-shirts,' she tutted. 'And by the time he left, I felt so exhausted. I'm so pathetic.'

I shuffled her inside so that she didn't let out all the heat of her house.

'Don't be silly, it's not pathetic at all. And I'm happy to help.'

'But what about getting you to the airport?'

'I've got my case,' I said, wheeling it in behind me and closing the door.

'But you were supposed to be going with Graham. It's your first mini-break.'

Her eyes looked red and puffy and I wondered how long she'd been crying for.

'It's fine; he was meeting me at Heathrow anyway. Made no sense for him to come to mine first.'

'And your mum?'

'She's getting the coach straight there too. It's fine, I'll get the train or a taxi with you, OK?'

'OK.' She took a deep breath.

'It's not good for you to get stressed. Come on then, where's your case?'

'In our room, but—'

'Then that's fine.'

She wiped at her tears and we headed upstairs. There was a mountain of clothes on the bed.

'Where's the case?'

'Under there somewhere,' she said, sitting down. 'I couldn't get it closed.' Her head fell into her hands.

'It'll be alright.' I painted a cheery smile on my face, not wanting to upset her anymore, despite the work that we had cut out for us.

'Bloody hell,' I muttered, poking and prodding at first, not sure where to start. I winced looking at how many jumpers, tops and trousers she'd packed. 'I'm not sure you need quite this much.'

'I'm growing at a rate of knots and nothing fits me. Plus, I don't know what I'll want to wear.'

'We're going for three days; I don't think that the baby is going to grow that much. These are out,' I said, picking out a pair of spindly heels. 'Firstly, I think Dublin has cobbled streets and stilettos and cobbles do not mix. And secondly, we're not going anywhere that dressy.'

I kept rooting and picked out fleecy pyjamas.

'Right, now you're taking the piss.'

'But I like to be cosy.'

She hugged the furry top to her chest.

'It's no good, I'm going to have to take hold luggage,' she whined.

'You are not taking hold luggage.' I held my hands up like I was trying to calm down a crowd. 'We're going for three days. Right, it's got to be done.'

I tipped the case out on the bed. Amy gasped.

'It's fine, we've got at least an hour to do this.'

She tried to prop herself up against the pillows.

'You know you get so much more in if you roll your clothes up.'

'Oh, I know that.' Amy was usually the most organised of all of us, and I was surprised that she hadn't packed last week. 'I just don't know what's happening to me. It's like I'm in a constant fog, and I'm tired; why am I so tired?'

'You're growing a living creature in your belly.'

She wrinkled up her nose. 'Still, I feel like I've been on a week-long bender. In fact, I don't think I was this tired after Ayia Napa and I slept for a week when we got back.'

I shuddered at the memory of that holiday. Being twenty-one, our mantra at the time had been something like 'go hard or go home'.

'That feels like a lifetime ago.'

'I know,' she said, laughing. 'Remember our dodgy sunburn?'

'I swear I still see the strap marks when the sun comes out.'

'Didn't stop us going out that night though, did it?'

'Looking back, we must have had really bad sunstroke.'

I held up a questionable dress that I'm pretty sure dated from that holiday.

'In case we went clubbing.'

'Um, well, we're not going clubbing in two thousand and five, so I think this can stay here.'

She groaned. 'I can't think straight anymore.'

I made piles of clothes and looked in her drawers for a couple more staples. 'I've got your back.'

Tears started to roll down her face.

'Oh, Amy, we're almost there; why are you crying!'

'Because,' she said, between sobs, 'you're being so nice. These bloody hormones.'

'Only another four months to go. It sounds like you need this trip away.'

'I do,' she hiccupped.

'We'll take it nice and easy. I'm sure we could all do with a rest.'

'Yes, a rest is exactly what I need. But I did manage to do us a bit of an itinerary.'

'I would expect nothing less,' I said, squeezing in some extra maternity leggings just in case.

My phone started to ring.

'Hey, Mum.' I cradled the phone under my ear and started to push the case down to zip it up.

'Hey darling, just to let you know that I'm here.'

'At the airport?'

'Yes, are you here too?'

I looked at my watch, in a slight panic that we'd taken longer than I thought, but we still didn't need to be there for another hour and a half.

'I'm at Amy's helping her pack. We're leaving in a bit, so we'll be there about eleven. Why did you get such an early bus?'

'Because you said to meet at nine.'

'No, I said, get the bus at nine. Our flight isn't until one p.m.'

Mum tutted loudly. 'Oh bloody hell. I'm sure you said ten.

What an idiot. Oh well, I brought a good book with me; might give me a chance to read it.'

'Be on the lookout for Graham. He's always early too.'

'OK, love, let me know when you're here.'

'Will do.'

I hung up and shook my head.

'Your mum is at the airport already?' asked Amy. She was pushing herself into a more upright position.

'Yeah, she got the times wrong.'

'Let's go then.'

'We'll have to wait around.'

'It'll be fine. It takes me ages to get anywhere these days so maybe if we leave now we'll arrive on time. I'm just glad your mum's coming with us.'

'I know. I can't believe she agreed to it.'

It had taken a lot of convincing that none of us had any style to cramp, and that it would be pretty tame with Amy being pregnant. She'd let me buy the tickets as a Christmas present, and I hoped it would pave the way for getting her to let me pay for a New York trip in the future.

'Let's get this show on the road then.'

'Are you sure that I don't need this?' Amy picked up her dressing gown.

'Come on. Anything you don't have you can buy there. I hear they have shops in Dublin, you know,' I said, heading down the stairs. 'All you need is your passport, wallet and phone.'

Amy froze in horror.

'Shit, my wallet.' She went back into her room and appeared back a few minutes later with it in her hand.

'Do you want me to check your hand luggage?'

'I can't believe we're here,' squealed Amy, as we stepped off the airport bus into the centre of the city. We were almost all together. Caz's flight from Manchester had already arrived, but she was waiting for her new boyfriend Bertrand to fly from Paris, and Mags would be joining us tonight after a big appointment with an investor.

'I can't quite believe we made it either, or at least you did . . . ' Amy had packed her old expired passport rather than her current one. Thank goodness I'd checked before we left.

'Don't remind me,' she said, looking sheepish, 'and thanks for not telling Paul. He's terrified of what the baby brain is going to do to me when the baby is actually born.'

'Your secret is safe with me.'

'So, what's up first on the plan then?' asked Noah, climbing off the bus and joining us.

'I've factored in a little more free time for me to have naps, but we'll still be doing the important things. Like going to the Guinness factory. Seeing some Irish music.'

'You do realise that you won't be able to drink at the Guinness factory?' Paul slipped his arm around her.

'I'm sure I could have a sip or two. Didn't they used to give women Guinness on maternity wards to boost their iron?'

'Pretty sure that we shouldn't be trying to go through this pregnancy on fifties medical advice,' he said. 'Didn't you make me turn off that midwife programme that was set then as it was freaking you out?'

The two of them bickered in that sweet way they did, with little shoves and playful looks.

Graham pulled a map out of his hand luggage and started to study it.

'Is it far to the hotel then? Do we need to get a taxi?' asked Mum, looking around her, trying to take it all in.

'I think it's a short walk.' Graham slipped the map into his pocket and reached down for Mum's case. 'I'll take that.'

'You will not.' She pulled it back. 'I'm not that old. But you can walk with me; I want to hear more about this beer you brew.'

Graham's eyes lit up. 'With pleasure.'

They headed off and Amy and Paul followed after. I waited for Noah to slip his backpack on his shoulders. Unlike the rest of us, he didn't have a suitcase. It was probably far more practical for the city streets, but it didn't fit the image he now had. He was wearing a long wool coat and dark khakis rather than the jeans that used to skim his bum, and a V-neck jumper. He looked like he'd stepped out of a Gap commercial.

'Can you believe how far those two have come?' he said, pointing at Amy and Paul, who'd got over the bickering and were now swinging their hands as they walked.

'I know, and it was all thanks to us.' I liked to take credit, even though I'd done nothing to get them together other than convincing her to go to their party.

'Yeah, I know. Although, I think they would have met anyway.'

'With campus being so small?'

'No, fate.'

I tutted. 'Why does that not surprise me? Of course you would be a believer in fate.'

'Come on, looking at those two, can't you see it? I'm pretty

153

sure they would have found their way to each other.' We watched as Paul squeezed Amy in tight as they walked and planted a kiss on her head.

'The trouble is, if you look hard enough you see coincidences and twists of fate wherever you look. It's just an endless stream of decisions that lead us to a particular point.'

'There she is, ladies and gentleman; there's the cynic that we know and love.' Noah gave me a wink. 'I still like to think that the universe has some kind of plan.'

'Yes, I'm sure a universe with infinite numbers of galaxies has a plan just for you, one of seven billion people on Earth.'

I went to step off the kerb and Noah put his arm across my chest. I looked up in surprise to see a tram approaching.

'You probably would have made it in time, but just in case.'

'Yeah, thank you. I guess I have to look out for those.'

'Um-hmm.'

'I bet you're going to say that it was fate that I introduced you to Mags.'

'Ha, I wasn't . . . ' he said with a pause.

It was funny we'd become so close over the years and shared so much about our lives, but we never spoke about him and Mags. I guess that's what happens when you are friends with both parties: neither want to confer with you for fear of it reaching the other person.

'Speaking of,' I said, 'what time's she arriving?'

'I don't know, around five? Maybe six? I just hope she makes it on the plane. She was only supposed to have one meeting today and then she scheduled another.' He shook his head.

'She'll be here. It's your birthday.'

'Of course she will. Don't get me wrong, I love that she's

driven and she's thrown herself into the business. I just wish that she didn't have to be on all the time.'

'It must be a busy time for her. Getting the warehouse and everything.'

'Yeah.' He nodded, before he let out a deep breath. 'Listen to me. I sound ridiculous. Of course I'm super proud of what she's doing, and I'm pleased those bloody boxes are out of our house. Don't tell her I said any of that, right?'

He looked pained. I knew more than any of us he wanted Mags' business to succeed, and not just because his mortgage depended on it.

'Well, I can't promise,' I teased to lighten the mood. 'A few whiskeys tonight, and who knows what I'll come out with.'

'You wouldn't. Don't forget I can tell Graham some choice things. What story would he like to hear first? The time that you crawled into my wardrobe and went to sleep after that night out in Clapham? Or the time when you dressed up as a mermaid and fell off the bar and split your skirt tail all the way up to your knickers?'

'Do you have any idea how hard it was to walk in that skirt, let alone dance on a bar in it? I'm surprised I didn't break any bones.'

Noah let out a snort.

I looked at Graham walking with Mum further up on the pavement. They were chatting away animatedly. It was nice that Mum got on well with him. It was one of those boxes to tick off on that mental checklist.

'I guess we both know enough to blackmail each other into silence on any subject,' I said, thinking over our eight-year friendship. 'Questionable outfit choices. Dodgy haircuts.'

'Oh, there you go. I was just waiting for you to drop in the frosted tips. The fishtail story comes out and the gloves come off.'

I tried my very hardest not to cackle at the image of Noah primed in front of the mirror with tiny plastic gloves trying to bleach the tips of his spiky hair.

'Or more like the gloves stayed on.'

'Easy.' He threw me a warning glance. This was a dangerous game we were playing. We both had far too many embarrassing memories of the other in our arsenal.

'I still wish I'd got a photo of you with the frosted tips before you shaved it off.'

He shuddered. 'That was not a good look for me.'

'The frosting or the skinhead?'

'Either.'

My cheeks were starting to ache from trying not to laugh. 'How did we even get on this topic?'

'I think I was trying to blackmail you into not telling Mags.'

'That was it. Don't worry, your secrets are safe with me. And don't worry about Mags; I'm sure it'll all calm down soon.'

'Yeah, I know.' He nudged me with his elbow. 'Especially with you set to join her.' A tightness drew over my belly. Mags had initially asked me to come in on the business fifty-fifty at the beginning, but it was too big a risk, so we decided I'd go in when it was more established. I'd get less reward in terms of shares, but there'd be less risk. I'd done a bit of freelance work for her, but now the business was growing she needed someone full time. I'd be overseeing the marketing like I did now for clients, but being in-house meant that I'd be more hands on with the e-commerce and social media. It could be a brilliant move, but the closer it got the scarier it seemed.

'And what about you? How's work?'

'It's alright, I guess. It just about pays the mortgage.'

I recognised the forlorn look on his face. It was the kind of look that Mum had on her face at the end of the month when she balanced her cheque book. She was always trying to find money somewhere.

'That good, huh?'

'Mags keeps saying I should move. Chase the new title, the bigger bonus.'

He put his hands in his pockets. Maybe I'd misread the look and it was more than just the size of his mortgage.

'But you like your job, don't you?'

'Does anyone?' There was no emotion in his voice.

'I do,' I said, taking myself by surprise. I'd put up with Fucking Francis for too long, but when I'd moved for a promotion at a rival company, I'd rediscovered the love of my job. 'I get out of bed, excited to go to work every day.'

'Bloody hell, what's that like?'

I smiled.

'Perhaps you should work for Mags. Take the job she wants me to do.'

'Uh, no. That would be a recipe for disaster. And I doubt that would help with the mortgage anxiety.'

'You've got a beaut of a house though. And you're homeowners. Actual real-life house owners. I thought they were an urban myth, especially in the home counties.'

'I know. I'd have never believed I'd own a house like that.'

The wind whistled along the river.

'My ears are freezing.' I put my hands up to them, wishing I knew where in my suitcase my hat was.

'Yeah, it's not warm. Why couldn't we have a birthday in summer?'

'I know, or go somewhere hot?'

'Yep, hot would be good. Maybe next time, huh?'

'Maybe next time.'

'Although haven't you always fancied New York?'

I looked out at the river, a little guilty that I wished I was there when here was so pretty.

'I did. But I still really hope that I'll go with Mum one year, and Graham and I talked about it. You know, maybe later in the year, if we're still . . . ' I tailed off. I always got a bit freaked out in a long-term relationship; most people liked looking to the future with a partner but it made me feel trapped.

'That'll be good.'

'Yeah.'

It might have been freezing, but the sun was out and the sky was blue. If it wasn't for the wind, it would have been pleasant.

We weaved our way through the tourists as we got closer to Temple Bar. The wide avenues started to give way to smaller streets and cobbles appeared.

'I can't believe it's this busy on a Tuesday in February,' I said, trying not trip anyone up with my suitcase.

'I know. But I guess that this is the most touristy area.'

'Right,' said Paul, as we caught up to him on the corner, 'this is where we're staying. We should see if they'll hold our luggage then I think it's time to get on it. This pub looks like an excellent place to start.'

Someone walked out and we could hear the sounds of folk music coming from inside. It looked exactly as I'd imagined a Dublin pub to look. The windows were made up of tiny windows steamed up from condensation, and there were wooden beams running along the outside of the building.

Amy coughed and stuck her belly out so that it protruded from her coat.

'Of course, we don't have to get on it. I just meant, soak up the atmosphere.'

'And by atmosphere did you mean whiskey?' she asked, with an inquisitive eyebrow.

Paul bowed his head. 'Maybe.'

'Let's just dump the bags, and go from there. We might be able to check in early. I could do with a nap. We're not booked on the tour at the Guinness Storehouse until four.'

'There was a time when checking in early meant other things,' he muttered under his breath.

'Yes, but that's how we found ourselves in this situation, isn't it?'

'They're like a comedy double act,' whispered Graham in my ear. He rested his hand on the small of my back. 'It must be exhausting. Hope we're not like that when we've been together that long.'

'Oh, they've always been like this.' I tried not to read too much into what he said. We were at the age when so many of our friends were settling down – it seemed that I couldn't open up Facebook without an ultrasound photo or a blingy ring announcement – but anytime that I was dating someone and things even hinted at any form of commitment, I felt too young for any of it. We weren't even thirty yet.

'Glad we're not like that.' He leaned over and slapped me on the bum as we walked into the hotel. He'd started to do that a lot lately. I'm pretty sure it was his way of showing affection.

Our equivalent to Amy and Paul's bickering, only I think I'd rather have the bickering.

'You alright, Mum?'

She was staring at her phone. 'Yeah, I'm fine, I just can't get it to send a text. I wanted to send a message to Gloria at work.'

'Have you activated your roaming?'

She looked at me blankly, so I took her phone and toggled it in the settings.

'I don't understand these phones anymore. I miss my old BlackBerry.'

'Got to move with the times, Mum,' I said, and she sighed.

'Listen to me, I sound like a dinosaur.'

'You don't.'

I handed it back to her and she sent her message.

'There, done. Now, I feel like I've been on the go for hours. I need a good shower and then I'll be ready to take on this city.'

Mum's cheeks were glowing and if I'd been nervous of how she was going to fit into our trip, those fears disappeared as I watched her cackle her way over to the reception desk with Amy.

Chapter 13

'All these years, I never thought I liked Guinness . . . ' said Graham, as we walked away from the Storehouse.

'I know, me too,' said Caz. 'It's a revelation.'

'It doesn't taste like that in London,' said Noah. 'That was different.'

'Yeah, yeah, Guinness is great, blah, blah, blah.' Amy was still a little bitter that she couldn't get involved like the rest of us.

'After the baby's born I promise I'll bring you some tins,' I said, and she pulled a horrified face.

'I don't think I mind missing out that much. I've got a bigger list of alcohol I want after the birth. A good bottle of Rioja for starters.'

'Rioja, noted.'

'Don't be fooled by the baby-kicking routine,' Paul said, slipping his arm around her shoulders. 'She just wanted a comfy seat.'

'I did get an incredible view over the city.' She gave me a little wink.

We were huddled on the street in front of the Storehouse, and it was freezing.

'What's on the itinerary now?' asked Graham. 'I feel like I've brought my PA on holiday. It's amazing. Makes me feel like

I need one for the rest of my life. Fancy taking up the position?'
He looked at me as he spoke and I gave him what Noah would
call my murderous look. He laughed. 'I'll take that as a no then.'

'Not unless you can give me the same sort of return I'll get
from Mags' company.'

I joked, but in truth I hadn't made my final decision about
leaving. I'd written my resignation letter a million times in my
head, but I didn't know if, when the time came, I'd have the
balls to actually type the words, let alone hand it to my boss.

'Fair enough,' he said. 'So, Amy, where's next?'

She pulled out her phone and brought up a list.

'We should probably head back to the hotel, get ready for
dinner.'

'Code for Amy needs a nap.' Paul coughed.

'I don't usually hear you complaining.'

'Well, every man and his dog keeps telling me to bank my
sleep whilst I can.'

'Ah, come on,' said Noah. 'We've got a while until we go
out tonight. I bet we could stop off for a cheeky little drink.
Somewhere with comfortable seats for Amy.'

'And a view?' she said.

'Demanding much? OK, with a view. I'll see if I can Google
something.'

He pulled out his iPhone and tapped away before telling us
we were better heading closer to the hotel.

I watched Caz holding hands with Bertrand. It was weird
to see her with someone other than Nick. We'd got to know
him so well over the years. But Bertrand seemed nice. He was
younger than us, and a little blunt at times, but he clearly
adored her.

I turned to make sure Mum was OK. She had her arm looped through Amy's, looking perfectly happy.

'This is fun,' said Graham, lowering his voice to me. I snapped my head round and smiled at him.

'You say that like you're surprised.'

He pulled a face. 'I guess we haven't spent that much time all together. And at your dinner party, everyone seemed a bit more . . . uptight?'

I thought back to the first time he'd met my friends and I guess things were a little off that night. Amy was in the early stages of pregnancy and, whilst I had been sworn to secrecy, no one else knew. She'd spent most of it swapping her wine glass with Paul's and scraping extra food onto his plate as she was too sick to eat it. The result had been Paul absolutely hammered, slurring about the most random topics. Mags and Noah had arrived late and both looked exhausted. And Caz had bailed on the whole thing, shocking us all by going to Paris to meet Bertrand instead.

'Yeah, that was an odd night, but this is a much better representation of what they're usually like.'

'What a relief; there's nothing worse than when you don't like your partner's friends.'

Up until that point I'd always thought of it as the group putting the new partner on trial, rather than the other way round.

The best bit about being on the group trip was that a twenty-minute walk went by in the blink of an eye with so many people to chop and change talking with.

'So, Graham,' said Paul, sidling up to us, 'Lucy says that you support Spurs?'

I watched the two of them walk away, not too sure that it

was such a good idea for them to talk about that. Paul was still holding a grudge about the former Portsmouth manager and many of the players defecting to Spurs that signalled the downfall of the club.

'What are those two talking about?' asked Noah, taking Graham's place next to me.

'Graham's a Spurs fan.'

Noah pulled a horrified face. 'It was nice knowing him. Even if it was only temporary.'

I laughed, but I was a little worried that it might destroy the harmony that we'd built up as a group this afternoon.

'I was thinking that whilst we're here we should do a little sightseeing.'

My brow wrinkled a little. 'Isn't that what we've been doing?'

'No, I mean just us, um, two. It's sort of our tradition on our leap year birthdays. Our trip around Calais and then our morning in London.'

I nodded; two of the highlights of my last big birthdays.

'Um, yeah, that sounds fun. I know Graham wanted to go for a run tomorrow morning. He's training for the London Marathon and he needs to get his miles in.'

'Wow. Good for him and, I guess, good for us. I'll obviously have to run it past Mags when she gets here; we all know she wears the trousers.'

'We do.'

Noah laughed.

'It'll be nice to spend some time together,' I said. I couldn't remember the last time that Noah and I had done anything just the two of us. Since he'd moved in with Mags, I'd seen more of him than I ever would have done normally. But Mags was always there, and if she wasn't, Amy and Paul were.

'It will.'

'So where are we going to go then? Do you fancy an art gallery or a walking tour?'

I looked up at the blue sky. It was cold and crisp and somehow it made the sky look bluer than in London. If it wasn't for the biting wind I could have been lulled into thinking it was a spring afternoon.

'I've got something in mind; it's a surprise.'

'A surprise? I'm not really good with those.'

'Well, learn to be.' He wiggled his eyebrows in a way that made me laugh.

The others had stopped up ahead, having found a pub that ticked many of the boxes, and, with a view over a park, it almost ticked Amy's too.

Noah held the door for me.

'Why thank you, kind sir,' I said, with a little curtsey.

'You're welcome.' He nodded back. 'Why is that you're the only person that can get away with saying stuff like that?'

I shrugged. 'I think most people are far too cool.'

'That must be it.'

The pub was busy, but it was large enough that we found a table near the back that could just about accommodate us.

Graham and Paul, still arguing about football, found their way to the bar, and Noah went over to act as referee. Bertrand was about to sit down next to Caz but she suggested he join the boys.

'Everything OK?' I asked.

'Yeah, fine. I'm just encouraging him to branch out a little.'

She smiled. 'I want him to get to know them and there's no chance if he's always cuddling up to me.'

'True.' I nodded, watching him at the bar, where he was hovering on the periphery.

'So, are we going to play some sort of drinking game?' asked Mum, slipping off her big winter coat.

'Um, no, not if you want any of us to make it to dinner. Those days are long gone,' I said. 'Plus, I'm not sure how many drinking games you can actually play with an Irish coffee.'

'Shame. I always thought they looked fun.'

'Don't worry, Mrs A, when Lucy gets married and I'm planning the hen do, we'll do drinking games a plenty,' said Amy, patting her on the arm.

'Hey, don't be holding your breath thinking that any hen do is going to be forthcoming.' A cold sweat broke out on my forehead. Inviting Graham on the trip had been enough of an agonising decision.

'Yeah, too right,' said Mum, looking over the bar. 'You don't want to be rushing into anything.'

'Oh, I wish you were my mum.' Caz sighed. 'All she talks about it is me hurrying up and getting engaged or I'm going to be left on the shelf.'

'That sounds like my mother, and I sometimes wonder where I would have been in my life if I hadn't listened.'

It's funny, I'd never really thought what Mum's life would have been like if she hadn't married Dad.

'But then you wouldn't have had Lucy.' Tears started to form in Amy's eyes.

'You're right, my life would have been empty without her. Those pregnancy hormones, huh, they're a bitch.'

'The worst.'

Mum squeezed her hand.

'Of course I'd always want to have had Luce. I just mean, that I wish there hadn't been that pressure to settle down. But back then, I was a complete hopeless romantic anyway. Given the choice I probably still would have thought your dad was Prince Charming.'

'Speaking of Prince Charming,' said Caz, 'are you still dating?'

Mum shook her head. 'I gave up on that. Honestly, the amount of baggage and hang-ups people had. Me included.'

She smiled and shrugged. 'I've realised I quite like being on my own. Doing my own thing. I've got friends who are still married and now they're coming up to retirement, they're dreading having to spend time with their partner.'

'I'm dreading Paul's paternity leave; he's going to be fussing all over me.'

'Oh, you'll be glad of him being there, believe me,' she said. A look of panic flashed over Amy's eyes and Mum squeezed her hand again.

'But don't you miss having someone?' Caz's voice was a little hollow and I wondered if there was more to the question. There so often was with Caz. Unlike Amy, she didn't give you a running commentary on her thoughts and feelings; you had to wait until she was ready to share.

'No, I've made some friends at my allotment and believe me that gives me enough of a male fix. Plus, I've always got my friends in the bottom drawer of my bedside cabinet.'

'Mum,' I practically shouted.

Caz snorted with laughter and Amy's cheeks flushed.

'What did we miss?' asked Graham, putting down the drinks.

'Believe me, you do not want to know.' I held up my hand.

'OK,' he said, backing away slowly. 'I'll leave you to it.'

He headed off towards the toilet and Mum and the girls burst out laughing.

'I'm not even going to ask,' said Noah, sitting down next to me.

'Best not to.'

'I already know it's got something to do with you, Mrs A.'

Mum gave him a wicked smile. 'Of course; it's where Lucy gets it from.'

'Oh, I bet Lucy's got a bottom drawer full of toys too.' Caz cackled again.

Noah tilted his head. 'Oh, that's what we're talking about? Rabbits and all that.'

I elbowed Noah to stop, worried Amy might go into labour with the amount her body was shaking with laughter.

'What's so funny?' asked Bertrand. He slipped in next to Caz, his arm around her within seconds.

'We were just talking about rabbits,' said Mum, her face deadpan.

'Rabbits? That you eat or you pet.'

The others started to howl and poor Bertrand wore a blank expression, wondering what he'd said.

'This is all your fault.' I pointed at Noah.

'Excuse me. You lot were talking about it before I even sat down. I can't help that's what you all talk about when we're not around.'

'You're loving this.'

He grinned, the dimple in his cheek appearing.

'So, Noah,' said Mum as the conversation started to fracture as everyone came back to the table and people got swallowed into smaller conversations, 'how's your mum?'

'She's good, thanks. But I have to say, she would kill me if she knew you were here. She'd be so jealous.'

'She should have come,' I said, thinking of Sandra and her warm hugs.

'Oh, that would have been nice. Two oldies together.'

'Yeah, no. As much as I love my mum. You know she'd have been giving us lectures along the way. Don't be drinking that Irish coffee after three p.m., the caffeine will keep you up.'

'Oh, blimey, she's right though.' Mum stared into her cup. 'I hadn't even thought of that.'

'Which is why you're here and not her.' Noah's nose wrinkled a little. 'And she certainly wouldn't be discussing any type of rabbits.'

I nudged him again. We might be twenty-eight now, but he was still eighteen at heart.

Mum rubbed under her eyes. 'I need a drop more cream. Anyone else?'

When we all shook our heads, she headed up towards the bar.

I rolled up my sleeves, trying to cool myself down. A warming Irish coffee had seemed a good idea when we were outside in the freezing cold, but now we were in a pub belting out the heat, I wished I'd gone for a Bailey's with lots of ice.

'You're wearing the bracelet.' Noah reached for my four-leaf clover charm. My skin prickled at his touch.

'I am. It seemed fitting, coming to Dublin.'

He let go and smiled at me.

'It still looks alright, considering I bought it at some market in Sydney.'

'No expense spared.'

He winked. 'You know me.' He took a gulp of his coffee and almost spat it out. 'I forgot this had whiskey in it, for a minute I was going to pound it like my morning coffee.'

'This is definitely one to sip.'

'Yeah, it's good though. I feel my cockles warming.'

'What even are cockles?'

Noah wrinkled up his nose. 'I don't know. It sounds like it should be your toes.'

'It means your heart,' said Mum, butting in. I hadn't realised she'd sat back down. She shot me a look I couldn't decipher. 'It's from the Latin word for the heartstrings – don't be asking me what the word is – but that's why you say warm the cockles of my heart.'

'Huh,' said Noah. 'Every day is a school day.'

'That's why you bring your mum,' I said.

Mum smiled.

'There you all are.' I looked up to see Mags standing over the other side of the table.

'Ah, you made it,' said Amy. Mags leaned over and gave her a hug.

'You made good time,' said Noah. 'If I'd have known you'd be that quick, I'd have ordered you a drink.'

'I know, I got the taxi to come straight here when I got your text. Figured I could drop off my stuff later.'

She started to make her way round the table, giving everyone hugs.

'I'll go get a drink.'

'Stay, I'll get it,' said Noah. He slid out from the table and gave her a quick kiss as he passed.

'You know, you need to pay attention to who it is that warms the cockles of your heart,' whispered Mum.

I turned to look at her.

'What are you talking about?'

'I think you know.'

She looked over at Noah propping up the bar.

'Mum,' I started before I shook my head. 'Friends can warm cockles too.'

I kept my voice low. Not that anyone else at the table was listening.

It was true, that once upon a time I'd had feelings for Noah. But it was at times like this that I was glad that I'd never acted on them, or else we might not all have been sitting here now.

'I think there's more of that hopeless romantic left in you than you thought,' I said, finishing off my coffee and not even flinching at the strong taste. 'But you're barking up the wrong tree.'

Noah looked over like he knew he was being talked about. I smiled, and he smiled back.

When I turned back to Mum she was giving me that knowing mum expression.

'Perhaps there's more of a hopeless romantic in all of us that we try not to let out . . . '

My fingers instinctively rubbed over the charm. I used to do that so often for luck, but I hadn't needed to do it in a long time.

Chapter 14

Wednesday 29th February

I'd done my best to hide from Mags since she'd arrived yesterday evening, not wanting her to pin me down about the job. It was surprisingly easy, with the pub we'd gone to last night being so loud, and with so many other people to talk to. But I knew that luck couldn't last forever.

'Does anyone want more coffee?' asked Noah, standing up.

'I'm good, thanks,' I said, and Mags shook her head.

'I'm going to get some more of that soda bread.' Graham followed Noah, before I had time to ask for some.

I braced myself, waiting for Mags to ask if I'd made my decision, But to my surprise she just pointed at her plate.

'This was hands down the best hotel breakfast I've had in ages.'

'Tell me about it. I'm already looking forward to the same tomorrow.'

A silence hung over the table and Mags looked at her watch. She hadn't stopped checking it since she'd sat down at the table.

'Everything OK?'

She looked up, and planted one of her fake smiles on her face. The kind she'd always given to Francis at our old work.

'Yeah, fine. Just got to send a few emails before we head out for the day.'

I nodded.

'How did your meetings go yesterday?'

'Productive.' She ran her hand through her hair, fluffing out the ends. 'But we shouldn't talk about that. It's your big birthday and I promised Noah there'd be no shop talk.'

She picked up her phone for a quick scroll and then put it down again, looking over her shoulder at where Noah was battling with the coffee machine.

This wasn't like Mags. Promise or no promise, she'd usually be making the most of squeezing the conversation in until he came back. Not that I was complaining; it gave me more thinking time.

She followed my gaze. Her hands were almost shaking.

'Lack of caffeine, I might just go and get another coffee. Do you want some?'

'Um, no,' I said, watching her get up. She was jittery and un-Mags like. An uneasy feeling washed over me. Like something was wrong.

'I got you some soda bread,' said Graham, popping a slice on my plate. 'I know how much you like it.'

I was snapped out of my thoughts about Mags. There was me thinking he'd been selfish not offering, but instead he'd almost read my mind.

'Thanks, just what I wanted.'

He raised his eyebrows at me and took a seat, looking proud.

Noah came back to the table alone, small coffee cup in hand, but he didn't sit down.

'Mags has had to go back to the room, so I'm going to head out too. I'll see you in the lobby in half an hour, Luce?'

'Sure.'

'And good luck with the run, buddy.' He tapped Graham on the shoulder. 'Although I don't think you'll be running fast with that in your belly.'

'Gotta stock up on the carbs,' he said. 'There's got to be some perks for running fifteen miles.'

'What's my excuse?' I asked.

Graham laughed. 'Hotel breakfast included.'

'Yes, that's it.' I dipped the fresh slice of soda bread into my runny egg, trying to push thoughts of Mags and how weird she was acting out of my mind.

Half an hour later, Noah and I were strolling away from Temple Bar.

'At what point are you going to tell me what we're doing?'

'When we get there,' he said with a shrug. 'I don't want you to change your mind.'

'Is that a possibility? It's not anything that I'm going to hate, is it? Am I dressed right?'

'You look OK to me. I mean, the hat is a bit dodgy, but apart from that.'

I gave him a quick jab with my elbow.

'It's fashion,' I said, tugging it down.

'It's something.'

'At least my ears aren't cold like yesterday.'

'That's true. And you've always got the option to be an extra in a gangster movie set in the twenties.'

'I would make a fabulous moll,' I said. 'It's like the one I wore in the school production of *Bugsy Malone*. But I mainly packed it because it's wool and it's warm.'

'I know; I thought it was cold yesterday, but now it's arctic.'

'The Irish guy at work told me to come prepared, that you quite often get all four seasons in a day.'

'I can well believe it.'

I still couldn't wrap my head around being in Dublin. It felt so different to London. Everyone was still in a hurry but there wasn't as much stress and no one seemed to blame anyone irrationally for holding everyone up.

We walked past an impressive stone building.

'Is this where we're going?'

'Nope.' He pulled out the map of the city that the hotel gave us. He squinted a little as he found the art museum on the map to get his bearings. 'No, but we're almost there.'

I wondered where we were going. Mum had headed off on her own for a full day of sightseeing – a literary walking tour, followed by a trip to the decorative arts museum – and Caz, Bertrand, Paul and Amy had headed to the gaol.

'Before you ask, no, not there either,' he said as we passed the large park.

'Good, I hope it's indoors.'

'Well, you're in luck.' We rounded the corner. 'Tadaa.'

He held his hand out and I read the sign chiselled over the door. 'The National Museum of Natural History.'

'Uh-huh, also known as The Dead Zoo.'

I screwed up my nose.

'Yep, you're going to love it. Forget all that CGI graphic stuff, this is proper old school, filled with—'

'Dead animals.' I shivered. 'Hmm, you know I've heard really good things about that art gallery we walked past; you know, very famous pieces that would be a real shame to miss out on.'

'Oh, is that, right?' He folded his arm. 'Go on then, name one.'

'Name one what?'

'Name one piece of art hanging in that gallery that we have to see.'

'Um . . . well, there's that Irish one . . . you know that's really famous and culturally significant.'

'Can you even name an Irish artist?' The corners of his mouth were twitching.

'Can you?' I struggled to think of a single one. Musicians, plenty. Writers, heaps. But artists? 'That's surely the point – if neither of us can name an Irish painter; shouldn't we go and educate ourselves?'

'Lucy, what's going on?' He sounded like a teacher trying to coax a pupil into a confession.

'I just think that it would be a better use of our time, than . . . '

I looked at the natural history museum and shuddered.

'Why don't you want to go in there? Come on, it's supposed to be great.'

'But you said it yourself, it's the Dead Zoo; how does that sound attractive to you?'

I turned my back on the museum, digging my heels into the ground and he started to laugh. At first it seemed like he thought I was joking but he stopped laughing and narrowed his eyes.

'If you must know,' I said, with a huff, 'the animals freak me out.'

'You're kidding, right?'

I shook my head. 'Nope, taxidermy scares me.'

I could barely say the word, let alone spend an afternoon looking at it.

'Taxidermy scares you? What, like ladybirds?'

I bit my lip. The problem with friends is they always seemed to remember your quirks.

'No, I don't like ladybirds on me because I hate the way their tiny little legs tickle my skin and they're poisonous.'

'Actually, I looked that up. They're only poisonous if you ingest them.'

I shut my eyes and gritted my teeth. 'They still freak me out.'

'So, what's worse in the Lucy scale of irrational fears, ladybirds or taxidermy?'

'Taxidermy. Every time.'

Noah laughed. 'Well, then it's time to conquer the fear. How does someone become scared of that anyway?'

I shivered again. 'My nan had a taxidermy fox that lived in the hallway of her house and my cousin told me that it came to life at night.'

Saying it out loud sounded ridiculous and I knew that Noah was trying to keep a straight face.

'Does that mean to say that you've never been to the Natural History Museum in London either?'

'Nope. I was ill the day we went with the school.'

'Ill?' He didn't do air quotes but they were implied. 'I feel, it's time to cure this fear.'

'Noah.'

'You're brave enough to conquer this. It can't be any worse than the time we ended up at that death metal gig.'

Now it was my turn to laugh. We thought we were going to The Killers at a secret gig, but it turned out we'd got the wrong end of the stick about The Axe Murderers. He was right. I had to get over this. It might technically be my seventh birthday, but I wasn't really seven like I was when my cousin tried to trick me. I knew they weren't going to come back to life.

'OK, but no trying to make me jump, and if I see a fox . . .'

'Got it,' he said, pursing his lips. 'No foxes.'

'And if it's really bad, we'll go to the art gallery?'

'OK, deal.' He took hold of my hand. 'I've got you, OK.'

'OK.'

'They're behind glass anyway, so even if they did come to life . . .'

He started to laugh and I whacked him on the arm again.

Stepping into the museum was like stepping into a time machine back to the Victorian times. I found myself not marvelling at the animals, which were just as freaky as I thought they'd be, but at how they'd interpreted the space. We'd managed a loop of the bottom floor with only one close-call with a fox family, and headed upstairs where the views were quite spectacular.

'I tell you, he's looking at me,' I said, walking one way and then the other, maintaining eye contact.

'The moose is not looking at you.'

'He is, look at how his eyes follow as I move.' I shivered.

'It's just like the Mona Lisa; her eyes follow you wherever you go and she doesn't freak you out.'

'She does a bit.'

'Huh, and you were the one that wanted to go to an art gallery.'

'Yeah, maybe I'm not good with museums in general.'

'Good to know, for the next birthday.'

'You know, you lied,' I said, looking over the balcony onto the main gallery below. 'You said all the animals would be behind glass.'

'I thought they would be.' Noah leaned on the railing. 'But it's kind of cool being able to wander next to the bigger animals.'

'Is it?' I scrunched up my face.

'You're doing well, really. Aside from the foxes.'

'The vixen had the same eyes as Felix.'

'Felix?'

'My nan's fox.'

'Why did your nan even have a taxidermy fox in the first place?'

'Her mum used to work for a fancy country house and she was given it when she left.'

'Nice.'

'Was it? I'm sure she'd have preferred a fancy box of chocolates, or smelling salts, or whatever you gave people in the olden days.'

Noah chuckled.

'Where's Felix now?'

'I don't know. My dad and his sister fell out not long after my nan died, and Dad doesn't have it, so I like to think that it's there haunting my aunt or my cousin.'

'Just as long as it's not haunting you, right?'

'Exactly.' I looked down at all the animals below. So many of them. The hairs had been up so much on my neck that I worried they were going to turn into a permanent fixture. 'I'm so glad that I didn't come here as a kid; I would have been terrified. I mean it. That elephant out on the loose, and all these stag heads.'

'It's like that film, *Night at the Museum*, where everything comes to life.'

'I haven't seen it.'

'Probably for the best.'

We carried on out of the gallery and back down the stairs, to where we'd come in.

'What's the verdict then, is taxidermy still scary?'

I slipped my coat back on, in denial that we were about to leave the warm museum and head on outside into the cold.

'Um, let's just say that I wouldn't like to be here alone at night, but with all the people around, it wasn't *that* bad.'

Noah laughed. 'That would make an excellent online review. *It wasn't that bad.*'

'Would recommend, but wouldn't visit again.'

'I can see a new career for you in passive aggressive reviews.'

'I'd be excellent at that.'

It had clouded over since we'd gone inside and the light was starting to fade.

'And it was something different; thanks for bringing me.'

'I really did not bring enough layers for this trip,' said Noah.

'Here.' I put up his coat collar. 'Keep the back of your neck warm.'

'Thanks, that is much better. I feel a bit like a model in a catalogue.' He put his hands in his pocket and struck a pose.

'Yeah, well, you don't look like one.' I pulled a dismissive face.

'Hey, thanks for the ego boost.'

'You're more than welcome,' I said, with a laugh.

The trouble was he did suit it. It might not make him look like a model, but it was the kind of look that oozed confidence and if I'd been passing him in the street, and been single, it would have been enough for me to do a double-take.

I looked up at the clouds; they were such a dark-grey colour but they looked almost luminous.

'Have you spoken to Mags much since she arrived?' asked Noah. He now had his arms folded, his hands tucked under his armpits.

'Um, no not really. Why?'

'I've felt like she's been acting pretty strange since she got here. She's been a bit jumpy and then she's gone off today. I thought she was headed back to the room to do emails but she'd gone by the time I got back after breakfast. Left me a note to say she'd see me later.'

The unease I'd felt at breakfast started to creep over me. I hesitated, wondering whether I should tell him how odd she was acting, but I didn't want to worry him.

'She's been working so hard lately, and don't forget she arrived late. She probably just needs a rest.'

'True, yeah. Maybe she'll be alright by tonight.'

'Yes, I'm sure she will. I'm looking forward to more live music tonight. I absolutely loved it.'

'It was awesome. Brings the whole pub to life.'

We weren't far from the hotel now, and the closer we got, the slower we were walking.

'This has been fun, just the two of us,' said Noah.

'Yeah, it has.'

'We don't do this often enough anymore.'

'I know. Life changes,' I said. I rarely saw my friends now, or at least not like I used to. Gone were the days when you'd text at the drop of a hat to see who was free to hang out. Now it would take us days of pinging emails back and forth to get dates in the diary, and they tended to be full group meet-ups. Everyone too busy trying to fit their lives into the hours they weren't working, and as people climbed the corporate ladder those hours got fewer and fewer.

'That's the weird thing about only having our proper birthday every four years – it always makes me stop and think how much has changed since the last one.' I came to an almost stop as I dodged out of the way of a tour group.

'Yeah, I guess, I hadn't really thought about it.'

'Like now, you're living with Mags, and Amy and Paul are having a baby. Last time, you hadn't even met Mags, and Amy and Paul weren't married, or even engaged. What's going to happen by the next one? Amy and Paul might be well on their way to having their own five-a-side football team by then.'

'You're right. I've never really thought about it. I can't think what our lives are going to be on our next one. I mean, if you'd asked me on our trip on the pedalos last time to predict what was going to happen, I certainly wouldn't have guessed any of that, with Mags, or my job.'

The streets were getting more crowded and we were walking closer together. The wind almost lifted my hat off my head and I gripped on to it.

'What would you have predicted?'

'I don't know. I'd just got back from Oz and I was all optimistic that I'd get some job at an ethical company.' He rolled his eyes. 'And then, I don't know. I guess I wouldn't have thought I'd end up with someone like Mags. I still don't know what she sees in me.'

'I know, it was a shocker.' It was out of my mouth before

I realised how bad it sounded. 'I mean, you know, you both being my friends. Not what she sees in you; don't put yourself down.'

He smiled. 'And now, you're with Graham. Do you think that you'll be with him in four years?'

We were walking so slowly that we'd almost come to a standstill and the light tone that had been in Noah's voice had all but disappeared.

'I don't know. It's still early days.' I turned to him. 'How do you know when you've met the one?'

Noah looked straight at me and it was the kind of gaze that made me catch my breath. The street around us was busy but in that moment, it was as if we were the only two people in Dublin. My heart was starting to burn and I wondered if it was the cockles, and if my mum was on to something.

'You just know,' he said, and he took a step closer towards me. I held my breath, my heart beating rapidly. He reached his hands out and I audibly gasped. If this had been a movie, this would be when the hero would sweep the heroine off her feet, scooping her up into his arms and kissing her for all he's worth.

He grabbed hold of my hat and pulled it further down my head.

'Careful, you almost lost it,' he said, and I came back down to earth with a jolt. My life wasn't a movie.

'Thanks,' I muttered. Putting my hands up to where his had just been, adjusting it even though it had already been adjusted.

'I guess,' he said, 'all you can do is go with your gut.'

'My gut? Right. Yeah,' I sounded a little breathless despite us standing on the spot. 'Is that how you know about you and Mags?'

He shrugged. 'That's all any of us can do.'

I nodded, but I knew in my gut what I was feeling. The same thing that I had been feeling four years ago when I'd pushed him away in the club. That I wanted him. And here I was, going to do the same thing that I did then. Absolutely nothing. Because this time I couldn't; he was with one of my best friends. Something I had done nothing to stop happening.

'How did this conversation get so deep? It was supposed to be one of those *where will you be in five years' time* chats,' he said, putting on a mock gameshow-host-type accent for the last bit, and I forced myself to laugh. 'But, seriously, trust your gut. Don't be with someone just because you think you should settle down.'

I knew he was talking to me, but there was something about the way he said it, so soft, that it sounded like he was saying it more to himself than to me.

He looked into my eyes. There it was, that moment again; the charge between us almost electric. Snow started to fall from the sky.

'What the actual—?'

'You guys,' said Mags, appearing as much out of nowhere as the snow itself, 'this weather is crazy.'

I planted the best smile on my face that I could.

'Four seasons in one day,' muttered Noah.

'That is certainly true. But isn't it beautiful?'

She planted a kiss on Noah's cheek and grabbed hold of his arm. She was like a changed woman from this morning. 'How was your sightseeing?'

'Lucy didn't like the Dead Zoo.'

'It's not that I didn't like it,' I said, worrying that my voice would betray me. 'It was just taxidermy animals. Not my thing.'

Mags pulled a face.

'I don't think it's anyone's type of thing, Noah. What are you like? When you said you were taking Lucy out on a birthday adventure, I thought you'd go for high tea or something.'

'Where's the fun in that? It had to be memorable.'

'It's always memorable,' I said, before I could stop myself.

'Well, I'm glad you had a good time anyway.' She brushed Noah's hair to the side and smiled back at me. 'I should get my shopping back to the room. We'll see you later on.'

I watched them go. Noah gave me a look over his shoulder but I turned away. I was too busy trying to ignore my gut and what it wanted me to do, because seeing them together I knew I could never do that.

Chapter 15

Whilst the boys went to a whiskey distillery, we had opted for the tame option of a pampering session.

'That colour is gorgeous,' said Amy, pulling at my hand to check out my purple nails.

'I know, I love it.'

Mags was admiring her own. She'd gone the whole hog and got full acrylics done.

'They look stunning,' I said, a little jealous at how amazing they looked.

'Thanks. I just need to get the rest of me looking as good. Speaking of which, I've got to get moving to my hair appointment. I'll see you all back at the hotel.'

'Oh right, yeah, see you later.' I barely had a chance to reply before she went.

'That was abrupt,' said Amy. 'Did you know she was leaving?'

'Nope. But she's been like that the whole trip. I guess she's making the most of not working, catching up on all her beauty appointments.'

'Oh well,' said Caz, 'just us then. Your mum still on her tour?'

'No, but she was heading to a museum after.'

'She's brave going off on her own.' Caz ran a hand over her freshly painted nails. 'I think mine would be sticking to us like glue.'

'Yeah, I get the impression she didn't want to intrude, no matter how many times I told her she isn't.'

'Oh bless her, she's so sweet.'

I nodded, so pleased I'd managed to convince her to come, even if she did want to give us space.

'Any ideas what you fancy doing now then? I'm guessing the boys will still be at the distillery.'

Amy rolled her eyes. 'God knows what state they'll make it back in.'

The four of them had gone off like excited schoolboys.

'I think I'm going to have to bail. I need to have a snooze,' said Amy, screwing up her face. 'I'm so sorry, but I really want to make it tonight.'

'Of course,' I said, as we walked out onto the street. 'That's fine. What do you reckon, Caz? You fancy some chill-out time?'

'No, I'm alright. Shall we go for a walk? I quite fancy a nose around Trinity.'

'Yeah, that sounds good.'

We headed to the hotel to drop Amy back.

'I'm just going to run in and change jumpers,' said Caz. 'The snow threw me off and I'm baking in all these layers.'

'I'll wait here.' I pulled out my phone. I had a missed call from my dad so I called him back.

'Hey, it's the birthday girl,' he said cheerily, causing me to smile. 'Are you having a good time?'

'Yeah, Dublin's great. We've seen a lot of it.'

'Have you been to the Guinness factory?'

'Yesterday,' I said, keeping moving to stay warm, taking small steps so I didn't go too far.

'Ah, I'm jealous. I'll have to go and take Tania; I'd love to see it.'

'I'm sure you'd both love it. Mum enjoyed it.'

It came out before I could stop myself. There was a slight pause on the other end of the phone and I wondered if I'd told them she was coming. It was the kind of pause that I used to get from Mum when I'd say to her that I was going to do something with Dad, something she was no longer part of. It was one of the reasons that I'd stood back from Dad's new life so much when I was a teenager.

'I'm glad. It's lovely that she's getting to spend the time with you.' There wasn't any malice in his voice, but I knew I should make more of an effort to see him.

'Tania and Gilly OK?' I asked in a bid to change the subject.

'Yeah, they're good.' His tone instantly brightened. 'Gilly's got a job interview next week and we've been helping her to prep.'

'Oh, wish her luck from me.'

'I will. You can text her to tell her too. She'd like that.'

'Yeah, um, OK. I'll try and remember.'

'It's important to her.'

I thought of all the important things in my life that Dad hadn't remembered when I was growing up. Exam dates. My first day at uni. My graduation.

'I'll text her.'

'Good. Thanks.' There was a sigh. 'I should let you enjoy your trip.'

'Yeah,' I said. 'Thanks for ringing.'

'Thanks for phoning back. I'll call you soon.'

I hung up and was just putting my phone back in my bag when I heard a familiar laugh. I looked down a nearby alley and saw Mags. She was standing by the back door of the pub next to the hotel, talking to a man dressed head to toe in black that I recognised as one of the musicians from last night. His head was bent down over her and he looked as if he was whispering something in her ear, whilst her hand was on his arm.

Panic flooded my body. Mags' odd behaviour. I'd assumed it was about the business, but what if it wasn't?

She'd rushed away, saying she was getting her hair done, but here she was, with some guy in an alleyway. The hackles on the back of my neck went up, imagining the worst.

I couldn't watch anymore so I started walking, as quickly as I could, back to the hotel. I never thought that Mags would hurt Noah like this. But it all seemed to be fitting into place. Why she had been acting so strangely. Why she kept disappearing. I thought of Mum and the fallout after Dad left, when she'd found out that everything she'd known about their relationship had been a lie.

I bumped straight into Caz in the hotel lobby.

'What's wrong? Changed your mind about the walk?'

'No,' I said, trying to put what I'd seen out of my mind. 'Just getting out of the cold.'

I pulled my coat tighter round me and we headed back out. I couldn't help but look down the alley, bracing myself for what I was about to see, but it was empty.

'Oh, look,' said Caz, reaching out. For a split second I wondered if she'd spotted Mags and the mystery man, but I followed her gaze to a couple in the middle of the street. A woman was down on one knee with a crowd forming around them. 'Look, a proper leap year proposal. I wondered if we'd see one in Ireland.'

'I thought it was a myth.' I watched as the man pulled her up and into his arms. The crowd clapped for the newly engaged couple and we carried on.

'You not tempted to do a leap year proposal to Graham then?'

'Um, no. Firstly, it's such an outdated tradition, and secondly, it's way too soon.'

Caz laughed. 'Shame. We could do with another wedding. Plus, I like Graham a lot. I think he's great.'

'You just like him because you can talk about mergers and acquisitions and all the things that none of the rest of us understand.'

'Ha, yes, that's probably true, but you know you'd be able to understand them too if you actually paid attention when I talked about work. I know when you drift off; I can see your eyes glazing over.'

'I can't help it,' I said, laughing. 'That's just how my face goes. But I'll have you know that when I'm looking gormless, I'm doing my best listening.'

'Speaking of doing your best listening . . . Are you sure you're alright? You looked like you'd seen a ghost in the lobby.'

'Did I?' I tried to shrug it off, but that was the problem with spending time with your best friends, they could smell bullshit from a mile away.

I wasn't sure what to do. If I was going to say anything to anyone it should be Noah, but if I said something to him, there'd be no going back. And if I said something to Mags, I risked jeopardising us working together.

I sighed. I needed to talk to someone and, out of everyone, Caz was the safest choice. Amy was married to Noah's best friend and it would put her between a rock and a hard place.

'I know this is a given, but you can't say anything to anyone about this.'

'OK,' said, Caz, her pace slowing. If it wasn't for the cold I'm sure we would have stopped completely.

'It's about Mags. I saw her out the back of the pub we were in last night . . . with one of the musicians.'

Caz pursed her lips. 'They were . . . ?'

I shook my head. 'No, I didn't see them actually doing anything.'

She sighed with relief. 'Oh, for a minute I thought you saw her cheating.'

'Well, I felt like I did; he was whispering in her ear and she was laughing.'

Caz turned, a stern look on her face.

'Lu, that's not cheating. That's flirting, maybe, at a push.'

'Are you going all lawyer on me?'

'No, I'm going all "this has the potential to stir up unnecessary shit" on you. Are you going to talk to Mags?'

'I don't know, I just don't want to see Noah get hurt.'

Caz looped her arm through mine and guided us gently across the road. She looked up at the impressive-looking Georgian building with large wooden doors pinned back to keep them open.

'We're here already,' she said, pointing across the road. 'Trinity College. Come on, let's have a walk around.'

We passed through the archway into a courtyard. There was a mix of tourists and students milling about. Some on bike, some on foot, and I didn't know if it was just being at a university but every student I saw gave me pangs of jealousy. What I wouldn't give to be back on campus with Caz, Amy, Noah and Paul. Things were so uncomplicated in those days.

'I don't think you should say anything to Mags,' Caz said as we weaved our way round a group. 'You didn't see anything. Not really. You saw Mags being flirty, but we all know she's a flirt.'

'But why was she down a dark alley with a musician? Come on, that's sketchy.'

Caz stepped to the side to dodge a person on their phone from crashing into us.

'It is sketchy, but it's also not enough to go on. It's not like we're their age anymore.' She pointed to the students huddled in groups. 'Noah and Mags have got a house and a mortgage together; it's not that simple. Plus, even if she had snogged him, it's just a kiss.'

'I know. I know you're right.' All I could think of was Noah telling me to trust my gut. 'It's just that she's been acting really strangely since we got here, and you've seen what my dad's cheating did to my mum.'

'Lu' – she stopped and took my hand – 'I know what your dad did was awful, for you and your family. But you can't assume everyone else's relationship is the same. No one really knows what goes on behind closed doors.'

I shut my eyes tight. She was right.

Perhaps it was the moment in the snow, making me look for some reason that they shouldn't be together.

'Look, I know what this is really about,' said Caz.

'You do?' I braced myself for what was to come.

'Yes. No one can blame you with what you've been through with your parents' break-up. It's only natural that you're going to see infidelity in very black and white terms. But this isn't even a grey area.'

It stung as she said it but I nodded.

'What if Noah gets hurt?'

'Then he's going to get hurt whether you get involved or not.'

'But . . . ' I started but I didn't know how to finish.

'I know you just want to be a good friend, and that's one of the things that we all love about you. But trust Mags, and trust that you've got it all wrong.'

'And if I haven't?'

She gave my arm a little squeeze before we carried on walking.

'People make mistakes and unfortunately all you can do is let them.'

I watched her blink back a tear before we carried on walking. There was something in the way that she was talking and the look in her eyes that made me wonder if we were still talking about Mags and Noah.

'Mistakes like letting people go?'

Caz turned to me, surprise written across her face.

'Am I that obvious?'

She looked away, and wrapped her scarf tighter around her neck.

'Oh, Caz. You miss Nick.'

Her lips were quivering. I reached over and hugged her as the tears started to roll down her cheek.

'Don't be nice to me. It makes it worse.'

I wiped away one of her tears with my glove.

'But I'm so confused; you and Bertrand, you look all loved up.'

'I know, that's the problem. It's just so full-on. At first it was exciting when I was at the Paris office and we'd flirt. And then when I went back, after I'd broken up with Nick, and we got together it was amazing. And exciting. Sneaking off to Paris.' She opened her mouth and then sighed heavily.

'And now the novelty's worn off?'

'Yeah. I feel so stupid. Like a kid that wanted a shiny new toy only to get it and wonder why they wanted it in the first place.'

She ran her hands through her hair and walked away from me.

'Hey.' I steered her to a bench and sat her down.

I tried to wrap my coat around my bottom as much as possible as I sat, but I could still feel the cold seeping into my bones. 'Don't beat yourself up.'

'But I broke Nick's heart, and now I'm going to break Bertrand's, and mine ultimately because I can't get Nick back.'

'Do you know that for a fact?'

She spluttered a laugh. 'He didn't even come and get his stuff from our flat; he sent his brother. And he's moved. He's down in London now.'

'Another reason for you to move down.'

She laughed, causing her to hiccup through the tears. 'Any opportunity to get that in.'

'Can't blame a girl for trying. But look, Caz, it's never too late.'

She smiled weakly. 'How did we even get on this topic anyway?'

'I get the feeling you've been wanting to get it off your chest for a while.'

She nodded. A group of girls walked past, giggling and teasing one another, and both our eyes followed them. What I wouldn't give for that to be us. In those days if we had a dilemma in our love life we'd head to the nearest bar on campus and do shots. By the time the night was over and the hangover had set in, the pain had gone and a decision been made, albeit usually via an ill-judged drunken phone call.

'What are you going to do about Bertrand?' I asked, and her weak smile fell.

'I don't know. Part of me was just hoping that it would naturally fizzle out after this weekend.'

I scrunched up my face. 'I somehow don't see that happening.'

'Me neither. I guess, in that case, I'm going to have to let him down as gently as I can.

'I sort of wish we were still back at uni. Didn't we just used to snog someone else if we wanted to break up with someone?'

'Or just not reply to texts.'

'We were awful,' said Caz.

'To be fair, the people that we dated were pretty awful in the first place.'

'Not like Bertrand. He's a nice guy, just a bit . . . dull.'

'Dull?'

'Yeah, or perhaps things get lost in translation.'

We sat there people-watching for a while, until the cold started to bite.

'I'm not sure if I fancy traipsing round here anymore; it's just making me really jealous that we're not that age anymore,' I said.

'Tell me about it,' said Caz. 'Fancy going for a walk along the river? Blow some cobwebs away.'

'Yes, and then we can go get an Irish coffee on the way back to the hotel.'

'Deal.'

I relooped my arm through hers, and gave the students one last wistful look. I wished we could be their age again, when things were less complicated, and decisions didn't have such life-changing repercussions.

Chapter 16

The pub next to the hotel was exactly as you would imagine an Irish pub to be. Wood-panelled ceiling, long granite-covered bar with glasses hanging over it, leather upholstered booths and stained-glass windows running about the top. With the live music ringing out, it felt as traditional as we could have got.

'Aren't they great?' said Mags, leaning across the table.

'So great,' I muttered back.

I saw the man that she'd been in the alley with, tapping his foot as he played the fiddle.

Between Mags' acrylic nails, her new haircut and what must be a designer outfit, she looked fantastic and I hoped that the effort wasn't for the man on stage. She was still acting jumpy, but I was going to take Caz's advice and let it all go.

'Are we planning on spending all night here?' asked Caz. 'It's just that I saw this really nice bar round the corner, and they had a Corrs tribute band, and I—'

'We've got to stay here.' Mags shot her a look. 'The craic's great.'

'Just a thought,' Caz muttered into her drink.

I watched the interaction, knowing that I needed to talk to Mags. Caz had been right: I shouldn't jump to conclusions. But something was up and I wanted to get to the bottom of it.

'Does anyone need another drink?' I asked and there were a few nods around the table.

'I'll give you a hand,' said Paul, climbing out of his chair. He wobbled a little as he stood up, and Amy had to steady him.

She rolled her eyes behind his back and I smiled compassionately back. Perhaps more drinks weren't what he needed.

The boys had come back from the whiskey tasting having tasted what seemed like all of the whiskeys in Dublin. Luckily for them, and I guess for us, the food in the pub had been giant portions, and it had gone some way towards soaking up the alcohol.

We found a quiet end of the bar, which gave us space, and Paul took advantage of it to lean on, propping himself up.

'I don't think we're going to get served here,' I said, watching the barmen who spent most of their time at the other end of the bar. The quietness down here suddenly made sense.

'We're not in a rush, are we? We've got all night.' He grinned.

I liked drunk Paul. He was all happy and smiley, and would get the giggles at everything.

'That's true, I guess. The music's good.'

'And the company's even better.'

'Of course it is.' I looked over at the table where Caz and Amy were deep in conversation. Bertrand looked like he was doing his best to follow what was being said, but I couldn't help feel for him after what Caz had told me. Graham, Mags and Noah were watching the band, Mags leaning over to Noah to point things out every so often.

I took in Mum's empty chair; she should be back by now. She'd headed out a while ago to get cash from the machine, but it shouldn't have taken this long. I knew I should have gone with her, but she'd laughed me off when I'd suggested it.

'I wish we didn't have to go back tomorrow,' said Paul.

'All good things must come to an end.'

'I know, but it's been the best, hasn't it? Yours and Noah's birthday celebrations, they're always such belters.'

'I'm not sure the one where I met you guys was for you, with the oysters.'

He pretended to retch.

'You know, I've never eaten once since. But I guess I was talking about the last one, in London, when Noah came back.'

'Yeah, that was a great night.'

I looked over my shoulder at the door when it opened, and my stomach sank, still worrying about Mum when it wasn't her coming through it.

'So good,' said Paul, leaning even further onto the bar. 'But I think I was more gutted than Noah when you two didn't get together that night.'

It was like I'd been winded and for a second I couldn't speak. I snapped my attention away from the door and back to Paul, and he pointed his finger in my direction.

'Don't think that I didn't see you two grinding on the dance-floor, and when you snuck off upstairs.'

I still got shivers over my spine when I remembered Noah's hands creeping up my thighs.

'But I don't think Noah was gutted.' I gripped my hands onto the bar; still, after all these years, the memory hurt. 'He seemed pretty relieved the next day.'

'That's not the way I remember it.'

'Well, that's the way it happened.' I was snappier than

I should have been, but clearly Paul had had so much whiskey that he was rewriting the past. 'Noah was quite clear the next morning that he'd been a bit drunk and horny.'

He gave an eye roll much like Amy's, only his wasn't quite as polished. She was obviously far more practised in them.

'Yeah, because his pride was dented when you pushed him off. That's all he kept banging on about when we stayed at his parents'.' He went to shake his head, stumbling after as he tried to regain his balance. 'He'd come back from Australia and he was convinced that you two were going to get together.'

My knuckles turned white as I gripped harder, grateful to the bar for keeping me upright.

'It probably wasn't a bad thing though, was it?' Paul shrugged. 'If you hadn't shot him down, he wouldn't be here now with the lovely Mags. And Graham's a top bloke too, even if he is a Spurs fan.' He turned to the table, and raised his arm at them, oblivious to the can of worms he'd just opened.

The room was starting to spin and I felt lightheaded. All those times in the dark of the night when I'd let my mind wander to that day and night, thinking of Noah, his touch, his words, thinking I'd imagined it all. But what if what Paul was saying was true and that hadn't been a figment of my imagination?

Paul's eyes were closing and I gave him a quick nudge.

'Shall we get you back to everyone?' I said, giving up all hope that we were going to get served here, and right now a drink was the furthest thing from my mind.

I led him back to the table, and I grabbed my coat and muttered something about getting some air then headed outside.

The ice chill of the wind hit my cheeks, causing them to burn and the cold crept around the rest of my body through my open coat, but I didn't care. The coolness was grounding me and helping to slow the breath I was struggling to catch.

'Lucy.'

I turned to see Noah and my knees almost buckled. He was coming from the entrance of the hotel, his big digital SLR in his hands.

'Hey,' I said, biting my lips together. I took in the details of him like I was looking at him afresh. His coat was pulled up around the back of his neck and I remembered my fingers brushing across his neck this morning when I'd done the same.

'You alright? You're looking a little pale.'

'Just needed some air,' I said, closing my eyes for a split second, trying to shake the thoughts away. 'Where did you get off to?'

'I just popped up to our room; Mags thought we should take some proper photos.'

'You didn't see Mum?'

He shook his head.

'Do you want me to help you look for her?'

'No, it's fine. You go get back in the warm.'

I stood back to let another woman into the pub.

'I don't want to leave you out here alone. You must be freezing.'

He took a step towards me and pulled my coat across me and tied the belt and I instantly felt the heat, but I don't think it had anything to do with the coat.

Thoughts were racing around my head. About me liking him four years ago, and him liking me too. About this afternoon and the conversation in the snow. About Mags and the musician. What if it was all pointing to the same thing, that I should tell Noah how I feel? That I should follow my gut? Wasn't he telling me that's what I should do? Maybe he was hinting at it because he still felt the same? Maybe he feels the inexplicable magnetic pull that I do?

He was still so close to me, close enough that I could reach out and touch him.

There was a ringing and I didn't notice at first that it was coming from my bag.

'Are you going to get that?' said Noah, nodding towards it with his head. 'It could be your mum.'

'Yeah . . . yeah.' I scrambled, my hands shaking to get the phone, and it was Mum. 'Hey, where are you?'

I could hear a din in the background; wherever she was, it was noisy.

'I'm in the Stag's Head, but I can't see you all. Did you move?'

I took a couple of paces back and looked at the sign over the door.

'We're at Callaghan's, by the hotel.'

There was a pause on the line.

'I can't hear you, hang on.'

I closed my eyes and took a deep breath.

'Is she OK?' Noah asked.

I covered the mouthpiece of the phone. 'Wrong pub.'

'Right, I can hear now. Where are you?'

'We're at Callaghan's.'

She tutted loudly.

'You could have waited for me to come back before you moved.'

I rubbed at my brow.

'Mum, we've been there all night. That's where we ate. You know, by the hotel.'

There was a pause.

'But. Hmm. OK, um.'

'I'll tell you what. Stay there, I'll look on Google Maps and I'll come and find you.'

'No, I'm sure I can—'

'It's fine. I'm hanging up now, but I'll come and get you.'

I hung up the phone and waited for Google Maps to load.

'She OK?'

'Yeah, she just went into the wrong pub and thought we were there.' I furrowed my brow; it didn't make any sense.

'I get that. All these streets look the same, and the pubs too. Is it far?'

He leaned over my shoulder.

'No, it looks like it's only a few streets away.'

'Hey, what are you guys doing out here? It's freezing,' said Caz.

'Mum's gone to the wrong pub; I'm just going to go and get her.'

'I'll come too,' said Noah.

'You don't need to.'

Caz put her hand on Noah's arm. 'I'll go; I think Mags is looking for you, anyway.'

Noah looked between us, and nodded. 'I'd better give her the camera.'

'It's this way,' I said to Caz, trying to work out if I was following the dot on my phone the right way.

'Everything alright there?' I could hear in her voice what she was really asking.

'Yeah, fine. I wasn't going to talk to him about Mags.'

She gave my arm a squeeze. 'I know you just want to be a good friend.'

I felt guilty; the thoughts I was contemplating were far from that.

We weaved our way through the crowds in silence for a bit, double-checking on the phone that we were heading in the right direction.

'It's quite nice being out of the pub for a bit.' Caz tugged to loosen the scarf around her neck. 'It was stifling in there.'

'From the heat or Bertrand?'

She laughed; her non-response spoke volumes.

'You know, Noah gave me some advice earlier. He said that you just have to trust your gut.'

'Is that him still doing his agony uncle crap?' she tutted. 'He's right, though: that's all we can do. The trouble is, it's not easy when you know your gut's going to hurt someone.'

I knew she was talking about her and Bertrand, but I couldn't help but think of me. What would I be doing if I told Noah I'd also had feelings for him four years ago? It wasn't just me that could be hurt. There was Mags. And Noah. What if he did what Caz did, broke up with someone for that chance of something with someone else, only to regret it? The shine falling off the new toy quickly.

'There you are, love,' said Mum, walking towards us. She wrapped me up in a big hug as if I had been the lost one. 'I don't know what I was thinking. I was sure it was this one.'

'It's easily done,' said Caz.

Mum blew on her hands as she rubbed them together. 'Let's not hang around here, it's freezing.'

'Where are your gloves?'

'I must have left them at the hotel.' She shoved her hands in her pockets.

'Someone had too much Guinness with dinner,' joked Caz and Mum held up her hands.

'Guilty.'

They laughed and we walked the way we'd come.

It didn't seem to take us as long to find our way back. She'd been so close, but in the dark and the twinkling lights I could see where she'd gone wrong.

The pub was quieter when we walked in, except for a few hushed whispers. We made our way back but the rest of my friends had their eyes fixed on the stage. I followed their gaze to see Mags standing next to the musician I'd seen her in the alley with.

I made my way to the table, all the while watching Mags. She was smiling but she looked terrified, fanning her face with her hand and taking deep breaths.

'What's she doing?' I asked as I reached the table. Not to Noah or anyone in particular but to myself. Mags couldn't sing. She didn't play any instruments. As far as I could tell, she had no reason to be on that stage.

'Ladies and gentlemen,' said the musician. 'Today is February twenty-ninth, which is of course leap day. Now, some of you might know that in Ireland we have a very special tradition that can happen on that day.'

There were a few excited cheers and whoops in the crowd, but I was stunned into silence.

'Women are allowed to propose and the man they propose to must say yes.'

There was more cheering in the crowd and I turned to look at Noah. He was staring at Mags and I wondered if his heart was beating as quickly as mine.

'And so, with that in mind,' said the musician, turning to Mags, 'I wanted to give this lovely lady the stage.'

Mags took the microphone and tucked her perfectly styled hair behind her ear. The last-minute trip to the hairdressers and all her nerves now made sense.

'Wow, um, thanks for that. This sounded like such a good idea when I dreamt it up at home.' Her voice was shaking. I'd seen her do presentations and pitches on countless occasions and I'd never once seen her nervous.

'Um, this time four years ago, on a leap day, something happened that I never thought would be possible. I met the most amazing man. And in those four, wonderful years,' she said, her smile starting to shine through, 'I've realised that I don't want to spend any years without him. When I heard we were coming to Ireland on this date I knew this was absolutely meant to be. A sign that I should do this.'

Tears stung my eyes.

'And you heard the man,' she giggled, 'you have to say yes.'

The musician grabbed hold of the mic.

'Let's get him up here, come on.'

'Noah.' Mags beckoned him.

Everyone looked around at our table to stare at him, starting to clap. Paul sprang out of his chair, slapped him on the back and nudged him forward.

He passed me and I wanted to reach out and take his hand. That's what my gut was telling me to do. To tell him what I should have told him four years ago. Only I couldn't do it.

How could I? It was all clicking into place, what I'd seen in the alleyway; this was what it was all about.

The crowd was still clapping and cheering, and Paul wolf-whistled. My fingers started to turn the four-leaf clover on my bracelet, the one Noah had given me four years ago, the one I kept as my talisman. Only it wasn't bringing me much luck.

Paul clapped me on the back just like he had Noah. 'I just can't believe this is happening, can you?'

I tried to smile with even a hint of his enthusiasm. My cheeks burned as I fought against every other muscle that was trying to stop me.

'So, Noah?' boomed Mags out of the microphone, her eyebrows raised. She got down on one knee and I wasn't the only person holding their breath. You could have heard a pin drop in the pub. 'Will you marry me?'

Noah was looking down at her and then a smile crept over his face. I knew then whatever had been between us was in the past. This is what his gut was telling him to do.

He nodded and laughed. 'Yes.'

'Yes?' Mags didn't sound like she believed him, so he repeated it, and held out a hand to help her up. He pulled her into him and they kissed. The pub went wild with cheers and applause.

Amy was crying.

'Hormones,' she muttered through happy tears. My eyes were glossy too, but there was nothing happy about mine.

I felt two arms wrap around my waist and I froze until I realised it was Graham. My boyfriend Graham.

'Isn't that romantic?' he whispered as he squeezed me that little bit tighter.

'Uh-huh,' I said, nodding. I knew what my gut was telling

me to do about him. I shouldn't be with him if I had feelings for someone else.

'I'm going to get some champagne.'

Mum was still standing up, and she reached over to take my hand. She didn't say a word; she didn't need to. She'd always been able to see right through me, and see when I was lying, even to myself.

I wished I could turn the clock back four years to that night, before Noah met Mags. Before I talked myself out of whatever was about to happen. But that was me all over. Too scared to speak up. Too scared to take a risk.

Chapter 17

Thursday 1st March

There was only one topic of conversation the next morning at breakfast. The happy couple were yet to make it down, but that hadn't stopped us poring over the details.

'She's such a dark horse,' said Amy, dunking a croissant into jam. 'Who can keep that big a secret? I'd have told the whole world.'

'I wish you'd done it; it would have saved a whole lot of nerves on my part.' Paul looked greener this morning than he had the time he'd had food poisoning with the oysters.

'But then I would have had to choose my own ring.'

'I think that's the best bit though. At least Mags got something she loved,' said Caz.

'She wouldn't have had it any other way.' I should have known that Mags was going to do it. As Noah said, she wore the trousers in their relationship and it was so fitting. 'I just wish that women would know they could do it the rest of the year too, not just on a leap day.'

Bertrand made a pfft sound, and we all turned to him.

'It's not right. It should be the man.'

'Bollocks should it,' said Caz, pulling a face. 'Anyone can propose.'

He shrugged. 'There isn't much romance these days; I think the proposal is one of the last pieces.'

'And women can't make romantic gestures?'

'There's a time and a place.'

'What I think we're all missing,' said Amy, jumping in before they started to argue, 'is that we're going to get another wedding. How fun is that going to be?'

I was stirring my coffee and I dropped the spoon into my drink. Of course I'd realised that with them getting engaged they'd get married, but I hadn't thought about the fact that I'd have to watch them.

'I wonder if you'll be bridesmaid, Luce,' she continued.

'Hmm.' It was a possibility, I guess. Mags was one of those people with lots of friends but few close ones.

'I'm obviously best man.' Paul attempted to put his head upright, but collapsed again onto his arm. 'He hasn't asked me yet, but it's a given. Who else would he pick?'

I'd not been feeling the best this morning – the celebrations had gone late into the night, but I didn't think that was why I was feeling queasy.

'I think I might go and get some fresh air. Too much fizz last night.'

'Tell me about it,' said Paul.

'Do you want me to come with you?' asked Graham.

He had a full plate of cooked breakfast that he'd barely scratched the surface of.

'No, you stay. I won't be long.'

'And then we'll go to the castle about tenish,' said Amy.

'Gives us plenty of time to do that, have lunch and make it to the airport.'

'Sounds good. I'll knock and let Mum know.' I squeezed Graham's shoulder as I went. 'See you back in the room.'

I kept the smile on my face until I walked into the lift. As the doors slid shut, it fell. I rubbed at the bridge of my nose. Why did Paul have to tell me about Noah's feelings last night? Why couldn't he have kept quiet? Then I could have got swept away with all this wedding talk, rather than wondering what might have been.

The lift doors pinged open and I walked out into the lobby, spotting Mags sitting on a sofa in the corner. She was looking at her phone, a huge smile on her face. She must have sensed I was there as she lifted her gaze and waved.

'Morning. How are you feeling?'

'I've been better,' I said, walking closer. 'I was just heading out for fresh air. How about you?'

'I think I could be having the worst hangover ever, but I'm too happy to care.' Her smile was wide and infectious and I couldn't help smiling back.

'It was an amazing night.' Aside from everything I was thinking, I was genuinely pleased for them.

She tapped the seat next to me, ring sparkling on her finger. I still felt like I needed air, that I couldn't quite breathe, but I knew I couldn't go anywhere.

'Let me see the ring then. It was so dark in the pub.' She held out her hand. It was a platinum band with a princess cut diamond, and it caught the sunlight streaming in the windows. 'It's stunning.'

'Thank you. Of course that's the benefit of me proposing to Noah: I got to choose it.'

'Very wise.'

She took her hand back and held it out so she could admire it herself.

'You know I'm a control freak, and I know what I like. I just can't believe he said yes.'

She placed her hands back on her lap, scooping up her phone.

'I should leave you, if you're busy doing emails.'

'No, it's fine, in fact' – she held on to my arm as I stood to leave, pushing me gently back down – 'I wanted to talk to you.'

I thought of what Amy had said about me being a bridesmaid and my whole body went rigid.

'I was too nervous to think about anything else yesterday, but um . . . I know I've been hounding you about quitting and joining the business . . . '

My shoulders sank with relief; it was just business chat. This I could handle.

'I wouldn't say you've been hounding me as such.'

'Please, I have been, and I guess I've been thinking that it's probably been too much for you.'

It took a moment for the words to sink in.

'Oh no, Mags, it hasn't.' I shook my head. 'You know me, I'm just cautious.'

'Exactly, and I feel like I'm pushing you to do something that you don't want to do. And whilst I think this whole thing is going to be a success, it's still a risk and I'd feel awful if I'd pushed you into something and it had all gone wrong.' Mags put her phone back on her lap and fiddled with her fingers. 'So, I took a meeting with Aiden Vance, do you remember him? He was an account manager when we first started the grad scheme? Well, he's worked at a couple of tech firms since, including a start-up, and I think he'd be a great fit. And he's agreed to come on board.'

There was a throbbing in my head, part hangover, but part trying to connect the dots.

'I think deep-down you didn't want to leave,' she said, quickly, filling the silence. 'And this way it gives you a way out without thinking you've let me down. I know what you're like.'

I nodded slowly, trying to process it.

'He'd be a really good fit, and this way you get to keep your job.'

It was true, I liked my job, but there was a pain in my chest because it hadn't been my decision.

'It sounds like he'll be exactly what you need.'

The familiar sinking feeling washed over me. She was right, I was reluctant to give up everything, and this probably was for the best, but I couldn't help thinking that I'd thrown away an opportunity again because I wasn't brave enough.

She patted me on the knee, her ring still twinkling. 'Oh, you would not believe how worried I've been about telling you. You have to promise me that you'll still meet me for lunch. I miss my work wife.'

'Of course.' I planted a smile on my face that hurt my cheeks as I fought against every muscle in my face.

She stood up, tucking her phone into the back pocket of her jeans. 'I guess I better get ready.'

'Yeah, wasn't Amy's plan to head out for a bit to see the castle before we go for lunch?'

'Actually, I've booked Noah and me different flights home; we're going to spend a couple of nights at a spa hotel in the countryside. It's going to be manic when we get back with everyone wanting to celebrate and all the wedding planning. His mum's already going into overdrive and has invited over his entire family for us to celebrate at the weekend. I thought it would be nice to have some time just us two.'

'Good idea,' I said, thinking of the big family get together with Sandra and Peter and the rest of Noah's relatives, giving me a little pang of jealousy.

'You still heading out for that walk?'

I stood to join her; I needed it more than ever.

'Yeah, a walk along the river will do me good. Cure the hangover.'

Mags gave me a look of pity, then she leaned over to hug me.

'I'll see you before we go?'

I nodded and she hurried off. The sinking feeling remained. I hoped that I didn't regret not jumping at the job offer when I'd had the chance, as much as I regretted not telling Noah how I really felt all those years ago.

Text message – Mags to Lucy: May 2012

Thanks so much for coming last night and the lovely engagement pressie! We had an absolute ball at our party and cannot wait for the wedding now!!! Sorry to have heard about you and Graham, such a shame. Don't worry, you'll have at least another 18 months to find a plus one! X

Text message – Lucy to Amy: August 2012

Congratulations!!!!!!!! Paul just sent a photo and I am in love. What a gorgeous little boy. I can't wait to meet Patrick Michael Hansen. Whilst you were at the hospital I filled your fridge with some food, and put some ready meals in the freezer. Do remember to get Paul to look after you. Mwah.

WhatsApp message – Noah to Lucy: December 2012
We're going to have to bail on the ice-skating, Mags has booked some wine-tasting experience for the wedding. Let me know if you can't cancel our places and I'll ping you over a bank transfer. Sorry to be a pain; I did tell her we could just do a booze cruise to Calais, but she said booze cruises weren't really a thing now.

Voicemail – Lucy to her mum: April 2013
Hey Mum, it's me, again. Um, can you call me back please? Um, I'm at work, but my phone is on. Call me back. OK?

Voicemail – Paul to Lucy: September 2013
Hey Luce, this is top secret, but I'm thinking of organising Amy a surprise birthday party for her thirtieth and I don't know if it's the world's best or worst idea right now. I can't seem to do anything right at the moment and need to get back in the good books. Perhaps you can give me a call back during working hours so she doesn't overhear. Ta.

Text message – Lucy to her mum: December 2013
Hiya, don't worry, I'm up. They're probably under the sink? Isn't that where you usually keep that type of thing? If not, I'll order you some online and get them sent out x

Hi Sophia, thanks for reaching out. I'm excited for Mags' hen do! I'm voting for Marbs over Las Vegas, and definitely a weekend rather than a week. Not sure my liver (or bank balance) could handle a full-on week there. Thanks for organising x

Email – Lucy to Caz: July 2014

Hi hun,

Sorry we keep missing each other. Work's been busy and I've been spending loads of time at home with my mum. She's in a bit of a funk at the moment; she keeps forgetting things. Doctor thinks it's probably stress, so I'm trying to help out where I can.

And that's my life in a nutshell. And no, before you ask, nothing is happening on the romance front. I'm mainly trying to dodge dinner party invites from Mags who's desperate for me to have a date to their wedding. I think I'm upsetting the table plan or something. Plus when did we get to the age where we had dinner parties???

Hope you're having more luck with your love life.

Miss you and hope we finally speak soon x

WhatsApp message – Amy to Lucy: September 2014

Hey girl, where did you disappear to last night? You were on the dancefloor and then poof you were gone. Amazing wedding though, right? They looked proper loved up. Anyway, hope you're well and that your mum's OK xx

Email – Hampshire Social Services Health Team to Lucy: December 2014

Dear Lucy,

Further to our meeting today. I have now started the process on the file for your mother. Following the assessment at the memory clinic and the recommendations from her medical team, we will arrange a visit to her home to assess what her needs will be.

Yours Sincerely.
Annabel Henshaw

WhatsApp message – Lucy to Mags: March 2015

OMG I just read the article about Lovely Lenses in the *Financial Times.* So proud of everything you've accomplished x

Text message – Lucy to Amy: May 2015

Hey, thanks so much for you and Paul helping with the move. It feels like the end of an era, doesn't it? I've got such great memories of that flat, and most of them with you. Anyway, I'm getting soppy in my old age. Give Paul a big hug and thank him too. Once we're in more of a rhythm with the carers and we get everything sorted for Mum, I'm sure I'll be able to spend more weekends up with you guys xx

Facebook messenger – Noah to Lucy: August 2015

Hey you! Long time no see. How's it all going? You're more than welcome to come stay with me and Mags anytime if you need a night away?

Voicemail – Lucy's Dad to Lucy: October 2015

Hey Luce, I thought I'd get to see you more with you now being closer. But I know things must be tricky with your mum. Just to say if you need me and Tania, we're here. Let's try and do dinner one night, or lunch, whatever's easiest.

Text message – Mags to Lucy: December 2015

Hiya, we're having an apres-ski themed New Year's shindig. So dig out your salopettes and I'll have the Aperol Spritzes at the ready. I'm sure you're very much in need of a party right now!

Text message – Caz to Lucy: December 2015

Merry Christmas, lovely! I hope you and your mum have a lovely day. Xx

WhatsApp messages – Uni group: late January 2016

Caz:

Hey, it's not long until the big birthday. Are we doing anything @Lucy and @Noah?

Mags:

I'm whisking Noah off to the Maldives, so you'll have to count us out this time. Hope you have a good one, Lucy x x

Amy:

Alright for some. We obviously can't go far as Oscar will only be nine weeks.

Lucy:

I'm going to have to be counted out too. I can't really leave Mum for any great length of time at the moment, and she's not letting any carers come in the house. Perhaps we can do a rain check?

Caz:

Of course. We'll do something when you're ready. Xx

PART FOUR

2016

Chapter 18

Monday 29th February 2016

'I can send that right over,' I said, clicking desperately through my files, trying to find where the hell it was.

'That's great. Thanks, Lucy.'

'No problem.' I put the phone down, before sighing loudly and gently knocking my head on my desk.

'Lucy, I think there's someone at the door,' shouted Mum from down the corridor.

I shook my head; she might be losing her memory but there was absolutely nothing wrong with her hearing.

'Just me, Mum. I was tapping on my desk.'

I could hear her padding down the hall and I found my whole body tensing.

'Whilst you're not busy, did you fancy a cup of tea? I've got some nice biscuits in?' She poked her head around the door then walked in and sat on the old sofa.

I rolled my lips together, trying to muffle the sigh. The trouble with my mum when she sat was that it was almost impossible to get her up again.

'Um, actually I'm in the middle of finding something for a client and I've got to get it to them ASAP so no real time to chat.'

I went back to trying to find the file on the server but I kept getting blocked. I'd changed companies when I'd moved in with Mum, and I'd never really got to grips with their computer system in the office, let alone now that I'd switched to home working in the mornings. The arrangement was supposed to make it easier, in case Mum needed me, but between her constant interruptions and the IT failing, it wasn't working.

'Oh, of course. You're busy. All those essays to write. Sorry, love, it's just I'm trying to make the most of you being here before term starts again.'

'Hmmmm, yep, on a deadline. I'm here for a while.' I didn't correct her that I wasn't still at uni. 'So you don't have to worry. I'm not going back to Canterbury anytime soon.'

'Good, OK. Right, well, I'm going to make the tea and have a biscuit. I think I bought some Jaffa Cakes or Hobnobs. Which are the ones you like?'

'Both.'

'Oh, that's good. I have both. I think I prefer Jaffa Cakes.'

She turned her head to look out the window, in no hurry to get out of the chair.

'Mum?' I tried to be as gentle as possible.

'What's that?'

'The tea. You were going to make me some tea. And I wanted a Jaffa Cake.'

'I don't have any Jaffa Cakes. Surely you're too old for Jaffa Cakes?'

I closed my eyes and counted to three.

'That's OK. Just the tea.'

'Tea, right, OK. I better go and let you get on.'

'Yes, yes, please.'

She rested her hand on my shoulder and gave me a gentle squeeze.

'It's nice to have you here.'

'It's nice to be here,' I agreed.

She nodded and headed out of the room and I went back to my computer files, not sure whether I'd get tea or not, or whether there'd be biscuits. But I knew that, whatever happened, I didn't have long before the next interruption, so I wrote a quick email to Kat in the office to send me the file I was missing.

A notification flashed up on my screen and I felt instant relief that it wasn't an out of office for Kat. It was from Caz.

Email – Caz to Lucy
Hey Birthday Lady!
Just wishing you a good one. I know it's not the birthday of dreams, but hope you're having a good one. Chat tonight?

I sighed. I'd been burying my head in the sand about my birthday, pretending that it wasn't happening. I hadn't even bothered to take the day off. What was the point? I couldn't go anywhere as I couldn't leave Mum for that long, and getting her to leave the house had become such a battle at the best of times, there was no point doing it unless I really had to.

Email – Lucy to Caz
Thanks, it's pretty shit, to be honest. Think I underestimated how crap it would feel working and dreaming of the type of holiday I could have gone on if things were different.

I hit backspace and watched the letters disappear one by one.

Thanks! Yes, let's catch up tonight. Not up to much.
Working and going to knock off early and head out for
a bit. Making the best of it.

I was lying, but Caz didn't need to know. She'd only worry, and it
wasn't like she could do anything about it. She'd recently moved
to Edinburgh, too far to pop down and see me.

I sent the email and pulled up Facebook. My notifications were
going crazy with weird and wonderful friends and people I went to
school with that I haven't talked to in fifteen years messaging me.
I ignored them; it was bad enough that I'd moved back home and
spent most of my dashes to the big Tesco's trying to avoid them and
their brood of kids. There were the Timehop memories: a photo
of us all on the night out in London, a couple from the flat before
we went out, then there was the trip to Dublin. I clicked through
the photos I'd been tagged in. The big green leprechaun hats, the
endless pints of Guinness. I shuddered. I hadn't had a pint of it
since, and then of course there was Mags bending down on the
stage with Noah towering over her, his face saying it all.

I clicked on his name, unable to help myself. I stared at the latest
photos that Mags had tagged him in. In my head, the Maldives
were the kind of place that you went to get away from everything.
The perfect place to do a digital detox, yet Mags didn't seem
to share the same vision. For the past four days she'd uploaded
a stream of photos that looked even more polished than the
generic ones on Instagram, full of crystal-clear turquoise water,
bungalows that hung on stilts over the water, private pools. Their
holiday, according to the photos, had been mostly lounging around
said bungalows looking toned, trimmed, and now bronzed in their

swimwear, and all of it felt like they were lording it over the rest of us stuck at home in Blighty in a particularly miserable February.

Not that I was jealous, of course.

'Hard at work, I see,' said Mum, walking back in the room, no tea in hand. I wondered how far she'd got through the process. Sometimes I found cups in rooms, forgotten about and undrunk, but more often than not I found the kettle warm and a cup with a teabag in, waiting to be filled with water.

'I'm having trouble concentrating.'

My email pinged and I saw Kat had sent over the file. I quickly checked over the document to make sure it was OK, before sending it across to the client.

Mum started arranging the books on the bookshelf. Picking out one and putting it back; then taking out the next one. This was ridiculous. I was just sitting here feeling sorry for myself.

'You know,' I said, typing an email to my boss, 'I think I'm going to take the afternoon off.'

'You are?'

'Yeah. It's technically lunchtime. I'd only need to take a couple of hours out of my flexi.'

'Great.'

I waited for a response from my boss, double-checking that I didn't have anything I needed to do urgently, but I couldn't see anything.

Rachel sent back an email confirming that it was OK, and I put on my out of office.

'Why don't we both go out?' It had become a leap day tradition of mine to go sightseeing. 'Why don't we head to see that seventies exhibition they've got on at the museum?'

'Oh, I don't think I fancy a museum today.'

'Come on, it'll be nice. Birthday treat.'

'Whose birthday is it?'

'Mine, remember? The flowers arrived this morning, and then Hannah from the allotment brought the veg basket over?'

'Oh, I meant who's treating you. I am, of course, but I wasn't sure if one of your friends was coming.'

'No. Just us. Why don't you go and get ready?'

I finished off what I needed to do and headed downstairs to wait for Mum, scrolling on my phone, making myself feel miserable looking at Mags' pictures of the Maldives.

'Are you still looking at that phone?' said Mum, coming into the hallway, her hair unbrushed, still wearing her slippers.

'I was waiting for you. We're going out in a minute; let's get you ready.'

I picked up the brush and ushered her to the mirror.

'That's right. Yes. I was just looking for my brush.'

'Mmm-hmm,' I said, nodding along. She started to brush but anytime it met resistance she took the brush up to the top. 'Do you want me to do it for you?'

'I can brush my hair. You've always been the same, always wanting to play the mum. You used to do that with your dolls, you know. It's a good job you never had a sister or you'd have been dressing up her too.'

I winced at the matt of hair appearing. I wished I could get it out for her, but I knew better than to suggest it. It was difficult enough getting her out of the house as it was, let alone upsetting her and making her think she wasn't coping with something.

'How do I look?'

'Great,' I said, scanning the coat rack. 'But you might want a hat. It's quite drizzly still and it's cold.'

'It's raining again?' She peered out the window pane next to the door. 'Maybe we should stay in? We don't want to catch a cold.'

'I'm driving. We'll be fine.'

I picked up the coat, not wanting to break the momentum.

'Oh, but you said I might need a hat; if it's that bad I don't want to go out.'

'No, it's fine,' I said. 'Forget the hat. Looks like it's stopped.'

I slipped her coat on, but she started to take it off again.

'Wouldn't you just rather have a cup of tea and we could see if that programme is on that you like?'

'Hmm, I'm sure it would be on when I got back.'

I didn't know what programme she was talking about and I don't think she knew either. This was the pattern of behaviour that happened anytime I wanted her to leave the house. She tried to find a reason for us to stay in, and sometimes when I saw that she was getting distressed and it wasn't urgent, I gave into her. But not today. Today was my birthday and we were going out.

I helped Mum put her coat back on, and ushered her out of the house and straight into the car. I quickly locked the front door and joined her. At least she was fastening her seat belt, which meant that I might have pulled this off; we might actually get out.

'Which way are we going?' she asked, looking out the window.

I'd noticed this with Mum, when she couldn't remember where we were going, she'd ask what route we were taking or how we were getting there. Anything to not admit or to show that she'd forgotten.

'I thought we'd go through the city centre, and then up past the station and over to the leisure park that way?'

'Right,' she said, watching the buildings pass.

The roads were quiet in the middle of the day and the weather, despite my reassurance to Mum, was downright miserable. If it wasn't for us spending far too much time in the house then I would have agreed. But it was my big birthday; I felt that I deserved at least a trip out somewhere.

We pulled up outside of the museum. The rain had eased off but the air still felt damp, like it could start again at any second.

I looped my arm through Mum's and we headed towards the reception.

Mum startled as she got inside. It might have been quiet on the roads but it was busy in here. Mum stood back to let some children run past her and gripped her bag even tighter towards her chest. I began to wonder if this was a terrible idea.

'You OK?' I asked her.

'Yes, why wouldn't I be? I'm pleased to be here.'

'Good.' We took our place at the front of the queue and I paid for us both. The woman handed me a map and our tickets and we headed towards the stairs. I took hold of Mum's arm as we reached the step and she knocked my hand away.

'I'm not an invalid, you know. I'm only sixty—' she paused as if she was going to correct herself, but she carried on. We walked into the downstairs level of the museum gallery that had old-fashioned shop fronts and cobbled streets. 'And before you ask, I can walk over cobbles just fine in these boots.'

'I wasn't going to say anything.'

'Oh sure you weren't.'

I smiled, but I couldn't help it; that was a kind of feisty

comment my mum of old would have made. I knew rationally that it was her mind that was failing her, and that, for the moment at least, she was physically fine, but the whole process had aged her and sometimes I forgot that she was only just sixty.

'So is there anything in particular we're looking for?' Mum stopped outside the old-fashioned sweet shop. 'I remember when I used to go to the tuck shop and they'd weigh out my sweets. God, that makes me sound really old. It's the kind of thing my gran would have said.'

'Don't forget I grew up with Woolworths' Pick 'n' Mix.'

'Woolworths' Pick 'n' Mix.' She almost snorted at the memory. 'I miss Woolworths.'

'Me too. I still grieve for it every September.' There was something about the autumn leaves falling that gave me a strong desire to buy a new pencil case and stationery, despite not needing either.

'Hmm, but I definitely don't miss it when Christmas shopping.' She shuddered. 'Shall we take a look inside?'

We waited as a family, all clutching paper bags, left the shop, before heading inside. It was like the sweet shops I imagine my nan probably went to, all glass jars in rows and rows.

'Oh, look, we can buy some,' I said, pointing at the sign. 'I wonder if they'll have any cola cubes.'

'Or rhubarb and custards.' She didn't wait for me before she asked one of the dressed-up people behind the counter for some.

'Ah, a classic choice, madam,' said the man dressed in a white shirt and candy striped waistcoat. 'How much would you like?'

'I'll take an ounce, please.'

'Anything else?'

'Cola cubes for me, same amount.'

If I was honest I had no idea how many we were going to get, but the bags were just the perfect portion size.

Mum slipped one of her sweets into her mouth before offering me one.

'I don't think I've ever had a rhubarb and custard before.' I reached into her bag and took one. 'Oh, that's not quite what I was expecting. You can taste the rhubarb and the custard.'

'And would you expect any less?' Mum laughed at me.

'No, it's just . . . I think I'll stick with the cola cubes.'

My mum smiled and I couldn't remember when I had last seen her this relaxed. Her face lately had looked tired and worn, but when she smiled it was as if all the lines made sense, and they drew a completely different picture.

'My mum used to have one of these when I was growing up. A dolly.'

I looked down at the metal contraption in a bucket.

'That's a toy?'

'No.' She laughed and she picked it up, before looking around. 'Am I allowed to touch it?'

'I think so.' There were interactors walking round in costume, and a woman dressed in a Victorian gown with bustle walked over.

'Did you want to know how it was used? It's a clothes dolly; it was used to wash clothes.'

'My mum had one, before we got a machine.'

'Hard work,' said the woman, going on to show how they would have ground the clothes into the bucket. 'They'd push it down and use the motion to gently wash the clothes, and then of course came the mangle.'

She moved over to a contraption with rollers.

'Oh yes, we had one of those too.'

'I had a gentleman in last month and he said his nan still used hers.'

I pulled a face. 'It must take ages.'

'And it was physically demanding too.' The woman put a shirt into the press and turned the handle. 'It would have taken four hours on average for a woman to do one load of laundry.'

I stared in horror.

'I'll never moan again that the quick cycle on the machine isn't quick enough.'

'No,' said the woman, laughing.

I muttered a thanks and we carried on walking. Mum kept pointing out weird-looking objects along the way and we headed straight into the seventies exhibit.

'Waterloo' was playing from a record player in the corner, and everything was an explosion in colour.

'Look at this furniture,' I said, pointing; 'it actually looks like stuff you find in IKEA now.'

'It all comes back in. If you keep hold of it long enough. Oh, look at that poncho. I had one when I started my first job. It was green with tassels, pretty much identical to that one.'

'I remember I had one when I was in sixth form.'

Mum looked at me, her eyes scrunched.

'The black and grey stripey one?'

'Yes,' I said, almost about to compliment her on remembering. I'd forgotten all about that, and yet here was Mum who could barely remember what day it was and she could remember it. Only I couldn't share the irony with her.

'And look at this, it's a poster for a Led Zeppelin concert. I went to that. Your dad was there too, only we didn't know each other then. We found out years later when we worked out that we'd been in the same room so many times and never met.'

I braced myself for the smile to fall and her to drift into the inevitable melancholy that they were no longer together or the bitterness that she used to get after their messy divorce, but it didn't. She was caught up in a better time of her life, far from where they'd ended up.

For the first time since I woke up this morning, I was glad it was my birthday and that I'd come out. Seeing Mum like this was quite possibly the best present I could have been given.

Chapter 19

The afternoon at the museum passed quickly. Mum was practically buzzing when we got home. She was animated and even made us dinner, something that she'd been struggling to do. I was on hand to help but it was like muscle memory had kicked in and she cooked us a shepherd's pie.

It felt like a normal day, until the adrenaline started to wear off and she tired quickly.

'Why don't you go and sit in the living room? I'll do the washing up,' I said, after we'd eaten.

'I'm alright.'

'No, I insist. Go and see what's on telly.'

She nodded and I soon heard the sound of the TV flicking between the channels.

I ran the tap, starting to fill the washing-up bowl when the doorbell rang. We didn't get a lot of visitors.

'Maybe it's Martin, forgotten his key,' said Mum, coming out of the living room. She didn't often talk about Dad; maybe the museum had brought him back into her mind.

'It's probably a delivery. You stay in the warm, I'll get it.'

'OK, good idea.'

She turned back into the lounge, and I opened the front

door. I peered through the spyhole and thought my mind was playing tricks on me.

'Surprise,' said Amy as I opened the door. 'I couldn't not see you on your birthday, it's tradition.'

Baby Oscar was in a car seat slung on her arm, fast asleep.

'Hey, you, come on in, it's freezing outside. Is it just you two?'

'Yes, Paul's putting Patrick to bed. I couldn't face bringing him out in the evening, he'd be far too overtired.'

'Paul or Patrick?'

'Ha!' She laughed out loud, startling Oscar. She winced and, when he didn't stir, she leaned over and gave me a quick hug.

'This is for you.' She handed me a present.

'What is it?'

'Open and see.'

'Who is it, love?' said Mum coming out of the hall. Her eyes flitted between Amy and Oscar.

'Hello, Mrs Adams, I'm Amy, one of Lucy's university friends.'

'Yes, I know, Amy. But this one I haven't met before though.'

'No,' she said, relaxing. 'This is Oscar, he's nine weeks old.'

'And fast asleep.' She put her hand to her mouth in a sshing noise. 'Do you want me to make some tea?'

'I'll do it, Mum.'

'It's fine. You've got your friend. Go and sit down.'

Amy shrugged her shoulders and I shrugged mine back. 'OK, thanks, Mum.'

She went off into the kitchen and we headed to the lounge.

'Just to check is it decaf? It's just I'm still feeding Oscar and he doesn't sleep as it is.'

'Yes, don't worry. All decaf.'

'Perfect,' she said, relieved. 'Your mum seems great. Like you wouldn't know that anything was wrong at all.'

'That's the tricky thing.' I switched off the TV and sat down on the sofa. I tucked my legs under me and Amy did the same. 'Today's been a great day with her, actually. It felt like things were normal, even though they're not.'

I scrunched up my face, willing the tears not to fall as I told her about our trip to the museum.

'Oh, Lucy. That sounds really nice.'

'It was. I just wish it was like that all the time.'

'I know.' Amy reached over and squeezed my hand.

I let out a deep breath. 'I knew this was going to be hard, and weirdly today was so nice that it's made it seem even harder, because it feels like it's reminded me of what I'm missing. She's so young and it's not fair.'

Amy's eyes were welling up too. 'Baby hormones,' she said, fanning her face. 'It's not fair, not fair at all.'

'I just want to do more, but I know it's only going to get worse.'

I stared at the gas fire, watching the flames dance.

'Look, you're doing a great job; don't be so hard on yourself. You're here, aren't you? You've given up so much to look after her.'

I nodded and wiped under my eyes, grateful that I hadn't bothered to put any mascara on this morning.

'Anyway, that's enough about me; what are you even doing here? I barely let you in the door without bombarding you with my crap.'

Amy tutted.

'That's exactly why I'm here. I figured that this was going to be a hard birthday for you and I know you said that you didn't want to do anything or see anyone, but I thought you might have changed your mind.'

I nodded, and finally let a tear fall.

'Thank you.'

'You're welcome. And on a purely selfish note, Oscar is a terrible misery guts in the early evening, but he's great in the car seat so I figured a sleep on the way here, a sleep on the way back, it beats listening to him scream his lungs out for two hours.'

'Oh, that sounds rough.'

I took in the black circles under her eyes and her ashen skin. I had no idea how she looked after one child, let alone two.

'Yeah, but we'll get through it. The hardest bit is getting Patrick off to sleep when he's kicking off. Once he's asleep it's no problem, we could throw a rave in his room and he wouldn't wake, but when he's in that trying to fall asleep state it's a nightmare.'

I smiled weakly, wishing I had any advice to offer.

'And how about you? I thought you said you were just going to stay here for a few months to get your mum sorted before you found somewhere nearby? Hasn't it been almost a year?'

'But that was before I moved in and saw how bad it was all the time. I don't think she'd do anything dangerous or that she'd harm herself, but sometimes she's so confused and I worry what she would do if she was on her own. The thought of her being here alone and who she'd let in. People to read the gas meter when she doesn't have gas. Anyone could tell her anything.' I shuddered.

'I don't know how you do it.'

'And I don't know how you have kids.'

She laughed and tipped her head back, staring up at the ceiling.

'I guess we're going through a similar thing. That feeling of being trapped by other people that are dependent on us. Unable to just drop everything and go out and get drunk and all those things we used to do without question.'

'I would love nothing more than us hitting up the Red Bar right now,' I said, thinking how we practically lived there when we were at uni.

'Tell me about it. I'd even go on a night out in Clapham.'

'You hate Clapham.'

'I know; that's how desperate I am.' She sat back upright again. 'I'm sorry, I shouldn't moan. Motherhood is a gift and I'm lucky that I have healthy children. It's just sometimes I get tired.'

Now it was my turn to give her hand to squeeze.

In a funny way, it was comforting to know that Amy felt this way. It was so easy to click on her photos on Facebook and Instagram and see her beaming with pride as her children did weird and wonderful things and think that she had the perfect life.

'You know there's that really shit advice that people give mums. That it's all a phase and this too shall pass.' She put on a voice for the last bit, then she smiled. 'It won't be like this forever.'

There was a pang in my chest, because, unlike Amy whose children would grow up, I didn't want to think about what it would mean for the next phase for Mum.

'This is nice. We haven't done this for ages,' she said, and I snapped out of my dark thoughts.

'I know.' I nodded.

'I should come out without Patrick more often. It means we

actually get to have a conversation without me losing my train of thought every two minutes.'

'Oh, but it's nice to see him,' I said, thinking the same as Amy but not wanting to suggest that he wasn't welcome.

I glanced at the clock above the fireplace and it hit me that Mum had been a while. 'I might just have to check on the tea situation. Mum has this habit of starting one thing and I'll get in the kitchen and she'll be defrosting the freezer.'

'Oh, I do that all the time. Not defrosting the freezer. There are leftovers living in there that I think I've had longer than Patrick. But do a completely unrelated job. I should probably check on Oscar too. I'm sure he's due a feed and he's probably roasting in his fleecy onesie.' She tried to push herself up. 'Do you remember the days that we'd be on the dancefloor doing slutdrops all over the place and now I can barely get off a sofa?'

'I know, what is that about? We're only thirty-two.'

'And it's only going to get worse,' she said, finally standing up and I followed suit. We headed into the hallway and froze as we saw Mum cradling Oscar in her arms.

She was rocking him and singing gently to him. Neither Amy nor I moved for a split second. I was so in shock that Mum had him. She'd broken that unwritten rule that there is about not picking up other people's babies without asking.

'That's so cute,' said Amy, in a whisper. 'But I probably should take him for a feed.'

'Of course. Um, Mum?' She didn't look up. She just kept rocking Oscar. 'Mum.'

'Sshh, you'll disturb the baby. It's taken me ages to get her off to sleep.'

Amy smiled at me but the look on her face had changed and

fear was creeping into her eyes. She wasn't the only one starting to panic. Mum hadn't done anything like this before.

'Actually, that's a he; it's Oscar,' said Amy, taking a step forward.

Mum stepped back and seemed to tighten her grip around him.

'OK.' I held out my hand towards Amy to stop her walking forward.

Mum's moods could change dramatically and quickly when she was confused or agitated, and the last thing I wanted was this to escalate any further.

I put my arm around Mum, trying to steer her back towards Amy.

'Ah, she's beautiful, what's her name?'

'Lucy.'

My heart started to crack a little more.

'She's gorgeous. Amy here's come to see her, can we take her?'

She looked up at Amy with an air of suspicion. Amy was still doing her best to smile but her hand was starting to shake.

'Just for a second,' said Mum. I held my breath as I leaned across and took hold of Oscar. 'Make sure you cradle her head,' Mum fussed.

I did as I was told, terrified that she'd snatch him back, but she didn't.

Oscar looked up at me with his bright-blue eyes and then he started to wrinkle his nose like he was going to cry. I swiftly handed him to Amy who kissed him on the top of his head.

'Did you want help making the tea, Mum?'

She was staring at them, transfixed.

'Mum, Amy's going to feed Oscar, *her* baby and you were making tea. Shall I help you?'

She looked between Oscar and Amy again. 'No, I don't need help. I'm perfectly capable of making tea,' she snapped and walked off.

I closed my eyes and breathed a sigh of relief. Since my mum was diagnosed with dementia, I'd done a lot of research on the topic, scouring websites, reading books, even taking a few deep dives into medical papers that I could barely understand. One of the things they talked about was the mood swings and aggression. So far, Mum had got cross, but she'd never been aggressive. Seeing her standing with Oscar in her arms, I seemed to have imagined the myriad of different ways that scene could have played out. If she'd left the house with Oscar. If she'd rocked him too hard. The more I thought, the worse the possibilities became, and I felt sick.

'Are you OK?' I said, turning to Amy. 'I'm so sorry.'

'It's fine.' But her voice gave her away that it wasn't fine. I knew that she was lying, and I didn't blame her. I barely felt OK.

Oscar was getting unsettled and starting to whimper.

'I wonder if it's time I should be getting back. Maybe this wasn't such a good idea. It's after eight and it'll take a while to get home and—'

I knew that no matter what I said, she wasn't going to stay. If I was her I wouldn't want to either.

'I understand. It was lovely of you to come.'

She bit her lip as she bent down to the car seat. I noticed her hands were still shaking as she buckled Oscar in.

'She wouldn't have done anything, you know, to hurt him.' The words were out before I could stop them. They sounded so quiet and pathetic.

She stopped fastening and turned to look at me, her face softening.

'I know. It's just . . . it's this thing, with all the hormones. I don't even like Paul taking him out for a walk in the pram. It's a mum thing.'

'Right.'

The closeness that we'd shared before started to drift apart. We were no longer the same in her eyes.

'It was nice to see you. Happy birthday again.'

'Yeah, thanks for coming.'

She gave me the quickest hug, like she was going through the motions rather than with any genuine affection.

'Are you sure you're OK to drive?'

'Yeah, I'll be fine.'

'Text me when you get home. And take care in case there's any ice.'

Amy nodded, but I knew she wasn't really listening. I'd never seen her so keen to leave anywhere before.

'Bye,' she said. I watched her clip Oscar's seat in and get in the car. I waved and she gave me a brisk smile before she drove off.

I shut the front door and rested my back against it, not entirely sure what had happened.

'Right, I've made the tea and I managed to find some KitKats, your favourite. It's cold, have you had the door open?'

I took the tray from Mum.

'Yes, Amy had to leave.'

'Oh, I didn't say goodbye.'

'She needed to get back, Oscar needed a feed.'

'Right,' she said, nodding. 'But her tea.'

'It's fine. We can leave it.'

I carried the tray through to the lounge and popped it on the coffee table.

'But I've made it for her.'

'It's fine,' I snapped. 'It's just a cup of tea.'

Mum looked wounded and I felt awful for losing my temper. It was all her fault that Amy had left so suddenly and yet I knew I couldn't blame her for it. She didn't realise that what she'd done had scared Amy, or she might not even remember what she'd done at all.

'I'm sorry, Mum. It's just, this birthday hasn't really turned out like I planned.'

'Whose birthday?'

'Mine,' I said. 'It's the twenty-ninth today.'

'It is?'

'Leap day.'

'Did you know there's a one in a thousand chance of being born on a leap day.'

'I nodded. One in one thousand four hundred actually.'

'My daughter was born on a leap day,' she said, smiling. She had that look on her face like she'd had in the museum. Lost in another time and place.

I wanted desperately to correct her, to remind her that I was her daughter, but with the smile on her face, I wondered if in her mind she was somewhere better. Somewhere less focused on finding my favourite biscuit in the cupboard.

My chest ached. Amy's words echoed in my mind, that this too will pass, and I knew it would, and that thought was enough to break my heart.

Chapter 20

Mum had a strict bedtime routine that would give Amy and her toddler wrangling a run for her money. She watched a drama that finished at 10 p.m., she did some stretches, she brushed her teeth, washed her face and went to bed. She never deviated from it, and as I heard her switch on the TV to find the drama to watch, I slipped into my bedroom upstairs.

My bedroom was the boxroom in the two-up, two-down semi. It brought back memories of my late teenage years, lying in what felt like a room with the walls closing in, trying to mend a broken heart from whatever crush I had at the time. I had to work hard in my darkest moments to remind myself that my life hadn't failed because I'd ended up in the same place. It was different now. I had a job, good friends, and I had my friends from the allotment.

The allotment had been the biggest surprise of the move, finding a peace I'd never known in my London life. I'd initially gone for Mum, to help with her patch, but I'd soon found myself suggesting we went more. I never thought I'd be the type of person to get a buzz out of watching something go from seed to plate, but I loved it. And I loved the people too. There was a real community feel and, at a time like now, it was exactly what I needed.

But having new friends from the allotment didn't make me miss my old friends any less. I picked up my phone, refreshing the screen. Hoping to see that Amy was back, but there was nothing. I sent her a message, apologising again for what happened, and asking her to let me know she was OK.

I opened up Facebook and stared at Mags and Noah's photos of the Maldives, again.

It felt weird not spending today with Noah, and it made me miss him in a way I hadn't for years. Over the last few years we'd drifted apart. In some ways the whole group had. We all had new friends that suited where we'd found ourselves in life. Amy and Paul with fellow parents, Mags and Noah with other power couples, and me with my allotment crew. But I wondered sometimes if I made less of an effort with Mags and Noah, because of my regrets about the past.

Watching Noah in his life with Mags had made me realise how different we were and I no longer felt that he was the one that got away. But the same couldn't be said for Mags' glasses business. That had gone from strength to strength, and whenever I saw her and heard about it, tiny pangs of jealousy and regret crept in. I'd been almost grateful when they were going away and didn't want to do a group meet-up, to save me from those feelings. But I hadn't expected to miss him so much. Sightseeing with Mum had been brilliant in so many ways, but it made me pine for the friendship we had once upon a time.

I clicked to send a message:

Lucy to Noah

Hey you! Technically I don't think it's our birthday anymore where you are, but I still wanted to say Happy 8th Birthday! I hope you had a good one. And that you kept up the tradition of going to see something weird and wonderful. I get the impression that whatever you saw in the Maldives was more exciting than the living history museum I went to today. Anyway, hope you're OK x

I put my phone down, not expecting a reply, but it started to ring. Hoping it was Amy, I turned it over to see Noah's name on the caller ID.

I hesitated before I picked it up, not being able to remember the last time we'd spoken on the phone and wondering if he'd dialled accidentally.

'Hello?'

'Hey, Luce, can you hear me?'

'Yeah, I can. What time is it over there? I didn't expect you to be up.'

'Yeah,' he said, with a groan. 'I'm all over the place with jetlag and I keep finding myself up in the middle of the night.' He paused. 'But you know, it's a lovely time to take a moonlit stroll on a beach.'

'On your own?'

'There's a couple of night security that I wave at every so often.'

'Oh to be a man in the twenty-first century,' I muttered under my breath not imagining what it must be like to wake up in the middle of the night and feel safe enough to wander outside alone.

'How about you?' he said.

'Why am I up at nine o'clock at night?'

'No, what are you up to?'

'I'm currently lying in my teenage bedroom.'

Whilst the walls had been white-washed after I'd gone, the Artex ceiling was still there. The speckled pattern of tiny drops of plaster that I'd spent my teenage years thinking were about to drop onto my head at any second.

'Nice.'

'Yep,' I said with a laugh. 'We can't all be in paradise, unfortunately.'

Noah laughed. 'Well, paradise isn't always paradise.'

'Looks pretty much like it to me in your photos.'

'Ah, the joys of Facebook when you're on holiday.'

'Is it even a holiday if you don't post photos?'

'Now you sound like Mags.' He sighed.

'So, come on then, what did you do for your birthday? You're going to have to work hard to convince me that it's not as blissful as it seems.'

'The same as we've been doing all week. We lazed around, ate breakfast on the deck of our bungalow. Did a little snorkelling in the sea. Ate seafood at the restaurant at the beach.'

'Sounds awful and quite hellish; nothing like the dictionary definition of paradise at all.'

He laughed.

'Yeah. But there was no living history museum. What even is that? In my mind that's almost scarier than the Dead Zoo. Kind of a zombie museum.'

If I closed my eyes, I could imagine the dimple on his cheek that would be making an appearance.

'It's where they have people dressed up in costumes and they have houses and shops kitted out from different eras, full of objects from the past. No zombies in sight.'

'Nice, although zombies would have taken it to the next level. I take it there was no childhood trauma associated with this one.'

I thought of the afternoon. I kept seeing the smile on my mum's face and I felt the squeeze on my heart.

'Nope, none. I learned a lot. I took my mum and we had a really nice afternoon. There were a few moments where it felt like she was fine and she was talking about memories, and I mean memories from years ago, stuff that I'd never heard about her childhood, about her meeting Dad.'

'That's why you sound so sad.'

It stopped me in my tracks.

'How could you tell?'

'I can hear it in your voice.'

I bit my lip. I missed Noah. I missed how someone could know you so well that even with all these miles between us, between the silly banter and the jokes he could hear that something was off.

'Believe it or not, that wasn't the saddest part of the day.'

There was a pause and faintly in the distance I could hear the rhythmic crash of the waves on the beach.

'What was?'

I didn't want to tell him. I was embarrassed about what he'd think of Mum.

'Lucy?'

I sighed. I'm sure Paul would tell him anyway.

'Amy came over tonight and she was barely here before Mum picked up Oscar, thinking he was her baby.'

'Oh.' He smacked his lips together.

'Yeah, it was all fine. She just held him and I quickly got

him off her. But it rattled Amy, which it would, of course; she's a mother.' I could still feel the fear that had taken hold of me. 'But it also rattled me. I keep thinking what if something had happened, would Amy have ever forgiven me? And she hasn't texted to say she got home OK and now I'm worried because she was in a state when she got in the car.'

My mind still felt like it was in a heightened state of fear and I couldn't do anything but imagine worst-case scenarios.

'Breathe. Amy will be fine. She's probably got home and been sucked into looking after the kids. If Paul was doing bedtime, Patrick was probably still up and running riot. And she'll understand; of course she will. It was just a shock.'

'Still, I—'

'And as for running things that could have happened through your mind, they didn't happen, did they? Thinking about the what if's isn't going to help.'

'But—'

'But nothing. It sounds like you've got enough on your plate without thinking about what might have happened.'

I knew he was right, but it didn't make it any easier to accept.

'I didn't realise things were so bad, with your mum.'

There was a concern in his voice. Whenever anyone started to sound caring about me, it made me want to cry.

'I knew you'd moved in with her but I thought it was just to keep her company. I had no idea that it was at this stage.'

This was why I didn't want to tell him what had happened. Now he's judging Mum.

'It's not always this bad.'

'But it is sometimes though. Are you getting enough help?'

I scrunched my eyes tight.

'We have a person that comes in a few times a week; she sits with Mum whilst I go to work.'

'That's not what I asked. I asked if you were getting help? Is your dad supporting you?'

I blinked back a tear.

'He tries. But it's tricky as Mum gets agitated if she sees him, and he's busy with Tania and Gilly. But I'm fine, really. I'm coping.'

'It sounds like you need some more support.'

There was a stabbing pain in my chest and for a second I couldn't breathe. It was the thought that I didn't want to admit to myself.

'We're managing.' I could hear the hardness in my voice, and I didn't mean to sound snappy, it was more that I was trying not to cry.

'Look,' said Noah, breathing out, 'I know I'm not the best person to dish out advice at the moment, I feel like we haven't . . .' There was a pause. Neither of us had really acknowledged that things had changed between us. 'I know I haven't been there like I could have been. And I know you've always been the wise one in this friendship. But, if I was going to say something, I'd say that you don't have to do this all by yourself. You've always looked after everyone, and that's one of your absolute best qualities. It's why you make such a great friend.'

I closed my eyes; it was getting harder and harder not to cry.

'But,' I said, sensing the pause.

'But,' he said, elongating the word, 'sometimes you've got to admit that something isn't working and that things have to change.'

'But it works. I mean, Mum's getting more confused, but we've got a routine and—'

'Lucy, no one will think anything less of you if you get more help. When was the last time you went out?'

'I told you I was out this afternoon. And Mum and I go to the allotment, though not so much in this weather.'

'I mean out by yourself doing something for you. I'm not talking about work or going to the supermarket. I mean you putting yourself first, doing something that you want to do. Didn't you and Amy used to go for spa days?'

I couldn't remember the last time we'd done one of those. It would have been long before she got pregnant with Oscar.

'It's not that easy.'

'I never said it would be, but I think you've got to face facts that it's not going to get any easier.' He sighed. 'I know I've been a bit of a shit friend over the last few years and I've probably got no right to say all this when I've done nothing to help, but I've got to say something.'

I didn't respond, not because of what he'd said, but because I was trying not to cry.

'Sorry, Luce. I blame these damn big birthdays. We've always had too much talk of where will be next time; it makes me think.'

'Yeah, me too,' I said, letting out a deep breath and pinching the bridge of my nose in a bid to stop the tears. 'I guess we were both wrong with our predictions. I did not have me living at home in the boxroom, caring for my mother.'

I tried to laugh but there was a bitter edge to my voice that I couldn't hide. What I wouldn't give to go back four years. Not to change what had happened with Noah, but to be with the mum from those pubs in Dublin, with her how she used to be. When she knew where she was and she planned for the future, before that future was cruelly ripped away in what felt like a blink of an eye.

'And I never thought I'd be on a beach in the Maldives.'

'Yes,' I said mock sighing. 'There's no need to rub it in.'

'No, no. I didn't mean it like that. I meant, me being here. On this kind of holiday . . . I don't know. I'm being a dick, holding a pity party for one over here.'

'I'm getting my tiny violin ready for you.'

He laughed. 'Look, I guess I'm just trying to say that sometimes we all need to put ourselves first.'

I wrinkled my face up. I knew that he was giving me advice, but there was something in the way he was talking that made me wonder if he wasn't just speaking to me.

'Is everything OK with you?'

There was a pause, and it was hard to tell on the line but there was a slight mumble like he started to say something and thought better of it.

'Yeah, everything's fine. I'm in the Maldives, how could it not be?'

I couldn't help but hear sarcasm in his voice.

'Listen, I should probably get back to the bungalow in case Mags wakes up and freaks out that I'm not there.'

I wanted to talk to him more, to get to the bottom of whatever it was he was hinting at. I worried about him being alone in the night on a deserted beach.

'Noah, you know I'm here, if you need to talk?'

There was a pause and I couldn't make out the noise on the other end of the phone.

'I know,' he said, eventually.

'OK, well, I mean it.'

'Thanks, Luce.'

'OK, well, um, thanks for phoning.'

'You're more than welcome. I'm just sorry that we didn't spend it together. Feels weird, right?'

'Yeah.' I nodded, without him being able to see. 'It does.'

'We'll do something again for the next one.'

I hoped that we would and that this wasn't a one-off phone call that was a kneejerk reaction to nostalgia and birthdays. I wanted him back in my life, and if that meant swallowing the petty jealousy I had of the life he and Mags were living, then so be it.

'I'd like that . . . as long as there aren't any dead animals involved.'

'Noted. Take care.'

'You too.'

I hung up the phone and I let the tears I'd been holding flow down my face. It wasn't for the fact that today had been a birthday of extreme highs and lows, or that I missed having Noah in my life, but because he was absolutely right with what he said. I wasn't coping and I needed help. I just didn't know if I was brave enough to ask for it.

There was a knock at my door.

'I'm making a cup of tea. Do you want one?'

I almost laughed through the tears. At this rate my blood was ninety per cent tea.

'OK, thank you.'

'Great. I think I've got some ginger nuts, they're your favourite, aren't they?'

I heard her footsteps pad down the hallway. Ginger nuts were my favourite and I clung on to the tiny bit of hope that it was a sign that Noah and my gut were wrong.

Facebook messenger – Amy to Lucy: March 2016

You don't need to keep apologising. Nothing happened! Besides, I think if it had been less of a shock, I would have marvelled at how at peace Oscar was with her. He usually hates strangers. Hope you had a nice birthday, and we'd love to have you to stay if you can get someone to look after your mum overnight? Or, failing that, an afternoon?

Text message – Mags to Lucy: May 2016

It's that time of year! We're having our annual summer BBQ! Saturday July 16th, 6 p.m. Let me know dietary requirements. Dress code cocktail. RSVP

Voicemail – Caz: July 2016

Hey Lucy, I heard from Amy that you can't make the Matthews' annual summer bash. Did you know last year that they had actual lobster on the BBQ, just in case that makes you change your mind? But if it's tricky leaving your mum, I wondered if you were free the next morning for brunch? My train back up to Edinburgh isn't until 4, so I think I could make it to Basingstoke and back in time? Call me.

Email – Hampshire Social Services Health Team to Lucy: February 2017

Dear Lucy,

I'm sorry I don't have better news but we're unable to change your mum's care package at this time.

There is a list of reputable private care options on our website that might help you to fill the gaps you're looking for.

I also attach the information about respite care for short stays in residential homes, and the costs associated with it.

Regards,
Michelle

Email – Paul to the Group: December 2017
Hi everyone,
Long time no see, although maybe it seems much longer through lack of sleep. We were thinking that it would be nice to get us all together before Christmas? I know it's a squash and a squeeze at ours, but it would be easier for us than trying to get someone to look after our little darlings. We were thinking lunch – as there might be a chance we get one of the children (or both!) to nap – optimistic, I know. But also thought that, Lucy, you could get someone to watch your mum for a couple of hours?
Let me know thoughts.

P

WhatsApp message – Lucy to Amy: December 2017
Thanks you guys for making me come, I'm sorry I couldn't stay longer. Food was lovely and the company even better. Mum was fine, and you're right, I should do it more often. Have a great Christmas xx

Voicemail – Lucy to Noah: May 2018
Hi Noah, I am so sorry to cancel at such short notice but it's Mum; she's having [sigh] a bad day and I can't leave

her. I know that you're not often down this way, so I hate that I'm going to miss you but I can't go. And she's so agitated that I can't even suggest you coming to the house. I hope you're well. Catch up soon.

WhatsApp message – Lucy to Caz: August 2018

Sorry I missed your call again. The evenings are tricky at the moment. I'll try and call you maybe from work. I'm OK, hope you are too. Did I see from Instagram you were in Paris? Did you see Bertrand? Xx

Email – Lucy to everyone: February 2019

Hi guys,

I'm sorry to bail on another birthday – sorry, Noah, hope you have a good one. Dad is coming over for us all to have a birthday lunch. I have no idea how that will go, but hey. Have a great time. X

WhatsApp message – Dad to Lucy: July 2019

Hi Lucy. How are you getting on? Is your mum doing any better? Tania wanted to know if you wanted to come to us on Sunday for lunch? Or any Sunday?

Facebook messenger – Andrew to Lucy: September 2019

Hi Lucy! Hope you don't mind the DM. But your bushes need trimming. Just wondering if I could trim them for you?

Yep. I hit send before I read that back. Your BLACKBERRY bushes need trimming. Sorry for inadvertent creepy message.

Also, sorry, it's Andrew, from the allotment.

Just to say, I'll be thinking of you all day. I'm sure that your mum is going to settle in just fine. Call if you need me. Or if you want me to come and stay in the house with you. Love you. xx

Thank you for helping me with the pruning, I would have got rid of most of the raspberry plants without your intervention. And I honestly was sorry I couldn't go to the pub after. Hopefully we can go another time?

Amy:

Paul and I have been thinking and we thought perhaps we could try and all get together for Noah and Lucy's birthday??? I don't think we could stretch to anywhere as fancy as the Maldives. Short of selling one of the kids, and I don't think we'd get much money for them, we won't be able to afford to go too far. But we were thinking a weekend in London?

Lucy:

I'd love that. Mum's happier in the home but I still don't feel like I can go that far afield, so London would be perfect. I know it isn't really picnic weather but maybe we could do a walk in one of the parks to keep the costs down. Looking forward to seeing you all! And thanks so much for suggesting it. @Noah, are you going to be able to make it, or are you off to another paradise for it?

Noah:

What are you saying, Lucy, that London isn't a paradise in its own right? Yes, I can make it. Looking forward to it.

Caz:

Love this for us. Do not love the walk idea. It's going to be freezing. What about a museum? British Museum? Natural History? Lucy, are we going to meet the new man???

Lucy:

NO DEAD ANIMALS, although the dinosaur bones look cool. And no to new man, it's still early days.

Amy:

Museums are a great idea. Leave it with me, I'll come up with a plan.

WhatsApp message – Lucy to uni group: February 26th 2020

Guys, are you watching the news? Are we still going?

PART FIVE

2020

Chapter 21

Friday 28ᵗʰ February 2020

I finished brushing my mum's hair and put the brush on the side, next to the photograph of me and her walking up Snowdon. It had always been one of her favourite pictures. I looked hideous in it, my cheeks flushed red, from the cold or the exertion, my skin clammy and my hair both frizzy and sticking up in as many directions as it could, thanks to the constant drizzle of rain that had plagued us all day. Mum, on the other hand, looked radiant. Her red cheeks were rosy and healthy and her smile was wide. We were both smiling. It was the toughest of days, but the best of days.

'Did you want to take a walk today to get a coffee?'

Mum turned her head and looked out the window.

'Looks like rain.'

'It's February, it always looks like rain.' I took the coat off the hook on the back of her door.

She stayed sitting in the chair in the corner of her room and she pulled her pashmina further round her.

'I don't think so. Not today.'

I put the coat back on the hook. Sometimes Mum went willingly to the café on the edge of the park, and sometimes she just wanted to stay in. I couldn't force her, she'd only get agitated, and my point was to try and brighten her day, rather than make things worse.

'How about a game of Scrabble?'

'I'm a bit tired.'

'OK, did you want me to go?'

'No.'

'Right.' I sat down in the armchair next to her and looked at the same view that she had. I could see the elm tree out of the window, and there was a squirrel running along its branches. 'Look at that.'

'He's always in that tree.'

'Huh. Have you named him?'

She paused and tilted her head. 'Martin.'

'Martin.' Just like Dad. I wondered if it was deliberate or just the first name that came to hand for her. 'I've always thought that squirrels were essentially vermin.'

Deliberate then. At least on a subconscious level.

She was smiling with a mischievous look on her face, which made me smile too. Martin the squirrel it was. It was these little moments in our exchanges that kept me coming back. They reminded me that my mum was still in there somewhere. That sometimes her mind might take her back to the right place.

'Has Dad been to visit you lately?'

'Dad? My dad's been dead years.'

She wrinkled her brow, shooting me a look that made me feel like I was the one with the memory problem.

'No, I mean, my dad.'

'Your dad? How would I know your dad? I've not even met you before.'

No matter how many times this happened, it didn't hurt any less.

'Mum, it's me, Lucy,' I said, trying to keep my voice as soft as possible. The first time she'd thought of me as a stranger it had broken my heart, not that there was a lot left to break. It had been gently cracking and fissuring since her diagnosis and now it was so brittle that the tiniest thing would shatter it into pieces.

I'd thought that it was the start of it. That once she forgot who I was, she'd never remember me again. But most days, and most of the time, she knew me. I was the one that got the panicked phone calls at any time of day when she was spiralling about whether or not she'd put the bins out, despite not having bins anymore, or why she hadn't got Marion's number in her phone, her sister that had died of cancer two years previously.

I shelved the topic and went back to the squirrel.

'Do you think he has a nest in the tree?'

'Who?'

I nodded. 'I think I might get a fancy coffee from the café on the corner. Do you want to come?'

'No, it looks like rain.'

In Mum's world, it always looked like rain. If she didn't want to go somewhere, that was always the reason, whether it was perfect, cloudless blue skies, or whether the heavens were teeming it down. Today, it was cloudy and on the way here it had been drizzling.

'I can bring you one back?'

'No, thanks. No need to come back. I'm going to have a little sleep.'

'OK, Mum,' I said, reaching over and taking her hand.

She let me hold it for a second but snatched it away soon after, not making eye contact.

'I'm going to go then. I'm away tomorrow overnight, but I'll be in on Sunday afternoon.'

She looked up and smiled, but it was the smile I'd seen her do countless times in my life when she was being polite to strangers.

I walked to the reception at the end of the hallway.

'How did you find her today?' asked Carol. She was tapping away at her keyboard and staring up at me at the same time. I wish I could multi-task like her.

'Mixed,' I said, wrinkling my nose. 'But she seemed calm.'

'Good, calm is sometimes the best we can hope for.'

This is usually the point that I'd wish her well and walk off, but I found myself lingering and Carol stopped typing. She glanced up at me again.

'Is everything OK? You're not going to be talking to me about this virus, are you? Did you see the news today?'

'I'm trying to ignore that.' I turned away from the newspaper on the counter. Every day the tickertape on the news channel was getting more alarmist. 'I just wanted to let you know that I'm going away.'

'OK, that's fine. Let me bring up your mum's file.' She started clicking again. 'How long for? And is there someone that you're nominating to be an emergency contact in the meantime?'

'It's only tomorrow for the night to London. But it was just in case that something happened and—'

Carol tilted her head and looked down over her glasses.

'Lucy, you're going for one night. Enjoy yourself. Your mum is fine here. Fine.'

'I know, it's just sometimes she rings and when I'm at home I can pop down.'

'She'll be fine. Honestly. Have fun. Are you doing anything nice?'

'It's my birthday, actually. I'm meeting up with some friends.'

'Nice, well, happy birthday.'

I nodded and turned to go.

'Do you think I should be worried about the virus and Mum?'

Carol tutted. 'You don't need to be finding extra things to fret about. Don't worry, we've asked relatives who have been abroad to maybe wait before visiting those in here.'

'That's sensible.' I nodded.

'Relax, enjoy yourself. Have a nice birthday.'

'Thanks.' I gave one last look towards Mum's corridor and left. Carol was right, she'd be fine, but saying it and believing it were two different things.

I was early to meet Andrew for lunch, but he was still there before me, waiting on the wall outside the restaurant.

'Here she is, here's the birthday girl,' he said, beaming when he saw me.

'Here I am.'

We were in that awkward stage of dating, still finding our feet with each other, and he hesitated for a moment before kissing me on the lips. My hand found his stomach and we stayed there for a little longer, his hand grazing the small of my back.

I pulled away, and he smiled, the little lines at his eyes creasing.

'Have you got something behind your back?' I asked, taking a step back.

He was standing with one arm behind him, and he bobbed his head from side to side.

'Um, I do,' he started, pulling a face.

'For me?' He nodded. I tried to grab at the back of him but he stepped away.

'Now, wait.' He held out his free hand to push me back gently. 'Before you get too excited, this was something that seemed like a really sweet idea at the time, but now I'm just thinking it's mega cringe.'

'Mega cringe. Ooh, is it over-the-top flowers?'

'No,' he said, shaking his head. His face looking apologetic. 'I wish it was that cool. That would have been much better.'

'What is it?'

I tried to turn him to the side. But he laughed and kept walking backwards until we'd gone in a circle.

'You promise you won't think any less of me?'

'Promise.'

'OK.' He took a deep breath. He'd really built this up now. He brought his arm round to reveal a bouquet of sprouting broccoli in beautiful purples and greens.

'Andrew, they're beautiful,' I said, taking them, and not knowing quite what to do with them I sniffed them. 'No idea why I did that, but they smell fresh.'

'Picked this morning. I went to the allotment on the way to work.'

'Ah, that's so sweet.'

'Yeah. The jury was out with my colleagues; some thought it was romantic, some thought corny.'

'Well, my verdict is kind of romantic.'

'Kind of romantic?' He did a fist pump. 'I'll take it.'

'So, shall we get some food? I'm starving.'

'Me too.' I followed him into the café.

We sat at a table in the corner, and ordered quickly as Andrew was on his lunchbreak.

'How was your mum this morning?'

'She was mostly good. She's named a cheeky squirrel Martin, after my dad.'

'Is your dad a cheeky squirrel?'

'Once upon a time he was. But not anymore. Now he lives a normal life with his second wife, Tania.'

I used to tell the story so differently, and whilst I'd never advocate the way that he went about it, the fact that he'd been with Tania for twenty years, far longer than he'd been with my mum, changed things.

'Are they local?'

'Yeah, I probably should make an effort to see them more. It's so stupid but for a long time I felt disloyal to my mum hanging out with Tania.'

'His new wife?'

I nodded.

'Doesn't sound silly. Divorces are tricky for the kids; they're often caught up in the middle. I know that first hand, from my parents. It was why me and my ex were so reluctant at first to split. I didn't want Jack to go through that.'

'But he's doing OK?'

'Yeah,' he said, nodding. 'It helps that I get on well with his mum and her new husband.'

Andrew always looked different when he talked about Jack; there was a mixture of pride and love written all over his face.

'How old were you when your parents divorced?'

'I was about five, so I can't remember it any other way. Two Christmas days. Lots of presents. I've had three stepmums.'

'Three?'

'Yep, my dad was a truly cheeky squirrel,' he said, his face wrinkling almost apologetically.

'What's his name?'

'Eddie.'

'Just so I know what to name the next squirrel if there's another one at my mum's.'

He laughed with his whole belly and I couldn't help joining in.

'That makes Dad sound really bad. But he's had a bit of a run of bad luck. We'll talk about that another day.'

I nodded. These early stages of a relationship were very much like sketching a picture, and slowly we'd go back and add the colour and definition. It was the bit that I both loved and loathed. It was that exciting time of butterflies and lust, but I missed the moments that came later when you really started to know and understand each other.

The waiter popped our coffees down on the table.

'So, I have a question to ask you.' Andrew pulled out a sugar packet and shook it.

'That sounds ominous.'

'Ha, does it? It's just, I don't know if it's a bit soon to ask, but my mates are organising this trip to Bilbao, in Spain, to learn to surf. I think it's one of their things to do before you're forty bucket lists. Anyway, there's a whole group of us going, hiring a big house. And I guess I want to know if you want to come too? It's in July, early on before the schools break up.'

My eyes were blinking, taking it all in. Bilbao. Friends. House. July.

'Oh, um . . . that's quite a while away.'

He had the same look of embarrassment on his face that he'd had when he'd pulled out the broccoli. I'm not sure he realised how cute it made him look.

'I know, I said it was too soon, but they're booking and I think it'll be fun. That part of Spain's supposed to be pretty too. Have you been?'

I shook my head. 'Do I have to decide now?'

'I was going to book it pretty soon, before the prices go too high for the flights. But I understand if it's too much pressure or you think it's too soon.'

By the time July rolled around, if we'd become a proper couple we'd have been together over six months, but what happened if we booked and then broke up? Or worse, stayed together because of the holiday?

'Can I think about it?'

'Yeah, of course. But you know,' he said, stirring his coffee, 'I look pretty hot in a wetsuit, in case that swings your vote.'

'Oh really now? Is that a thing, looking cute in a wetsuit? Does anyone?'

He smiled. I could imagine that he'd suit a wetsuit. I'd been watching Andrew garden through the seasons on the allotment, and he looked good in most things.

'Hang on.' He pulled his phone out of his pocket and scrolled. 'Here you go.'

He passed me a photo of him coming out of the water in a wetsuit, a surfboard under his arm. He was true to his word, it was working for him. But I squinted at the phone; he also looked a lot younger and baby-faced than he did now.

'When was this taken?' I said to Andrew, giggling.

'About twenty years ago. It was the time me and my mates learned to surf the first time. Dec, who's organising it, sent the pictures, hoping it would spur us on.'

'So you can all already surf?'

'No. That's the whole point. We went to Newquay a million years ago to do it, but after half a day of lessons where we barely got on the board, we found the nightclubs, and the rest, as they say, is history.'

'You suit your hair longer,' I said, passing him back the phone.

'I also suited less wrinkles.'

'Don't we all?' Although I didn't agree with him. I liked the lines on his face; they gave him character.

The waiter put our food down in front of us.

'Oh no,' he said, looking down at his plate after the waiter had left, 'we've got a problem.'

'What?' I studied his plate, wondering if they'd got his order wrong.

'We're going to have to hide the broccoli bunch; don't want them thinking they'll be next.' He unfolded the menu and put it up like a screen around the bouquet.

'You are ridiculous,' I said, secretly loving the fact that he really didn't care that he was being silly.

'Ridiculous, but slightly romantic.' He gave me a wink, picking up his cutlery. 'I'll take it.'

Chapter 22

Saturday 29ᵗʰ February

I walked across the bridge from Southbank, breathing in the fresh air. The light drizzle from this morning had cleared, and London was trying its best to show blue skies amongst pockets of clouds.

I was glad to get off the train. I'd tried to read my book but found myself obsessively checking my phone, checking to see if Mum had called, checking to see what the latest on the news was. Neither was conducive to a relaxing journey.

I headed down the stairs to the end of the bridge towards Embankment and saw Noah standing at the bottom. He had a takeaway coffee cup in one hand and his phone in the other, immersed in his own little world of scrolling. Still, after all this time, I felt that flutter in my belly when I saw him. It was always the same, that fleeting feeling that washed over my body before my brain kicked into gear and reminded me that I wasn't supposed to feel that anymore.

He was wearing a down jacket with a black hoodie underneath. It was the first time I'd seen him in anything so casual in years. It almost reminded me of the Noah that I'd met in Calais. I'm pretty sure he'd been wearing a hoodie that day, his Abercrombie

& Fitch one that I saw degrade over the years, fading from a brilliant blue, to pale with little holes around the cuffs.

I felt nervous about seeing him, not for any residual feelings that lingered, but because I barely saw him anymore. In another life, finding ourselves childless in a sea of married friends with toddlers in tow with endless conversations about PTA groups, and playdates and routines, might have bonded us together. Given us a common purpose, the last of us hanging on to the life that we'd once had. But in truth our lives couldn't have been more different.

I walked down the steps to meet him, and when I neared the bottom I stopped. A ripple of déjà vu jolted through my body. When we'd spent our birthday in London all those years ago, that was the spot that he'd caught me as I slipped, the first time I'd felt real butterflies from being with him.

He looked up and I raised my hand in a wave. He smiled and slipped his phone into his pocket.

'Hey,' I called, as I walked over.

'Hey yourself.' He leaned forward to give me a kiss on the cheek, and not knowing what way he was going, we ended up doing that awkward dance, both of us tilting the same way, trying to correct ourselves, then going the same way again.

I coughed. 'Shall we settle for a hug?'

'That's a much better idea.' He wrapped me in his arms. I lingered for a little bit too long, caught up in a wave of nostalgia and gratefulness that we'd actually managed to meet up on the big birthday.

'So,' I said, embarrassed that I'd spent too long in the hug, 'you're the first one here. Where's Mags?'

He took a sip of his coffee and gave a little shrug.

'She's not coming.'

'Work?'

'You know Mags,' he said with a sigh. He was trying to laugh it off, but there was a rawness in his voice and I wondered if they'd had an argument. 'Was the train ride up OK?'

'Yes. I got a seat. That's what passes for a good journey these days, isn't it?'

He smiled. 'I guess so. Somewhere to rest those old knees.'

'Hey, less of the old, thank you.' I put my hands on my hips and straightened up a little, feeling my shoulders twinge. 'We're still in our thirties.'

'Barely. Happy birthday, by the way.'

'Oh, yes, you too.'

In years gone by, this was the moment that we would have pulled out silly presents for each other. Tacky gifts full of thought. But we no longer did presents; I barely did for any of my friends. Now their children were the recipients at Christmas and birthdays, despite the fact that in hindsight it was probably their parents that needed the little treat – the children already far too spoilt by doting grandparents and the whole class from school when they were invited to a party.

'Ah, here they are,' said Noah, pointing behind me, a little too much relief in his voice that there were people to rescue us from the awkwardness that had descended. I turned and saw Amy and Paul.

Amy gave me a squeeze so tight that I almost couldn't breathe.

'I'm so glad you made it,' she said, letting me go.

'Well, it is my birthday.'

'I know, but you know . . . '

I nodded. I did. I didn't add that I'd thought of cancelling when I got to the station. If the train ticket I'd bought in advance hadn't been so extortionate then maybe I would have.

'Where's Caz? Didn't you meet her at the hotel?' Amy asked.

'No, she was running late. She went to meet up with Nick.'

Her eyes almost popped out of her head. 'Nick, as in *Nick* Nick?'

'The one and same. He's living in Walthamstow now.'

'Huh,' she said, her brow wrinkling. 'I'm not sure what's more surprising: that she's meeting up with him, or that Nick's moved to Walthamstow.'

'It's not only East 17 that live there now, it's massively bougie,' said Noah, chipping into the conversation.

Amy playfully hit Noah on the arm.

'You make me sound like a snob; I just meant that Nick moved down south. He's more Mancunian than—' She paused like she couldn't think of a cultural reference from Manchester.

'Than Oasis?' said Noah.

'What is it with you and your nineties references today?' I turned to him.

'I've been listening to a lot of Radio 2.'

'Mate.' Paul shook his head. 'How can you do that?'

'Do you know, I'm not even sorry. The music actually sounds like music.'

Amy snorted with laughter. 'OK, Grandad.'

'What are you talking about? You listen to Smooth Radio in the car. And don't you pretend you don't; it's always on when I get in,' said Paul.

Amy opened her mouth and shut it again before she shrugged. 'It sends the kids off to sleep near nap time. And it's kind of habit.'

'Admit it, you do it for the Celine Dion power ballads.'

She giggled. 'Is there a greater pleasure in life than belting out "It's All Coming Back to Me Now", safe in the knowledge that no one will hear you?'

Nods rippled around the group like a Mexican wave.

'Fuck, guys, we're ancient.' Noah tutted. 'I feel like we should head to the nearest pub and get shitfaced.'

Amy looked at her Apple watch, and turned her nose up. 'If I started drinking now, I'd never make it to the dinner reservation.'

'Yeah, you can't handle your drink at the best of times.' Paul laughed a little, but it fell flat when Amy didn't join in. 'Speaking of us all getting old though, you guys at least don't look it. What is it with you two not ageing? Does being born on a leap day give you magical powers for eternal youth.'

'Well, it is only our ninth birthday,' I said.

'What are you trying to say, that I look haggard in comparison to Lucy?' Amy had her hands on her hips, not in the same mocking way I'd done earlier with Noah.

'No,' said Paul, slowly. I could see the beads of sweat forming on his forehead. 'That's not what I was saying.'

'Do you want to know the key to eternal youth? It's not having two kids.'

She poked him sharply with her finger.

'And that's my fault, obviously,' he muttered under his breath.

'So,' said Noah, jumping in before things escalated any further, 'speaking of the kids, where are they today?'

'My mum's got them. Overnight too.' Paul was raising his eyebrows at Amy but she rolled her eyes.

'And I am looking forward to a lie-in the morning, and that is all. I do not want four kids in the house.'

'You realise we only have two . . . oh, I get it, I'm the third child, and right, judging from that look, if I want to have any chance of ever having sex again, I should just keep quiet.'

'And finally he's learning. Only taken umpteen years,' she muttered.

This wasn't like Amy and Paul. They were like an old married couple in a cute way, but there was nothing cute about this. Usually their type of bickering showed everyone how well they really knew each other, but this was like Paul's mere act of breathing was annoying her.

'Sixteen actually. In fact, sixteen to the day that I met you in our kitchen.'

'Sixteen years,' said Noah. 'It's not already, is it?'

'Bloody hell, not another anniversary that we have to celebrate,' Amy muttered. 'Paul's big on anniversary's – first date, first kiss.'

'Sorry for being romantic.'

'Well, I for one am pleased that I met you both sixteen years ago,' I said, shooting Noah a look in the hope that he'd help plug up the sinking ship.

'Me too. I can't believe it was that long ago that we were in Calais with you dressed in . . . ' He started to laugh.

'Oh god,' I groaned, looking at Amy, and she tried not to laugh too. 'The Parisian chic.'

'We watched too much *Sex and the City* back in the day,' said Amy. 'I think we dressed you in something we thought Carrie would have worn.'

'That hat.'

I gave Noah a look. 'That hat was of the time.'

'You know, I've still not had an oyster since then.'

Noah gave his shoulder a squeeze in solidarity. 'If you hadn't then we might have not been standing outside getting air, and we might not have met Lucy.'

'I wonder where we would have been if you hadn't,' said Amy, a little too wistfully for my liking.

'Ah, there's Caz,' I said, waving at her walking out of the Tube exit.

She didn't see me; she was walking and typing on her phone, a frown on her face. She shoved the phone back in her pocket, but as she looked around to find us, she saw me and her angry look evaporated, a smile unfolding.

'The gang's all here,' she said, making her way round the group, hugging and air kissing.

'Good meeting?' I whispered and she wrinkled her nose up.

'He cancelled.'

'Oh, Caz.' My heart went out to her. I know how much she'd been looking forward to seeing him.

'Maybe we can chat about it over a nightcap?'

I nodded.

Even though Caz had had boyfriends since Nick, he'd always been 'the one that got away'. It was rare we chatted on the phone these days; instead our once long chats had been replaced by snatched WhatsApp messages. But occasionally when we were late-night messaging, one of us would phone, we'd chat and her regret would spill out.

I'd half hoped, when she'd texted to say that she was meeting him, that it might be the start of something new. The selfish part of me had hoped it because Edinburgh was a really long, long way away and the thought of having her in Walthamstow was an attractive proposition. But now that wasn't going to happen.

I blew on my hands to warm them up, as there was a cool, crisp wind coming off the river.

'Speaking of ages. Happy birthday, you two,' said Caz. 'I should give you your present before you turn into an icicle. You're such a southern softie.'

'Yeah, for all the years you've lived up north, I still don't think you can say that if you were born in Sussex.'

'Whatever,' she said, mock-rolling her eyes. She handed me a little bag and I pulled out a furry snood.

'Bloody hell, I haven't seen one of these in years.' I immediately slipped it over my head. 'That is much better. OK, before I freeze to death, what is it we're going to do today?'

We turned to face Amy and Paul. In their only show of unity, they dug into Amy's bag and pulled out some envelopes.

'OK, so here are the options. All free museums.'

'We thought it was in keeping with the sightseeing you guys always do,' said Paul.

'Birthday tradition. Can't mess with them.' Noah raised his eyebrows and I nodded back.

I thought of Mum and our trip to the museum on the last leap year. It was one of the rare good days we'd had over the last few years. My heart tightened and I had to fight the urge to call and check up on her.

'We couldn't pick what to do, so we've put a different one in each envelope and you can choose,' said Amy, fanning them out.

'Ooh, this feels like we're on a game show.' My hand hovered around the red one, and then the blue one, before I finally went for the green. 'And the winner is . . . '

Paul started to do a drum roll on his thighs until he got a look from Amy.

I pulled the card out of the envelope. 'Tate Modern.'

Amy air punched in victory, I knew it was her very favourite gallery and I tried to share her enthusiasm. I'd been a few times before, though not for years, and it wasn't that I didn't love the buzz of the gallery or the scale of the building, but nothing changed the fact that I just didn't get a lot of the art. I'd tried really hard to appreciate it like everyone else, but I'd never been able to.

'What's on in the turbine hall?' asked Caz. 'I think the last time that I went was with you guys when they had those slides.'

'I remember those. I remember going on them after I'd had a few G&Ts. Not recommended,' said Paul, turning up his nose. 'I'm not sure what's on at the moment though.'

'Well, let's go and find out.' Amy was brimming with enthusiasm. 'Shall we walk or get the Tube?'

'How about we take the Clipper?' said Caz. She held a hand up before anyone protested. 'I know we're keeping costs low, but it's my treat. Just think of it as you're indulging me in my fantasy of pretending I'm a Bond Girl.'

'It's the Clipper – not a super yacht,' said Paul.

'It's about as close as I'm going to get. Besides, these big birthdays warrant a bit of a fuss.'

'I do love the Clipper,' said Amy. 'Always makes me feel like a tourist.'

'Which we all know is exactly what we try to be on leap days,' said Noah, bowing his head. 'I approve.'

Chapter 23

It didn't take us long to whizz up the Thames on the boat as it was only a couple of stops from where we were. We really could have walked, but Caz was right, it felt more of an event cruising down the Thames. I'd found myself standing next to her at the back of the boat, the spray hitting us as it blew up in the wind.

She wasn't ready to talk about her meeting with Nick, so we talked about her job up in Edinburgh. The one I still thought of as new even though she'd been there for five years. It was going well, as I'd expect from Caz; she was always going to be one of those people in life that succeeded. She'd always achieved what she put her mind to. But the more she talked about the world that I didn't understand, one that she obviously did, the more I got the impression she was just going through the motions of telling me about it.

The old power station, home to the Tate Modern, never failed to impress. It was always so much bigger than I remembered it to be.

'I'm glad the Edinburgh move was a good one.'

'Jury's still out on that,' she said, with a sigh.

'Workwise?'

'Oh, no workwise, best decision I ever made. And probably financially too, buying when I did.'

An unspoken look passed between us; I knew there was more to it. But now wasn't the time or the place. We were sharing a hotel room tonight, and I hoped that away from everyone else I'd get to find out what was really going on, because her sparkle was missing and it was making me worry.

'Right then, gather round,' said Paul.

'Um, can't we just walk around and soak it up?' asked Amy. 'We've all been here before.'

'Are you feeling OK?' I put my hand to her forehead. 'Since when do you want to just wander?'

'Amy's been tired lately so I thought I'd prepare something,' Paul said, reaching into his backpack and pulling out a clipboard and flipping through pages until he found the right one. 'I've been preparing for this all week.'

'Right, so that's what you've been doing when I've been trying to tackle the laundry mountain. Nice.'

'Obviously I didn't know which envelope was going to be picked, so I had to be prepared.'

'Where's first on the list?'

Paul shot me a grateful look. 'Glad to see someone is enthusiastic, Lucy. We're going this way. Onwards.'

He reminded me of the tour guides you'd see in city centres, with his backpack and his clipboard in hand; all he needed was a colourful umbrella to hold above his head and he'd be all set.

'Please, Sir, can I go to the toilet?' asked Noah, causing us all to giggle.

'Be quick, there's lots to squeeze in.'

We walked into the Turbine Hall and it was busy, as you'd expect on a Saturday, but it was the large fountain that dominated the centre. It was so high; I'd never seen anything like it.

'A whole day of art galleries,' said Caz, as we got ready to go through the bag check. 'That reminds me of when we went to Madrid.'

Amy and I winced.

'Don't mention that; I think I can still feel that hangover,' said Amy, clutching her head.

The three of us had had a long weekend there in our early twenties and after a long night drinking too much rioja, we'd headed to an art gallery with raging hangovers.

'I just remember how long it took us to walk between rooms,' I said, laughing at the memory of the slow shuffle we'd had to do.

'Thank goodness they had all those benches.'

'And a lot of toilets.' Amy shivered, her face pale. 'At least today we'll be able to enjoy the experience and walk at a decent pace.'

'That's true. And maybe I'll remember what I saw. I can't think of a single thing we saw in Madrid.' No matter how hard I wracked my brains, I could only remember the floors of the gallery. I'm not sure I could even lift my head.

'Everything was too hazy.' Caz shrugged.

'And that had nothing to do with the modern art,' said Amy.

Caz laughed, and then sighed.

'We should do another one of those trips; I think that was the last time we were away just the three of us.'

'I'd love that.'

'Me too,' said Amy, looking over at Paul. 'I've had to endure far too many weekends alone with the kids whilst he's off on stag dos. I'm pretty sure when the kids were babies he invented friends to go on weekends away. If it was just me rather than us as a couple, we'd be able to afford it.'

'We don't have to go far,' said Caz, 'and I'm sure we could get a cheap B&B or a triple hotel room to keep the costs down.'

'Sounds great,' I said, trying to ignore the kernel of anxiety starting to grow in my belly at the thought of going abroad and not being there for Mum in an emergency. I closed my eyes and tried to stop it, reminding myself of what Carol said this morning: that they were there and not to worry.

'I can just imagine it now,' said Amy, 'lie-ins in the morning, leisurely breakfasts, long lengthy dinners, a bed I can starfish in.'

Caught in her imagination, she stretched her arms out, and knocked into a passing man.

'I'm so sorry.' She turned to us, her face drawn. 'I think I got a bit carried away. It's just that it's been so long and I need a break.'

'You know that you can come to mine anytime, don't you?' I said. 'Not that it's that luxurious a break or anything.'

'And you're always welcome at mine too,' said Caz.

'Now that's much more glamourous.' Even I'd love to go there for a holiday. Caz's flat was in a converted factory with floor-to-ceiling windows; it had that industrial modern vibe that made it feel like you were staying at a hotel rather than a home.

'Don't tempt me,' said Amy.

Noah reappeared and Paul got his clipboard ready. 'Right, we're going to head to the Start gallery, which, does exactly what it does on the tin.'

'So you spent all week preparing this, and you're going to take us to exactly the place that the gallery suggests you start?'

Paul sighed. 'Don't forget I didn't know what envelope she

was going to pick; not all the attractions had such an obvious place to start. Although, I'll have you know I have a few places up my sleeve too.'

Amy folded her arms, seemingly unimpressed and I looped my arm through hers as we followed Paul.

For a while we all moved as a group round the gallery. It brought back the feeling of being on a school trip: Noah was the class clown; Amy, the sulky disinterested teenager: Caz and me the studious ones. Paul was taking his role of educator seriously and it might have been to the detriment of the laundry pile, but his tour was a good one and he'd even gone a bit above and beyond with facts that had needed more than your average Google.

'I'm impressed,' said Noah, patting Paul on the back once more. 'I didn't realise you were so good with the old art history.'

'I'm not just a pretty face.'

'It was great, thank you,' I said, still not convinced by modern art, but at least I felt that I'd learned just a little.

'It wasn't that bad,' said Amy, and she gave him a thumbs up. It might not have been the highest compliment, but judging from Paul's face exploding into a beam, it might as well have been.

'Now then, I figured that we'd have a bit of a mill about for the rest of the time. I quite fancy going to see the tanks in the new bit.'

'What have they got in?' asked Caz.

'Performance art,' said Paul.

Caz wrinkled her nose up.

'I think I need a coffee or something,' said Amy. I was surprised she hadn't jumped at it; it sounded right up her street.

'That sounds like a plan to me.' I wasn't going to question why she wasn't going; a coffee was just what I fancied.

'Shall we meet at three p.m.?' Amy led me and Caz away without waiting for an answer.

I turned over my shoulder to see Paul shout that was fine and give us a wave before they headed off.

'I think I might go for a little wander, by myself,' said Caz, pointing towards a gallery.

'You sure you want to be alone?' I asked.

She nodded. 'I'll call you in a bit. See where you are.'

Amy watched her go. 'Is she OK?'

'I don't think so. But you know Caz, she'll tell us when she's ready.'

Amy nodded. That was the thing about having long-term friends. I knew that Caz was one of those people that needed to be left alone to tell what was bothering them in their own time. Unlike Amy, who wanted to be nudged about how she felt so she could spill all that was on her mind.

'How about you?'

'How about me what?' she asked confused.

'Are you OK?' We stood back to let a large, organised group walk into the gallery with a tour guide who would have given Paul a run for his money.

She sighed.

'Perhaps a conversation for over coffee?' I suggested, peering at the signage to work out where we needed to go.

'Definitely.'

It took us a while to get our bearings without Paul and his clipboard, but we eventually found our way to the terrace bar. I dispatched Amy to get a table whilst I ordered.

'There we are,' I said, placing the tray down and handing one of the matching flat whites to her. I gasped at the view behind us of St Paul's. 'That's stunning.'

Amy looked up from her phone. 'What is?'

'The view!' I pointed behind her.

'Oh yeah, it's pretty good.'

'Pretty good? I wonder how much money you usually have to pay for a view like that.'

She laughed and shoved her phone back in her bag.

I put a chocolate tiffin in the middle too, cutting it into bitesize squares. 'Couldn't resist.'

'Too right,' she said, picking one up and eating it. 'Oh, that's amazing.'

'So,' I said, after taking a sip of coffee that was far too hot, 'what's up with you and Paul?'

She hung her head.

'You noticed that, huh?'

Unlike with Caz who you had to handle with care when addressing a problem, with Amy it was always better to jump straight in.

'Um.' I knew I had to tread carefully. In all the years that Amy and Paul had been together, I'd never heard her say a bad word against him, or at least not one that was more than the usual gripe about living with someone. It was uncharted territory and I was unsure how to navigate it. 'You just seem to be niggling at each other.'

'Not at each other, I'm niggling at him,' she said. I didn't like to point fingers, but it did seem to be coming more from Amy than it did Paul. 'I don't know, it's just that every little thing that he does at the moment annoys me and because I'm being a bit shitty it seems to have spurred him on to be more romantic and that makes him even more annoying in my eyes.'

There was so much to unpick that I didn't know where to start.

'What are you trying to say?' I scrunched up my face; none of this made any sense.

'It's hard to explain. . . It's just I've been wondering a lot about what life would be like without him. And I know it would be hard being a single mum, and it would mean splitting time with the kids, but . . . ' she shrugged ' . . . I guess I just wonder sometimes if we're together because of logistics, that it's cheaper and easier to manage the kids as a united front, than a split one.'

She was holding her cup steady in her hands and looking at me like this was a perfectly normal conversation to be having.

'You don't really think that's all there is to your relationship, do you?'

She shrugged. I was shocked into silence. Out of all the couples I knew, Amy and Paul were one of the most solid. If they fell, what hope did the rest of us have?

'But you and Paul,' I said, 'you're Amy and Paul.' I was struggling to get my head round it.

She put down her drink and sighed. 'I know, that's the problem: we're Amy and Paul and sometimes I want to be Amy again. Not a wife, not a mum, just me.'

She reached over and helped herself to another bite of tiffin.

'Oh, Ams, I had no idea that you felt like this.' I moved the plate closer to her; she needed the chocolate more than me. 'But it sounds like you're just a bit tired of your life, not of Paul. You still love him, don't you?'

She nodded. 'Of course, I love him. But it's not the same.

Like whenever the five of us are together it makes me feel like we're back at uni and it reminds me of who he used to be and who we used to be. If this was back then, Paul and I would have been sneaking off for a quickie in the toilets. I just miss all that buzz and excitement.'

'You miss being young,' I said, picking up my cup and letting the heat ground me. 'But look at the things that you do have, that you didn't have then. And I'm not talking about the kids.'

'Or the spare tyre round my midriff,' she said, with a pathetic laugh.

'We've all got one of those,' I said, smiling. 'I meant more, look at how much shared history you have. All those little in-jokes. How he's always surprising you, and he's so romantic.'

'I know. I know all that. And it makes me feel terrible that I'm moaning when I should feel so lucky to be with someone as great as Paul and for him to still want to be with me. Look at me. My hair has accidental balayage from neglecting my roots and dying it different colours from a packet.' She turned up the ends of her curls and examined them before letting them drop. 'And my face, I think I've got more spots than I did when I was a teenager, and don't get me started on the bags under my eyes.'

'Amy,' I said, shaking my head.

'But it's true, it's all true. And I'm worried that I'm with Paul because I don't think that I'd get anyone else.' She buried her head in her hands properly this time so that I could no longer see her. 'I'm a terrible person,' she whispered from underneath.

I could hear the pain in her voice and it made my heart ache for her.

'You're not a terrible person.' I reached over and squeezed her arm. 'You're just a real person. Look, I'm not exactly an expert in this. Bear in mind if we were in Regency times I would have been written off as a spinster aunt or a governess by now.'

Amy peaked out from behind her hands; I could see her smile twitching.

'But I think this is what marriage and family life is. This is probably what most people experience.'

She fully took her hands away and looked me in the eye.

'What, boredom and sticking through things because you're worried that you can't do better?'

'No, growing comfortable and complacent. It can't be fireworks and butterflies all the time.'

'But why can't it? If this was Regency times, I'd be the lady of the manor that has an affair with the gardener out of sheer boredom.'

I couldn't help but think of the TV adaption of *Lady Chatterley's Lover* that Mum had made me watch one Christmas, but it wasn't impure thoughts of Sean Bean I was having; it was the image of Andrew in his gardening gear causing me to blush.

'Then it's lucky that neither of us are in Regency times, isn't it?'

'Is it?' she said. 'A handsome rugged gardener?'

She was quiet for a moment and I felt I'd lost her to her fantasy before she jolted back to earth with a deep sigh.

'I think it sounds like you need a break,' I said. 'And not a break from Paul, a break from everything. I think you just need to be you for a little bit. Let's book that trip away, a proper girls' weekend.'

I pushed the thought of Mum out of my mind. Even if we were in Europe, we'd be able to get home quickly in an emergency.

This was the whole point of her going into a home, so that she could have that round-the-clock care, and I could start living my life again. Only life wasn't going to just start happening, I had to make it happen.

'OK, let's do it. And thank you, for not judging me.' She tilted her head and gave me a grateful look.

'Of course I wouldn't judge. Relationships are complicated.'

'Yeah. Don't I know that,' she said, taking her hair out of her messy bun and then scooping it up into an almost identical one. 'I'm sure it's just the news about Mags and Noah that's rattled us.'

'What news?' I didn't mean for my hands to jolt, but the mention of the two of them unsteadied me.

'Noah and Mags?' She finished off the last of the squares of cake and mumbled through the crumbs. 'They've split up.'

'They've what?' I pushed my cup and saucer further away from me, not trusting my hands to be steady enough to drink it. 'When?'

'About a month ago. He's moved out, he's renting a flat in Epsom.' She wiped her lips with a napkin.

'Why didn't he tell me?' I'm not sure what was more shocking, that they had split up or that neither had told me. I know that I'd grown apart from both of them and our separate friendships, but I didn't realise quite how far.

'I don't know, I thought everyone knew.' She checked over her shoulder and leaned closer. 'Look, I'm not one to gossip, but I think things haven't been right for a while and it all got a bit much for him. You know Mags has always been so ambitious, hasn't she?'

Mags' ambition was one of the things that I'd always admired in her. Noah too.

'I still can't believe it. Is that it? Divorce?'

The words caught in my throat. I'd watched them from the very first time they met, to their wedding. Divorce seemed so final.

'I think that's where it's heading. I think him actually renting a flat is a pretty big thing.'

'I can't believe it.' I tried to stitch together the clues that I'd been presented with today. The hoodie under his coat, his tired-looking eyes. His bitterness when he spoke about Mags and her work.

'I know, it was a massive shock. It hit Paul really hard. Although, we have got bets on how long it'll be before Noah moves on.'

'Moves on?'

There was that familiar pull on my heart, that one that had gripped tighter and tighter as Mags and Noah's relationship had strengthened.

'Yeah, come on, have you ever known Noah not to be in a relationship? Even when Hayley and him took that break at uni, he dated that other girl. What was her name? The one with all those earrings?'

I searched the rusty bits of my memory, trying to think of a name. In moments when I couldn't recall details easily there was that lurch in my stomach, that first hint of a worry that not remembering might be a sign that my memory would go early like Mum's. It didn't matter that the name wasn't important, that both of us could visualise the woman with the row of studs that ran from the tip to the lobe; in that moment I needed to remember it. 'Ruth?'

'Hmm, yes,' said Amy, pointing at me, and that moment

of panic yielded. 'That's the one. And then he'd barely broken up with Hayley and come back from Oz when he got together with—'

'Mags.' I started to feel a little sick, remembering what Paul had told me in Dublin about how if I hadn't pushed Noah away things could have been different. 'I guess he's just one of those people that can't be on his own.'

'Exactly, so I gave him three months; you know, a little bit longer as he's rebounding from a marriage. Paul reckons six months.'

'Six months?'

It seemed an awfully short amount of time considering how long they'd been together.

'I've eaten all the cake, let me get another.'

She was up before I could protest. I looked back out at the view but I couldn't take it in; I was too busy trying to process it all. I'd come today thinking that I was the odd one out, that everyone had their lives sorted, but the more I talked to my friends, the more I realised that none of us had it together. And for the first time in a long time, I felt a little less alone.

Chapter 24

Buoyant and caffeinated from our stop at the bar, Amy came to life a little more and we wandered a few of the newer galleries. I still didn't see what she did in the art, but it was nice to see her looking a little happier. We'd just met up with Noah and Paul on a landing, and were waiting for Caz to find us.

'Ah,' she said, 'I think I came up a different lift system.'

'Did you have some good thinking time?' I raised an eyebrow.

'Um, yeah, but actually Nick texted and asked if I could meet him for a coffee now. Do you mind if I catch up with you after?' She gestured towards the outside of the building. 'I'll be back for dinner.'

'Of course, go,' I said.

'Thanks.' She leaned over and gave me a hug before she went. Her face was full of nerves.

'It's just the four of us then,' said Paul.

I looked up at Noah and he smiled at me, but I only half smiled back. It stung that we were no longer as close as we used to be. Not close enough to be told his marriage was ending.

Paul reached over and took Amy's hand. I braced myself for the fallout if she pulled away, but she didn't; she let him take it and he looked relieved.

'Shall we head off and go and see Performance and Participant?' asked Amy, reading off her floor plan.

Noah winced and I couldn't help but smirk as that would have been my reaction too.

'Actually, I think I might go see some of the older stuff,' I said, taking a leaf out of Caz's book to have some thinking time.

'I'll come with you,' said Noah.

'Great.' I tried to add a little enthusiasm to my voice, but part of me wanted to be alone with my thoughts.

We arranged to meet them in an hour and we headed in two separate directions.

'I thought you would have gone to see performance stuff with Paul.' We drifted towards the nearest gallery.

'It isn't really my type of thing.'

'Huh, that surprises me, as Mr Gadget Man; I'd thought you'd be all over the tech stuff.'

'Well, unlike most gadgets, art doesn't come with an instruction manual.'

'Would it matter if it did? I doubt you'd read it any more than you read other instructions.'

'I'll have you know that they'd pre-drilled the holes in the wrong place.'

I was never going to let him live down the time he built a wardrobe for me in my first flat in London.

'Uh-huh. And they'd made it so the door hung wonkily. I bet even after that experience you still don't read them.'

'You know me so well.' He laughed.

Not well enough, I silently added in my head.

'So what do we have here?' he said, leaning over to read the text panel. 'Dada. What's that?'

'No clue.' I shrugged back.

We walked around the exhibit to what looked like an old-fashioned urinal mounted on a plinth. I stared at it, tilted my head, and moved slightly to examine it on an angle, just in case.

'Any ideas?' asked Noah.

We stood back to let other people look, watching as another couple whispered and pointed at it, nodding their heads in agreement of their clever observations.

I couldn't help but get the giggles and Noah did too.

'I don't get it,' I whispered.

'Me neither,' he said, with relief. 'Oh, thank god, I thought it was just me that was a philistine.'

'No, me too. If I'm honest, I think that's a bit of an anti-climax.'

'Much like life in general,' he said.

It was far from the glass-is-half-full Noah that I was used to.

'That's the kind of thing I'd say.'

'It's true though, isn't it? I mean, look at us now. We're almost forty.'

'What, we're really not. We're only thirty-six, still mid-thirties.'

'Approaching late thirties.'

We walked out of the gallery we'd not long entered, fighting against the heavy tide of visitors who hopefully would get it more than us.

'We could always cling on to the fact that technically we're only nine,' I said.

'But if you were really nine, you'd have to go through the teenage years again.' He shuddered.

'I can't imagine you as a teenager.'

'What do you mean? I was practically a teenager when we met.' He furrowed his brows and I noticed there was a hint of salt and pepper creeping into the sides of his hairline.

'You were twenty.'

'That day, but the day before I'd been nineteen.'

'Well, I guess that's true. I meant like a fifteen year old.'

He nodded. 'I know what you mean. But, to be honest, although I would have liked to have thought I was far more grown up and sophisticated when I met you, I was probably just as wildly immature.'

'You say that like you've grown up now?'

'Oh no, I'm still wildly immature. I've just got a new level of cynicism to go with it,' he said, shoving his hands into his hoodie pocket.

'Nice addition.'

'I thought so.'

We walked around a few of the galleries mostly in muted silence, but we drifted around, unable to connect with the art, and judging by our stilted conversation, unable to connect with each other either.

We covered the very basics – how my mum was; what we were doing workwise – but all the while it felt like we were both ignoring the elephant in the room. In the end we fell back into the silence until we walked into the Rothko room. Instantly it was as if the light had been sucked out.

'Fuck,' whispered Noah. 'This is moody.'

We shuffled into the space and I walked around, trying to take in the paintings. They were hung close together and their block colour of maroons and black created an atmosphere unlike anything I'd ever experienced in a gallery before. There was a reverent silence in the room, as if everyone could feel what I did.

I sat on the wooden bench in the centre of the room and gazed at the painting in front of me. The colour seemed to grow in intensity the more that I stared at it.

'I think I get this,' said Noah, as he sat down next to me on the other side of the bench so that he was facing the opposite way. We looked at each other and, in that split second, I felt a jolt.

'Me too.' I turned back to the painting in front of me, getting lost in the colour.

I don't know how long we sat in those spots; it was one of those times in your life where it could be seconds or it could be hours. Eventually the room started to fill up with a group of people talking loudly and the spell was broken.

'Do you want to get some air?' Noah tugged at the collar of his hoodie.

I nodded. I needed it too. 'Did you want to go to the viewing platform?'

'Can we just go all the way outside?' he said, picking up the pace towards the stairs. 'That was so intense.'

'Sure.' We started down the stairs. We might have left the room but its effect hadn't left me. 'I had no idea art could make you feel like that.'

'Me neither. Do you think that means we got it?' Noah puffed his chest out a little and gave a bit of fake swagger.

'Do you know, I think we did? I could have stayed looking at that all day.'

Noah shook his head. 'I don't know if I could. It felt like I was looking into my soul on a dark day and I'm doing too much of that at the moment as it is.'

A tone crept into his voice and I could hear the pain. I didn't want to tell him that I knew about Mags; I didn't want him to feel like we'd been gossiping behind his back. But I wanted him to know I was there for him. I reached out my fingers to find his, and I took hold of his hand. He squeezed mine back and neither of us acknowledged it. We walked out like it was a perfectly normal thing to do. And it felt like it was.

Chapter 25

Outside we started to slowly walk towards the river. It was still cloudy but it felt warmer. I was busy unwrapping the snood around my neck when Noah moved me aside to allow a group to pass. The group members were all wearing masks as they followed their tour leader inside.

'Does it freak you out that they're wearing masks?' I said, taking a wider berth.

'I think that it's probably more cultural,' said Noah. 'But yeah, I have noticed that I've moved away from people that have them on the Tube a bit more, just in case they're wearing them because they've been in contact with someone rather than as a precaution.'

I thought about what Carol had said at the home and tried not to let the fear get hold of me.

'This feels better,' said Noah. It was almost as busy outside the galleries as it was inside, but I knew what he meant: it was nice to be out in the open. 'I feel like I can breathe again.'

'Those paintings really did a number on you, didn't they?'

'Yeah, I've seen them in books, but never in person. Amazing.'

I nodded. They were definitely my favourite things I'd seen on our visit.

'You know, I'm working near here now,' he said, walking

along and pointing in the general direction. 'Just past London Bridge.'

'That's a nice place to be. Close to Borough Market.'

'Too close sometimes, far too much temptation,' he said with a laugh. 'But sometimes I run down here on my lunch break.'

'Impressive.'

'Well, when I say sometimes, I mean I've done it twice.'

I laughed.

'Still more impressive than me. I tell myself every week I'm going to go out for a lunchtime walk, and I'm lucky if I even leave my desk.'

'Sounds familiar.'

We walked along until we reached the railing and we stopped to take in the view. Although it was widely different from the view upstairs in the bar, it was still impressive in its own right.

'What's the story with Caz and Nick?' he asked, leaning his back on the railings.

'I'm not sure there is one.' I'd of course been hoping there would be. I always liked him. 'But I'm glad she's at least talking to him; it's always good to get things off your chest.'

'Speaking of getting things off your chest,' said Noah, taking a deep breath. 'I'm not sure if you've already heard . . . '

He turned and looked at me, and there was a strain on his face as if he didn't know how to finish the sentence. I nodded my head and automatically it tilted to the side.

'Amy told me, about you and Mags.'

He let out another deep breath and looked down along the river.

'I thought she would have done.'

It was getting colder, the chill starting to bite around us, but it didn't feel like the type of conversation to interrupt to go somewhere warmer.

'I was going to tell you, you know this morning, when you asked where she was.'

'Why didn't you?'

He shrugged and shoved his hands in his hoodie pocket.

'I don't know really' – he paused and I looked away – 'and maybe because it didn't feel like the right time to talk about it on our birthday. I didn't want to bring us down.'

'Come on, why break the habit of a lifetime? Isn't that our thing, analysing why we're unhappy on our big birthdays?' I said, thinking back to our phone call four years ago. Mum had seemed so distant then but I'd had no idea how much further she'd go.

'Analysing all the decisions we got wrong.' He looked up and into my eyes.

I stared back. The outside of the gallery was busy but I didn't see anyone else.

'Noah.' The words barely came out of my mouth. I didn't know what to say.

A large family group walked past, two of the children tugging at each other's arms in a fight and their mum stepping in to separate them.

We watched them go and then I turned back to him.

'I'm sorry, for what it's worth, about you and Mags.'

'Thanks,' he said, nodding. 'Things weren't great for a while, so it's kind of for the best.'

'Are you sure you just weren't working too hard? You know, not making time for each other?'

They'd always seemed like such a slick couple. Not the

homely, bickering type like Amy and Paul. Just two people on the same page.

'I think it was the opposite, throwing ourselves into the work to ignore what was going on.'

I turned to him and he bit his lip.

'I guess I've known, for a long time, maybe even since before we were married, that it wasn't right.'

'Then why did it take you so long to figure it out?'

'I don't know,' he said, with a simple shrug. 'Because I wanted to be who Mags saw when she looked at me.'

'And what did she see?'

'Someone confident. Someone that was going places. She's been my biggest cheerleader; she helped me rebuild my life when I came back from Australia and I loved it. You know Mags, you know how great she makes everyone feel. And she could have picked anyone to date, and she picked me.'

I knew exactly what he was talking about. She was one of those people that always built you up. Always believed in you.

'I've just been thinking so much lately about after I graduated, when I worked for that refugee charity, how I was making a difference. And I thought about my life now and I can't remember the last time I did any good for anyone.'

'I'm sure that's true for most of us.'

'Um, hello, you gave up your whole life in London to take care of your mum. You put someone else before yourself without even thinking. It's you all over.'

I closed my eyes a little. I know that he was saying his words to be nice, but they stung.

'Hey, why are you crying?' he asked.

I dabbed at my eyes. 'I'm not crying.'

'Looks like it,' he said, raising a sympathetic eyebrow.

'It's just . . . ' I searched for how to explain my emotions. 'You're making me sound like some kind of saint.'

'But you almost are. Not everyone moves in with their mum to look after them. I'm sure you could have put her in a home before now.'

'I know I could have and I think that's what hurts because maybe I should have. I think about it a lot; that maybe that wasn't me being selfless. Maybe it was me being selfish.'

'How could you moving back with your mum, possibly be selfish?' Noah screwed up his face in confusion.

I looked around for a free concrete bench. I motioned to him and we headed over to sit down. I pulled down my coat and popped my hands into my sleeves to fight the cold.

'I remember what she was like before the divorce. How she was when I was growing up and she was so . . . alive. All sparkly and magical. She had this huge smile on her face, most of the time, or at least she did when she was around me. She'd make us picnics to have on the carpet on rainy days and the day after my birthdays she'd let me have leftover cake for breakfast.' I sighed. Tears were starting to burn at my eyes but if I gave in to them, it would open the floodgates. 'And even when Dad left, when she hit rock bottom, she picked herself up and dusted herself down. Still smiling. Always making the best of things. And I don't know, I kept her at home for so long because of those rare moments where she smiled like that again. When I saw snippets of who she used to be.' I shook my head. 'God, this sounds so pathetic.'

'It doesn't at all,' said Noah, seriousness in his voice.

A tear rolled down my cheek and I wiped it away quickly, trying to stop others from doing the same.

'Weren't you supposed to be the one having a moment?' I said, trying to force a smile.

I held my breath, a pain burning in my chest. I knew I was powerless to stop the tears.

'Hey, come here,' said Noah, pulling me into him. My lip was starting to wobble and the tears were falling thick and fast. I could feel the puddle I was making on Noah's coat but I didn't want to move anywhere.

He stroked my hair and it only made me cry harder.

'I'm sorry,' I whispered.

'Sshh,' he murmured back.

It was like being in the gallery where time stood still. All I could do was cry, and when the tears gave way to the kind of silent sobs that took over my body, I pulled back and wiped my eyes.

'I'm sorry, I don't know where that came from.'

'I do,' he said, pulling out what looked like napkins from a fast-food restaurant from his pocket. I took them and wiped my eyes anyway. 'You've been holding all this in for years. And it's not selfish to want your mum back. I can't imagine how hard it's been to lose her like you have.'

I nodded and scrunched up the tear-stained napkin. 'It hasn't been the best time. And now that I'm back on my own again, it's like I don't even know who I am anymore. I've been caring for Mum for so long.'

'Do you think that's why you haven't really let her go?'

I took a deep breath, rolling my lip over to bite it, the pain grounding me.

'Maybe.' I looked up at the bare branches of the trees above us. 'But that's what's so scary. I don't know who I am if I'm not looking after her. I think I've forgotten who I was.'

'If it makes you feel better, I don't remember who I really am either.'

'You,' I almost spluttered in shock.

'Yeah, me.' He ran his hands through his hair and looked out towards the river. 'I spent New Year skiing, and we were in a bar in the middle of the afternoon halfway up a mountain. Beats were pumping out of the speakers and everyone was there drinking Aperol Spritzes in the sun, and there were these little wagons going over our heads on pulley systems taking magnums of champagne to the groups in the corners and it just hit me: what was I doing there?'

'Yeah, sounds truly awful,' I said, with heavy sarcasm.

'I know, I sound like a dick. I get that. But everywhere I looked there was just so much money being spent and it made me feel sick. Like it hit me that this was our life. Holidays in the Maldives, skiing in the three valleys, the house in Surrey.' He looked at me and there wasn't a hint of a smile on his face. 'I know that I'm living a dream life, and I sound so spoilt, but it's not my dream. It was never my dream.'

For years I've thought of them living in their house in the Surrey Hills with their five bedrooms all with ensuites and I've envied them so much.

'So where are you now?'

'I'm staying in a flat in Epsom.' He kicked out his legs in front of him and crossed his feet at his ankles. 'It's all grey, grey walls, grey furniture. and it's tiny. I mean, it's the most prison-like place I've ever lived, but weirdly I just feel free.'

I tried to picture what Noah was describing, but in my head I kept seeing him in his Instagrammable house he'd left behind.

'So that's it? You and Mags are finished?'

'It was supposed to be a trial separation, but . . . ' he trailed off.

'Is she OK?' I tried to think of the last time I'd seen Mags without Noah, and when it was that we'd stopped being proper friends in our own right. Years ago I would have had this conversation with her too, but we no longer had heart-to-hearts.

He nodded his head. 'Yeah, she is. As much as I'd love to flatter my ego that she wasn't, I think she's doing fine. She seemed more worried about how it would look to our friends, or her friends, as most of the people we hang out with are. It's a bit of a sad state of affairs, isn't it? The only thing she was bothered about in the break-up was the optics.'

'Deliberate pun?' I thought of Mags' glasses business.

'Unintentional. But I wish I'd been clever enough to think of it. I love a good pun.'

I was about to laugh, before the reality of it all sunk in.

'I'm sorry, Noah.'

'Thanks.' He turned and smiled at me, and I could see now there was a sadness there. 'Fuck, do you think we're ever going to have a birthday where we have a good day?'

'What, you mean where we don't do soul searching or drop an emotional bombshell on each other?'

He laughed and looked out at the river. He sat up a little straighter and I followed his gaze to the seagull waddling towards us.

'What's with you?' I laughed at how much he was squirming.

'They freak me out.'

'What do? Seagulls?'

I thought there was something quite cute about them, but the way Noah was edging up straighter, and tucking his outstretched legs in closer towards him, he didn't feel the same.

'Yeah, I think I read something in the *Metro* once about someone who got attacked by one.'

I looked at the seagull, which was tiny compared to us.

'Oh my god, all that crap you gave me when we went to the Dead Zoo.' I put my hands on my hips in mock annoyance.

'Yeah, but that was different.'

'Why? You've got an irrational fear of seagulls.'

'It's not irrational. People get bitten by them, plus, you thought taxidermy animals were going to come back to life. It's hardly the same thing.'

I started to giggle and he joined in. I hadn't meant to laugh as hard as I did, but it was like the tears – once I started, I couldn't stop.

I felt a little bit guilty to lose it at a time when he'd been bearing his soul.

'Sorry, I didn't mean to laugh so hard, it's just . . . I guess I needed that.'

'I'm glad that my seagull anxiety came in handy for once.'

We watched as the gull flew onto the balustrade and looked out at the river.

'Is it seagulls that mate for life?' he asked. 'I can never remember if it's them or swans. Which, in case you're wondering, are another bird that I can't stand.'

'Swans?' I shook my head. 'How can you hate them too? But yeah, I think it must be swans or penguins. Penguins mate for life.'

I tried to remember the bits of *Planet Earth* I'd watched.

'Huh.'

'Imagine that, knowing that when you find your one person, that's you for life. They're lucky.'

Noah turned his head towards me.

'Maybe they're not lucky; maybe they just act on their feelings.'

Our eyes locked and I didn't need to ask him what he meant; I could see it written all over his face.

'Noah.' I struggled to speak; the air felt like it had been squeezed out of me. He reached out and took my hand, and I studied our entwined fingers. I turned and saw the look Noah had in his eyes, and before I could say another word, he leaned in to kiss me.

He was so close my whole body could feel him. Our lips brushed together and I held out my trembling hand and rested it on his chest, hoping I didn't regret pushing him away this time as much as I had the last.

'You can't do that,' I said, my voice cracking. My whole body ached for him, trying to rebel against what my brain was saying. This time he didn't pull away and pretend it hadn't happened. This time he had to be able to see that I wanted him too.

'But you feel it, right?'

I looked away.

'It's not fair, Noah.'

'Come on, Lucy, there's always been this thing between us. Tell me that I haven't imagined it.'

I closed my eyes and sighed, my jaw starting to harden. I opened my eyes and looked at him again. 'Noah, you can't do this now. You and Mags.' I shook my head. 'This is like last time, in that club. You'd just broken up with Hayley. What am I? The rebound? That person that's always there when you're feeling, what was it, "lonely and horny".'

I stood up, my legs unsteady. Anger coursing through my veins.

'Luce, it's not like that. Believe me.' Noah went to grab my arm but I moved it away from him.

'Isn't it? Amy was right, you've never been on your own, but that doesn't mean you can keep messing with my feelings when you are.'

'What do you mean, keep messing with your feelings? You've never had feelings for me.'

Our voices were raised now, and I was aware that people were looking at us. But I didn't care.

'I liked you, Noah. When you came back from Oz. I pushed you away because I didn't want our first kiss to be somewhere like that. I wanted it to be special, and . . . ' I blinked, my eyes wet with fresh tears. 'I sound like such a moron, but I pushed you away because I wanted more. And then you told me you'd only done it because you'd been lonely.'

'But that's not—' His voice was softer, his eyes searching mine.

'No matter what you thought then, that's exactly what it was and I think it's no different now.'

My voice cracked at almost every word, because part of me wanted to kiss him, the part of me that had always wanted to kiss him. But my heart was hardening, going into protection mode.

'How can you stand there and tell me what I did and didn't feel? And you're wrong. I can be on my own; kissing you has nothing to do with that.'

I thought of what Amy had said earlier about how Noah jumped from one relationship to the next. I didn't want to be with someone who was with me until something better came along.

'Doesn't it? Even Amy and Paul have got bets on how soon it'll be before you have a new girlfriend.'

'Have they now?' he said, through gritted teeth.

I regretted it as soon as I said it; I hadn't wanted to get them involved. But I wasn't any less angry about him trying to kiss me.

'I shouldn't have said that. Look, I get it, Noah, I really do. You've been through this massive life change, and everything feels scary and you feel lost. But jumping into something else isn't the answer, not when you're playing with other people's emotions.'

'Playing with other people's emotions? Is that what you think I'm doing?'

'I do. If you did like me, like you think you do, you wouldn't have got together with Mags, or engaged to her in Dublin, let alone married her. And how do I know that you're not going to go back to her? You said that it was a temporary separation.'

'That's how it started—'

'But is that how it ended? Are you sure you're not just keeping your options open?'

'Right.' He nodded his head. 'Well, if we're dishing out home truths, maybe I do jump into things too quickly but at least I'm not afraid of letting myself fall in love, unlike you.'

'Unlike me?' I felt my voice get that little bit louder. 'What does that even mean?'

'It means that you never put yourself out there. You've always dated people who deep down you knew were never good enough for you, and that you didn't really like so you knew they'd never work out.'

'Oh, really? Is that what I've done, Mr I took one psychology course at university?'

'Yeah, it is.'

'Andrew, the guy I'm dating now, is really fucking nice.'

'Then where is he?' he half-shouted, arms out wide. 'If he's so great and you like him so much, why didn't you invite him to your one-in-four birthday? I'll tell you why: because you're keeping him at arm's-length and away from your heart. You're too scared that you'll fall in love and have your heart broken like your mum did when your dad walked out.'

Tears were stinging at my eyes, only there were none left to fall; instead I was left with a burning sensation.

'So, I'm sorry, if you think that I give my heart away too gladly, but I'd rather be that way than never give it away like you.'

I felt winded; it was as if he'd punched me in the gut.

We stared hard into each other's eyes, neither wanting to move, but eventually he shook his head.

'Tell the others I've gone home.'

'Fine,' I snapped as he walked away.

I watched him go, my whole body shaking. I'd never argued with Noah, or at least nothing like this before. I watched him get smaller and smaller, my fists forming tighter and tighter balls until they ached. All the while I replayed his words over in my head. I didn't know what was worse, the fact that he'd said it, or the fact that the words might be true.

Chapter 26

Sunday 1ˢᵗ March 2020

At first, after my argument with Noah, I'd thought that he'd come back, but as the day rolled into evening, I realised he wasn't going to. Caz's coffee had gone well with Nick and whilst there wasn't some grand reunion, I got the impression that the door that was once shut had been left open a tiny bit. Luckily it was enough to deflect from the fact that Noah had gone and wasn't coming back.

Unlike the other times when I'd regretted what could have happened, this time I might have been angry that Noah had tried, but I was angrier at myself for imagining for all these years that there was something real between us. I just wished that I hadn't been quite so nasty to him.

But despite feeling sorry for myself, it had done me good to go up to London and stay over. It was a small step in getting back on with my life; I needed to see more of my friends and start living again. There was even a part of me that thought Noah had been a tiny bit right, that I never really put myself out there for fear of getting hurt.

I walked into Mum's care home and said hello to Carol who was sitting as usual behind the front desk.

'I thought you were going away.'

'I did. I had twenty-four hours in London, and believe me, it feels like a lifetime.'

She shook her head. 'Well, you'll be pleased to know that she was fine. Her friend's popped in, and that seems to be cheering her up.'

'Her friend?'

Carol pointed to the visitors' book and I ran my finger down to see Dad's name.

I muttered under my breath and hurried along to her room, hoping that she wasn't too rattled. I knew that he'd visited with me before, but I couldn't believe he'd come alone.

I braced myself for what I was about to find. It didn't take much to get Mum agitated, and that agitation could turn so easily into anger or her getting inconsolable. I headed down the corridor to her and I heard the sound of her tinkling laughter before I reached the room. It caught me off-guard and I froze.

It was the high-pitched tinkling sound that was a precursor to a cackle, full-bodied and genuine, nothing out of politeness. It sent chills all over my body and I wondered when I'd last heard it. I heard Dad's laughter echo round the room to join in and if I closed my eyes, it reminded me of when I was little.

I didn't know what was going on, but I didn't want to disturb it. I crept back along the corridor and took a seat in the reception area.

'Everything OK, love?' asked Carol, still tapping away on her keys.

'Yeah, I just thought I'd let her and Dad talk alone.'

'Oh, that's your dad, is it?' She nodded. 'Nice of him to come.'

'Hmm, yeah.'

I was confused. He'd sent me the happy birthday text, but he hadn't mentioned that he was coming. I pulled out my phone and saw that I had a text message from Amy.

Amy

I am NEVER drinking shots again . . . but hangover aside, brilliant night last night. And thank you for making me spend time with my husband. Turns out he's not so bad after all, even if he does stack the dishwasher wrong EVERY. SINGLE. DAY. Xx

Me

It was an excellent night. Thanks so much. Needed it more than I realised. Here's to the next one in four years . . .

Amy

Bloody hell, I hope we see you before then.

Me

Just kidding. You will. I think you're going to get sick of seeing me you'll see me so much this year.

Amy

Impossible.

(That we'd get sick of you!) Can't wait xxxxxxxxxxxxxxxxxx

'Lucy.' I looked up from my phone and saw my dad standing in front of me.

He took the coat hanging over his arm, and slipped it on.

'Hey.'

'You,' he said, pointing at me like I was a naughty child, 'are supposed to be away.'

'I was, I just got back.'

He nodded, looking over his shoulder at Carol before turning back at me.

'Want to walk me to my car?'

I stood up and followed him, the jet of heat over the door hitting me and making the outside seem even colder.

'Did you have a good time? Happy birthday, by the way.'

'Yes, and thank you.'

'We've got a present at ours for you; I should have known you'd be here and brought it.'

'It's fine. I was thinking I should pop round and see you guys soon.'

We reached his car and stood awkwardly outside.

'Have you been to see her, on other occasions?'

He slipped his hands in his pockets and shook his head.

'No, I haven't seen her since that day with you, last year. I just thought that I'd come because I thought you were away and I know you were worried. I hoped that if I came, it might help you to know that she'd be OK, without you.'

'Mum seemed to approve. She was laughing.'

'She didn't know who I was.' He looked up to the sky and I wondered if he was going to cry. My dad didn't show emotions, he always made awkward jokes to avoid them, but here he was. 'She thought I was a stranger, and it reminded me of how she was when I first met her. She was so sharp, and so funny. And I guess I forgot that since . . . all that happened with Tania and the divorce.'

I put my arm on Dad's shoulder.

'I get it. She seemed happy to see you.'

'I know that you saw our marriage break down and I know you bore the brunt of it all. But when you were younger, we were happy. We were happy for a long time. We used to get on well.'

Dad opened the passenger door of his car and motioned for me to get in.

'It's brass monkeys out there.'

'Tell me about it.'

The car wasn't that much warmer than standing outside, but at least it was more comfortable.

'I'm sorry I didn't tell you I was coming.' He had hold of the steering wheel and was looking straight ahead despite the fact the engine was off and we weren't going anywhere. 'I didn't know how to explain it to you. It doesn't make much sense to me either. This was the woman who, for the past twenty years, I haven't been able to be in the same room with.'

'The woman that you once loved.'

He turned to look at me, and I could see the emotion in his eyes.

'Exactly.'

'Does Tania know?'

'Yeah.' He bit his lip. 'I thought she might be a bit funny about it, but I think she understands and I know she's always felt almost as guilty as I did about how I left your mum. I'm sorry I didn't tell you. It just felt like something I needed to do and I thought you'd be cross.'

'Why would I be cross?'

'I don't know, because it's me.'

'In some ways it makes it easier for me, to know that I'm not doing this alone.'

'Oh, Lucy. You never had to do this alone. Me and your mum, I still care about her, and I care about you, more than I've probably ever let you know. And if I can help then I will.'

I didn't know if it was his time seeing Mum and it being emotional, but Dad's face looked worn and lined and I had that ripple wash over me that I'd spent so long worrying about Mum that I hadn't ever stopped to think that one day I'd lose him too.

I reached over and took his hand.

'Thanks, Dad.'

He squeezed my hand back. 'I think I've got an eyelash in my eye,' he said, with a laugh and cough as he poked at his eye. He was back to being the joker, but he'd changed in my eyes.

When he left I headed back over towards the care home entrance, not caring that a tear had trickled down my face. It only made me more determined to do what I'd said to Noah. That I'd figure out my life for me, stop hiding behind excuses and start to live.

I waved as Dad passed as he drove away, and I pulled out my phone and typed:

Lucy to Andrew
I'm in – for July! Get that wetsuit and long hair ready 😊

WhatsApp messages – Uni group: March 18th 2020
Amy:
Fuck, they've just closed the schools. And there was me excited about Paul working from home. Now I'm going to have to home-school. Not sure we have enough wine.

Paul
Currently feel like I'm solving one of the kids' maths puzzles. How many bottles of wine do you need to see out home-schooling in a pandemic????

Noah
Yeah, sod the toilet roll. I've been panic buying gin. And in answer to the maths question – deffo more than you think.

Paul
More importantly, Lucy, are you able to visit your mum?

Lucy
No – will text later, we're trying to sort her out using FaceTime

Noah
Shit, Luce, sorry, that's really awful. Shout if you need help.

WhatsApp message – Mags to Lucy: April 2020
You're such a sweetie checking in on me. Things are mental at the moment, business is booming and the supply chain is grinding to a halt. And yes, I'm holding up OK. Better to have loved and lost and all that. Hope you're OK, and your mum? Xx

Text message – Andrew to Lucy: May 2020
Slight public service announcement: any chance you could not wear those dungarees to the allotment? Every time they slip off your shoulder when you bend down . . . it makes this whole two metre thing pretty tricky to observe. Not to mention I almost deadheaded an artichoke by accident.

Zoom chat – Paul's weekly quiz: June 2020

Noah is the host:

Noah: Hey, can you hear me?

Lucy: Yes. But I can't see you. Ah, there you are. Hi.

Noah: Hi! [waves]

Lucy: Hi . . .

Noah: Hi. Where are the others?

Lucy: I just got a text from Caz. She and Nick are wine tasting with his work. Virtually, of course.

Noah: I love that they're locked down together.

Lucy: Always the hopeless romantic.

Noah: Would you expect anything less . . . And I guess Paul and Amy are running late?

Lucy: Yep, ah, there's a message. They'll be here in five.

Noah: Right . . . So how are you?

Lucy: Good. You?

Noah: Good.

Lucy: I um—

Noah: Did you—

[Both laugh awkwardly]

Lucy: You go.

Noah: No, you. Really.

Lucy: I was just going to ask how you really were.

Noah: Pretty shit. How about you?

Lucy: Bit better than that.

Noah: I don't think I picked the best time to leave my wife, to be honest. It's not a great time to be living alone.

Lucy: Yeah. I can't imagine. Can you not bubble up with someone?

Noah: Mags suggested I came back but I thought it would confuse things. Instead, we've started divorce proceedings.

Lucy: Oh, Noah. I'm sorry you couldn't work it out.

Noah: At least now I've got a clean break. And now I've got time to be alone. If there was ever a time for me to get to know myself, being stuck alone in a global pandemic is probably it, right?

Lucy: I guess so. So what have you learned so far?

Noah: That I'm shit at making banana bread, and I don't like drinking alone.

Lucy: I tried to make a sourdough starter, but decided it used so much flour to feed it so now I just make pancakes instead.

Noah: Pancakes. Suddenly that bubbling up doesn't sound so bad.

Lucy: Too bad I'm with my dad and Tania.

Noah: How's that going?

Lucy: Better than being alone. Sorry, no offence.

Noah: None taken. My parents tried to get me to go to theirs. And Paul and Amy, of course – I think they wanted a live-in babysitter – but it's good for me. I've never lived on my own and it's kind of liberating.

Paul and Amy have joined.

Amy: Oh my god, sorry guys. Patrick threw an almighty strop because we wouldn't let him sleep in his den and then they all kicked off and—

Paul: Here's your drink. How are we all?

Lucy: Good, thanks.

Noah: Yeah, good.

Paul:

Great stuff, great stuff. Now have I found the quiz for you.

WhatsApp messages – Amy to Lucy: January 2021
Amy:

I can't do this again. Not another bloody lockdown. I'm not strong enough for home-schooling again. Are you going to your dad's, or can I live with you????

Lucy:

Actually Andrew's moving in this time. Guess it's one way to test a relationship!

Amy:

Yes, at least something good's coming out of all this!

WhatsApp messages – Girls: April 2021
Caz:

Some news . . . Nick and I just got married. Just the two of us! Sorry, couldn't face the whole Zoom wedding thing but just know if these were normal times you'd have all been with us. We're going to have the mother of all parties for this when we can.

Lucy:

You guys!! You melt my heart. I'm so happy for you. Although you better have that party because there's no way we're not celebrating this.

WhatsApp messages – Lucy /Amy: May 2021

Lucy:

I've just had Mum over to sit in the garden for tea!!!!!!

Amy:

That's amazing!!!!!

Lucy:

She of course flirted with Andrew. But we'll gloss over that . . .

WhatsApp messages – Uni group: November 2021

Amy:

So we've been trying to work out a plan for a Christmas do. We're going to borrow a gazebo from Paul's parents. We figure we could fire up the BBQ and all bring blankets?

Lucy, will you be bringing Andrew?? And Noah, would you have a plus one? Just trying to work out if we'll be able to fit all the chairs in the gazebo or if we need to buy anything bigger.

Paul:

We're not buying anything bigger. Couples can sit on each other's laps.

Noah:

No plus one. Still just me.

Lucy:

Hiya – I think it sounds great. Yes, Andrew will be coming, but it may have to be earlier rather than later in December as will be quarantining so I can see Mum on Christmas Day.

WhatsApp messages – Uni group: December 2021
Amy:

Paul and I were talking about the Christmas do and I really don't think it's a good idea, as much as I'd love to see you all. Thought perhaps we could do an online escape room or online gin tasting? Xxxx

WhatsApp messages – Uni group: August 2022
Noah:

Are we all on for next weekend? I've booked a table in the garden. Be there or be square.

Noah:

Yes, I know. I read that back. I've been spending way too much time on my own. See you next week.

Lucy:

Hey – just checking that you've booked Andrew in too?

Noah:

Yep, he's officially part of the group.

WhatsApp messages – Girls: September 2022
Amy:

Right, now that things are opening up properly, I'm thinking we're long overdue a girls' holiday. Think of it as a belated hen do for Caz. I'm thinking Ibiza?

Caz:

Love that for us, but might have to be a bit closer to home and also might have to be a bit more tame. Baby Brady due in six months' time.

Amy:

What??????!!!! Yes, welcome to the mum gang. I am ridiculously excited. Scratch Ibiza, let's go all-out pampering. Although no spa as I know they're tricky in pregnancy. But I'm thinking nice hotel, nice pool, nice food.

Lucy:

Congrats, Caz, so happy for you, and closer to home sounds good to me! x

WhatsApp messages – Uni group: March 2023

Lucy:

Hey guys, thanks for the birthday love. Rome was great or at least the little bits I saw. So nice to be abroad again though! I was wondering if you were all free for the coronation? We could do a mini garden party?

Amy:

Count me in. I'll do whatever, just want to see your beautiful faces.

Noah:

I'm afraid I'm not going to make it. I'm going to be in (drum roll) somewhere in south America.

Amy:

What??? Holiday?

Noah:

More like midlife crisis gap year.

Amy:

You're quitting your job?

Noah:

Leave/unpaid leave/remote-working combo – hybrid working. Welcome to the future.

Caz:

Jealous!!! Lu – count us in for the garden party xx

WhatsApp messages – Noah/Lucy: May 2023
Noah:

Hope the party went well. Here's me watching the coronation at this restaurant. And yes, that is a taxidermy anaconda. And yes, his eyes pretty much freaked me out for the whole meal. Have a good one x

Lucy:

Thanks for the photo of nightmares (the snake, not you, although that beard . . .)

Noah:

I've found my inner hipster, many years too late.

Text – Lucy to Andrew: June 2023
Lucy:

Sorry about last night. I hate it when we fight. Are you still seeing Jack after work? If not, we could do a make-up dinner? x

WhatsApp message – Lucy to Mags: August 2023

I can't believe you're selling the company! What's next on the agenda? I know you'll have another big idea in the pipeline.

I'm OK, thanks. Yes, you're right, it's been far too long. Andrew doesn't agree with horse racing, but I could come on my own? I'm excited to meet Rupert; it sounds like everything is going so well for you. Also, Mum's doing OK. Or at least as OK as she really can. She's content in the home and most of the time she's fine with me visiting. Let's set up a Doodle with dates to get something planned.

WhatsApp voice message – Caz to Lucy: September 2023

I've just listened to your message, and oh Lucy. I'm so sorry sweetie, break-ups are pretty shit even when they are 'conscious uncoupling's. How are you holding up? It's great that you and Andrew were on the same page with things, but I'm guessing that it still hurts? Let me know if you want me to come and stay, or if you want to come here? We're here for you xx

WhatsApp messages – Noah/Lucy: September 2023
Noah:
I just heard about Andrew. Are you OK? Do you need me to find some photos of taxidermy otters to cheer you up?

Noah:
Not sure why otters. But even taxidermy otters must be cute, right?

Lucy:

I'm OK, thanks.

Lucy:

I mean that I'm both OK, and absolutely no taxidermy pics.

Noah:

But I went out of my way to find this one [taxidermy otter dressed in a dress]

Lucy:

There's something wrong with you. But thank you, I needed a laugh.

WhatsApp messages – Noah/Lucy: December 2023

Lucy:

Saw this and thought of you. [Video of a flock of seagulls trying to steal a person's fish and chips]

Noah:

Is that how it is? [photo of a sloth] This sloth is real – I actually thought it was stuffed but it blinked.

Lucy:

Maybe it is stuffed. I told you that they could come to life.

Noah:

Now I'm just freaked out. Have confirmed with park ranger, it is 100% living and breathing.

Lucy:

Costa Rica treating you well?

Noah:

It's awesome. It'll be a hard place to leave.

Lucy:

I bet.

Noah:

Was hoping you might say you missed me.

Lucy:

I'd miss the animal pics more if you came back.

Noah:

Charming.

Lucy:

Always.

WhatsApp Voice message – Lucy/Noah: December 2023

Lucy:

Just wanted to wish you a merry Christmas, wherever you are now. Are you still in Costa Rica or did you make it down to Peru? Did Paul say that was the plan? Is it guinea pig for Christmas lunch? Not sure I'd fancy that. Although, to be honest, anything would be better than the turkey Dad just cooked. He went so over the top about making sure it was properly cooked that it was almost like eating charcoal. I'm rambling, that would be the Baileys. Merry Christmas.

Email – Girls: January 2024
Subject: Suggested Itinerary for NYC
From Amy:
Right, ladies, be prepared
Day 1 – 26th Feb – Arrive, cocktails and out / go to sleep and get up early
Day 2 – 27th Feb – Sightseeing – See Everything
Day 3 – 28th Feb – Shopping – Buy Everything
Day 4 – 29th Feb – Lucy's Birthday! (See and buy what we missed on day 2/3)
Day 5 –1st March – Fly home 😵
Did I miss anything?????? NYC BABY!!!!!!!!!!!!

PART SIX

2024

Chapter 27

Wednesday 28th February 2024

'My feet,' said Caz, pulling off her boots and collapsing backwards onto the monstrous bed. 'I thought I was fit running round after the twins, but that was extreme.'

I was taking a slower approach of taking my boots off, gently prising them off my feet in the hope of not angering the blisters any more than was necessary. I didn't even have the energy to lift my wrist to see how many steps we'd walked. My watch had long since buzzed to tell me I'd hit my 15,000 step target.

'You're such lightweights,' said Amy, picking through the bags on the bed to inspect her purchases.

Caz threw a decorative pillow at her before collapsing back onto the bed.

'Come on,' said Amy, with a groan. 'You can't flake out now, we haven't even had dinner yet.'

'I don't know how you can think of eating, that lunch was more food than I usually eat in a week.' I rubbed my belly, straining to break free of my jeans that usually were a little loose.

'You know how hard it was to get those reservations for the diner. We need to leave here in an hour. I'm going to jump in the shower. Power naps only,' she said, pointing a finger at us accusingly.

I saluted and fell onto my back, my body sinking into the firm mattress. It was so comfortable that I didn't want to ever move again.

The shower started to run and I rolled onto my side to face Caz who was flat on her back on the other side of the super king bed we were sharing.

'Do you feel like staging a mutiny and just advocating for room service?'

Caz rolled over and propped her head up with her hand.

'We'd never hear the end of it.'

'True. I guess I shouldn't moan. Thanks to Amy, we've seen more of this place than I thought we possibly could in two days. I honestly don't know what we've got left to see tomorrow,' I said.

'I know, it does feel like we've walked every square mile.'

'Perhaps we can head out across the Brooklyn Bridge; you're supposed to get great views of the city.'

'Hmm,' said Caz, 'you know Amy. She'll have everything planned.'

'Yeah, I guess so.'

Amy always did love to take charge, but since she'd become a mum she'd become even more of a planner. I guess that she needed to, working full time and slotting in everyone's activities. It had almost come second nature to her. And whilst I was grateful that she'd organised everything, part of me missed the travelling we'd have done in our twenties: ambling around a city, moving from bar to bar, picking up food in interesting-looking places along the way. But this trip had been different, tickets purchased, and time slots were booked, and some of the restaurants had been reserved months in advance.

'This has been just what I needed, some quality time with my girls,' said Caz. 'I feel like I'm surrounded by boys all the time, at home, at work.'

'You really are outnumbered.' Jacob and Max were the cutest little boys. It often felt when visiting that Nick was trying to relive his childhood with dens or imaginary explorations, the three of them heading off on chairs masquerading as boats to discover new lands.

'Speaking of work, have you thought any more about moving jobs?'

Lately I'd really started to notice how much I'd outgrown my job. It had happened a while ago, but I'd been distracted by caring for Mum, the pandemic and then falling in and out of love with Andrew. Only now that I'd had six months without him and time to really think about what I wanted from life, I'd realised that I needed to move on.

'I've actually started applying for a few things.' I winced as I said it. I'd wanted to keep it a secret, just telling people when I'd changed jobs.

'What? Why didn't you say?'

'I don't know really. It's been so long since I applied for anything, I'm worried that I won't get any interviews.'

'What, with all your experience? You'll be turning down the offers,' said Caz, shaking her head.

I wished I shared her optimism.

'Are you applying locally?'

'Yeah, but I've also applied for a couple of jobs in London too. I'm not saying I'd move or anything, but, you know, these days so much is hybrid that I'd only need to commute a few days a week.'

'Would you not want to move?' she asked softly.

'I'm not sure now's the best time.' I didn't often mention what was going on with my mum to the girls, it was too painful to talk about it. There was a sort of unspoken inevitability about what would happen to her, and we all knew that I wouldn't be leaving the area until any of that happened.

'Well, homeworking makes all the difference. Nick loves it. I think mainly because he gets to blast his death metal round the house whilst no one's in.'

'I still can't picture Nick liking death metal.'

She wrinkled up her nose.

'I might love him, but I don't have to love his music collection.' She laughed and then leaned back on her pillow. 'My whole body is aching.'

'Mine too.' I tried to stretch out my tight calves. 'What do you reckon Amy would do if we were fast asleep when she came out of the bathroom?'

'Wake up your arses!' she said, appearing with a towel wrapped around her and a hotel plastic shower cap on her head. 'Come on, we've got to make the most of tonight.'

'Why? It's not like it's our last night,' I groaned. 'We could have room service, and all get into bed and watch something on TV.'

I went to pick up the remote and Amy gently tugged it out of my hands.

'Get in the shower, you'll feel better. And don't you be going to sleep.'

Caz held up her hands. 'I'm awake. I'm awake.'

She rolled over towards me again.

'I don't think your plan is going to work. Do you want to shower first, or will I?'

Two hours later we were seated in a restaurant that I didn't even know how to begin to describe. The décor was exactly as you'd imagine a 1950's American diner: checkerboard floor tiles, red cushioned booths, and a metal-lined Formica bar with stools that ran along the back with the open kitchen beyond. But that wasn't the half of it. The most impressive part was the staff that kept breaking into song.

'Isn't this amazing?' said Amy, in between singing along with the waitress to 'Defying Gravity'.

'It's definitely stopping me from falling asleep.'

I laughed at Caz; there'd be no chance of that.

'I don't know how you found all these places.' I sipped on my Bellini, which was nothing short of delicious.

'You would not believe the amount of posts on Mumsnet dedicated to NYC itineraries. And this place is impossible to avoid on Instagram. I think every mum influencer and their dog have been here. It's like *the* thing to do. And unlike most things that you see on Instagram, this is definitely as fun as it looks on the grid.'

'Definitely,' I said, nodding. 'Well done you for such dedicated research.'

'Ha, thank you. You know you should tell Paul that. He's always giving off about how much time I spend on my phone. Even though he's the worst.'

'That's exactly like Nick. He'll be looking down his nose at me watching TikTok and then he'll be refreshing his football scores.'

'Do you ever wonder what we would have been like at uni if we'd had TikTok?' I asked. We'd always loved our choreographed dances and I could see us all cramming into one of our tiny rooms trying to perfect the moves to the latest craze.

'We would have been a nightmare. We'd have been all over campus dancing in the middle of the street,' said Amy, shaking her head. 'And can you imagine the kind of things we would have worn?'

'I'm glad we only started using Facebook after we left. We used to take far too many photos as it was, let alone if we'd been posting them.'

'Oh god, and could you imagine those pictures being up there in public and being reminded about them on an annual basis?'

'That photo of you with pizza boy,' said Caz, pointing at Amy.

I shrieked with laughter and Amy's eyes almost popped out of her head.

'How many love bites did you give him?' I asked, through the giggles.

'We promised we wouldn't talk about that night.' She hid her head in her hands, trying to fight the laughter.

'And there was that photo of you when you ripped your skirt,' I said to Caz.

'And you grinding on that pole.'

Now it was my turn to recoil in horror. Our uni days had been amazing but cringey to look back on.

'You know Paul's got copies of all those photos, I could scan them and put them on Facebook,' said Amy.

'You will not.' Caz glared at her with a stern look. 'It was bad enough when Noah tagged us in those photos a few years ago. I still haven't forgiven him for that.'

I shuddered. I'd done my best to untag myself, but anyone who was friends with Noah on Facebook would still be able to pick us out of the line-up.

'Speaking of Noah,' I said, 'do you know what he planned for his birthday in the end? Did he head back to Costa Rica? I feel like we haven't had an update in ages.'

'Yeah, I think he's been volunteering somewhere there, the place with the turtles or was it the cloud forest? You know what he's like, his plans seem to change at the drop of a hat.'

I nodded. He'd changed so much over the last few years since him and Mags split. At times I felt guilty for what I'd said to him outside the Tate Modern, but seeing what he'd achieved on his own, I knew it had been the right thing for him.

'I've got a chopped salad,' said a waitress, holding out enormous bowls. 'And two Mexican salads.'

Caz and I raised our hands 'Mexican for us.'

'These are ginormous, and there was me thinking the salad would be the lighter option.'

The waitress cackled like she'd heard it all before, and after checking we didn't need anything else she went off.

'I think the food has been my favourite part of this trip,' said Amy, tucking in, her face exploding as she tasted it.

'And there was me thinking spending time with us would have been your favourite,' I teased.

'Well, that's a given, but on top of your scintillating company, it's been so nice to eat out all the time and not have to think about what's for dinner.'

'Only because you thought about it months ago when you booked.'

Amy gave Caz a wink. 'And aren't you grateful? Don't you

remember what we used to be like when we went away? We'd walk around in circles trying to figure out where to eat, everyone too polite to make a decision.'

'I thought we were just being super laid-back,' I said, thinking back to our trips.

'Don't you remember that time we were in Nice and we ended up in McDonald's because we'd walked around for that long that all the restaurants had stopped serving lunch?'

I laughed. 'I'd forgotten that.'

'We kept walking up and down that street with all the boards outside, trying to work out where to go.'

'I thought we went to Maccy D's because it was cheaper? Then we had more money for wine?'

'Was that it?' said Amy, scrunching up her face.

'All I can remember from that trip was Caz trying to flirt with that guy with the boat, thinking we'd get to go for a drink on a super yacht.'

Amy snorted. 'And then it was that little dinghy.'

'How was I supposed to know it would be that small? It wasn't like they had *Below Deck* back then.'

'It's probably a good thing though – three women in their twenties going back to a yacht with a creepy old dude . . . ' said Amy.

'Old?' I said. 'I'm pretty sure he was only early thirties.'

'Was he?' she said. 'I just remember him being ancient. God, that's depressing. Do you think that young people think that about us?'

'Well, we are forty.'

'Speak for yourselves,' I said, holding up my hands. 'I've got another four hours of being thirty-nine, thank you very much.'

'Well, make the most of it; in four hours you'll be positively ancient like the rest of us.'

'Come on,' said Caz, 'it's not that bad.'

'Let's face facts, we're old. Skin is wrinkling, body parts are sagging.'

'I'm making your coffin now, Amy,' I said, scooping up another fork of salad. It barely looked like I'd touched it, but I seemed to have been eating it for ages.

'But some things are better with age,' Caz said. 'This trip for example. If we'd done this in our old style, we'd probably not have got further than the end of the block we're staying on.'

'That's true.' I pointed at Amy.

'Oh my goodness.' Amy's fork clattered. 'I've started eating this and I haven't taken a photo of it.'

Caz did a mock gasp. 'How will you cope?'

'How else will I make Paul jealous?' she said, laughing and taking a snap of her bowl. 'Selfie, whilst I'm here?' Amy leaned towards me, holding out her phone.

I gave what I hoped was a flattering smile, trying my best to angle my head down to avoid multiple chins.

'Lovely,' she said.

'We should do a toast.' Caz picked up her glass. 'To getting older, and Amy getting even more organised.'

We raised our glasses and chinked before drinking.

'And I'm going to propose a toast to Lucy. Here's to tomorrow being your best proper leap year birthday yet.'

'To Lucy and the best birthday,' chimed Caz as she chinked my glasses.

We all sipped our drinks, and I placed my glass back on the table.

'Right then, when are you going to tell me what we're doing tomorrow? I was thinking that Brooklyn seemed fun to explore.'

'Oh, don't you worry about anything. We've got plenty of surprises in store for you,' said Amy, and her and Caz exchanged a sneaky look with each other.

'Don't I get any clues?'

'Only that you'd be best off wearing your new trainers. More walking to do.'

I groaned. 'Don't you look so smug,' I said to Caz. 'You'll be walking too.'

'Uh-huh,' she said, a big smile on her face and it made me even more nervous as to what was planned.

I hadn't had the best of sleeps since being away. The concoction of jetlag and hectic sightseeing schedule had left my body tired and my mind constantly buzzing. Which meant at first when my phone started ringing that night, it took me a while to work out what it was.

Caz reached out, feeling for her phone and when she realised it wasn't hers she rolled back over. I hastily picked mine up, saw it was Mum and answered it, creeping into the bathroom so as to not disturb the girls any further.

'Hello,' I whispered into it as I fumbled for the light switch. My heart was racing in panic that something awful had happened.

'Lucy? Lucy?'

'It's me, Mum.' I flicked on the light and the brightness floored me. I shut my eyes, trying to adjust to it more slowly. 'What's wrong?'

'I've been looking for you upstairs and you're not in your room.'

I thought of the single-storey care home that she now lived in, with not a stair in sight. Whilst part of me relaxed that it wasn't the care home ringing from her phone, the other part of me tensed for one of these types of calls.

'I can't see you on the screen. Where are you?'

I flicked the call to video and I saw her face scrunched up, staring at the screen. She visibly relaxed when she saw me.

I barely recognised either woman on my screen anymore; me and Mum had changed so much. I scraped my hair back into a messy bun.

'I'm here. Are you OK?'

'I've been calling you upstairs.'

'I'm not upstairs, Mum. I'm in New York. I'm here until Saturday.'

'New York?' she repeated, the furrow on her brow that was almost permanently there deepened.

'Yes, New York, until Saturday.'

'Saturday. I always wanted to go to New York.'

'I know, Mum.'

It broke my heart that I'd never gone with her. We could have gone when I was living in London, one of my bonuses would have paid for it. I should have just booked it, pride on her part or not. Or we could have gone in the early days of her illness. Looking back, if I'd known how good she really was then, how much we could have made of her time.

'New York, New York,' she almost sang.

'That's right. And I'm here. Until Saturday.'

'Saturday. You won't be here today?'

'No, Mum.'

'Is it raining?'

I closed my eyes trying to wake up. I had no idea what time it was and the noise of the heating system provided the kind of white noise that made it impossible to hear the weather outside, even if it was hammering down.

'I don't think so. It was sunny yesterday.'

'It's raining here.'

'Is it now?'

'Pelting it down. All day.'

'Sounds bad.' I put the toilet seat down and sat down on it, balancing the phone on the vanity unit next to it.

'Doesn't matter to me. I'm staying inside.'

'Wise decision. Just you stay there.'

'I'm not going anywhere.'

We sat there for a moment in silence. This usually happened, after the initial panic of what had caused her to ring had subsided. If I was in the middle of something, I'd tell her that I'd speak to her later, and then I'd wait for the next call. But sometimes, like now, when I had nothing better to do, I talked and she listened.

'Shall I tell you about New York? It's just like we imagined it would be. The buildings really are as high as they look on TV, maybe even higher, and smoke really does come up from the side of the pavements.'

I looked at the clock in the corner of my screen. It was 3 a.m. It was officially my birthday. I was forty. I almost laughed at myself. This wasn't how I'd thought I'd be spending it, whispering into FaceTime whilst sat on a toilet. I leaned my head back against the wall and carried on telling her about the trip whilst the words washed over her. I was never sure whether she was following what I said or not, but it seemed to calm her and these days that was the best I could hope for.

Chapter 28

Thursday 29ᵗʰ February 2024

'Where's Amy gone?' I asked, looking round the street. We'd arrived at the tip of Manhattan, close to Wall Street, and with it being rush hour, the place was heaving. Police were directing traffic around it, buses and cars rushed past and people were hurrying in every direction. I stepped back to let a fierce-looking commuter by. 'We should have had an extra hour in bed, let things calm down here.'

'Well, you know Amy: she's got us a jam-packed day planned,' said Caz. She looked down the street and her eyes lit up as she pointed. 'There she is.'

I watched Amy bob into view, behind her a balloon with a big forty printed on it.

'Oh no.' I turned to Caz. 'What has she got? I am not taking that round with me.' I crossed my hands, signalling to her it was a no-go. 'Nuh, uh. No way.'

'Come on. It's your birthday.'

'This is supposed to be a joint one for all our fortieths.'

'Oh no, this is all for you.'

I watched as Amy kept having to apologise as the balloon got in the way of people rushing about.

'Happy birthday!' She didn't even wait for me to say anything before tying the balloon to my wrist.

'Did you really need to tie it?'

'I didn't want you to accidentally lose it.'

'Hmm, how thoughtful of you.'

At least it served one purpose, it seemed to be a commuter repellent. Balloon in hand, everyone was giving us a wide berth.

'Did you have to get my age printed on it? Forty's so depressing.'

'Oh hush now,' said Caz, who was the oldest amongst us. 'That feeling lasts for about a week and then you realise that your world hasn't ended and you carry on as normal.'

'A week you say?'

'Mine lasted a bit more than that,' said Amy.

'Come on, forty is the new thirty.'

I stared hard at Caz.

'You told me when I turned thirty it was the new twenty-one.'

'And I'll be telling you ninety's the new seventy when we're in our rocking chairs on the porch together,' she said, pushing the balloon gently so it hit me in the face. 'Besides. Without the balloon, how are you going to do one of those insufferable "This is Forty" posts on Instagram? Seriously, you're going to have to stop giving me those looks. The wind might change and you'll be stuck like that.'

Amy laughed. 'Right, ladies, as much fun as this is, we've got a schedule to keep.'

She reached into her bag and pulled out an envelope. It reminded me of the ones she and Paul had for us on the last leap year to pick where we were going. Only this time there was only one.

'What is it?' She handed it to me and I set about opening it.

'It's a treasure hunt.'

'We're going on a treasure hunt?' I looked down at the first clue. I was kind of excited.

'Well, you're going on a treasure hunt,' said Caz. 'We're just keeping you company.'

'You made this for me?' I looked down at the card and back up to them.

'Uh-huh, we thought it would be fun. After all, you did kick arse at all those online escape rooms we did on Zoom,' said Amy.

'You guys.' I was choked up with emotion that they'd done something so personal. I reached over and gave them both a hug at the same time.

'So you might need this,' said Amy, handing over the guide-book that she'd used like the bible since we'd arrived. 'And you'll need to keep your phone handy: every time you get to the right place, you have to take a photo of you in front of whatever the answer is, and you're going to send it to the group chat. And from there, Paul, who's going to be standing by his phone, will text you the next clue.'

'Wouldn't it be easier if you gave me the next clue?'

'We thought it added a bit more fun,' said Caz, with a shrug.

'And less work for us to make sure we got them in the right order,' said Amy, with a nod that let me know that that was the real reason.

'Sound good?' Caz raised an eyebrow.

'Sounds amazing.'

'Then what are you waiting for?' said Amy, tapping the card. The first clue took us to Staten Island on the ferry where we stopped for breakfast before I snapped a photo of myself in front of the Statue of Liberty – the gift from France that I'd been tasked to find.

'I'm so sorry I forgot the balloon.' I tried to hide my little smile.

'I bet you are.' Caz had a stern look on her face. 'We should have known tying it to your chair was a bad idea.'

'Although it did mean you got free pancakes,' said Amy, always looking on the bright side.

'Not that I needed them after that giant omelette.' I groaned and tugged at my waistband, wondering if I was going to be able to fit into any clothes by the time I left.

I stopped in front of the boating lake at Central Park.

'Right, I'm pretty sure this is the answer.' I turned to Caz and Amy for confirmation, but they were giving nothing away.

'Sure?' said Caz.

'Uh-huh.' I re-read Paul's clue one more time before taking a selfie and sending it to the group chat.

I turned and took in the park. The strangest thing about being in New York was that at every turn it felt like I'd been there before. There was a familiarity to it that I'd never experienced in any other city.

I looked over at the boat house that was case in point.

'I wish we could have lunch over there. Like Meg Ryan did in *When Harry Met Sally*.'

'I love that movie,' said Caz, looking over at it. 'Was it really in it?'

'Yep, when they're having lunch.'

'Not when she does the whole orgasm thing?'

'Nope,' I said. 'Not that bit. She was with her girlfriends chatting about men.'

'Ah, now that sounds more like it,' said Caz.

My phone beeped. Paul barely hesitated before he sent back a message, which I hoped was the next clue.

'What does it say?' asked Amy.

'*Whilst you're there, have a paddle, before you get back in the saddle.*' I looked up at her. 'These clues are getting weirder.'

'Yeah, well, we did drink an excellent bottle of pinot noir when we were writing them, so apologies for that. But I can translate this one: we're supposed to be going on a rowing boat,' she said pointing at the water that had patches of ice on it. 'That ain't going to happen.'

I shuddered at the cold.

'That's a pity,' I said. 'So what do we do now?'

Caz pulled her phone out. 'There must be a way we can go boating.'

'Watch out, you're going to sink me,' I yelped as Caz's boat came perilously close to mine.

'Sorry, but could you drive any slower, Miss Daisy?'

'Oi, watch it. I just want to get our deposits back.' I watched as Caz's boat did little loops of mine.

'I'm glad that the rowing boats were closed. I can't imagine letting you loose on a pair of oars.'

'I'll have you know, I'm an excellent rower,' said Caz and we turned to look at her. Amy almost crashed her boat into the side as she wasn't concentrating.

'You've rowed?'

'Yeah, in the gym.'

'On a rowing machine?' I groaned. That was not the same thing.

'Well, it can't be that different.'

'Other than it's anchored to the floor,' I said.

'And you don't actually move.' I high-fived Amy and Caz rolled her eyes.

'Whatevs, I guess now we'll never know. So how about we make this interesting. A race from one end to the other? Loser buys lunch?'

'And winner picks where?' said Amy.

'Within reason, no Michelin stars. Just in case it's me that's the loser,' I said, knowing that was a likely possibility. 'That shopping spree yesterday was not kind to my credit card.'

'Agreed. Cheap and cheerful. So let's line up the boats.' Caz started to laugh. 'Lucy, we're having the race this century.'

The others were already at the starting line and mine was lagging behind.

'What? I'm not burning out the engine before we start.'

'Ready . . . steady,' said Caz.

'Go!' screamed Amy and she pushed the lever on the remote control and her boat whizzed along. She ran alongside and when her boat pipped Caz's to the post she whooped with joy. 'Hot dogs.'

'What?' I looked at Caz who was equally as confused.

'We're having hot dogs, from one of those little carts. They smell amazing.'

'When I said budget, I didn't quite have one of those in mind.'

Amy did a victory lap with her boat, running circles around us. 'We had a bet. Besides a hot dog off a street vendor is peak NYC tourist.'

*

I started to take the museum steps two by two. 'Is this actually the museum that Ross was supposed to work in in *Friends*?' I said, turning back to the other two who were keeping up.

'Ooh, I thought you were going to say *Night at the Museum*,' said Amy.

'I haven't seen that.'

'My kids love it, and I think you would too. Robin Williams, Ben Stiller.'

'New York really is a movie set,' said Caz.

'Isn't it? That's why I love it,' said Amy. 'That and they have snacks at every corner.'

'I still can't believe you made us eat those hot dogs. You have no idea what meat was in them.' Caz was turning her nose up. 'And those pretzels, I don't think my thirst will ever be quenched again.'

'Oh please, like we didn't eat worse on nights out.'

I thought of some of the dodgy fried chicken and kebab shops we'd frequented in the past.

'But then we were too drunk to notice.'

'Well, it tasted delicious. And look, we're all still alive.'

A thought flicked into my mind of Paul with his oysters on the day I met him. I hoped Amy was right and she wouldn't suffer the same fate.

'Right, let's figure out this clue,' I said, really getting into it.

From plains to prairies, marsh to mountains. You'll find me living the same life day after day after day.

I looked up at the girls. 'I'm guessing it's too much to hope for that it'll be the dinosaur bones?' I picked up the floorplan and looked at the different rooms, knowing that description could only be talking about the hall of North American Mammals. 'You've got to be kidding.'

'Don't worry, we'll be there with you,' said Amy, linking her arm through mine. 'Plus, I'm pretty sure the things in here only came to life at night-time.'

I shot her a look.

'Oh, on second thoughts, you don't want to be watching the *Night at the Museum* after all. Might not help that fear.'

We headed into the gallery, where all the taxidermy was fixed into dioramas to be shown in its natural habitat. I didn't know if that made it better or worse. I read the rest of the clue again and looked at the list of the animals before the answer leapt out at me: The Groundhog.

Of course, it was located on the far side of the gallery so I had to pass all the other exhibits. As we walked through the gallery it struck me that the last time that I'd been anywhere like this had been in Dublin with Noah. We'd walked around the whole museum then, and I'd managed it unscathed. I could do this.

When I reached it, I stood as far back from it as I could and took the photo.

'How can that freak you out? It looks so cute,' said Amy.

'It's a marmot, isn't it? Is that what a groundhog is?' Caz peered at the text panel to get more detail.

'Look at it on its hindlegs. It's freaky.' I shook my head. It definitely made it worse that it was surrounded by prairie land. It looked even more lifelike and like it could pounce on me at any minute. 'Can we wait for Paul's reply in the lobby?'

Amy nodded and guided me out. I passed the grey fox, and, as he eyeballed me, I got flashbacks of my nan's taxidermy fox. It was camouflaged amongst the foliage, but it had the same eyes as Felix. Where once it might have scared me, now it didn't. It wasn't that I would choose to have one in my hall like Nan,

354

but perhaps the WhatsApp photos over the years from Noah, and the jokes everyone had had at my expense, had finally done their job. Exposure therapy worked after all.

My phone pinged in my pocket.

'Next clue is in.'

I noticed the looks between Caz and Amy.

'Do you guys know what's coming?'

'That would be telling.'

'Right, *The first word of "Bohemian Rhapsody" with an American spin*. What does that mean?'

'We can't help you,' said Amy.

'But we can sing it if you like?'

Amy and Caz giggled as they started to sing Queen's famous song, other visitors to the museum giving them a wide berth.

'Mama – that's the first word, with an American spin.' The more I went over it in my mind, the less sense it made. 'Mama? Mama?'

'What do American people call Mama?'

'Mom? Is it like an abbreviation M.O.M.?'

'Moma,' coughed Caz. Amy glared at her. 'Oh, come on, she was never going to get it and time is ticking on.'

'Moma? What's moma?'

'Check the guidebook,' said Amy.

I pulled it out of my bag and scanned the list, before I found it. 'Oh MOMA. The Museum of Modern Art, of course.'

'Got there eventually,' said Caz.

'Yeah, thanks to you.'

'What, it'll be dark soon.' She raised an eyebrow.

'You're right, you're right. Come on,' said Amy, leading us out.

It was mid-afternoon, and fun as it had been scrambling between the places all day, when Caz suggested we get a taxi, we all leaped at the chance.

We pulled up outside of the gallery and Amy squealed a little.

'I've been dying to come here,' she said. 'How about you do this clue by yourself? I really want to go and see *Starry Night*.'

'Me too,' said Caz.

'I can meet you there then, once I've taken the photo.'

'Uh-huh,' said Amy, 'and this is the last clue to find. We've only got one more place to go after this.'

Amy paid for us at the counter and took her guide book back. 'You won't be needing this. Send Paul the photo and he'll send you where you're going.'

She gave me a quick wave and it was like they couldn't leave me quick enough. I hoped I was able to solve the clue without them.

It must have been well into the evening back in the UK and I hoped that Paul hadn't got sucked into doing the kids' tea and bedtimes and forgotten about the treasure hunt. But no sooner had I sent it, than a text pinged back.

Time for a little maths. Your new age times the age you are in reality plus three.

I read it over twice, my brain trying to make sense of it all. Forty times ten plus three equalled four hundred and three. I started climbing the stairs until I found myself on the fourth floor and I knew almost instantly where I was heading as soon as I caught a glimpse. MOMA's Rothko exhibition.

It was the polar opposite to the room at the Tate Modern, which had been moody and atmospheric. This was all whitewashed walls and space between the paintings. And the paintings themselves were full of colour. Yellows and blues and bright red.

But despite the differences, they still had the same effect. I was drawn to one with the familiar reds and purples. People bustled around the gallery in a way that they hadn't in London. There I'd felt you could have heard a pin drop, but here it was full of life, like the colour in the paintings themselves.

A couple that had been sitting on the bench in front of a red and purple painting got up to go and I took their place. I found myself getting sucked in, just as I had at the Tate.

I turned to my side, for a second wishing that Noah was here. This had been our artist, the one that we'd both connected with. I looked over my shoulder, and for a second, I scanned the gallery for him.

I took out my phone, snapped a photo of the artwork in front of me, and I sent it to the group. Then I opened up my messages to Noah. He hadn't seen the Happy Birthday text I'd sent him after I'd finished on the phone to Mum last night. There was no point in sending him another one.

I couldn't help but think about him though. It felt like such a strange coincidence that Paul would send me here. And to the taxidermy. A shiver ran down my spine as I started to connect the dots. The boating lake in the park. The ferry to do French sightseeing. It was all there. It had been all day.

This wasn't a treasure hunt the girls had put together out of coincidence; this was a treasure hunt of mine and Noah's leap years.

My phone beeped and it was another message from Paul.

I know you don't believe in fate, but you'll know where to go. Sometimes all you need is serendipity.

I gasped out loud. The room starting to spin around me. Noah. It had to be him. Was he here?

I read the message again. *Serendipity.*

The ice rink, like the film.

Chapter 29

The security guards gave me suspicious looks as I ran out of the gallery. I pulled my phone out of my bag whilst spinning round to get my bearings. I had no idea what part of the park had the ice rink, or where I was in relation to it. I was so lost at this point, I'd have to get another cab.

I hailed a taxi, with as much frantic arm flapping as I had in Calais, and hopped in.

'I need to get to the ice rink,' I said, almost out of breath. 'The one in Central Park.'

I didn't want a repeat of Calais, getting taken to the wrong one.

The taxi lurched away and I found Amy's number.

'Hello,' she trilled. 'Do you need a hand with the clue?'

'No, I've figured it all out by myself.'

'Good girl.' She squealed down the phone.

'I'm in a taxi, but I didn't want you to be waiting for me at the gallery.'

'Don't worry, we're not. Good luck and we'll see you soon.'

I hung up and shoved my phone back in my bag. We were there already.

'Woolman rink's just through there,' said the driver as I tapped my card on the keypad.

'Thanks so much.'

'Have a great day.'

'I will. You too.'

I ran at first but I found my steps slowing the closer I got, doubting that I'd got this right. I'd leaped to all these conclusions and what if Noah wasn't there? What if I'd read all this into the clues because I was so desperate to see him? What if it was just Amy and Caz?

I stopped to scan the horizon, and then I saw him, standing by the ice rink, a balloon in his hand. My balloon, the one I'd left in Staten Island this morning.

He was looking towards another entrance and I caught my breath as I watched him. He was searching the crowd, hope on his face. He must have sensed me watching and he turned and our eyes met. His smile widened, and even if I couldn't see it from here, I knew his dimple was there on his cheek.

My legs were unsteady as I willed them towards him. It was the opposite to my arrival. Slow at first, and then I sped up until I was there, in front of him.

'Hey,' I said, still half convinced that he was a figment of my imagination.

I reached out and he grabbed my hands. I almost jolted at the crackle of electricity. There was no denying he was real now. It was Noah, in the flesh.

'What are you doing here?' I asked, unable to believe that it was really him.

'Well, I missed one birthday with you, I wasn't going to miss another one. Not when we only get them once every four years.'

'And what? Are you going to lead me to the treasure?' I said, trying to keep my breathing steady.

He shrugged, and he bit his lip as he smiled. 'I hope so.'

My heart was hammering in my chest as I wondered what the treasure might be and what him being here might mean.

'I was worried you wouldn't get the clue. It felt like I'd been waiting here for hours,' he said, and I noticed then that his hands were like blocks of ice.

'Serendipitous. It's one of my favourite words.'

'Mine too, now,' he said, nodding.

'When did you get to New York?'

'Last night. Paul got in a couple of hours before me.'

'Paul's here too? He's been texting me from here?' My mind was whirring.

'The gang's all here. Well, Nick's still holding the fort at home with the twins. We were at Central Park this morning, and saw you racing your boat, terribly may I add. Did you run out of batteries?'

'I can't believe you saw that. I was being cautious, someone had to protect the deposit,' I said. It burned my heart that he'd been here and I hadn't seen him until now. 'I'm glad you're here. It didn't feel like our big birthday without you.'

'I know,' he said. He turned to look at me and he took my breath away. 'It's good to see you.'

'You too, you're looking well. Travelling always suits you.'

'I actually had a mud bath a few weeks ago; it's supposed to have taken ten years off me.'

'I wouldn't go that far.' He laughed again. It was the best sound in the world.

'Thanks very much.'

'You can always count on me to tell you the truth.'

'That I can. I remember how much from our last big birthday,' he said, nodding his head.

361

I felt instantly guilty about our argument at the Tate Modern. I'd been angry about the near kiss, but I hadn't needed to turn it into a personal attack. We'd never really talked about it properly; we'd swept it under the carpet like so much that had gone unsaid when we got used to the new normal in the pandemic.

'About that day. I've never said—'

He shook his head.

'You don't need to say anything.'

'I do, I need to say sorry, and I need to say thank you.'

'Thank you?' He wrinkled his brow.

'Yeah, what you said to me at the Tate. That I should put myself out there. Take a risk in love? And that's what I did with Andrew.'

His hands started to tremble.

'You didn't get back together?'

I shook my head. 'No, we didn't. But we had a wonderful two and a half years, and whilst it didn't work out, it made me realise that I'd quite like to be in a relationship. Having someone to say goodnight to. Someone to be there for you when you need them. Someone to finish—'

'—your sentences for you,' he said, a small smile spreading over his face. 'Are you just quoting what I said about love when we first met.'

'Kind of, although it's a bit rusty. But wasn't that the gist of what love was to you?'

'Love's a lot of things to me.'

The sun was setting, taking with it any heat from the day, but holding Noah's hands, I felt like I was on fire.

'You know, I want to thank you too for what you said that

362

day. I mean, it was harsh, but fair. You were right, I shouldn't have kissed you then. I needed to be alone. And maybe if you hadn't said that, I would have spent lockdown with Mags. But instead, to prove a point to you, I stayed on my own. I'm not going to lie, it was pretty shit at the beginning, but then I kind of got into it. Especially when things opened up again and I could see people. I liked that I could be who I wanted to be, go where I wanted. Travel when I wanted to travel. No one to answer to. I've loved it, being me, just for me.

'But . . . I've been thinking, lately, since you broke up with Andrew and you're now single, and I'm still single. I've been single for four long years, may I add.'

'Nothing to do with the pandemic happening for a lot of those, making it tricky to date people for at least two of those years?'

He smirked. 'Still counts though.'

I spotted a small group of people that looked like they were watching us. I was about to point them out to Noah when I realised it was the rest of our gang. Paul was standing with his arm around Amy, and Caz had her head on Amy's shoulder.

I waved at them, and they waved back enthusiastically.

I went to move towards them, but Noah tugged at my arm.

'Hang on.' He turned me towards him.

He was so close to me that I could feel his heart racing as much as mine.

'I tried to kiss you four years ago, not because I couldn't be on my own, not because I felt lost. But because it was you. I don't know what happened in Calais, when we went on that wild goose chase trying to find something open. I didn't care where we went, I just knew I wanted to go with you.'

'You did?' It was starting to sink in what this might mean.

'I did, I wanted to see where the adventure took us, and look where it has. Sightseeing in deserted towns, boating on lakes, trips to Dead Zoos, bonding over being art philistines, and that's just our big birthdays. I could have filled the treasure hunt with late-night trips to kebab shops, and divey dance clubs, Tesco runs in the middle of the night to get the ingredients for banana splits.'

A tear rolled down my cheek, and Noah wiped it away, his hand lingering there.

'That day in the car park when I saw you playing with the charm on your wrist, I didn't know that I was looking at a friend for life, one that I'd slowly fall for.

'And so I hope, Luce, that four years is long enough to prove to you that I can be single, because I don't want to be anymore, and I certainly don't want you to fall in love with anyone else. That was awful to watch, and to think that I'd spurred you on to do that when really I was trying to tell you to take a chance on us.' He screwed up his face.

'You were?' I spluttered, in shock about everything he'd said.

'Yes. The trouble was, you'd hit a nerve so it came out a bit angry and, um, not quite to the point. So instead I've spent the last four years thinking about what I'd do if I got the chance again.'

I took his other hand in mine so that now both our hands were touching.

'And what would you do?'

He brought his head down to mine and I held his gaze for a second.

'I don't know, I thought I might do this,' he said, and he

leaned in and kissed me. It was so soft and gentle but before it had even started, he pulled away. 'I mean, if that's OK with you?'

I let go of his hand and tugged at his coat and pulled him into me.

'It's more than OK.'

He smiled, and wrapped his arms around me before kissing me harder this time. His hands found the small of my back to pull me in closer.

I could hear whooping and it took a few moments to realise it was our friends. I took a step back and laughed.

'I think they've been waiting for that for a while.'

'As long as us?' I said, biting my lip.

'I don't think anyone's been waiting longer than us.'

He leaned in and kissed me again and this time I forgot about our friends.

'Do you think we should go and see them?' I asked, looking over towards them when we finally pulled out of the kiss. They were grinning almost as much as we were.

'Before you do, you need your treasure,' he said, reaching into his pocket. He pulled out a Tiffany blue box and I gasped. 'Woah, don't have a heart attack. It's not that.' He laughed and I loved how he knew without me saying a word what I was thinking. 'I'm not trying to spook you.'

He handed me the box, which thankfully was bigger than a ring box, and I flipped it open. It was a bracelet, like the one I used to wear, only this was beautiful. It had a solid silver chain, and the four-leaf charm was silver too. It was a sophisticated, grown-up version of the bracelet he'd bought me before.

'Can I?' he asked.

I nodded and he slipped the bracelet over my wrist so that the four-leaf clover hung from my wrist.

'I thought we'd be waiting for you two for ever,' said Amy, the group coming to us.

'I'm sorry; Noah had to give me this bracelet.'

Caz raised her eyebrows in approval and had a look at it as I shook it from my wrist.

'We're talking about the twenty bloody years I've had to hear this one whine about it,' said Paul, nudging his wife.

'I've always said they'd be perfect.'

'Sometimes it's all about timing, isn't it?' said Caz, with a wink. She knew more than anyone how much it took for the stars to align in a relationship.

Caz joined in then and the five of us had a group hug. My heart couldn't swell any more than it already was.

When we eventually let go, I realised Noah still had my hand in his, and he kissed me on the top of my head.

'Ah,' said Amy, a tear in her eye. 'Young love, gets me every time.'

'I don't think they're young love anymore. They're ancient now,' said Paul, poking at the balloon. 'Just like the rest of us.'

'Speaking of not getting any younger, are we going to get on this ice or what?' said Caz.

'Let's do it,' said Noah.

He didn't let go of my hand as we made our way around the ice, skittish and wobbling, clinging to each other for dear life.

The daylight was fading and the lights of the buildings were springing on and starting to sparkle.

'This is beautiful,' I whispered to Noah as we clung to the

side after we'd nearly fallen over. 'I'm so glad you added this to the end of the hunt.'

'Something touristy for the leap year birthday. A new adventure.'

'A new adventure,' I echoed. It certainly seemed like one and I couldn't help wondering where we were going to spend the next leap year, and the one after that, and the one after that. We'd had twenty years of leap years together, and that was only the start of our story.

Epilogue

Four Years Later: South Downs

Noah took my hand and helped me up the steep path.

'You don't have to do that, you know. I'm fine on my own,' I said, using him to balance anyway.

'I know you are, but you've got precious cargo.'

I knew where I stood in the pecking order.

Barney, our Labrador, ran up, as if to remind me. He dropped a ball, and Noah ran a few steps to tease him as he threw it.

'Are you sure this is all going to be worth it?' cried Amy. 'These wellies aren't really made for rough terrain.'

'I told you to buy walking boots.' Paul held out his hand for her but she didn't take it. She pushed him gently with her arm as she passed.

'Believe me, it's worth it,' beckoned Caz. She and Nick were already up there. Mainly as the twins had charged ahead, and they wanted to keep an eye on them in whatever tree they were climbing. They were in their daredevil stage, big enough to do most things at six, but still young enough to not do the most thorough of risk assessments.

When I reached the top of the hill, I looked down at the view below and I gasped. We'd lived in our little town in the South

Downs for nearly two years and we still hadn't fully explored the area.

'Are you OK?' asked Noah, putting his hand on my back.

'I'm fine. We've only walked a mile at most.'

'I was talking to this one,' he said, pulling down at Mia's little hat. I shot him a look and he laughed. 'Alright, I was asking about you. But only because she's heavy now. I don't want you wrecking your back.'

'It's fine, we're both fine.'

'And no, she's not too hot or too cold,' said Amy, peering in at her and cooing.

'Don't you be getting any ideas.' Paul gave her a stern look, hands on his hips as he caught his breath.

'Yes, I can get signal,' muttered Patrick, fingers moving like lightning across his phone screen.

'What? Mum, you said no phones. Why has Pat got one? That's not fair. That counts as screen time.' Oscar went off following Patrick, protesting the unjust nature of it.

'Believe me, I've got no ideas on that front. If they could stay this size forever . . . ' she said, still cooing.

'Really? This stage?' said Noah, running his hand through his hair. 'Do you see the bags under our eyes?'

I stroked at Mia's feet, laughing as the group descended in, discussing the optimum age of parenting, each thinking the others had the best age. I looked around my group of friends, all of us in such different stages of our lives. Paul and Amy had teenagers, actual real-life ones that grunted and everything. But still, no matter what was going on, we still found time to get together.

'Hey look, there's the Fox and Hounds,' said Noah, pointing down the valley. 'You have to squint a bit.'

'Oh yeah.' I could see the thatch of the roof of the pub restaurant I had helped to rebrand last year. They were one of my first clients when I set up my small marketing agency. I might not have the drive of Mags who sold her first business for multiple millions and was onto her next one, but it felt good to be working for myself.

After Mum had died, we made the move to the South Downs to be nearer Noah's parents. We bought a bungalow that needed more than a little work, but it was now just about habitable and there was even a small veggie patch out the back of the garden that we were slowly bringing back to life.

Noah had settled into the area as if he'd never left. He loved, like I did, that we were close to his parents, and they in turn were excited to be living so close to their first grandchild. He'd got a job as a development officer at a youth charity, and he finally had a job that he looked forward to getting up in the morning for. Even if he wished Mia would let him have a little more sleep in the night.

And of course there was Mia. Mia Jane Matthews, her middle name after her grandma, who'd she'd never meet. Having Mia had been bittersweet. It made me miss my mum in ways I'd never imagined, but at the same time, it spurred me on to be the kind of mum she was to me.

'Another leap year,' said Noah.

'I've almost lost count of how many we've spent together,' said Paul. 'Although you do realise that you missed a trick with not getting Mia to share the birthday too.'

'Bloody hell,' said Caz. 'What would the chances be of that? The two of you is freaky enough.'

'I'm just glad that she gets to have her birthday when it's

warm. Picnics, day trips to the beach, I'm jealous of the stuff she and her friends will be able to do for it.'

'What are you saying?' said Noah, slipping an arm around me. 'That you don't like the fact it's always Baltic on our birthday? Or that it often rains?'

'Speaking of Baltic, how far is that pub that we're going to?' Amy rubbed her hands together. 'And shall we start walking? These wellies are freezing.'

'Should have brought walking boots,' Paul said, smugly, walking off.

'That man,' said Amy.

Noah laughed and kissed me and Mia. Barney, never wanting to miss out, jumped up my legs.

'I haven't forgotten about you either,' I said, tickling him behind his ears in the exact spot he liked.

I went to follow the others, who had descended down the hill, but Noah held me back.

'What?'

'Just taking a moment.'

'Taking a moment?' I raised an eyebrow.

'Yeah. I know we always think about where we've come from and where we're going on our birthday. But today, I just want to take it in. Where I am . . . ' he said, squeezing us all a little tighter ' . . . is exactly where I want to be.'

'Oh Noah, now that's cheesy.'

'And I don't bloody care.' He leaned over and kissed me. I kissed him back, only pulling away when Amy hollered.

'Come on, the teenagers will eat us if we don't feed them soon.'

'We'd better go. Mia's starting to stir anyway; I've stopped for too long.'

We headed off, holding hands, following our friends down the path.

'You do realise, you're going to be that embarrassing dad that'll be all, "Mia, once upon a leap year—"'

'Oi,' he said, pulling his hat further down on his head, 'my voice doesn't sound anything like that.'

'I was more trying to capture the corny radio voice that you do when you're being cheesy.'

'OK, well, in that case,' he said, going full-on cheese voice. 'Once upon a leap year, I met the love of my life, and it changed me forever.' He started to laugh as he heard the words out loud. 'Please don't let me be that cringey a dad.'

'Oh believe me, you will be. She'll hate it, but I'll love it. Just like I love everything about you.'

He stopped again and pulled me in tight.

'Everything, huh? Even the way I make the tea?'

I wrinkled up my nose. Milk before hot water was never going to be the right way.

'Almost everything,' I corrected and he broke out into a smile.

'And I love almost everything about you too.'

He leaned down and he kissed me, and this time as my hand slipped into his open jacket to pull him in closer towards me, I didn't care that we were in danger of a mutiny from hangry teenagers. I wanted to kiss my husband properly and take it all in, because he was right about every single thing.

Once upon a leap year, I met the love of my life, and I count my lucky stars every single day that I did.

Acknowledgements

I adored writing this book and at times Lucy and Noah's story felt like it wrote itself. I loved how they grew up and evolved over the years as I caught up with them at each big birthday. Four years sounds like such a short amount of time, but life really can change quickly. In the last year, my life has changed dramatically – we lost our trusty Labrador, Rex, who is very much missed, and we moved from France to Northern Ireland.

I'd originally written a first draft of a completely different novel but something about it didn't feel right. I kept coming back to the leap year idea and I phoned my editor at the time, Melanie Hayes, and pitched it to her. I want to say a huge thank you to her, Emily Kitchin, and the rest of the HQ team for embracing the idea and letting me write it instead. Thank you to Clare Gordon too, for cheerleading it from the first read-through and all the helpful edits since. Thanks to Donna Hillyer for the eagle-eyed copy edit. Thanks also to the rest of the staff at HQ – in particular Becci Mansell, Caroline Østergaard, Georgina Green, Brogan Furey, Angela Thomson, Sara Eusebi, Angie Dobbs, Halema Begum and Charlotte Phillips.

Thank you to Viola Hayden, and the team at Curtis Brown, for all the patience and your editorial steers. Thank you also to Hannah Ferguson and the team at Hardman and Swainson.

The storyline relating to Lucy and her mum was a tricky

one to get right and any errors are entirely my own. Dementia is sadly an illness that has touched so many of my friends' and family members' lives in some way. In researching the topic, it became clear how different every single person's story is, but what they had in common was how heartbreaking they all were.

The other elements of research for the novel were more upbeat. Thank you to Laura Pearse for letting me pick her brains about Working Holiday Visas in Australia for Noah's story.

I want to thank Tyler Shepherd for bidding on my lot in Book Aid for Ukraine in 2022. His bid was to name a character in the novel. After hearing that he wanted to name the character after his late sister Lyndsey, who was also a writer, I thought it much more fitting to dedicate the book to her. Thank you to Tyler and his family for agreeing.

As always thanks to Steve, Evan, Jessica and Prue for putting up with me whilst I squirrel myself away writing. To both sets of parents – Mum and John, Heather and Harold – for all the babysitting. To the screenwriting crew for our monthly meets. To Vicky Walters for keeping me sane. To Katie and Rich for always cheerleading and listening to plots. To those friends that I'm so lucky to have and know you're always there to help when needed: Debs, Jon, Laura, Kaf, Hannah, Jo, Sam, Ross, Sarah, Sonia, Ali, Christie, Janine and Ken, and Lynne and Ric.

Lastly, I really want to thank you, the reader, for picking up and reading this book! I wouldn't be here without you. If you've enjoyed the book and are able to leave a review on Amazon, they really do help. If you'd like to keep up to date with my future books or find out about my previous ones you can head to my website (www.annabellwrites.com) and you can even sign up to my newsletter – where once in a blue moon I do get myself in gear and send out an update!

Fallen in love with *Once Upon a Leap Year*? Try one of Anna Bell's other heartwarming novels...

It's never too late to follow your heart.

One summer's day seventeen years ago Edie and Joel meet.

Their connection is instant and a friendship is born,
although Edie can't help but wish for more. But
just as she builds up the courage to lay her heart
on the line, one night changes everything . . .

Edie's moved on from the heartbreak of years ago. So the last
thing she expects to receive on her thirty-fifth birthday is an
email . . . from her eighteen-year-old self. As more emails arrive,
she starts to remember what – or rather *who* – she left behind.

Following her own advice, Edie heads back to the place
where it all began, and finds her path unexpectedly crossing
with Joel's once more. Could this finally be their chance
at love? Or are some things better left in the past?

Available now!

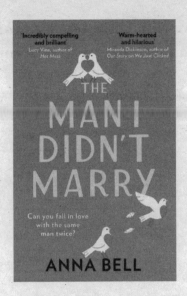

What happens when the man she married can't remember her?

Ellie has the perfect life: a happy marriage, a gorgeous daughter and a baby on the way. But when her husband Max develops amnesia, he forgets everything about the last five years . . . including their relationship.

Now the man she said 'I do' to has become a stranger, and she has no idea why. Yet Ellie is determined to reconnect and find *her* Max again – he has to be in there somewhere, right?

As they get to know one another afresh, Ellie finds herself seeing Max clearly for the first time. But then she discovers that before his memory loss, Max was keeping a huge secret from her. Will their new beginning prove to be a false start, just as it seemed they might fall in love all over again?

Available now!